Prologue

THE CARIBBEAN SEA – AUGUST 21ST, 1714

The Marauder was a fast, three-masted frigate that had been constructed in Portsmouth just under two decades earlier. Having spent the first years of her life as a well-armed escort ship for the English transatlantic merchant fleet, she was now roaming the warm seas of the Caribbean with a very different purpose and in the service of very different men. With her sleek and strong hull made of oak, a solid keel made of elm, and large square-rigged canvas sails on her three tall fir masts, she was fast and nimble despite her extensive armaments, and she was able to carry a respectable amount of cargo. In other words, she was perfect for her current role.

For almost a decade now, she had been captained by Jack Flynn. The rugged-looking captain was at the helm, having taken over from the designated helmsman during this final and crucial stage of the operation. A lean and muscular man in his mid-thirties, he was tall and sported a short, black goatee to go with his ponytail and dark brown eyes. On his head was a well-worn, black leather tricorn hat. He had always been a handsome man, and although his face was weathered beyond his years, he struck an impressive figure standing atop the vessel's aftercastle with his feet slightly apart and his hands gripping the ship's heavy twelve-spoke wheel tightly.

As was his custom, he wore dark brown leather trousers and a slim, worn-looking black knee-length frock coat with a raised collar that was festooned with ornate nickel buttons and grey button loops. The coat was open, its tails flapping gently in the fresh breeze as he steered the ship, and underneath it, he wore a simple white shirt that had not been washed for several weeks. Slung over one shoulder and reaching across his chest was a wide leather baldric, which he used variously for attaching either his cutlass or his flintlock pistols, depending on the need. It also had small pouches for gunpowder and lead bullets. Today, it was the flintlock that had been attached, since he expected to need that before the cutlass. Also attached to the baldric was a large, square brass buckle that was now tarnished by years of weathering at sea, but still clearly visible was a small circular embossed symbol. It was a medieval broadsword and battle axe crossed in front of a tall kite shield adorned with laurels around its edges. It had been the Flynn family crest for centuries. However, none of his crew knew of his noble birth back in England. Not even his long-time quartermaster, John Mercer, and that was how Flynn preferred it. It was better if the men remained entirely unaware of his past life.

Along with his older brother James, Captain Jack Flynn had been born into the relative wealth and privilege that came with belonging to minor English nobility, and the expectation for both of them had been to join their father's business once they came of age. Sir Archibald Morley Flynn, the wealthy proprietor of the highly successful Flynn East India Trading Company, wanted both of his sons to take over the family enterprise, but to the great disappointment of Sir Archibald, this had never happened. Jack and James had often joined him on his trips from their home in Marylebone to the docks in East London, where merchant ships from India and the rest of the burgeoning English empire unloaded their precious cargo. While waiting for their father to conduct his business, the two young boys would sit wide-eyed on the long quays, looking dreamily at the huge Royal Navy sailing ships leaving for the high seas. Their hulls were as tall as three-storey buildings, and their impressive, fully rigged masts towered over them, seemingly reaching as high as the top of the new St Paul's Cathedral that was in the process of being rebuilt after the previous cathedral had burnt to the ground in 1666.

The idea of cruising the world's great oceans aboard the best and most advanced warships ever constructed had proved irresistible to the two young boys, and it had made a future life managing the Flynn East India Trading Company appear about as dull as dishwater. But as the boys became young men, their father had at first denied their request to join His Majesty's Navy, despite the fact that his political connections would easily have been able to facilitate their enrolment as officer cadets at the Naval Academy. However, Sir Archibald had eventually, and only then very reluctantly, consented to them signing up with a merchant ship captained by an old acquaintance of his. And with that, at the ages of 15 and 17, respectively, the two brothers had finally set to sea.

Life aboard the merchantman called the Sea Flower had soon proven much harder and more challenging than either of the two could have imagined. But they had soon grown into their roles as deckhands, maturing quickly among the experienced and hardened sailors aboard the vessel, not least due to their intense rivalry. Ever since they were very young, a fierce contest of will and skill had developed between the two brothers, spurred mainly by Jack being the younger of the two and always being desperate to do as well or better than his older sibling. James had responded as any strong-willed boy would and had given no quarter. What resulted was a relationship aboard the ship that became ever more competitive, and although the captain was pleased with his two latest hard-working recruits, he had to pull them aside on more than one occasion to attempt to dampen their rivalry, if for nothing else, then simply for their own safety aboard what was a dangerous place to work.

An additional and even more serious and incendiary point of contention between the two brothers had its origin far away across the seas yet always nearby in both their hearts and their minds. Her name was Charlotte Cavendish, and aside from being just about the most exquisite thing the two boys had ever seen, she was also the niece of Lord Cavendish, the Duke of Devonshire and First Lord of the Treasury. In his ongoing efforts to cultivate his political connections, Sir Archibald Flynn would invite Lord Cavendish for dinner roughly twice a year, and the Duke would always bring his beautiful and demure wife as well as his young daughter.

Jack and James had been equally smitten and mesmerised the instant they had first laid eyes on Charlotte, and she had always smiled sweetly at them both during the dinners. As the boys grew older, their attraction to her transformed from one of mere blind infatuation to thoughts of one day perhaps marrying her. But there were two of them, and only one Charlotte. On that, at least, they could agree. She was utterly captivating and exquisitely unique. And from then on, it was only ever a question of who would win her heart. In the end, the issue had remained unresolved, and when the two brothers joined the Sea Flower, they had both carried with them a letter from her, believing themselves to have been chosen by the girl who had by then grown into a gorgeous and radiant young woman.

One day, while docked in Tangier and waiting for the ship to be resupplied with fresh water and food for the onward journey south along the west coast of Africa and around the Cape of Good Hope to the Indian Ocean, James had accidentally knocked one of Jack's books onto the floor. It was a copy of the tome '*History of the Buccaneers of America*', first published in Dutch in 1678 and written by the sailor Alexandre Exquemelin who had served in the Caribbean with the famous English privateer and pirate Henry Morgan in the 1660s and 1670s. Having been translated into English in 1684, both of the Flynn boys had devoured the book many times, and it had poured further fuel on the fire that was their desire to venture out onto the high seas. Full of stories about fearless, swashbuckling pirates, daring raids and golden treasure, it had quickly become a sensation amongst the learned gentry, including Jack and James. However, as Jack's copy of the book thudded heavily onto the wooden floor next to their hammocks, a letter had fallen out. When James picked it up, he realised that not only was it from Charlotte Cavendish, but it was almost word for word a copy of what she had secretly pressed into his palm shortly before their departure on the Sea Flower. Feelings of embarrassment, betrayal and red-hot rage had welled up inside him, and when he found Jack standing by the railing looking out over the exotic Moroccan city, he had launched himself at his younger brother. The two siblings had rolled around on the deck of the ship, writhing, punching and clawing at each other until two burly midshipmen had grabbed them roughly and pulled them apart, finding that James had in his hand a knife which he mercifully had not yet had the opportunity to use.

Soon after, Jack and James found themselves sitting inside the captain's quarters, bruised, bleeding, sweating and panting heavily. As they eyed each other icily, the captain yelled at them, threatening to put them ashore to make their own way home and continue the journey to India without them. Eventually, the two young men reluctantly shook hands and promised that no such incident would occur again. They had stayed true to their word, but ever since that day, their relationship had never been the same. In that fight on the deck of the Sea Flower in Tangier, all of their pent-up rivalry, as well as intense feelings of jealousy, envy and general frustration since childhood, had spilt out, and there was now no way back to the way things had been before.

After completing their trip back to England several months later, they had both separately declared to their father that their minds were set. They wanted a life at sea. Sailing on a merchantman had been a useful learning experience for them both, but if they truly wanted a maritime career, the Royal Navy was the only real option. As promised, Sir Archibald had pulled strings in Whitehall to help them to be enrolled at the Naval Academy. However, there was a catch. The only way for their father's arrangement to work was for them to sign on at the same time and join as cadets on the same ship, the HMS Valiant. And so they did in the year 1698.

The next two years had been challenging, to say the least, and not just because of the punishing life of a late 17th-century naval cadet. Jack and James avoided each other as much as possible, but whenever they found themselves having to work together, their rivalry would re-emerge, although thankfully mostly without physical altercations ensuing. During this time, the HMS Valiant crossed the Atlantic multiple times and spent months patrolling the Caribbean sea lanes and protecting the interests of the Empire from the French, the Dutch and the powerful Spanish, as well as the ever-present threat of privateers and pirates.

The HMS Valiant was a powerful warship that was bristling with guns and capable of projecting power across the Atlantic from London to the Caribbean Sea, but its effectiveness depended entirely on the skill and discipline of its captain and crew. With a few exceptions, her crew was everything a good captain could hope for, yet Captain Lennox proved less than perfect by a significant margin. Appointed by the Admiralty and Marine Affairs Office mainly on the back of family connections rather than aptitude and experience, Captain Lennox was cruel, drunken and incompetent. He took the already harsh naval discipline to its extreme, personally flaying sailors with his cat o' nine tails for even minor infractions of Royal Navy regulations, and he seemed to positively revel in the corporeal punishment of his men, even going as far as to keelhaul a sailor for falling asleep in the crow's nest. The poor soul did not survive.

When, after having lost several of their crew during a botched and ill-judged engagement with a French vessel off the island of St Kitts, the crew finally mutinied. Jack joined the mutineers, but James went into a small pinnace with the officers, still believing that his future lay with the Royal Navy. And that was the last time the two brothers had seen each other, although they heard whispers and stories in the years to come.

While James made it back safely to St Kitts after two days at sea in the pinnace, Jack fell in with the crew of the now commandeered Valiant. The mutineers spent several weeks raiding merchant ships in the Lesser Antilles of the eastern Caribbean, but they eventually ran the ship aground in rough weather near the island of Martinique. The HMS Valiant broke up on the rocky shores and was lost, and soon the entire crew had scattered to the four winds. They realised only too well that capture meant a short trial that would swiftly end in an appointment with the hangman's noose, so they melted away into the often chaotic and badly governed new frontier world of the

Caribbean colonies and disappeared. Some managed to find a place on a new ship, many changed their name, and some were never heard from again.

After finally making his way back to London under a false identity, but having now acquired a taste for piracy, Jack once more sought out his old father and eventually managed to enlist his help. By paying a very substantial bribe to the appropriate officer clerk in the Admiralty, the now somewhat frail Sir Archibald was able to have Jack Flynn's name struck from the official records of the mutiny aboard the HMS Valiant, and he was instead issued with a coveted letter of marque. This document, officially giving him the status of privateer, would allow him to engage in legal piracy on behalf of the British Crown against French and Spanish merchant vessels in the Caribbean. For this purpose, his father helped him finance the purchase of a fast and manoeuvrable sloop, which Jack named The Scoundrel. When James learnt of this, he was incensed. But by then, Sir Archibald was too old and feeble of mind to see sense, and all James could do was stew and quietly hope that the sea or the Spanish would soon claim his brother, lest the disgrace of the Flynn family become known to the wider London society.

Jack took to his new privateer vocation with gusto, capturing about a dozen vessels in the Caribbean over the following handful of years. James, on the other hand, rose steadily through the ranks of the Royal Navy to become captain of his own warship. Eventually, driven by a dangerous mixture of greed and boredom, as well as the desire to work only for himself, Jack turned his back on the privateer business to fully embrace piracy. Much to his older brother's fury and shame, news eventually found its way to him through dockside gossip that Jack Flynn had begun attacking vessels regardless of the flag they flew. When he and his new crew chased down, boarded and commandeered a large English merchantman and marooned its crew on a small island, there was no way back. Jack was now officially designated an outlaw and a pirate, his life forfeit if he should ever be captured, and as far as James Flynn was concerned, he no longer had a brother.

'Sails!' shouted the lookout suddenly from the crow's nest high up on the foremast. 'Sails nor'-east! Merchant vessel.'

Jack Flynn extracted his brass and leather monocular telescope from a pocket in his coat, extended it and placed it in front of his right eye. As he squinted through the optics, he saw that the lookout had been correct. On the horizon, some eight nautical miles away, he could see the tops of the masts of a two-masted ship. From the arrangement of the sails, it was already clear that this was not a military vessel but most likely a schooner carrying cargo, but that didn't mean that the ship wasn't armed. Even merchant ships carried guns for self-protection, and only a fool would allow himself to become complacent and approach the ship as if it presented no danger. Judging from the direction and the way its sails were rigged, the merchant ship appeared unaware of the approaching danger.

'What flag is she flying?' Flynn shouted up at the lookout.

'English!' came the reply, at which point Flynn hesitated for a brief moment before making a decision.

'Mr Mercer,' he said, turning to his quartermaster, who was standing beside him next to the wheel on the raised quarterdeck at the rear of the Marauder. 'Raise all sails. Topgallants and jibs too. Tighten the braces on the starboard side. We need all the speed we can muster.'

'Ay-ay, Captain,' said Mercer, who was a burly, barrel-chested man with large side whiskers and a ruddy complexion. 'Raising all canvas.'

Without a moment's hesitation, the quartermaster then stepped forward and bellowed Flynn's orders out across the ship, repeating them word for word and receiving a return confirmation from the master of sails. Immediately, the deck became a hive of activity as some men grabbed winches and pulleys while others climbed up into the rigging. Yet others tightened and shored up the multitude of ropes and pulleys that released and controlled the many separate sails. Only minutes later, the frigate was surging across the waves, sails straining in the wind and ropes creaking as she reached her top speed of 7 knots.

'We're gaining on her, Captain!' shouted Mercer after a while.

'I believe you are correct,' said Flynn, once more putting the telescope to his eye. 'Another twenty minutes and she's ours. Ready the cannons and prepare to board.'

'Man the cannons!' roared Mercer to the crew. 'Prepare to board! Mr Riley, get ready. You know what to do.'

Tom Riley was the crew's resident sharpshooter, and while much of the crew began opening the gunports and preparing the cannons for firing, he fetched three pre-loaded muskets from a locker inside the aftercastle. He slung them over his shoulder and ran forward across the weather deck to the foremast, where he began climbing up into its rigging. As soon as the lookout above saw him approaching, he vacated his perch in the crow's nest to make space for the shooter. Upon reaching the crow's nest, Riley lay prone and made himself as comfortable as he could in the small, cramped space that swayed considerably from side to side as the ship rolled in the swell. Shooting accurately under these conditions was an enormous challenge, but as Riley had learnt well, it was all about timing. It was about picking that brief moment when the momentum of the ship's roll was waning and the mast and the crow's nest seemed to hold still for a couple of seconds before rolling back the other way. This was the window of opportunity that he needed, and if he could hit his intended target, then Captain Flynn and the crew of the Marauder were practically guaranteed their prize.

During the following quarter of an hour, the Marauder steadily reduced the distance to the merchant ship, and eventually, the schooner raised additional sails to try to escape, but it was no use. Flynn's frigate was simply too fast.

'All guns ready!' announced the gunnery master as he stepped away from one of the 12-pounders and looked towards his captain. 'On your command.'

'Mr Mercer,' said Flynn. 'Once we have the signal from Mr Riley, we'll come hard to starboard and give her a broadside. We will then be on her leeward side, and I'll get us along her for boarding.'

'Very well, Captain,' nodded Mercer with a grin. 'Easy as pie. They won't stand a chance.'

Mercer turned away from Flynn, placed his large, calloused hands on the quarterdeck railing, and bellowed orders to the boarding crew to prepare their grappling hooks and weapons, which mostly consisted of cutlasses and other slashing or stabbing blades along with a few flintlock pistols.

'Mr Riley!' Flynn shouted, peering up through the rigging at the sharpshooter.

'Almost there!' responded Riley, who was struggling to acquire his target on the other ship's deck.

'She's coming around!' Mercer suddenly shouted. 'They mean to fight!'

He was pointing forward at the merchant ship, which was now attempting to make a hard turn to port to fire a volley from her deck guns in a last desperate attempt to fend off the attack. As it did so, the distance between the two vessels began to close rapidly since the Marauder was still going at full speed.

'Steady!' shouted Flynn, now sensing tension in his men as the merchant ship lined up her guns at her pursuer. 'We'll let her fire once, and then I'll bring us about for a broadside of our own.'

Moments later, a cannonade of ten 12-pounder guns erupted almost simultaneously from the merchant ship, and plumes of white gunpowder smoke exploded from their barrels as the spherical roundshot cannonballs tore through the air and then covered the distance to the Marauder in a couple of seconds. One smashed into the forecastle, ripping out chunks of wood and sending splinters flying through the air. There was a scream as a sailor was peppered with sharp pieces of debris. Another cannonball tore through the mainsail on the mizzenmast mere metres from Flynn, and the canvas ripped audibly as the projectile punched through it and continued onwards behind the pirate frigate. However, the rest of the incoming fire either whizzed past harmlessly or smashed into the waves nearby.

Almost immediately thereafter, a dry crack rang out from the crow's nest, and across the gap between the two ships, Flynn saw the burst of red as Riley's lead bullet smacked into the head of the merchant ship's helmsman. The helmsman was dead before he knew what had happened, and as he let go of the wheel and fell limp to the deck, the wheel began to spin as the wind drove the ship around and the rudder was pushed aside by the water. Within moments, the merchant ship had turned so much that its sails lost the wind entirely, and they began flapping uselessly in the strong breeze. The merchant vessel immediately began to lose speed fast, and within moments, she was dead in the water and unable to defend herself.

'Coming about!' shouted Flynn as he spun the wheel to one side. 'Gun crews at the ready! At 200 yards, open fire!'

Flynn turned the wheel hard to starboard, and seconds later the Marauder curved to the right as her guns began lining up with their target. When the ship was perfectly side-on to the merchant vessel, he issued the order.

'All guns, open fire!' he roared.

The gunners in charge of firing the cannons had already lit the wicks on their smouldering linstocks, and they immediately lowered them to the touch holes of their designated cannons. A fraction of a second later, the gunpowder inside the barrels ignited, and the Marauder's sixteen portside 18-pounder guns erupted in a deafening barrage of smoke and fire. Roundshot projectiles as big as a man's head covered the distance to the merchant ship in a fraction of a second and tore into her side, where they chewed up the wooden cladding of her hull and smashed through railings and sailors alike. One even hit the base of the ship's foremast with an explosion of splinters, cutting it clean off near the deck like a rose snipped by a set of secateurs. Amidst the groaning of wood and the snapping of ropes, the huge mast fell and crashed over the side of the ship, tearing the sails of the main mast into ragged strips of canvas as it came down.

Moments later, when the drifting curtains of smoke from the Marauder's guns cleared, they revealed a scene of utter devastation aboard the crippled merchantman. There was blood and severed limbs, screaming sailors, mutilated bodies and burning debris everywhere, and those of her crew who had been prepared to put up a genuine fight were now scrambling for cover in a desperate attempt to save their lives. Seconds later, a white flag was hoisted.

'Lower sails!' shouted Flynn as he spun the wheel and used the momentum of the Marauder to begin pulling alongside the battered merchantman. 'Secure the guns! All crew! Ready for boarding!'

Seconds later, when the two ships were mere metres apart, the boarding crews flung their hefty, rope-tethered grappling hooks over the railing. The boarding crew was led by one of Flynn's most loyal men. A tall and handsome boatswain named Larkin. Despite his success with the womenfolk whenever they docked at a harbour, he was known onboard the Marauder as 'Dandy' on account of his penchant for elegant, tailored clothing as well as his eagerness for personal hygiene and generally looking well-groomed at all times.

The hooks clattered onto the wooden deck of the merchantman, and then the boarding crew hauled them back in as they stuck into the wood of the merchantman's railing. The ropes went taut as Larkin's boarding crew hauled the two ships close. As soon as they touched, the crew went over the top, wielding pistols, cutlasses and long, sharp boarding pikes. Men shouted oaths and curses, pistols fired, blades slashed and clanged, and the deck of the merchantman ran red with slippery blood. In the end, the battle was brief and one-sided, and within minutes, the few members of the merchantman's crew who had attempted to resist the attack had been subdued, being either killed outright or wounded beyond the ability to resist any further.

When Captain Flynn finally made his way over to the captured merchant ship with his flintlock pistol drawn and Mercer by his side, Larkin's men had already found the merchant captain. He was standing unsteadily on his feet near the entrance to the aftercastle, held up by two of Flynn's men. He looked shocked and dishevelled, and blood was trickling from a deep gash on the side of his forehead. By the looks of it, he had attempted to hide and had then put up a struggle when the pirates had found him in his cabin.

'Your name?' said Flynn with a hard look as he sauntered up to the vanquished captain.

'Talbot,' stammered the bleeding man, shaking with fear of what might happen to him next. 'William Talbot of the British South Sea Company.'

'And what are you carrying?' said Flynn, eyeing the prisoner through narrow eyes.

'Sugar, sir,' said Talbot warily. 'Just sugar. From Jamaica. We were heading for the Virgin Islands to refit before setting out for home.'

'And where might home be?' said Flynn.

'Bristol, sir,' said the captain.

The disappointment in Flynn's eyes was plain for all to see as he pressed his lips together and glanced at his quartermaster.

'Mr Mercer,' he said. 'Examine the cargo hold. Make sure he's telling the truth. Then search for valuables. And call for Mr Frasier. Have him go through the ship's manifest and find a complete inventory.'

Mercer nodded and barked an order back towards the Marauder for the bookkeeper and bursar, Elijah Frasier, to be found and join them on the captured vessel. Frasier was by far the most learned of the Marauder's crew, and aside from being the man to always keep a perfect record of all items of plunder being brought aboard the ship, as well as making sure that the men were being paid on time and in full, he was known for keeping a meticulous diary written in his own neat but fast shorthand.

Flynn cast a brief glance across the ruined merchantman and gave a bitter shake of the head. This was just the latest in a run of dubious luck. Sugar was not the worst cargo to steal, although it was bulky and could be difficult to shift to black market traders in Nassau in the Bahamas or Tortuga off the coast of Hispaniola, but it was also far from the most valuable loot. Ideally, they would have hoped for high-priced tobacco and rum. Those were much easier to sell, and if need be, they could be used as payment to the crew in lieu of hard currency. A well-known way for pirate captains to compensate their crews during lean times.

'The ship is yours, Mr Mercer,' said Flynn. 'Report to me as soon as we know what we have.'

'Ay-ay, Captain,' said Mercer. 'And the crew?'

'See if there are men willing to join,' said Flynn. 'We could use two or three. Leave the rest.'

'Do we sink her?' said Mercer, glancing briefly at the stricken merchantman, at which its captain tensed and regarded Flynn with obvious fear in his eyes.

'No,' said Flynn with a quick shake of the head. 'We're not savages.'

Crossing back over to the Marauder, Flynn strode purposefully to his captain's quarters inside the aftercastle and shut the door behind him. His private quarters took up almost half of the interior of the aftercastle's lower deck, and they were spacious and comfortable to the point of being palatial compared with the cramped hammocks that the rest of the crew were issued with.

He sat down by the large, dark hardwood desk that was bolted to the floorboards near the centre of the room and yanked the cork from a bulbous bottle of spiced rum. Pouring himself a glass, he downed it in one gulp and then poured himself another. Then he slid a large map of the north-eastern Caribbean Sea in front of himself and reached for his compass and his brass dividers, which he used for measuring distances.

They were already preset to the scale of the map, and he placed a small marker to indicate the current position of their ship as estimated by his navigator shortly before they had taken the merchantman as a prize.

Walking the dividers across the map a couple of times yielded a less-than-perfect conclusion. They were roughly 140 nautical miles south of the port city of Santo Domingo on the island of Hispaniola, which was controlled by the Spanish. This meant that they were almost 800 miles from Nassau in the Bahamas, so that would be too far to travel. However, Tortuga was less than 450 miles away, which was just about possible for the heavily damaged merchant ship. It had to be Tortuga. Once Mr Frasier was back from the vessel, he would ask him to estimate the black market value of the sugar and produce an estimate for the value of the shares going to each of his men. This would then have to be paid out in coin at the earliest opportunity. Flynn downed the rum and lifted the bottle from the desk to pour himself a third glass when there was a familiar rap on the door.

'Enter!' Flynn called.

The door opened, and Mercer walked in carrying a large leatherbound book. He was followed by Elijah Frasier, the bookkeeper.

'Captain,' said Mercer as they approached.

'What's your report?' said Flynn. 'Casualties?'

'One dead,' said Mercer gravely. 'Mr Coles. A pistol shot to the chest. Another three injured. Cuts mostly. But they should recover within a few days.'

'Alright. Very well,' said Flynn, giving a brief nod of acknowledgement.

'There's something else,' said Mercer. 'Something you'll want to see.'

'Go on,' said Flynn.

'It turns out,' said Mercer, 'that our prize was carrying quite an important passenger.'

He walked up to Flynn's desk and dropped the heavy book in front of him. It landed with a thud that caused the bottle of rum to wobble. Flynn glanced up at Mercer with a dubious look.

'What's this?' he said, then eyeing the book in front of him.

Mercer looked over his shoulder and nodded at Frasier who stepped forward and opened the book on one of its last pages.

'We found the harbour master of Port Royal aboard the merchant ship,' said Fraiser. 'He has been recalled to London and was on his way to the Virgin Islands for onward passage. This book is his ledger. It shows all the ships that have anchored in Port Royal so far this year.'

Flynn had used Port Royal in Jamaica himself many times during his stint as a privateer, but since he had turned to piracy, it was now off-limits to him and liable to end in the Marauder being sunk by the fearsome 24-pounder gun batteries sitting above the natural harbour on the thick stone walls of Fort Charles. He leaned forward and looked at the neatly written but yellowed and smudged page in front of him. The page contained columns of immaculately handwritten ship names, dates of arrivals and departures, as well as several lines of text on the right-hand side describing the nature of each vessel's visit, be it commercial or somehow related to the Royal

Navy, which these days had a significant presence in the port.

'Alright?' said Flynn, studying the ledger. 'What's so special about this page?'

'Look there,' said Frasier, leaning forward to place a finger on the entry that was third from the bottom. 'Look at that ship. It arrived three days ago just before the harbour master left for his voyage back to England.'

Flynn peered at the handwritten name Frasier was pointing to, and then his eyes narrowed and his mouth fell partly open.

'El Castillo Negro,' he said in a near-whisper, before looking up at Frasier and then at Mercer, who nodded affirmatively.

'One of the Spanish treasure galleons,' said the brawny quartermaster. 'The one they call the Black Galleon. Armed to the teeth with 24-pounder guns. 86 of them in total. A formidable beast.'

'What the hell is she doing in Port Royal?' said Flynn, his eyes returning to the entry in the ledger as if to confirm that he had not been imagining things.

'That is indeed the question,' nodded Mercer.

'The harbourmaster,' said Flynn curtly as he sat back in his chair. 'Get him in here now.'

A couple of minutes later, the door opened again, and Mercer returned with a short and portly middle-aged man with a pink, puffy face and greying, short curly hair. He was wearing a light blue tunic that was stretched tight across his paunch, beige breeches and black leather latchet shoes with polished brass buckles that very clearly set him apart from anyone else on the stricken merchantman. He did not appear to have been harmed during the boarding operation, but his face was a picture of dread as Mercer walked him up to Flynn's desk and roughly sat him down opposite the imposing pirate captain.

'What's your name?' asked Flynn calmly.

'Henderson,' said the man, looking eager to please. 'Benjamin Henderson, esquire.'

'Esquire indeed?' said Flynn, with an amused and faintly mocking tone. 'Expecting to be a knight, are we?'

'Well,' said Henderson meekly. 'It is customary for former harbour masters in the colonies to be considered for…'

'Alright,' Flynn cutting him off with a wave of the hand. 'So, you're the harbour master of Port Royal?'

'Yes, sir,' said Henderson. 'On my way back to…'

'Yes, I know about all of that,' said Flynn, gesturing to the tome in front of him. 'Is this your ledger?'

'It is,' nodded Henderson apprehensively.

'Good,' nodded Flynn. 'Now, what can you tell me about the Black Galleon? El Castillo Negro.'

Henderson blinked and swallowed nervously as Flynn went on.

'What is she doing anchored in Port Royal of all places?' he said. 'She's one of the largest Spanish treasure galleons.'

'Indeed,' said Henderson, giving Mercer a brief, nervous glance over his shoulder. 'She had been on her way from Vera Cruz on the Spanish Main laden with gold and silver. But she became separated from the rest of the treasure fleet in rough weather. She was passing through the Bahamas when she was captured by the Royal Navy northeast of Havana nine days ago. There was a gun battle where the navy lost a man-o-war. Went down with almost all hands. But our ships managed to board and take over the galleon. Apparently, one of the Spanish gun crews suffered a terrific explosion of a cannon on one of the gundecks, and in the confusion, the ship was boarded and taken over by the crews of two Royal Navy frigates. A very bloody affair, to be sure.'

'I see,' said Flynn, intrigued, glancing up at Mercer, who nodded as if to confirm that it sounded at least plausible to him as well. 'And then they took her to Port Royal?'

'That's right,' nodded Henderson vigorously. 'To repair the damage and refit. They mean to escort her across the Atlantic to London and deliver her directly to the new King. Her treasure will be of great help to the Crown.'

'The king,' sneered Flynn.

'Well,' said Henderson uncertainly as he wrung his hands. 'It *is* his property under the law, now that Cromwell is no longer…'

Flynn raised his right hand to silence the flustered harbormaster. He then stood and rose to his full height, drew a dagger from his belt and walked around the desk. Placing a rough hand on Henderson's right shoulder, he placed the tip of the dagger on the harbour master's tunic directly over his heart.

'About that gold,' said Flynn, his eyes boring into Henderson's. 'How much is she carrying?'

'I don't know,' said Henderson anxiously. 'Truly. They would never tell me. In fact, no one has mentioned any gold to me at all, but since she is a treasure galleon, I simply surmised that…'

'West or east?' said Flynn, twisting the dagger slowly as its tip pushed into the tunic.

'I don't understand,' stammered Henderson.

'The Spanish galleon,' said Flynn coldly. 'Was she going west, or was she going east when she was captured?'

The implications of the pirate captain's question suddenly dawned on the harbour master, whose face was now covered in a thin film of sweat.

'East,' he said hurriedly. 'Most certainly east. That much I was able to glean from the Royal Navy officers. Like I said, she came from Vera Cruz.'

'In other words,' said Flynn, 'she was heading back to Spain, and her cargo hold would be full of gold and silver from the Spanish colonies.'

'Most definitely,' nodded Henderson as a bead of sweat formed under the tip of his nose and glinted in the light from the oil lamp. 'I am quite sure.'

'When is she scheduled to set sail?' said Flynn.

'In four days,' said Henderson, looking mystified. 'If the repairs go as planned.'

'And you are sure about this?' said Flynn.

'Yes, sir,' replied Henderson as Flynn's intent began to dawn visibly on him.

'Surely you don't mean to…' he said before being cut off by Flynn's sharp voice.

'What I mean to do is none of your concern,' he said.

'But she is guarded,' Henderson blurted out. 'Day and night. A dozen soldiers and an officer, if I understand correctly. And she's anchored right under the guns of the fort. You'll never…'

'What do you know of guard changes?' said Flynn. 'You were the harbor master. You would know such things, am I correct?'

'Twice a day,' stammered Henderson. 'At eleven o'clock, morning and night.'

'Who else knows about this aboard your ship?' said Flynn, tightening his grip around the handle of his dagger.

'No one,' said Henderson with a nervous shake of the head, the bead of sweat dropping onto the front of his tunic. 'Only I know about it. It's not the sort of thing I'd want to tell anyone. That would be... unseemly. And it would make me a traitor to the Crown.'

'Ah, yes,' said Flynn mockingly. 'The Crown.'

'I would never betray my king,' said Henderson firmly, seemingly mustering all the courage he could, despite the present company.

'He may be your king,' said Flynn, 'but he isn't mine. As far as I am concerned, he is just the latest in a long line of inbred parasites sitting on a pretty throne with a crown on his head made from stolen gold. He's no better than any of us. But we here are free men. The subjects of no king.'

Henderson looked confused and appeared for a moment as if he was going to say something, but then his courage seemed to melt away, and he merely swallowed and nodded weakly.

'Now,' Flynn said, pressing the tip of his dagger against Henderson's chest. 'Are you quite certain that there is no one else aboard that merchant ship who knows anything about this ledger?'

'I swear it,' breathed the harbour master pleadingly, his jowls wobbling as sweat now trickled off his brow. 'I would never tell a soul. I myself was sworn to secrecy by the governor before departing Port Royal. On pain of death.'

Flynn regarded him intently for a moment, and then a thin smile spread across his face.

'How very ironic,' he said icily, his left hand gripping the harbormaster's shoulder tightly as he drove the dagger hard into the man's chest.

The sharp, pointy blade cut through the tunic and continued into Henderson's chest, slicing through the skin as it slid between two ribs and pushed through the man's beating heart. Henderson gasped and seemed to hold his breath, his mouth opening and his eyes widening as the cold steel entered his chest. His weak hands then gripped Flynn's powerful arms, his legs kicked as blood bubbled up onto his lips, and he looked up into Flynn's cold eyes. He blinked several times with a bewildered look on his face, as if not quite able to grasp what was happening to him or why. His jowls quivered, and then he coughed up some more blood. Flynn pushed the dagger into his chest all the way to the hilt, and then he watched as life ebbed away from the harbour master, and he slumped limply down into the chair.

'Mr Mercer,' said Flynn evenly, releasing his grip on the dead man's shoulder, pulling out the knife and straightening to face his quartermaster. 'Plot a course for Port Royal.'

★   ★   ★

Delicate streaks of cloud high up in the night sky draped a thin veil across the full moon as the rowing boat approached the Black Galleon quietly from her stern. Inside the small vessel were Captain Flynn, Mercer and four other men from the crew of the Marauder. The pirate frigate was anchored in a small cove several miles east along the coast from Port Royal, and Flynn had instructed them to wait for him to return. Should he and the five others fail to do so before dawn, their orders were to set sail, head back out onto the open sea and then return to Nassau on New Providence Island. If Flynn and his small boarding crew did not meet them there within a week, he had given them leave to presume them all dead and proceed to elect a new captain and quartermaster of the Marauder. Flynn had pointed to no favoured successor in case of his death, since unlike on Royal Navy ships or those of the merchant fleet, pirate captains were elected by the entire crew, and most decisions were taken jointly rather than being handed down from on high.

At two o'clock in the morning, the normally bustling Port Royal was quiet except for a few groups of rowdy sailors staggering home through the dusty, unpaved streets holding bottles of rum and ladies of the night in their arms. The cramped port town at the end of the long, sandy isthmus enveloping Kingston Harbour was barely a couple of hundred years old, but it was now one of the busiest and most prosperous settlements in the entire Caribbean. It had begun life when the Spanish explorers brought settlers to the island of Jamaica in 1509, some fifteen years after Christopher Columbus had first set foot on it, and the indigenous Taino population was soon displaced and virtually wiped out.

As part of the Anglo-Spanish War and the English invasion of Jamaica in 1655, England took permanent control of the island and the port, soon building a fort on the tip of the isthmus to prevent any attempt by the Spanish to retake it. This had initially been named Fort Cromwell, named after the Lord Protector of the Commonwealth back in England, before then being renamed Fort Charles after the restoration of the monarchy in 1660.

During those years, Spain was still the most powerful empire in the world, and its mighty navy was more than a match for that of the English. For that reason, English governors issued letters of marque to dozens of well-equipped privateers in Port Royal, allowing those captains to chase down and attack Spanish merchant vessels as well as ensuring protection for Port Royal itself. Legal piracy through the actions of privateers was thus encouraged, as long as only Spanish ships suffered, and the successive governors of Port Royal were particularly generous in handing out letters of marque that allowed for such seaborne raiders to operate. In return, the Crown received a generous percentage of the takings, mostly consisting of trade goods but sometimes also including gold and silver from the mainland of New Spain. Other beneficiaries of these ventures were the local traders, who would often finance the privateers themselves and then take healthy cuts from their profits, making for a sometimes uneasy mutual dependency between the unlikely triumvirate of governors, wealthy merchants and opportunistic and lawless cutthroats.

Aside from it being a way to harass the Spanish Empire and curtail its influence and strength in the New World, privateering was also part of a religious war where the Protestant English and Dutch in particular saw themselves as righteous in their attacks on the Catholic Spanish. At least, that was how the Crown and the government back in London liked to present it. But Flynn suspected that it was only ever really about money and power. In his experience, those were ultimately the only true drivers of most of what happened in this world. And the way privateering in Port Royal had developed over the years seemed to prove his point. Before long, many of those captains who had been issued with a letter of marque succumbed to the temptation to capture vessels from other nations, and the line between privateers and pirates soon began to blur.

Through the decades since Port Royal had come under the control of the English, and with the help of successive local governors, tacit or otherwise, the town had become a pirate haven from which ships set sail to perform maritime raids on whatever they could find. Those ships would then return to the burgeoning trading hub and sell their ill-gotten gains to local merchants who were only too happy to buy them at huge discounts in order to then sell them legitimately on European and North American markets. Thriving off the back of privateering, piracy and general trade, Port Royal had now become home to roughly seven thousand people, making it the largest town in the Caribbean. Many of those people had acquired significant wealth and were living very comfortable lives rivalling those of the most well-to-do aristocrats in London.

During the day, the bustling town was a hive of activity. It was filled with merchants plying their trade from warehouses full of goods, including sugar and tobacco from the island's hinterlands that had been brought to Port Royal through Spanish Town on the other side of the bay. There were a plethora of taverns selling ale and rum to thirsty sailors while also serving as gambling venues, hidden drug dens, a multitude of busy brothels offering their high-priced services, and markets selling almost anything a person could ever need or want. Groups of redcoats from Fort Charles walked the streets of the bustling town to keep order amongst its often drunken and sometimes unruly denizens, and hundreds of people were milling around the docks as ships loaded and unloaded all manner of valuable goods procured illicitly from unwary merchant ships by privateers and pirates alike. Now, however, in the dead of night, the town was almost completely silent. There was only a gentle breeze sweeping across the isthmus, and in the outer harbour, several hundred metres from the port's main timber piers, the smooth waters were reflecting the moon and the stars like a gently rippling mirror.

The rowing boat slid calmly towards the galleon, its oars dipping smoothly and quietly in and out of the water as the six men propelled themselves almost silently towards their target. Flynn and the other five crewmembers in the inconspicuous vessel were all dressed in dark clothing. They were armed with various blades and flintlock pistols, and their faces and hands were painted black with soot so that only their eyes stood out in the pale moonlight. Flynn was sitting in the bow of the small vessel getting ready to lead his men from the front as any self-respecting captain would.

As they drew nearer to the enormous ship with its huge black hulk silhouetted against the moon and looming over them menacingly, its name suddenly seemed eerily appropriate. El Castillo Negro, which was rising up from the water like a black castle bristling with guns, had been placed in the outer harbour during her repairs in order to keep her away from the shipping lanes leading into Port Royal and onwards to Kingston Harbour that lay some four miles further inside the large natural bay on the southeastern coast of Jamaica. The chosen anchoring location was also selected due to a desire to make sure that she was well clear of the Royal Navy warships that lay anchored at Port Royal. In the unlikely event that Fort Charles was required to open fire on her with its gun batteries and sink her in order to prevent her recapture by a Spanish interdiction fleet, she had to be positioned well clear of any Royal Navy ships. However, her location and its considerable distance from the port was also a weakness that presented Flynn with the opportunity of a lifetime.

As the six men eyed the powerful galleon up ahead, it was not difficult for them to imagine the devastation that its three gundecks packed full of 18-pounder cannons could do to another ship up close. Certainly, in a straight fight between the two vessels, the Marauder would be shredded by those guns before she could put even a small dent in the treasure galleon.

As they drew nearer, Flynn spied a faint light coming from the small windows leading into the captain's quarters at the rear of the aftercastle, and as the ship lay there with only a few lanterns hung in a handful of locations around its deck, he slowly began to grow in confidence. If every detail of Henderson's account proved true, and Flynn had no reason to doubt it, only twelve sleepy redcoats would be guarding her tonight, along with a single Royal Navy officer who was no doubt drunk with rum or boredom or both. He might even be asleep. And it was precisely this complacency that Flynn and his small crew of raiders were hoping to exploit. And besides, their plan was so reckless and perilous that no one in their right mind would consider it, much less expect it.

The men lifted their oars out of the water for the last time and placed them quietly inside the rowing boat as its momentum carried it the final distance to the galleon. It bumped gently against the almost vertical stern of the huge warship as Flynn stood up and used a rope to secure it to the galleon's rudder. The rudder was taller than the rowing boat was long, and it had been constructed from several hefty pieces of wood that had been bolted together with large metal brackets. And although wet and slightly slippery, these brackets made it easy for the small band of raiders to climb up.

Without a word, all six men began scaling the rear of the ship, exploiting the fact that all Spanish galleons sported elaborate wood-carved and gilded open quarter galleries with narrow balconies at the rear of their tall aftercastles. This tradition of opulently decorating what were, at the end of the day, simply their warships was a way for the Spanish Crown to put its wealth and power on display for all the world to see. However, it also made it straightforward for Flynn and his men to climb up the rear of the ship and move up towards the captain's quarters. When they reached the lower gallery, they paused, and Flynn signalled for them to remain where they were while he listened for movement. On the other side of the small leaded transom windows were the officer's quarters, but there was neither light nor sound coming from inside. However, as the men sat there quietly, they heard the sound of dull footsteps from above, and then there was the sound of a man giving a brief cough. Flynn leaned out briefly from the balcony and craned his neck to look upwards. Past the captain's balcony above them, he caught a glimpse of one of the twelve redcoat soldiers guarding the ship that night. The man was standing by the railing to the rear of the very top of the ship's aftercastle smoking a small pipe. Had he not been smoking, he might have noticed the pirate captain looking up at him, but with white smoke drifting in front of his face and the glow of the smouldering tobacco impairing his night vision, he noticed nothing.

Flynn turned to look over his shoulder and gave a meaningful nod to a man named Nash. He was a short and lean man in his late twenties with cold eyes and a particular keenness for blades. Flynn knew little of his background, but he knew that he was unrivalled when it came to stealthy attacks and that he seemed to revel in putting his skills with a dagger to use. Nash began to scale the balcony above as deftly and smoothly as a cat burglar, and soon, he was only metres below the soldier who was still blissfully unaware of the approaching threat. While using the ornate wood carvings on the balconies to cling onto the exterior of the galleon's aftercastle, Nash unsheathed a long, sharp dagger that glinted ominously in the moonlight. Seconds later, the soldier turned around to face the front of the ship, and as soon as Nash sensed the movement, he covered the final distance with incredible speed. By the time the soldier heard a noise, Nash was already right behind him, wrapping one arm around his neck, drawing him backwards and then plunging the dagger into his chest three times in quick succession. The soldier's legs spasmed and buckled, and a few seconds later, he slumped to the floor in a pool of blood, but not before Nash had grabbed the musket slung over his shoulder to avoid it clattering noisily to the planks below. Then he signalled to the men below, and with Flynn taking the lead, they immediately began moving up past the transom windows into the captain's quarters to join Nash on top of the aftercastle. As they did so, Flynn noticed that there was still a faint light coming through from the inside. In all likelihood, the Royal Navy officer on duty was in there reading, drinking, dozing or whatever else he did to pass the time until he could return to Fort Charles the next morning.

Once they had all made it to the top of the aftercastle, they moved, crouched and quietly, towards its front, which afforded them a clear view down onto the rest of the galleon. The only sounds they could hear were the soft groaning of rigging and ropes and the gentle creaking of the yards up on the masts. Flynn spent several long moments scanning the decks and mapping out where the other soldiers were, but he ended up with a count of only eight. There was a solitary redcoat posted in front of the entrance to the captain's cabin just below them. Two were standing by the railing on the starboard side of the quarterdeck, another two were roughly ten metres apart on either side of the foremast, and three more stood atop the forecastle, but they all appeared to have their eyes directed longingly towards Port Royal where they would probably much rather spend the night. No doubt, they each had a favourite lady friend in one of the town's many brothels. The remaining three soldiers had to be located somewhere inside the ship. The soldiers that Flynn could see were all carrying long muskets, but those were designed to stave off threats at a distance and were as good as useless up close against hardened men who were highly skilled and experienced when it came to brutal close-quarter fighting involving only pistols and blades.

Flynn whispered instructions to his men, and they fanned out quietly to approach their designated targets and wait for his signal. Soon, only Flynn was left on top of the aftercastle, and he watched as his five men silently navigated the large, barely lit weather decks of the galleon, skilfully using masts, rigging, storage boxes, tall coils of rope and other obstacles to close in on their prey. Once he could see them all in position, he made his way down towards the soldier guarding the captain's quarters. Crouching as he moved, he quietly crept up behind him, rose to his full height, clasped a hand over his mouth and slit his throat with his dagger. Blood spurted out onto the deck as Flynn dragged him down onto himself and held him there until he had stopped moving. Then he shunted the dead man aside, got back onto his feet, and used his bloody hands to form a funnel over his mouth, after which he produced the call of an owl. Immediately, all five of his men closed in on their targets, slicing, stabbing and cutting until all four were dead. It took only seconds, but they then wasted no time in heading up to the forecastle and dispatching the remaining three soldiers quickly and quietly. Shortly thereafter, the five men returned to Flynn who was waiting by the door to the captain's quarters.

'Well done, men,' whispered Flynn. 'She's almost ours. Mercer and I will enter the captain's quarters and subdue the officer. Nash, you take the rest of the men below and search the ship for the last three soldiers. You know what to do.'

Nash nodded silently with a wolfish grin, and then he slinked off into the darkness with his small posse to hunt down the last surviving redcoats who still had no inkling of what was approaching and who would stand no chance against the oncoming threat. Flynn glanced at Mercer, who, like him, had large, glistening bloodstains on his dark shirt. Blood that wasn't his own.

'Time to signal the others,' said Flynn, walking to one of the few lanterns hanging near the stairs to the top of the aftercastle.

He picked it off its hook, climbed back up to the very top of the structure, and walked to the railing that was facing the inlet to the harbour. He raised the lantern above the railing and lowered it again five times, thereby sending the agreed-upon signal to the second rowing boat that was waiting just beyond the small headland by the harbour entrance. Within minutes, eight more of the Marauder's crew would be joining them. Enough of a skeleton crew to sail the galleon quietly out of the harbour under the cover of darkness and out onto the open sea before a pursuit could be organised and made ready to cast off. Having received a brief response signal from the headland, Flynn put down the lantern and rejoined his quartermaster.

'And now to pay that officer a visit,' he whispered with a grin. 'I'll let you do the honours.'

With a hard look on his face, Mercer nodded silently, and then he followed his captain to the door to the aftercastle. Mercer had spent almost a decade with the Royal Navy, suffering under the harsh, brutal and often cruel aristocratic captains of its fleet of warships but sticking with it in the hopes of advancement and the ability to one day retire comfortably. However, after arriving late from shore leave in St. Kitts with two of his best mates, the three of them had been flogged so viciously by their enraged captain using his well-worn cat 'o nine tails that strips of skin had been torn from their mutilated and bleeding backs. The punishment had gone on for hours, and with only rudimentary medical attention available to them, his two friends had not survived the ordeal. Ever since then, Mercer had carried a brightly burning resentment of the Crown, the Royal Navy and its landowning officer class in particular.

'My pleasure, Captain,' he said grimly, as his large hand closed tightly around the brass hilt of his dagger.

★   ★   ★

When Flynn and Mercer entered the captain's quarters, they found themselves in a small hallway with a closed door at the other end. Off to their right was a modest bedroom with what was almost certainly the only proper bed on the entire galleon, the rest of the crew sleeping in hammocks below deck. Directly opposite was a small storeroom lit by a single oil lantern and stocked with assorted supplies as well as what appeared to have been some of the personal effects of the now former Spanish captain. There was also a large, ornate wooden chest with sturdy-looking metal latches and a big lock, no doubt holding various valuables. However, it was not the chest that immediately grabbed their attention. It was the burly redcoat slumped down on top of it, clearly having been posted in the hallway but now taking a moment to rest his feet. He didn't move as Flynn and Mercer emerged in the doorway but instead continued looking down while stuffing his small beige clay pipe with dark brown tobacco.

'Oi! Jones!' he said lethargically, pinching some finely cut tobacco between his index finger and his thumb and then pressing it down into the pipe. 'I already told you, I ain't got no more tobacco for you, so you'll just have to…'

When he looked up, he froze as his mouth fell open and he glared up at the two terrifying apparitions standing in front of him. Armed with daggers and with their flintlock pistols drawn, their black-painted faces sent an instant chill down his spine. He immediately realised who and what they were, but for a moment, he found himself unable to move or cry out. Suddenly, he reached for the long and unwieldy sabre by his side while attempting to get to his feet, but before he could draw the weapon and charge, Mercer raised his pistol and fired. A burst of white smoke shot from the top of the flintlock pistol as the gunpowder ignited, and a loud crack rang out inside the small space as the pea-sized lead bullet left the muzzle and smacked into the soldier's chest near his heart. He immediately slumped back down onto the wooden chest and then fell forward, face-first onto the floor, dead. An instant later, Flynn and Mercer heard a commotion from inside the captain's quarters, and they immediately spun around, charged to the end of the short hallway and crashed through the door into the Galleon's largest and most luxuriously decorated room.

Flynn took the lead with his dagger in one hand and his pistol in the other. At the far end of the room, near the long row of small transom windows, was a large desk behind which sat the Royal Navy duty officer. He had clearly been half asleep and reclining in the captain's chair with his feet on the desk when he had heard the shot, and he was now scrambling to get back up and onto his feet. Next to him was another redcoat who immediately unsheathed his long, slightly curved sabre and rushed towards Flynn. With plenty of room inside the spacious cabin, the soldier raised his sabre to slice down and across in front of himself, hoping to cut the intruder and neutralise him. However, Flynn was as experienced in hand-to-hand combat as the rest of his crew, and he had seen the attack coming from the moment the soldier first reached for his weapon. He stepped inside the redcoat's reach, blocked his sword arm, and planted the muzzle of his pistol on the man's chest. The pistol fired and sent a bullet punching clean through the soldier's torso and punching out through one of the small windows, which shattered. Then Flynn pushed the dead soldier away and scythed across his throat with his dagger. Blood spurted from his neck as he fell to the floor, and he didn't move again. A dark pool of blood immediately began spreading on the floorboards around him.

Meanwhile, Mercer had drawn his own blade and was advancing towards the officer with a look on his face that spoke of resentment and hatred engendered by years of abuse, as well as the death of his two friends at the hands of men like the one before him. The officer raised his hands feebly in front of himself as if to ward off the imminent attack, and then his voice cried out.

'Please don't!' he pleaded. 'For the love of God!'

His terrified voice cut through the stale air of the cabin, reaching deep into Flynn's soul, and he suddenly lunged forward and gripped Mercer's sword arm.

'Stop!' he exclaimed. 'Leave him.'

Panting with blood lust, Mercer froze for a brief moment with his eyes narrowed and fixed on the petrified Royal Navy officer, but then he turned his head slightly to one side and glanced uncertainly at Flynn who only minutes earlier had promised him that he would be the one to finish the man off.

'Captain?' he grumbled, a look of mild confusion slowly spreading across his wrathful face. 'What's going on?'

Flynn pressed down on Mercer's muscular arm, and the quartermaster reluctantly lowered his dagger and stood aside.

'I'm sorry, Mercer,' Flynn said, eyeing the Royal Navy officer darkly. 'I know what I promised you. But things have changed.'

The officer lowered his hands tentatively, and then his expression seemed to change completely as he stared dumbfounded at Flynn.

'I don't understand,' growled Mercer, panting as he eyed his captain. 'What's got into you?'

'Please wait for me outside,' said Flynn evenly, his narrowed eyes locked on the officer. 'I need a moment alone with my brother.'

★   ★   ★

'Hello, James,' said Jack flatly, still holding his pistol in his right hand as he regarded his older sibling.

Mercer had now left the two of them alone inside the spacious captain's quarters of the galleon, and the estranged brothers were looking at each other, each of them trying to reconcile what they remembered from their childhoods with what they now saw in front of them. Jack's weathered face, dark beard and shabby pirate garb made him look older than James, although he was still the more handsome of the two. James, on the other hand, was clean-shaven with a braided ponytail, and he cut a dapper profile in his Royal Navy uniform consisting of a black bicorne hat, a dark blue coat with gold embroidery, silver buttons and epaulettes on the shoulders, white breeches, stockings and black shoes. The two brothers had always looked very much alike, and one could have easily mistaken one for the other had they been wearing the same clothes. Now, they could barely have looked less alike. However, even their very different appearances at this moment seemed to fall away as they regarded each other, and each of them now saw only their estranged brother standing in front of them. A heavy silence hung in the air between them for a long moment, but then James finally spoke.

'Hello, Jack,' he said coolly, having now mostly regained his composure. 'I never thought I would see you alive again.'

'You thought, or you hoped?' said Jack without a hint of warmth in his voice. 'I'm sure you'd be happier knowing I was dead.'

James did not reply but merely clenched his jaw as he gave a small shake of the head.

'What the hell is going on here?' he then said.

'I think you know why we're here,' said Jack.

'The gold,' said James evenly, giving a shake of the head.

'I assume it's still safe in the cargo hold of the ship?' said Jack.

'Of course,' said James. 'We're two days from setting sail for London.'

'Good,' said Jack with a sly grin that reminded James of long ago when a young but brazen Jack would steal sugary pastry from the butler's trolley without anyone noticing.

As Jack's plan finally dawned on his older brother, James's eyes widened and his lips parted, but for several seconds, no words came out. Then he finally managed to speak.

'You mean to steal it?' he said incredulously, his brow creasing as he attempted to make sense of the absurd notion of Jack attempting to steal the Spanish gold from a war galleon anchored under the guns of

Fort Charles. 'Jack, what the bloody hell are you thinking? Have you gone mad? How on earth are you going to do that? You'll never get it off this ship. Have you forgotten where we are? We're in Port Royal, for God's sake!'

'I am well aware,' said Jack. 'But I have a plan.'

'But there's too much of it,' said James, now growing angry as he considered the fallout on him personally if his brother ended up succeeding in his harebrained endeavour. 'You can fill your pockets, but that won't even make a dent in that hoard. And then you'll be caught. And then you and your murderous ragtag associates will hang right here in Port Royal.'

'Oh, ye of little faith,' said Jack, as a thin, roguish smile spread across his face. 'We intend to take all of the gold and the galleon with it.'

For a long moment, James couldn't speak but just stood there staring dumbfounded at his younger brother. When he finally spoke again, his voice was cold and laced with disdain.

'You really have lost your marbles,' he said. 'You belong in Bedlam with all the other criminals and lunatics.'

'Or perhaps,' said Jack, 'I am just crazy enough to come up with something so barmy that no one ever dreamed it could even be pulled off. And so here we are. The only question is this. Are you going to help me?'

'What?' James exclaimed with a derisive chortle. 'Help you? I am not even going to dignify that with a response.'

'Suit yourself,' Jack shrugged, calling over his shoulder towards the door. 'Mr Mercer!'

The quartermaster entered immediately, still holding the dagger in his hand, and behind him were the rest of the small boarding party eager to see what was going on.

'Restrain my brother,' said Flynn. 'I think it is time we had a look at that gold.'

A few minutes later, with his brother securely tied up inside the captain's quarters and guarded by the menacing-looking Nash, Flynn and Mercer descended the stairs down through the gundecks of the galleon into the cargo hold deep in the bowels of the ship. As they moved through the lower cargo deck, they passed dozens of wooden barrels full of supplies for the ship's crew and large square piles of various trade goods. There were textiles, tobacco, spices such as cinnamon and vanilla, corn, beans and a large volume of lumber. However, near the front of the cargo hold were twenty-four large wooden chests, each full of treasure beyond anything even Flynn could have imagined. Some were full to the brim with Spanish silver pesos known and used across the Caribbean as Pieces of Eight. Others were almost overflowing with the large gold coins known as Doubloons, with which anything and almost anyone could be bought. Yet others contained gemstones and pearls along with religious artefacts made of gold and silver that had been stolen from the indigenous peoples of New Spain. Piled up to around knee height across the very front of the cargo deck near the massive, rectangular copper-lined gunpowder storage, where hundreds of sacks of gunpowder were kept, were neat piles of gold bars with sheets of dusty canvas draped over them.

When Flynn and Mercer tore the rough fabric away and saw the gold gleaming in the light from their lanterns, wide grins spread across their faces.

'God's blood,' whispered Mercer, gawping at the glittering loot in front of them.

'Mr Mercer,' said Flynn with a crafty smile as he glanced sidelong at his quartermaster. 'You'll never have to work another day of your life after this.'

When the two men re-emerged onto the quarterdeck, the second rowing boat had just arrived, and an additional eight crewmembers from the Marauder were climbing up the side of the galleon and over the railing. They immediately began dumping the bodies of the dead redcoats over the side, and then some began climbing up the shrouds of the masts to the horizontal yards where, in well-practised style, they balanced out along the footropes under the yards to prepare the release of the ship's sails. Others readied themselves by the push bars on the huge rotating capstan to pull up the anchor so that the galleon could leave as soon as Flynn gave the order. Flynn himself headed back inside the captain's quarters, where he asked Nash to leave him alone with his brother once more.

'Did you find what you were looking for?' said James acerbically.

'I did,' nodded Jack, his eyes seemingly still gleaming with the glow of the galleon's treasure.

He lowered himself into the captain's chair and regarded his brother who was sitting on the floor with his hands bound and tied to a thick wooden support beam behind his back. Then he reached for a bottle of spiced rum, pulled off the cork and took a large swig.

'And just when I thought you couldn't stoop any lower,' said James contemptuously, giving a shake of his head. 'What the devil happened to you?'

'I woke up,' snapped Jack, abruptly sitting up in the chair and leaning forward to fix his brother with a hard glare. 'I realised that if I ever wanted to be free, I had to strike out on my own.'

'By becoming a filthy pirate?' James scoffed.

'Call it what you will,' said Jack. 'I am happier and wealthier now than I have ever been. And unlike you, I take orders from just one person. Me!'

'You're a traitor to your country and to your king,' said James.

'Ha!' said Jack derisively. 'He's not my king. Tell me. What does he pay you, this new king of yours?'

Jack reached into his pocket and extracted a single coin. It was one of the golden doubloons from the galleon's cargo hold. He tossed it onto the floor in front of James who stared down at it as it lay glinting in the light from the lanterns. A single coin made from 22-karat gold worth four pieces of eight. Enough to buy an expensive suit back in London.

'I now have more of these than I know what to do with,' said Jack. 'What have you got to show for your years of loyalty to your precious king?'

'My honour!' James blurted out, realising at that moment how feeble and almost laughable it sounded, but he persevered. 'Not everything in life is about money, Jack.'

'True,' nodded Jack. 'But it does make things a lot more fun. Out here, we live like kings with more pleasures than you can imagine. Women. Drink. Fine clothes. Whatever you want.'

'You're not the brother I remember,' said James, his voice subdued. 'You're nothing like him.'

'That's where you're wrong,' said Jack, his voice becoming louder and angrier the longer he spoke. 'That's what you never understood about me. The man I have become was always inside me just waiting to come out. Waiting to free himself from the shackles of the expectations that were always put on both of us. This is who I really am. You may not like it, but what you see here in front of you is the real Jack. Someone prepared to take what's his. Someone who isn't cowed by fear of what others might think of him. Someone who fears nothing, except a cage wrought by the expectations of so-called civilised society. That is the real me. It always was.'

'And what about our father?' said James sharply.

Jack glanced at him, his expression softening almost imperceptibly for a brief moment before becoming hard again as he gave a small shake of the head.

'Our father is a good man,' he finally said quietly. 'But he is no more of a loyal subject than I. He serves himself, and he has done well out of it.'

'He *was* a good man,' said James, fixing his younger brother with a stare. 'He died almost a year ago. But you wouldn't know that.'

Jack clenched his jaw and gave a faint, accepting nod, after which he sat immobile for a long moment before speaking again.

'I see,' he finally said, his voice tight. 'If I had been able, I would have come home for his funeral.'

'I doubt it,' said James bitterly. 'I am sure you would have been too busy in some whorehouse in Nassau.'

'Nothing wrong with a bit of entertainment,' sighed Jack, now beginning to grow weary of his brother's seemingly endless supply of disdainful words.

'Whatever makes you happy,' said James darkly, pausing a moment while looking at Jack's right hand before speaking again.

'I see you're still wearing your ring,' he continued, nodding at the signet ring on Jack's middle finger.

Archibald Flynn had given both of his two sons identical signet rings carrying the family crest, but on the inside of each ring was engraved their full names. At the mention of the ring, Jack's left hand involuntarily found it and spun it slowly around his finger as he had done countless times before.

'You still have yours?' he asked.

James raised both of his bound arms and turned his right hand to show his ring.

'Of course I do,' he said. 'But I don't know how you can still wear yours after the shame you have brought on our family. You no longer deserve to bear that crest. It's a good thing our father is already dead. Had he ever come to fully realise what you have now become, it would surely have put him in a grave.'

Jack didn't reply but simply shot his brother an icy look. Then he got to his feet, took another swig from the bottle and walked out of the room. As he climbed back up the steps and onto the top of the aftercastle, Mercer joined him, and the two of them walked over to the railing where they looked out across the water.

The dim lights of Port Royal were clearly visible about half a mile away, but there was barely a sound emanating from the town or its harbour area.

'Did you send the signal?' said Flynn.

'I did,' nodded Mercer. 'The reply came soon after. They are on their way to the fort.'

'Good,' said Flynn. 'Any time now. Get the men ready to cast off and set sail as soon as they see it.'

'Ay-ay, Captain,' said Mercer, turning and making his way back down to the quarterdeck.

Flynn peered up to the top of the galleon's masts, where a long, red and yellow pennant moved lithely in the breeze. There wasn't a lot of wind that night, but it would be enough to get the galleon underway. All they needed now was a distraction, and one was about to appear at any moment. He turned back to peer out across the almost still waters towards the port, and a few minutes later, it finally happened.

At the southern end of Port Royal near the seafront, a bright orange fireball suddenly bloomed up into the sky as one of the gunpowder storages at Fort Charles exploded in a roiling, scorching plume that rose from the fort and lit up the entire town and its harbour. A couple of seconds later, while the burning clouds of gunpowder still spiralled upwards into the night sky, the boom of the spectacular explosion reached El Castillo Negro. Immediately, its large mainsails dropped from their yards. At the same time, the men on the capstan began winching up the heavy iron anchor. Within seconds, the sails billowed as the wind began to fill them, and then the ship started to inch forward towards the rocky headland and the harbour exit.

Inside Fort Charles, it was pandemonium as burning debris rained down everywhere, and for the next hour or so, the fort would no longer be able to open fire on anything inside the harbour. The blast had rocked the entire town, and its citizens were spilling out into the streets looking bleary-eyed, shocked and confused by the burning spectacle playing out up at the fort. So much so that no one noticed the dark silhouette of the Spanish galleon slowly moving from its anchorage spot and heading out of the harbour towards the sea. When the fire at the fort had begun to abate, El Castillo Negro had disappeared from view behind the headland. By the time her absence was finally noticed by the crew of one of the Royal Navy frigates anchored in the inner harbour, it had been almost an hour since the explosion. During that time, the galleon's skeleton crew had managed to meet up with the Marauder, which had been hiding in a small cove during the hijacking operation. After a hurried transfer of enough men from the frigate to the much larger galleon to ensure that she could raise all of her sails, the two vessels got underway. As dawn broke and the Royal Navy finally managed to organise a pursuit, the Marauder and the Black Galleon were long gone. Using the steady wind out on the open water, they headed east along the coast of Jamaica towards a location known only to Captain Flynn.

★   ★   ★

Once the main pirate haven in the Caribbean, the small island of Tortuga, just off the northeastern coast of the major island of Hispaniola, lay in darkness. Having first been eclipsed by Port Royal in Jamaica and then by Nassau in the Bahamas as the preferred base of operations from which pirates set out to raid merchant vessels, it was now a shadow of its former self. It still served as a place for pirate ships to take on supplies and perform repairs, and above it on the hillside, its fort still remained. However, the location was much less busy than it had been not that many years earlier, and that suited Captain Flynn just fine.

It had been almost two weeks since the raid on Port Royal. He could still barely believe that they had managed to steal El Castillo Negro from under the noses of the Royal Navy, and with it an enormous amount of gold and silver that the Spanish had themselves plundered from Central and South America. And the way he saw it, stealing stolen goods from a thief was no crime at all. Of the huge galleon, there was not a trace. Residents and redcoats in Port Royal had glimpsed her disappear from view around the headland and fade into the darkness on that chaotic night, but since then, no sightings had been made.

Sitting low in the water, the Marauder was anchored in the small, shallow cove that had served as a natural harbour for pirates based out of Tortuga for decades. For the first time since arriving, her crew had been given shore leave two days ago, and the men had been only too keen to go into the small port town and spend some of their newly acquired pieces of eight in the taverns and brothels still plying a lively and lucrative trade there. They had been given strict instructions to tell no one about what had transpired in Port Royal three weeks ago, and none of them had done so. They all feared the wrath of their captain, but more importantly, all the men were loyal to the collective. None of them wanted to be the one to betray the mutual trust that had to exist amongst members of a pirate crew for it to function. And they all knew that if just a single one of them had a loose tongue, then more than likely, all of them would hang, and none of them would ever see another coin from the galleon.

Tonight, however, Jack Flynn had ordered everyone back to the Marauder. He had given no reason for this, but no one was so foolish as to question the motives of a captain, much less a pirate captain who was both respected and known to be as hard-nosed as he was skilful and cunning in battle. In addition, Flynn had proven to be capable of consistently securing the crew of the frigate a steady income in the form of captured merchant prizes, and at the end of the day, that was the only thing they really cared about.

It was now well past midnight, the ship lay in darkness, and almost everyone was asleep in their hammocks below deck. Many of them were still hung over and sleeping off the last effects of the raucous entertainment they had indulged themselves in for the previous few nights ashore. Only a small handful of crewmembers were on nocturnal guard duty, and a couple of those were asleep at their post. A few hundred metres away across the harbour and on the other side of the wooden pier was the town of Tortuga. It had now fallen almost quiet, although faint hornpipe and violin music could be heard emanating from a tavern somewhere near the harbour, and there was the occasional boisterous laughter from sailors and their female companions.

Out on the still water inside the captain's quarters of the Marauder, the voices of two men could be heard only faintly. The nearest guard stationed out on the quarterdeck could clearly hear the men inside, but with the door firmly shut, he was unable to make out precisely what their muffled voices were saying. They both had almost the same lilt and intonation, hinting at some familial relation, and they would have sounded almost the same had it not been for the fact that one had developed a more gravelly voice and a somewhat coarser manner of speaking. It was clearly Jack and James Flynn. At first, it sounded as if one of them was attempting through reason and appeals to personal riches to convince the other. Soon, however, the conversation grew into an argument with the other man dismissing whatever topic was being discussed in an increasingly angry and contemptuous manner. Outside, the guard could not make sense of the angry quarrel behind the door, except for a single sentence that was uttered with venomous contempt.

'These are your men!'

Eventually, slights and insults were being hurled through the air, and then suddenly there was a scuffle. As the guard listened nervously, the two men grunted, groaned and cursed as they struggled amidst the sound of furniture being knocked over, punches being thrown, and what could only have been the sound of a cutlass being swung violently, slamming into a wooden beam and singing as the steel of its blade vibrated. Then there was a heavy thud and then a crashing noise that sounded as if the two men had fallen onto the floor in a heap. More vicious punches were thrown, and groans and wheezes escaped their lips as they each strained for control in what had become a deadly and furious battle. There was the thick gurgle of someone choking and then suddenly the unmistakable sound of a dagger being drawn from its scabbard. Then a long, shrill groan emanated from within, and then there was silence for a long moment except for the sound of someone panting heavily.

Outside, the guard had heard the whole thing, but he had been so dumbstruck and frozen with shock and indecision that he had simply stood there listening to the macabre event unfold. At one point, he had almost moved towards the door to the captain's quarters and reached for the door handle, but he had found himself unable to move amidst the sound of the fierce struggle. Eventually, he heard the tired groan and the shuffling noise of someone getting up from the floor and back onto their feet. It was followed by the rustling of clothing and a few soft thuds. Then the guard heard a heavy, throaty voice speaking words that seemed laced with what he could have sworn sounded like bitterness and regret.

'I gave you a chance to see sense,' it said.

A moment later, the guard heard heavy, booted footsteps approaching the door, and he found himself taking a step back as it was unbolted and swung open. In the doorway to the spacious captain's cabin stood an almost perfectly black silhouette of a tall man against the light of the lanterns now spilling out onto the deck. His hair appeared tousled and matted with blood, and so did his short beard. The guard gazed dumbfounded at the man, and then he recognised Captain Flynn's long coat and knee-high leather boots. Standing there in the backlit doorway, his shoulders rose and fell as he breathed heavily. Then he stepped outside onto the dark quarterdeck, closed the door behind him and continued to walk past the guard as if the man wasn't even there. As he did so, his slashed, beaten and blood-covered face glistened in the weak light of the crescent moon, and it appeared blank and eerily devoid of emotion, yet his hard eyes seemed to gleam with malice.

'Captain,' stammered the stunned crewman warily, but he received no reply.

He remained where he was and watched silently as the bruised and visibly injured apparition continued unsteadily to a set of stairs and proceeded down into the ship. Then, for reasons he could not describe, the crewman suddenly grew troubled and glanced towards one of the other guards who was standing up on the forecastle with his back to the deck. After a brief moment of hesitation, he then hurried across the deck towards his shipmate.

Down below, the captain headed straight to the gunpowder storage at the front of the ship, where a fuse had already been prepared. He knelt down, examined the fuse to make sure it was long enough for him to escape, and then he extracted a small sheet iron tinder box from a pocket in his coat. Opening it, he picked out the charcloth and placed it gently over the end of the fuse. Then he took the metal fire striker in his right hand and the piece of flint in his left. Bringing the fire striker down hard onto the flint with a practised flick of the wrist, sparks then shot out from its underside and sprayed onto the charcloth. Small glowing specks appeared on the cloth, and when he leaned down and blew on it, the glow turned brighter, and then the fuse caught fire.

Once lit, the fizzing fuse immediately began to burn at a steady rate, rapidly inching closer to the large storage compartment that contained several tonnes of black gunpowder for the ship's cannons. He got to his feet, and despite his injuries, he walked hurriedly along the central walkway on the lower cargo deck towards a set of stairs leading back up to the main deck. However, when he arrived on the main cargo deck above, two figures emerged from the darkness. It was the guard who had watched him leave the captain's cabin and one other crewman. They were both armed and had their cutlasses drawn and their flintlock pistols tucked under their wide leather belts.

The quarterdeck guard, who by now appeared to have regained his composure, was about to speak when he spotted the lit fuse in the darkness behind the captain by the gunpowder store at the other end of the lower cargo hold. As the implications of what was about to happen dawned on him, his eyes went wide, and he launched himself forward with his cutlass raised. The captain, who until moments ago had appeared badly injured and almost incapacitated, deftly stepped aside, drawing his dagger as he did so. The cutlass sliced through the air near his head, and then he thrust forward and plunged the dagger into the guard's throat, cutting it open and causing blood to gush out violently. The guard instantly relinquished his grip on the cutlass and instead clasped his throat with both hands, but he was unable to stem the bleeding as his panicked heart kept pumping furiously. He fell to the floor as his cutlass clattered onto the floorboards, but not before the captain had reached out and snatched his flintlock pistol from his belt. In a fraction of a second, he cocked the hammer, raised it to point at the other sailor and pulled the trigger. The hammer struck down on the metal plate igniting the gunpowder, and then there was a boom as the weapon fired. Amidst a burst of smoke and burning gunpowder sparks leaving the muzzle of the pistol, a lead bullet punched a perfectly round hole in the forehead of the hapless second guard. He had barely crashed to the floor next to his dead shipmate before his killer stepped over him, took his pistol and made his way up the stairs.

As he emerged on the gundeck where the crew had been sleeping in their hammocks, he suddenly found himself face to face with quartermaster Mercer who had made his way to the stairs along with several other baffled crewmembers who had also been woken by the commotion and the sound of the shot.

'Captain,' said Mercer, looking confused at the bloodied man in front of him. 'What's happening?'

The captain took a step forward and embraced the quartermaster, putting his mouth close to his ear and placing the muzzle of the flintlock pistol on Mercer's chest just where his heart was.

'Thank you, Mercer,' he whispered in a tense, husky voice. 'For everything.'

Then he pulled the trigger. The bullet punched straight through Mercer's chest and exited out of his back near the spine, continuing on to smack into a wooden bulkhead. The fiery exhaust ignited Mercer's shirt, which began to burn as his lifeless body fell to the floor, but by then, the captain was racing up the steps to the quarterdeck. Momentarily stunned by what they had just seen, the handful of stunned crew who had witnessed the brutal act then gave chase.

However, the captain had now already made it up onto the quarterdeck, where he immediately raced for the side of the ship. His pursuers emerged a few seconds later, drawing their blades and cocking their pistols. However, just as the captain discarded his weapons, sprinted for the gunwale, launched himself over the side of the ship, and scythed into the water, the Marauder's massive gunpowder storage detonated.

Witnessed by a handful of people on the pier and one or two more up at the fort on the hill above the harbour, the entire front of the frigate was consumed by a huge, searing fireball that expanded almost instantly to envelop most of the ship. In the blink of an eye, sails were shredded, masts turned into splinters and kindling wood, and the once strong hull of the ship was reduced to a mutilated, fiery carcass. The thunderous shock wave raced across Tortuga town, rattling doors and windows and giving its residents the fright of their lives. Within seconds, what little was left of the vessel began to sink rapidly to the bottom of the cove, and after a few minutes, all that remained on the surface of the water were a few floating pieces of burning debris from the once proud and feared pirate ship. The mangled remnants of the Marauder and her cargo eventually settled on the sandy bottom of the cove, her entire crew killed by the devastating blast. Everyone who had been on board was dead, except for one man.

ONE

CYPRUS – PRESENT DAY

The scorching midday sun was beating down on the sprawling RAF Akrotiri airbase on the southern tip of Cyprus. Manned by several thousand Royal Air Force personnel and support staff, it served as home to a range of airborne elements of the British military, including fighter jets, UAVs, transport and tanker aircraft, search and rescue helicopters, reconnaissance aircraft and even a secretive detachment of the US Air Force operating the now decades-old U-2 high-altitude spy plane over the Middle East.

Huddled together on a parched grassy area near the end of the main runway was a group of five men. They had just completed their second test of a newly developed PHAOS system, which was short for Parachutist High-Altitude Oxygen System. Designed by a private contractor and offered to the Special Air Service regiment for consideration, the new system aimed to provide the special forces operators with better ergonomics and a more easily adjustable flow of oxygen than their existing high-altitude breather system. The five-man team consisted of four members of B squadron from 22 SAS at Hereford, and they had been joined for the test by someone who was no longer formally part of the regiment's active service element but whose vast experience and natural abilities made him a shoo-in for these sorts of assessments.

Andrew Sterling was slightly taller than average height, muscular and well-built with short black hair and a square jaw, and with his slim sunglasses, camouflaged jumpsuit, rolled-up sleeves and automatic weapons strapped to his torso, he looked the image of a special forces soldier. As usual, however, neither he nor his team were wearing any insignia or patches that hinted at their identity. Since its inception during the latter stages of the Second World War in North Africa, where the regiment had inflicted heavy losses on Erwin Rommel's army during a string of daring nighttime raids against German desert airstrips, the overriding priority of the SAS had been to be invisible. Operating covertly was the very essence of the SAS, and it extended to every part of what they did, including something as seemingly innocuous as the testing of new equipment and weapons.

'Well done, chaps,' said Andrew, as the four others converged on him carrying their bundled-up parachutes. 'That seemed to work well. Any complaints?'

'Not really, boss,' said McGregor in his dry, broad Scottish accent. 'Although maybe they could put a drinking nipple inside the mask. I'm thinking stout would do the trick.'

'Duly noted,' nodded Andrew, deadpan. 'Anyone else.'

'It fits snugly enough,' said Logan, who was one of B squadron's best recon specialists. 'But I think I'd like the adjustment valve for the oxygen mix to be closer to the front.'

'Yes, I agree,' said Andrew.

'The rubber around the edge of the mask could be more flexible,' said Dunn, whose expertise in explosives and breaching operations was second to none. 'It would make for a more snug fit.'

'Alright,' nodded Andrew as he committed the team's input to memory.

'Same,' said Wilks, the team's resident sniper, who was only ever brief and to the point. 'I had to adjust the mask a few times on the way down. Too much effort.'

'Says the man who spends all day lying down,' said McGregor with a grin, giving the sniper a friendly punch on the shoulder.

'How about the new quick-release catch?' said Andrew. 'Any thoughts?'

'To be honest,' said McGregor, giving a small shake of the head. 'Those things are about as much use as tits on a fish.'

'Right,' said Andrew dryly. 'I'll put that in my written report to the top brass and possibly rephrase it.'

'Well,' shrugged McGregor. 'The last thing you want jumping out of a plane at fifty thousand feet is to accidentally trigger it. I would just end up taping it in place. It's too risky.'

The other four grunted their approval as they rolled their black, lightweight nylon parachutes up into tight balls.

'Very well. That's enough for today,' said Andrew as he glanced over to one side to see a couple of tan-coloured Jeeps approaching that were going to take them back to the main compound of the airbase.

'Here come the taxis,' he said. 'Let's head back and get some lunch.'

However, the words had barely left his mouth before his phone, which was strapped safely into a velcroed breast pocket, began to vibrate. He pulled the pocket open and extracted the phone, and when he saw the brief text message, he looked up at the rest of the team.

'Sorry, guys,' he said. 'Lunch has been cancelled. We're going straight to Commander Singleton's office. There is a developing situation in Somalia, and we're the nearest assets. Let's move.'

From one moment to the next, what had up until then been a relaxed and jovial mood amongst the small group of special forces operators became focused and serious. Without a word, the other four men nodded affirmatively, exchanged silent glances, and mounted the vehicles for the short drive back to the administrative unit. Minutes later, they were seated in front of the desk of RAF Akrotiri's base commander, Group Captain Paul Singleton. He was a tall, balding man in his early sixties who, despite his age and busy schedule, did what he could to keep fit and set a good example for the rest of the personnel on the base. He was wearing a simple white shirt and dark trousers, and he was sitting with his hands folded on the desk in front of him.

'Gentlemen,' he said calmly, but with a slightly furrowed brow hinting at the seriousness of what he was about to relay. 'Thank you for coming so promptly. I know you were about to go and have your chow, but I'll have the cafeteria stay open so you can have your lunch after this meeting. And then I'm afraid you'll need to be on your way fairly swiftly after that.'

'Thank you, sir,' said Andrew. 'It's not a problem.'

'Here's the situation,' said Singleton as a grave look spread across his face. 'About half an hour ago, we received a message from Whitehall. They have been alerted by the UKMTO about a rapidly evolving situation in the Gulf of Aden.'

Despite its civilian-sounding name, the UK Maritime Trade Operations office located in Dubai was created and staffed exclusively by the Royal Navy. From its offices in the Emirati city on the southeastern coast of the Persian Gulf, it was tasked with coordinating and exchanging information with merchant traffic in the Arabian Sea and the Gulf of Aden. More specifically, its main job was to help counter threats to civilian vessels from Somali pirates operating from the coast of that war-torn and barely functional country.

'As you may be aware,' continued Singleton, 'there has been a recent surge in piracy against the maritime trade routes passing through the Arabian Sea to and from Europe through the Suez Canal. These are Somali pirates mainly operating from the coast of Puntland on the Horn of Africa, but some of them have also set up bases in Yemen on the other side of the gulf.'

The small group of SAS soldiers sat quietly and listened intently to the base commander as he laid out the information, but they all had a very good idea about where this was going.

'This sort of thing has obviously been going on for decades,' continued Singleton, 'but the recent increase in incidents may be related to, and possibly even instigated by, Iran, using the Houthis in Yemen to do their dirty work and harass European nations whilst maintaining plausible deniability. Over the past few months, we have also observed these pirate groups turning to human smuggling, using small skiffs to move migrants from Somalia across the Gulf to Yemen. Along with this, they also transport weapons, of which there is obviously an abundance in Somalia after years of civil war.'

Singleton, having painted a rough picture of the background of the developing situation, then began to lay out why the men were sitting in front of him.

'Eleven days ago,' he went on, 'a chemical tanker registered in the British overseas territory of Bermuda and loaded with phosphoric acid was hijacked about ten miles off the coast of Puntland.'

'Did it have any armed protection?' said Andrew.

'Unfortunately, no,' said Singleton. 'It was manned only by unarmed civilians, and as far as we can tell, the MO of the pirates was something we've seen dozens of times before. It began when a handful of them captured a fishing dhow further south, not far from Mogadishu. They then proceeded to sail it north along the coastline where they stopped at a pirate base and reinforced their crew with additional men who were aboard smaller skiffs. Using the dhow as a mothership, they then pushed out from shore, surrounded the tanker with the skiffs, and attacked and boarded her. The tanker was then captured and taken, along with its crew of six, to the coast of Somalia near the small town of Hafun, which is located near the cape of the same name. It's a small sandy promontory to the northeast of Puntland. The crew consisted of a British captain and first mate, along with four sailors from the Philippines.'

'Casualties?' said Andrew.

'One dead and one lightly injured,' said Singleton. 'Both of them are Filipinos. The pirates usually don't kill the crew since they are worth more to them alive, but it may have been a case of some sort of attempt at resistance, or perhaps the pirates were high on khat and just trigger-happy. We simply don't know. But needless to say, this has added a precarious and somewhat urgent aspect to this situation.'

It was common knowledge amongst members of the international anti-piracy coalition that Somali pirates were often chewing copious amounts of young leaves from the innocuous-looking khat tree. Containing a stimulant that is mildly psychotropic and similar to amphetamine in its effect, it would help keep them alert and often leave them slightly euphoric, impulsive and prone to rash and aggressive behaviour. Obviously, this was a bad combination for men pointing guns at the crews of merchant vessels.

'Now,' said Singleton. 'The pirates first contacted the shipping company four days ago and threatened to kill the crew and blow up the tanker unless a ransom of ten million Pounds is paid. As I am sure you know, aside from various industrial uses, phosphorous acid is used to make incendiary weapons such as white phosphorus munitions that ignite and burn at very high temperatures when in contact with oxygen. In other words, what we're looking at here is a possible atrocity against the crew of the tanker as well as an unprecedented environmental disaster for the Puntland coastline if that ship is damaged and the tanks containing the phosphorous acid are ruptured. And this is where you come in.'

Singleton looked briefly at each man in turn as if to emphasise the seriousness of what he was about to tell them.

'Whitehall has now authorised a rescue mission,' he said. 'It has been designated Operation Longbow, and it is to be carried out with the help of the U.S. 5th Fleet. The USS Dwight D. Eisenhower carrier strike group is currently moving into position in the Gulf of Aden a few hundred miles off the coast of Somalia. You'll each receive an ISR package with all the details.'

Picking up a stack of five manila folders from his desk containing identical intelligence, surveillance, and reconnaissance reports, he pushed them across to Andrew, who then began handing them out to the others. Singleton then opened his own folder.

'I trust you'll read this carefully,' said Singleton, 'but here's the gist of it. According to intelligence pieced together from satellite imagery, long-range footage from our Poseidon surveillance aircraft and some human intelligence sources on the ground in northern Somalia, the five remaining captives are being held in a small compound northeast of the town of Hafun, a bit less than two miles from the coast beyond a range of dunes and scrublands. As you'll see from the satellite imagery, there are three structures in the compound, two of which appear to be for the pirates, and the third is assumed to be where the hostages are being held. The buildings are likely made of brick and unable to withstand a blast from anything larger than a hand grenade. Therefore, no explosive devices can be employed during this raid. Needless to say, the safety of the hostages is paramount. You'll be taking off in three hours on one of our Atlas transport planes, and then you'll be taken to Camp Lemonnier.'

Camp Lemonier, located close to the Horn of Africa in Djibouti near the border with Somalia, was one of the largest US military bases in the world and the only permanent American base in Africa. Home to about 5000 military personnel and located just under 900 km from the pirate camp, it was an ideal location from which to launch a raid.

'I've already spoken to Hereford,' Singleton went on, 'and as far as I understand it, this will be a pre-dawn HALO insertion from the Atlas aircraft. Winds at the time of the insertion are likely to be from the southwest, so to minimise the risk of detection, you will touch down on the beach to the northeast and then approach on foot. Having made your way to the compound, you will eliminate the pirates and free the hostages, and as you do this, two Black Hawk helicopters from the carrier group will be holding station off the coast. After the compound has been secured, the choppers will arrive and exfiltrate you and the hostages back to the Eisenhower.'

Singleton gave the five men a few moments to leaf through the ISR reports before speaking again.

'Make no mistake, gentlemen,' he then said. 'The men in that compound are hardcore pirates with ten million reasons to put up a fight, so they should not be underestimated. If they have links with the Houthis in Yemen, as we believe they do, they are also likely very well-armed. And if they are anything like most pirates in that region, they will be dosed up on khat. This means that they are likely to be highly aggressive and impulsive. As I know you'll appreciate, this presents a very real danger of the hostages being put in peril if you are detected before you can get into position to launch the assault. Any questions?'

Andrew looked around at the serious faces of his four comrades, none of whom appeared to feel the need to ask questions. Then he turned to face Singleton.

'We're ready,' he said with quiet determination as he looked Singleton straight in the eye. 'Let's get this done.'

Two

Some fourteen hours later, just before 1 a.m. local time, the hulking RAF Atlas 400A transport aircraft took off from the enormous Camp Lemonnier on the coast of Djibouti to head southeast towards the Horn of Africa. Sitting in a row of jump seats mounted on the inside of the fuselage in its cavernous cargo hold was the small team of SAS soldiers along with two crewmembers who would be assisting in the high-altitude jump from the aircraft. The four-hour trip south from Akrotiri to Camp Lemonnier had gone without a hitch, and after a quick refuelling stop where the team had also checked their kit, readied their weapons and packed their lightweight parachutes, the plane had taken off again and headed out over the desert for the final roughly 600-mile stretch of the journey.

When the plane was almost at the drop location, it was just before three o'clock in the morning. Sunrise was about two hours away, and the team had to get down and into position no less than an hour before dawn. Since time immemorial, this had been the optimal time to strike an enemy unawares, especially if the initial approach and attack were covert in nature. The reasons for this were simple. The darkness would provide cover for the team's approach and minimise the risk of detection. More importantly, however, most of the pirates would be asleep, and the men on guard duty would be suffering from sleep deprivation. This would leave them groggy and disorientated once the assault began, and it would affect their reaction time and decision-making abilities, even if they had been chewing khat all night. In addition, the psychological impact on human beings of nearing the end of a dark night and instinctively believing that any nocturnal threat might be receding, only to then suddenly come under violent attack, also tended to significantly add to the chaos of confusion of gunfire erupting.

Aside from their identical black jumpsuits, tactical vests, boots, helmets and night vision goggles, the five men looked nothing alike. Tall and muscular, McGregor was built like a bear. Dunn was short and stocky. Logan had the physique of a marathon runner, and Wilks was all lean muscle. They were all at peak fitness, and each one of them was highly skilled and exceptionally motivated. Through years of training, they had spent thousands of hours in kill houses and on live-fire exercises all over the world, but this was what it was all about. This was the real thing. At this moment, sitting in an uncomfortable jump seat in the back of a noisy RAF transport plane heading out to complete a hostage rescue mission, none of them could have felt more alive than they did right now, and there was nowhere else they would rather be.

Their helmets were made of carbon fibre and painted matte black, as were all of the metal components on their weapons and other kit in order to make sure that none of them reflected any light. They were carrying Heckler & Koch MP5SD submachine guns that had been the short-range weapon of choice for the SAS for decades. It was compact, accurate and highly reliable, and with its inbuilt suppressor system, it was almost silent when fired. As a secondary weapon, they all carried a 9mm Glock 19 for close encounters in cramped environments where weapons like assault rifles or even submachine guns became cumbersome and difficult to operate. Wilks was the only one of them carrying a weapon that differed from the rest of the team. Lying across his lap and ready to be strapped tightly to his body for the HALO jump was the medium-range scoped HK417 sniper rifle. Firing standard 7.62 NATO rounds, it was accurate out to about 700 metres, and with a muzzle velocity of close to three thousand kilometres per hour, it packed a devastating punch. With that level of kinetic energy delivered on a target, any centre mass hit was not survivable unless that person was wearing heavy body armour. Something none of the Somali pirates would be doing, especially in the middle of the night. Dunn, on top of his submachine gun and pistol, was also carrying breaching charges just in case some unforeseen eventuality should crop up, as well as a compact and disposable M72 LAW. The short and light tube-shaped anti-armour weapon fired an unguided 66mm rocket-propelled grenade with enough punch and explosive power to take out most lightly armoured vehicles. With an effective range of about 200 metres, it could often serve as an ace up the sleeve in a tight, medium-range fire exchange where the team was pinned down by an opposing force with superior numbers and vehicles.

Roughly ninety minutes after taking off from Camp Lemonnier at an altitude of 43,000 feet, the Atlas performed a wide turn over the Gulf of Aden and headed straight for the jump point some fifteen kilometres off the coast of Somalia. With five minutes to go, the team got to their feet, strapped all of their kit to their bodies, and waddled towards the aircraft's massive rear cargo doors. They then stacked up and waited for the doors to open.

When the plane's interior lights turned from white to red and the doors finally opened, an icy torrent of air rushed inside. Then the jump lights turned green, and Andrew walked calmly out to the edge of the ramp and allowed himself to fall out and into the black night where the air immediately tore at his clothes as he spread out his arms and legs and stabilised himself. The rest of the team followed him out a few seconds apart, and soon the five men were plummeting towards the ocean below as the Atlas disappeared above them and began its turn back towards Djibouti.

Within less than a minute, the team had formed up in a loose wedge formation, and using their bodies to generate lateral speed, they began heading towards the coastline in the far distance. Falling at over 200 kilometres per hour, they were quickly able to convert a large portion of that energy into horizontal motion that almost matched their vertical speed, and with ice-cold air clawing at their jumpsuits, the five black figures raced silently across the sky towards their insertion point.

After about four minutes, with the coastline and the surf now clearly visible below them in the pale shades of green generated by their night vision goggles, Andrew checked the altimeter attached to his lower left arm. They were rapidly coming up on 3000 feet. Shortly thereafter, he pulled the cord on the parachute. It popped open, unfurled and yanked him up and backwards all within the space of less than a second. Immediately, the rest of the team followed suit, and then the five men steered themselves smoothly over the beach and landed in a small dip between a set of large, tall dunes on which grew tufts of lyme grass that wafted in the gentle breeze. They quickly huddled up and made sure that everyone was unhurt, and then they rolled up their parachutes and buried them in the sand.

'Listen up,' said Andrew in a hushed voice as the small group knelt silently around him, unstrapping and checking their weapons and equipment. 'We're a bit more than two kilometres from the compound. We'll yomp south from there and stay out of sight until we can get the lay of the land and get into position. Then we'll hit them hard. Watch out for sentries. These guys may be a bunch of pirates high on khat, but they're not stupid. They understand the value of what they have, and they won't want to give it up easily. Questions?'

The men glanced around at each other, but no one spoke. They all knew what to do, and they were now focused like laser beams on the task in front of them.

'Alright,' said Andrew. 'Let's move out.'

With Andrew in the lead, the SAS team began making their way southwest through the landscape, picking a route that kept them as low as possible between the tall shifting dunes. After a couple of minutes, he thought he spotted movement up ahead, and his right hand came up, forming a tight fist. Seeing the signal, the team stopped and went onto one knee while bringing up their weapons. A dark, mottled shape moved inside some parched bushes, and suddenly there were two glowing eyes looking their way. Then another pair appeared next to them, and then two more.

'Shit,' whispered Andrew, addressing the men over his shoulder. 'Hyenas.'

'What the hell are they doing all the way out here?' said McGregor. 'They shouldn't be in the dunes.'

'They must be starving,' said Andrew.

The words had barely left his mouth before a low growl emanated from their left. Andrew's head whipped around, and there, standing less than fifteen metres away inside a large clump of lyme grass stood another three of the powerful and fearless canine pack hunters. For hundreds of thousands of years, these predators had prowled the arid plains of Africa, hunting in packs of anywhere from a handful to nearly a hundred. This group looked particularly scraggy and famished, and as the group of three hyenas up ahead emerged from the bush and began to close in, they all started producing low growls as they bared their sharp teeth, slowly encircling the SAS team.

'Damn it,' said Andrew, his voice low and taut. 'We could do without this right now.'

'Scare them away?' said McGregor.

'No way to do that without alerting the compound,' said Andrew.'

'We need to drop them,' said Dunn. 'No other way.'

'I agree,' said Wilks. 'Nice and quiet.'

'Alright,' said Andrew. 'Pick your targets. On my command.'

The men released the safety catches, cocked their MP5s and set the fire selectors to single shot. Wilks extracted his suppressed Glock 19 from its holster and racked the slide quietly. Then they each took aim at one of the hungry beasts. Andrew prepared to take out two of the four in front of them, as did McGregor, who had inched up to kneel by his side.

'Ready?' said Andrew. 'In three, two, one. Fire.'

The weapons clicked as they fired, and there was a quick staccato series of muffled pops as the 9mm projectiles left the suppressed barrels and smacked into the musclebound bodies of the ravenous animals. A couple of them yelped as the bullets hit them, but they all dropped dead onto the soft sand like sacks of meat. For a moment, the team remained immobile, listening out for more hyenas or any other signs of movement. However, all they could hear was the faint whisper of the breeze in the grass atop the dunes, and after a few seconds, the team got back onto their feet.

'No time to hide them,' said Andrew, looking around at the dead predators. 'We'll just have to hope no one sees them before we reach the compound. Let's go.'

They continued through the undulating sea of sand, and after another twenty minutes, they glimpsed a faint light across the tops of the dunes up ahead. Bringing up his binoculars, Andrew could see the faint outline of a couple of buildings lit up by a campfire.

'That's it,' he said. 'Let's push up as close as we can. Stay alert.'

The men advanced across the final stretch of terrain, making sure to stay out of any line of sight from the compound. When they reached the final tall dune between them and the pirate camp, they climbed slowly up the sandy incline, and Andrew then went prone and crawled up to the top, looking over the crest and down into the compound. He had never been within five hundred miles of this place, yet after studying the satellite photos in the ISR package, the layout seemed completely familiar. There were two main single-storey buildings close to each other, as well as a smaller shack some thirty metres further north and slightly closer to their position at the top of the dune. Near the two main buildings was a large circular firepit edged by rocks where a handful of logs were burning. Huddled around the fire to keep warm during the chilly desert night were five armed men carrying what appeared to be the militants' weapon of choice the world over. The Russian-made AK-47. With almost 100 million of this particular model having been produced during the course of over half a century, in addition to its legendary durability and ease of use, it was no wonder that it could now be found in virtually every conflict zone in every country and territory across the planet.

Four of the five men were seated in folding chairs with canned drinks in their hands while the fifth was standing up by the edge of the firepit poking the burning logs with a stick. As Andrew watched them from his hidden perch, he noted that these five men would have inadvertently ruined their ability to see in the dark, which should give his own team a significant advantage.

In front of the smaller shack a short distance away was another man sitting with his weapon across his lap smoking a cigarette. Whenever he took a puff, its orange ember glowed brightly in the dark, and as he exhaled, grey smoke was carried off by the breeze. The fact that he was sitting where he was with his weapon ready to fire, all but guaranteed that the hostages were being held inside the shack precisely as the intelligence reports had indicated. Andrew slid back down into cover and turned to his men.

'Looks like the hostages are still here,' he whispered. 'Small shack to our right. There's a group of five tangos by the firepit, and I'm guessing there are more of them inside the two main buildings. Wilks, you flank right and try to get a bead on the guy by the shack. The rest of us will take out the men by the firepit.'

Wilks nodded and moved quietly back down the dune to circle right and begin climbing up to the top of another slightly taller dune some fifty metres away. This would give him a direct line of sight to the man guarding the hostages at a range of less than two hundred metres. And from that distance, he never missed. From his position, he would also be able to provide cover fire across the rest of the compound as Andrew and the others moved in to locate the hostages and secure the area.

While Andrew, McGregor, Logan and Dunn moved into position at the top of their dune and lined up their weapons on the five targets by the firepit, Wilks was nearing the crest of the larger dune when he suddenly spotted movement out of the corner of his eye. When he turned his head, he froze as he spotted a sentry less than thirty metres away. The man was clearly on a patrol around the perimeter of the compound and had somehow managed to walk right up on the SAS men without being detected. For a moment that seemed to stretch on forever, the two men stared at each other. Then, with lightning speed borne of endless practice, Wilks reached down and pulled his suppressed Glock 19 from its holster on his right thigh. In one smooth movement, he racked the slide, brought it up and aimed at the guard who was now in the process of unslinging his AK-47 from his shoulder. As the guard attempted to bring up the weapon, Wilks fired three shots in quick succession. Two of them hit the guard in the chest, and he briefly staggered backwards with his arms flailing before dropping heavily onto his back. As he hit the sand, his index finger tightened around the trigger, and the assault rifle produced a loud, dry burst of three rounds.

Over on the other dune, the heads of Andrew and the rest of the team instantly swivelled right to see Wilks lowering his weapon and glancing back at them. So much for the element of surprise. As Wilks quickly re-holstered his pistol and unslung his sniper rifle, the other four wasted no time returning their attention to the firepit where the four men in the folding chairs were now on their feet. The SAS team flicked their fire selectors to burst and lined up on their targets.

'Weapons free,' said Andrew tightly, and then they opened fire.

A hail of bullets immediately tore through the air and cut down three of the five men. The other two managed to bring up their AK-47s and open fire. However, without a clear idea of the direction of the incoming fire, and without the ability to see in the dark, they merely ended up sending long panicked bursts in the SAS team's general direction. The guard sitting by the shack had now also got to his feet, and because his eyes were better accustomed to the darkness, he had managed to spot the SAS soldiers at the top of the dune despite the fact that the inbuilt suppressors on the MP5SDs also did a good job of masking muzzle flashes. He brought up his assault rifle, took careful aim and squeezed off several well-aimed three-round bursts before a 7.62 projectile from Wilks' HK417 slammed into his chest. It punched straight through him and tore open a gory exit wound from which blood and tissue exploded as he spun and fell to the ground dead.

Andrew and the others found themselves having to duck down behind the crest of the dune as the incoming fire landed uncomfortably close to them, kicking up the sand and ricocheting off into the night. However, Wilks had not had time to mount the suppressor onto his rifle, so they all heard the dry crack as it fired, and they knew that whoever had been shooting at them was now no longer among the living. As they re-emerged and took aim again, the two remaining pirates by the firepit had gone prone and had begun returning fire, but their shots were frantic and inaccurate, and mere seconds later they were both dead. To Andrew's surprise, no more pirates emerged from the two main buildings, so he got to his feet and crested the top of the dune.

'I'm going for the hostages,' he said. 'Cover me.'

McGregor, Logan and Dunn quickly changed mags and took aim at the doors of the two buildings, and then Andrew began running down the slope of the dune towards the shack. He had barely made it to the bottom before both doors were suddenly ripped open and two groups of pirates emerged, clutching AK-47s and spraying fire around them, clearly uncertain as to the precise location of the attackers. When they saw Andrew sprinting across the flat stretch of ground between the dune and the shack, they immediately turned their weapons on him.

Andrew threw himself behind some rocks that were nowhere near large enough to provide him with full cover, but it was enough to buy him a couple of seconds. As he scrambled behind them, bullets slammed into the stone, and dust and fragments exploded into the air mere inches from his head. But then the rest of his team opened up. A torrent of lead came down from their submachine guns at the top of the dune, and every two or three seconds, there was a dry crack from Wilks' sniper rifle.

Andrew then decided that he had had enough of hiding, so he brought up his MP5, inched out to one side to get clear of the rocks, and immediately spotted a pirate who appeared to be sprinting straight towards him with his weapon raised. Whether the man was deranged, high on a particularly potent batch of khat or simply had a death wish, Andrew would never find out. He released a three-round burst that smacked into the man's torso, causing him to crash to the ground in a dusty heap, after which he rolled over and moved no more.

With the remaining pirates now seemingly suppressed by the incoming fire and running for whatever cover they could find, Andrew got back onto his feet and sprinted the final short distance to the shack. As he did so, shots suddenly came from inside one of the main buildings, and bullets pinged off the ground near his feet. Trying to get into cover as soon as possible, he raced past the dead guard who was missing the side of his torso and straight to the wooden door to the shack. Without stopping, he crashed into it and burst straight through as wooden fragments and splinters flew in all directions.

As soon as he was inside, he found himself face to face with another guard who had evidently been stationed there to watch the hostages. The man had an AK-47 slung over his shoulder, but in his hands was a semi-automatic Beretta M92 pistol. The guard had very sensibly elected to use the much more nimble pistol rather than the long and bulky assault rifle inside the shack, and Andrew only just had time to recognise the weapon before the man brought it up and fired.

There was a loud crack inside the small shack, and the bullet smacked hard into his chest. Thankfully, his ballistics vest stopped it dead in its tracks. However, the 9mm projectile carried enough kinetic energy to deliver a hefty punch that momentarily stunned him and caused him to stagger backwards a step. The guard pulled the trigger again, but this time the pistol jammed. As the man's eyes widened in sudden panic, Andrew brought up his MP5 and placed a three-round burst square into his chest. The guard toppled backwards and crashed onto the floor. Only then did Andrew notice the six hostages that were huddled in the far corner of the shack. He spun around with his weapon raised, and when he was able to identify no further threats, he flicked up his night vision goggles and switched on the torch that was mounted under the barrel of the submachine gun.

'My name is Sterling,' he said, his voice thick and rasping after the near miss from the Beretta. 'I'm with the SAS. We're here to take you home. Anyone injured?'

'No,' said the trembling voice of a man who was clearly English. 'I am Captain Miller. No one's hurt. We're dehydrated, but we're ok.'

'Stay here while we secure the area,' said Andrew. 'I'll be back soon.'

He left the shack, brought up his weapon, and emerged just as a lone figure burst out of one of the main buildings and raced around the corner towards the back. Andrew fired a burst at him, but the bullets hit the corner where they chewed up the brickwork. Seconds later, there was the sound of a car engine starting and revving up furiously, and a couple of seconds later, a pickup truck roared out from behind the building and swerved wildly as the driver attempted to escape across the uneven terrain.

'Dunn!' Andrew called into his mike.

'I've got him,' said Dunn calmly, sounding almost as if he had anticipated this exact scenario.

Seconds later, Andrew watched as Dunn fired the M72 LAW from the top of the dune, and the rocket-propelled grenade streaked through the darkness in a straight line towards its target below. It covered the distance in less than a second and connected with the back of the pickup in a fiery explosion that shunted the rear of the vehicle up into the air. When the mangled pickup crashed back down onto the sand, it had been reduced to a burning mess of metal, fuel and rubber that sent a black plume of smoke roiling up into the air.

'Good work,' said Andrew over the radio. 'Wilks, stay where you are. The rest of you, come down and clear the main buildings. The hostages are all in good condition. I'll radio for extraction now.'

About 45 minutes later, the five special forces operators and the six hostages stood on the beach as two Blackhawk helicopters from the USS Eisenhower touched down metres from the crashing waves. The SAS team formed a large, protective crescent formation around one of the choppers as the hostages scrambled up inside it, and after it had taken off safely and begun accelerating out over the ocean towards the carrier strike group, they converged on the second helicopter. Once they were inside and the sliding door was slammed shut, they all slumped down into their seats and exchanged satisfied nods and a few thin smiles. The running joke in the SAS was that they would complete their mission and be back home in time for tea and medals. Of course, they all knew that the best they could hope for was a cup of tea and a pat on the back, since, as a matter of policy, none of the missions carried out by the SAS were ever officially acknowledged. However, none of them were in it for the fame or the glory. In a case like this, it was only ever about the safety of the hostages. Aside from that, the only thing that mattered was making sure that everyone came home alive.

In the hours that followed, a team of U.S. Marines secured the captured tanker. At the same time, the hostages were taken to the Eisenhower for processing and medical treatment. The next day, after arriving back at RAF Akrotiri for a couple of days of rest and recuperation, they packed up their kit and boarded the plane back to RAF Brize Norton from where they headed back to the SAS's main base of operations at Hereford. All except for Andrew, who got into his dark green Jaguar DB9 and drove southeast towards his home in Hampstead in North London.

THREE

THE CHAGRES RIVER, PANAMA

It was a warm and humid afternoon as Lawrence Blake made his way from the modest parking area at the foot of the steep incline towards the fort. Birds were chirping in the trees, and there was the faint sound of waves crashing against rocks in the distance as he and his companions pushed up along the winding walking trail that ran through the dense tropical forest up to the imposing structure sitting atop a large coastal promontory on the northern coast of Panama. He was tall and slim and sported a short, neat beard, and he was wearing a thin, loose white shirt, beige slacks and brown hiking boots. He wore a smart, cream-coloured fedora, and on his nose rested a pair of expensive-looking designer sunglasses.

Ascending along the trail, he was flanked by two local uniformed police officers from the nearby city of Colón. Both men were short and somewhat overweight, and they were panting and huffing as they struggled to keep up with the Englishman. However, they had both been more than happy to receive an envelope full of US dollars to serve as his escort for the day. This would lend Blake's visit to the UNESCO World Heritage Site the appearance of legitimacy, and it would also make it straightforward to have it cleared of any remaining tourists and staff now that the site was coming to the end of its regular opening hours. Bringing up the rear of the small group and carrying a large, heavy holdall with tools was his assistant, fixer and general problem solver, Antonio Ortega. The tall, muscular Spaniard wore an olive green t-shirt, cargo trousers and hiking boots, and he sported black, slicked-back, medium-length hair and a thick moustache. He had a torso as wide as a door, and his arms bulged with the results of thousands of hours spent in the gym. With a long background in the Spanish armed forces, he was, however, not in Lawrence Blake's own direct employ. Instead, he had been provided by Blake's client, the illustrious Count Carlos Roberto Velazquez de Toledo. The Spanish aristocrat hailed from an old noble family from the Castilla-La Mancha region in central Spain, and as a descendant of one of the more prominent conquistadors of the New World during the 16th century, he was a keen collector of artefacts from that particular time period and that part of the world. And Blake was more than happy to oblige.

Relying on his natural skill as a treasure hunter, along with his deep knowledge of the history of the Spanish Main and the wider Caribbean, as well as the special access to valuable information about ongoing archaeological work that he often found himself in possession of, Blake had already completed a number of challenging assignments for the Spanish count.

And with a bit of luck, today he would be able to chalk up another success resulting in the full payment of his sizeable fee and almost certainly a nice bonus on top, if past experience with his benefactor was anything to go by.

Ever since Blake had been a young man, he had felt a longing for adventure, excitement and even danger, but circumstances back in England had eventually coiled their way around him and tied him down to a life much more ordinary and conventional than he had hoped for in his earlier years. A life of blissful domesticity had never appealed to him, yet that was somehow the situation he had one day found himself in. Precisely how it had ended up happening, he couldn't say. Perhaps it was the society he had grown up in. One that tempts with notions of comfort and safety at every turn, while neglecting the innate desire of men to seek out adventure and discover what might lie on the other side of the horizon. He had felt the crushing weight of it on his shoulders build with every year that passed. And so, one day he had decided to leave it all behind, at least in a manner of speaking, to take up his passion for treasure hunting. He had proven himself highly capable in this role, and he had mounted dozens of expeditions to scour the Earth for valuable artefacts, gold, silver, gemstones and sometimes historical relics that were unique and therefore worth a fortune on the black market. Now a middle-aged man, still handsome, fit and sharp of mind, his new life was everything he had hoped it would be.

As the group reached the end of the trail and emerged near the top of the promontory, the impressive ruins of Fort San Lorenzo rose up in front of them. It had been constructed during the late 16th century with almost vertical rocky escarpments on all sides except for a narrow and steep approach from the southeast, and its extensive gun batteries had provided protection for the Spanish ships in the bay below. It sat on a virtually flat, rocky promontory overlooking the mouth of the wide River Chagres that meandered about ten kilometres through the rainforest from the dam at Lake Gatun. The enormous artificial lake had been created as part of the construction of the Panama Canal during the first two decades of the 20th century. However, in 1502, when Christopher Columbus first arrived here and discovered the river, it had stretched far to the southeast, reaching more than halfway to Panama City on the Pacific Coast.

Over the course of more than a century after that initial discovery, the Chagres River had provided the Spanish conquistadors with a way to transport gold, silver and other valuables north from Peru up the coast of South America and across the Panamanian isthmus by mule trains to the Gulf of Mexico. From there, the stolen valuables could then be loaded onto treasure fleets and transported back to Spain via the ports of Nombre de Dios and Portobelo on the northern coast of Panama.

This virtually constant flow of precious metals through arduous terrain and poorly defended port towns naturally attracted the attention of many Caribbean pirates. The most famous of these men was the privateer and later lieutenant governor of Jamaica, Henry Morgan, who led an entire pirate fleet from the island of Tortuga to launch a successful attack on Fort San Lorenzo in December of 1670. He and his men then went on to cross the isthmus and sack Panama City itself in January of the following year. The expedition had become known mainly for the sacking of what was one of Spain's most important and wealthy cities in the New World at that time.

However, Blake, who had become highly adept at masquerading as an archaeologist carrying the official accreditations and all the proper paperwork, was not interested in Morgan's trip to Panama City. He was here because of a fascinating account he had unearthed back in England. It had been written soon after the raid on Fort San Lorenzo by a man called Joseph Bradley, who was one of Morgan's lieutenants. Bradley had led the assault on the fort, which was protected on the land side by a moat, palisades and gun emplacements that had their cannons facing inland. Launching a frontal assault, Bradley's men managed to take over the fort, although with heavy losses. And apparently, after the raid and the routing of the Spanish forces, the fort's royal liaison officer, a man named Luis Gamboa who was also in charge of handling special items and artefacts, had run to his private residence, where Bradley had found him attempting to hide inside a secret compartment in the cellar under one of the back rooms.

Along with Gamboa and a large cache of pieces of eight, Bradley had also found two magnificent, identical Aztec figurines made of intricately carved and burnished jade. They depicted *Huitzilopochtli*, the Aztec god of sun and war, and no one who laid eyes on them could deny their exquisiteness. Joseph Bradley had killed Gamboa and stolen the valuables in the secret compartment, but not before the terrified liaison officer had revealed to him an incredible story.

Supposedly, the twin figurines had been taken from the Aztec capital of *Tenochtitlan* on the 22nd of November in the year 1529 by a man named Pedro de Alvarado. He was a prominent conquistador who travelled with Hernan Cortés himself, and he was later to become governor of the Spanish territory of Guatemala. The two polished idols were said to have been the personal possessions of Moctezuma II, who was the 9th emperor of the enormous Aztec Empire. An empire that Cortés ultimately conquered and destroyed. According to Gamboa, Alvarado had taken the relics from an altar inside the Great Temple that the Aztecs called *Huēyi Teōcalli*, meaning Great House of the Gods. This happened immediately after the infamous and well-documented massacre at that temple, in which Alvarado interrupted a religious celebration and then slaughtered all the noblemen and warriors there. As the Aztec capital's elite lay dying in pools of their own blood spreading across the temple floor, Alvarado helped himself to the two figurines and sent them off to Fort San Lorenzo with the intention of having them shipped from there back to his wife in Madrid. However, the fort commander at that time appeared to have been equally enraptured by the twin pieces of Aztec art, and he had taken them for himself and hidden them in a metal chest inside a secret compartment in the cellar under his quarters. This was where Gamboa had eventually found them more than a century later, and he had left them where they were, planning to one day take them back to Spain himself.

Bradley, proving less restrained than Gamboa, had killed the hapless liaison officer, left one of the figurines in the chest, and taken the other with him.

However, soon after this, he died of wounds sustained in a battle with the Spanish. One figurine thus remained in the fort, but as for what happened to the one Bradley was carrying, nothing more could be found, and its whereabouts had been a mystery ever since. However, Bradley's diary had recently been unearthed, and it had revealed the story of the jade idols and the secret stash at the fort. Having come into the possession of this diary, Lawrence Blake had now arrived at Fort San Lorenzo to find the centuries-old prize so that he could deliver it to his paymaster.

As Blake and his small entourage approached the gate to the fort, the last tourists were just leaving, and a lone site warden was in the process of locking the gate with a chain and a padlock.

'*Por favour!*' one of the pudgy police officers called out to the warden, who turned with a look of puzzlement on his face as he regarded the approaching quartet. '*Espera un momento!*'

Blake waited as the officer and his colleague walked up to the warden and engaged in a quick exchange in Spanish. At one point, the officer glanced back at Blake, who nodded affably, and the warden mirrored his gesture.

'*Hola!*' Blake said cheerfully as he gave a small wave with a clipboard onto which was affixed an official-looking document with the UNESCO logo placed prominently in the top right corner.

After a moment's hesitation, the warden shrugged and unlocked the gate. Then he wiped his brow, put on his grubby straw hat and ambled off down the walking trail towards the car park. The fort was now deserted except for the four new arrivals.

'Thank you very much, gentlemen,' said Blake jovially in a clipped accent, addressing the two police officers as he walked confidently up to open the gate with Ortega following close behind. 'That'll be all for now. If I could ask you two to remain here and stop anyone from entering the fort while we are inside, I should be very grateful.'

The two officers glanced at each other, shrugged and stepped aside.

'Lovely,' smiled Blake as he pushed the gate open and walked through it before calling over his shoulder. 'We shouldn't be long. See you in a bit.'

Blake and Ortega left the two officers behind and made their way further into the large compound. Aside from having been a fort, it also at one point encompassed a small village that for close to a century sustained itself on the traffic that passed through this strategic location by the mouth of the Chagres River. Most of the buildings were in ruins, but since the entire fort had been built with blocks of dark granite, there were several partly overgrown and lichen-covered dwellings that were part of the main structure, which were in remarkably good condition. At the far end of the flat promontory, some thirty metres above the crashing waves at the foot of the sheer escarpments, were the bastions overlooking the water from which gun batteries with dozens of 24-pounder guns had once protected the Spanish treasure fleets from the threat of sea-borne raiders. Beyond it, as far as the eye could see, the wide river meandered south through a dense carpet of dark green rainforest that was blanketed by a faint mist rising up from the jungle.

'This way, Antonio,' said Blake brightly.

He strode across the main courtyard to a set of structures that were integrated into the perimeter of the surrounding fort. Following a few steps behind, Ortega lugged the heavy bag along with him, but he made it look as if it contained feathers rather than heavy-duty tools. Stopping to consult a copy of the original plans for the fort that his paymaster had helped retrieve from the *Archivo Histórico Nacional* in Madrid, Blake looked up and pointed.

'It should be this one,' he said as he entered one of the dwellings. 'Follow me.'

Ortega, who had barely said a word since the two men had touched down on a flight from the Spanish capital three days earlier, followed the treasure hunter inside the building. He was used to taking orders, and he had soon become accustomed to the Englishman's aloof and somewhat arrogant demeanour.

Inside the structure was a small number of cramped, low-ceilinged rooms connected by doorways that forced both men to stoop. Not only had interior space been at a premium when the fort had been constructed, but around five centuries ago the average height of the Spanish soldiers in this place had been several tens of centimetres shorter than both Blake and Ortega. The flagstone floor had been worn smooth, and of the once perfectly rendered and painted walls, there was now only the exposed brickwork left. The small square holes in the exterior walls where the windows had once been let in only a limited amount of light, but a few beams of warm, late afternoon sunlight cut in through them to illuminate the space.

'Now,' said Blake as he pushed into one of the back rooms, studying the fort's floorplans intently. 'This room appears to have a cavity between it and the fort's exterior. 'Antonio. If you wouldn't mind.'

Blake gestured to the back wall in the dimly lit room, and the large Spaniard dropped the holdall on the floor with a heavy thud, knelt next to it and extracted a sledgehammer. He then got to his feet again, walked over to the wall and gave Blake a glance.

'*Aqui?*' said Ortega in a low, husky voice. 'Here?'

'Be my guest,' smiled Blake cordially, giving a small wave of the hand. 'Let's see if I am right.'

Holding the sledgehammer's handle in his large hands, Ortega brought it up and back over his shoulder, and then he swung it forward in a wide arc with as much force as he could muster. He grunted as the steel hammerhead connected with the wall amid a loud thump that instantly cracked several of the bricks and sent dust and masonry fragments flying out. Along with the sound of the impact, there was a clearly discernible, hollow reverberation that hinted at the void behind the wall.

'Again,' said Blake, excitement creeping into his voice.

Ortega swung the hammer again, and this time several of the bricks crumbled and fell out onto the floor, leaving a small hole.

'Again,' Blake repeated, circling around to get a better view while staying clear of the sledgehammer's arc. 'Keep going.'

Ortega kept pummeling the ancient wall until it had been reduced to a heap of broken bricks revealing a dark space roughly a metre deep and two metres wide. As Blake stepped closer, he saw the stone steps leading down.

'Bloody hell,' he whispered. 'I was right.'

He extracted a small but powerful torch from a pocket in his trousers and stooped low to step inside the cavity. It was dusty and slightly damp, and the air smelt of some sort of decay. One careful step at a time, Blake descended a narrow stairwell whose sides were draped in thick curtains of ancient cobwebs. He continued down into the musty darkness and eventually emerged into a small cellar with exposed brick walls that contained only a chair and a tiny wooden table with a candleholder placed on top of it. To the left of the table was an alcove set into the wall, and sitting inside it was a dust-covered metal chest roughly the size of a small picnic basket. He stepped over to it and examined it. It did not appear to be locked, so he held the torch between his teeth and gripped the lid with both hands before immediately releasing the chest and pulling back his left hand. A small cut in his skin had been made inside his palm by a sharp corner of the metal chest, and as he watched it, a small trickle of blood emerged.

'Oh,' he whispered, still with the torch between his teeth. 'I guess you don't want to give up your secrets so easily. Let's try this.'

Once again, he placed his hands on the lid, more carefully this time, and he now managed to get a firm grip without the risk of injury. Holding his breath in anticipation, he lifted it up, and immediately a faint golden glow filled the tiny underground space. As he removed the torch from his mouth, a wide grin spread across his face.

'Bradley, you old sea dog,' he said quietly. 'You may have been a pirate, but you were no liar.'

The chest was almost full to the brim with gold doubloons, but on top of it lay the very thing he had come all this way to find. The roughly thirty-centimetre-tall Aztec jade figurine seemed to shine with a strange green translucency as he regarded it, and as he picked it up, he was amazed by how heavy it was despite its small size.

Turning it over in his hands, he suddenly realised that he had once seen one very similar to it. In fact, standing there with the ancient relic in his hands, he could have sworn that he had laid eyes on an identical figurine several years earlier in the British Museum. And unless his memory failed him, which it rarely did, it had been correctly identified as Aztec in origin, but its exact nature and provenance had been listed as 'uncertain.' But now he understood. What he held in his hands was one of the two figurines from the Great Temple in the Aztec capital, and the other was now held somewhere in the British Museum in central London. And incredibly, the curators there had no idea what they possessed.

After a moment, a thought suddenly came into his mind. The figurine that he had just found would secure him a very handsome payment from the Spanish count. However, if he could somehow retrieve its twin, then the two of them could be sold to his client for many times what they would have been worth individually.

'I guess we're heading back to Old Blighty, then,' he said to himself.

He placed the jade figurine carefully back inside the chest on top of the gold, and then he began carrying the treasure back up the steps and into the golden sunlight after almost half a millennium spent in darkness.

Four

Hampstead, London

It is often said that a picture is worth a thousand words, and in this particular instance, Fiona Keane had to agree wholeheartedly. The attractive Irish thirty-something blonde had lived in the UK capital for a couple of decades, and she had worked for the British Museum as an archaeologist and historian for almost half of that time. Living with her partner Andrew Sterling in their shared house in Hampstead, she often had the luxury of being able to pick a topic of research and then spend her time freely engrossing herself in it. On this sunny day in her light and airy, west-facing home office, she was gazing at her computer monitor, which showed a picture she had taken with her phone the day before. Her friend and colleague, Emily Butler, who was the curator of Renaissance Collections at the British Museum, had given her access to one of the collection's most captivating items. The Renaissance was not a time period that Fiona was very familiar with, but lately, she had developed a fascination with Queen Elizabeth I.

Elizabeth had reigned for an impressive forty-five years until her death in 1603, after what had been a tumultuous reign in a number of different ways. And on more than one occasion, her own life as well as the very existence of the Kingdom of England hung in the balance. However, as Fiona had discovered, the highly intelligent and shrewd monarch had navigated those treacherous waters as well as or better than any ruler before or since.

She leaned forward and gazed intently at the image in front of her on the computer screen. It was a small, twenty-by-thirty-centimetre paper hand drawing of Elizabeth produced in 1575 by the Italian artist Federico Zuccaro. The Tudor queen was wearing a bell-shaped farthingale gown with puffy sleeves, a bodice and an elaborate ruff. Around her neck hung also a necklace with a large pendant, and in her hand was a fan with a small handle. The drawing had been willed to the British Museum in 1799 by a private collector, and every few years it was retrieved from its climate-controlled storage to appear in various public exhibitions around London. However, Fiona had been allowed to see it for herself and even take a photo of it, and now she was struggling to take her eyes off it. Not because of the detailed depiction of her outfit, but because of the queen's face. At first glance, it appeared delicate and perhaps even vulnerable, but if Zuccaro had depicted her appearance accurately, and Fiona believed that he had, there was an impressive strength emanating from her eyes, which seemed to gaze directly and unflinchingly at the observer. For all her frailty of form, she exuded both confidence and determination, and in that sense, the drawing had captured perfectly the essence of her character.

Suddenly, Fiona was pulled from her reverie by the sound of the front door opening and closing, followed by the heavy thud of a bag being dropped onto the floor in the hallway.

'I'm up here!' she called cheerfully, and then she heard the sound of footsteps coming up the stairs to the open-plan kitchen and living room on the first floor.

'Hey,' said Andrew as he entered, looking somewhat weary. 'How's it going?'

'It's going well,' said Fiona, as she got off her chair and came over to him for a hug. 'How did it go?'

Andrew gave her a squeeze that instantly reminded him of the bruise on his chest where the ballistics vest had stopped the bullet from the Somali pirate's gun. He pulled back a bit as his hand found its way up to the tender spot on his torso. Then he shrugged, and she looked up at him with a quizzical face. He knew that he wouldn't be able to tell Fiona any details of the mission on the Horn of Africa, but she seemed to have a sixth sense for the nature of these things whenever he returned from an operation abroad. He tried to shield her as much as possible from the sometimes gory details of his job and the dangers he faced, but somehow she always understood. And the more he tried to downplay it, the better she seemed to be able to intuit what might have happened. At this point, he might as well have the mission debrief he had delivered at RAF Akrotiri turned into a neon sign and worn it on his head.

'It went about as well as we could have hoped,' he finally said, giving her a kiss on the forehead. 'Some people were in trouble. And we got them out.'

'I'm glad,' she said. 'And I'm happy you are back safe. That's all I need to know.'

'What have you been up to?' he said, moving slowly towards one of the two large cream-coloured sofas.

'I'm still deep into my research on Queen Elizabeth I,' said Fiona. 'She was amazing.'

'Oh yeah?' said Andrew as he flopped onto the sofa and looked up at her with a smile. 'As amazing as you?'

'Well,' smiled Fiona coyly and winked. 'Perhaps not quite. But in all seriousness, have a look at this.'

She walked over to her desk and picked up her laptop, carrying it over to sit down next to him.

'Look at this face,' she said, sounding enthralled. 'What do you see?'

'I don't know,' said Andrew, regarding the picture of the hand drawing for a moment and then turning to Fiona with a twinkle in his eye. 'Someone who needs to get out into the sun a bit more? She looks a bit pale.'

'Alright, fine,' said Fiona, with a nod and a smile. 'That might be true, but look at her eyes. It's almost as if she is watching you watching her. And don't they just say, 'Come at me if you think you're tough enough'?'

'Yes,' said Andrew after a beat. 'I suppose I can see a bit of that. Who is this?'

'Queen Elizabeth I,' replied Fiona. 'And I am quickly coming to the conclusion that she was the best monarch this country has ever had. In fact, if it hadn't been for her, there would probably be no England.'

'Really?' said Andrew, raising an eyebrow.

'I believe so,' said Fiona. 'She was as tough and clever as they come, even if she had to convince everyone that she could do the job as monarch as well as any man. In a famous speech at Tilbury Fort in Essex in 1588 when the Spanish Empire was threatening invasion, she actually said this.

"I know that I have the body of a weak and feeble woman, but I have the heart and stomach of a king."

'That might sound a bit odd to us,' said Fiona, 'but it was quite a thing for a woman to say in those days. And she really meant it. And at that point, I think it is fair to say that she had already proven it.'

'I vaguely remember learning something about her in school a very, very long time ago,' said Andrew. 'Wasn't she the daughter of Henry VIII?'

'She was,' nodded Fiona. 'The king who famously had six wives and who founded the Protestant Church of England. And also a man who, quite interestingly, was born the year before Columbus arrived in the Americas. So, as he was growing up, the scale and potential of the New World were just beginning to become clear. Anyway, his daughter Elizabeth only became queen because her half-brother and half-sister died, and then she suddenly found herself next in line to the throne. Although, it is a bit more complicated than that.'

'Right,' said Andrew, his brow furrowed as he tried to retrieve some almost forgotten information from the recesses of his mind. 'Was her mother Anne Boleyn?'

'That's right,' said Fiona, impressed. 'Boleyn was Henry VIII's second wife who was beheaded for treason three years after Elizabeth's death.'

'Blimey,' said Andrew. 'That must have been tough for that little girl.'

'No doubt,' said Fiona. 'And she was then actually declared an illegitimate heir. But she was incredibly intelligent, by all accounts. She was tutored by some of the most educated men from around Europe, who all gushed about how gifted she was, and by the age of twelve she was apparently translating the works of Greek and Roman philosophers into several other languages.'

'That's very impressive,' said Andrew. 'So how did she end up becoming queen?'

'Well,' said Fiona. 'Again, it's complicated, but I'll give you the skinny version. Basically, Henry VIII had broken with the Catholic Church in order to marry Anne Boleyn. When Elizabeth's half-brother Edward died at a young age in 1553, the crown passed to her Catholic half-sister Mary, who soon after married the heir to the Spanish throne, Philip II.

'Right,' said Andrew, trying to keep track of the names in his head.

'Mary then promptly and brutally attempted to restore Catholicism in England,' Fiona continued. 'This spawned a Protestant rebellion that was swiftly put down, but because the eighteen-year-old Elizabeth was suspected of supporting it, she was imprisoned in the Tower of London. She narrowly avoided having her head chopped off and was released after about two months, but she was then placed under house arrest. Then, after Queen Mary failed to provide the Spanish King Phillip with a child and an heir, he simply abandoned her, which by all accounts made her even more crazed and hell-bent on ridding England of Protestantism. And it was because of her religious persecutions that she became known as Bloody Mary.'

'Right,' said Andrew. 'Like the cocktail.'

'Precisely,' said Fiona. 'Now, Mary eventually died of an illness, most likely a tumour, and Elizabeth was then crowned the new queen in 1559.'

'All that in less than twenty years of life,' said Andrew. 'It must have made her into a remarkable person, if she wasn't one already.'

'Certainly,' said Fiona. 'But anyway, this whole thing ended up leading me astray a bit.'

Andrew glanced at her and smiled knowingly. Having watched Fiona employ her considerable intellect many times in the past, he knew only too well what was going on. Whenever she began to delve deeply into a subject matter, she invariably found herself derailed and distracted by a related topic. This would then quickly become a rabbit hole that she would find herself going headlong down into. The only question was. What was it this time?

'Alright, let me guess,' he smiled fondly. 'You stumbled across something even more interesting.'

'Well, yes,' Fiona smiled self-consciously. 'How did you know?'

'Go on,' said Andrew. 'Tell me.'

'Queen Elizabeth's Sea Dogs,' said Fiona.

'Sea Dogs?' said Andrew. 'Who, or what, were they?'

'Well,' said Fiona. 'Because of Phillip II's marriage to Queen Mary, England had been funded to a significant extent by the wealth of the Spanish Empire, whose treasure fleets had been hauling gold and silver back from the New World for almost a century at that point. But when Mary died, that source of income fell away, and it left the English Crown and Queen Elizabeth with a serious cash flow problem. And so, she hired a bunch of young strapping men like Francis Drake to sail out and attempt to establish trade routes to the Far East and the Americas through diplomacy. And if that should fail, she authorised them to use force to attempt to achieve those goals.'

'Francis Drake,' said Andrew pensively. 'What was his claim to fame again? Was he the first or second man to sail all the way around the world?'

'Second,' said Fiona. 'The first was Magellan. Drake was also part of the English fleet that beat the Spanish Armada when it tried to attack England in 1588, so he was really in the thick of things. But as I have now discovered, there is a lot more to Drake than just those two achievements. Apparently, he was ordered by Queen Elizabeth to harass Spanish merchant ships. This was partly because England had lost the Port of Calais as a trading hub to the Spanish, and that seriously hobbled her ability to conduct seaborne trade. On top of that, England was unable to access the New World because the Spanish effectively had a monopoly on trade with that whole region. And this is where I think I need someone much more knowledgeable about this than I am.

Because, as far as I can tell, Drake essentially became a kind of pirate, although he never would have thought of himself in that way. But some of the things he did in the Caribbean can really only be described as piracy, even if they were legal in the eyes of the queen and the law here in England.'

'Interesting,' said Andrew.

'It really is,' said Fiona. 'And as I began to look into this, I ended up looking at the next century or so in the Caribbean, and that's when I came across a story that I found completely fascinating.'

'About Drake?' said Andrew.

'No,' said Fiona. 'It is about a Spanish ship that was called El Castillo Negro. It was a massive galleon that was part of the Spanish treasure fleet and known at the time as the Black Galleon. Apparently, it was laden with treasure when it was captured by the Royal Navy off the coast of Havana in 1714 and taken to Port Royal in Jamaica for repairs before a planned trip back to London. But it never made it. You see, it was commandeered by a group of pirates led by a man called Captain Jack Flynn. In a raid that is about as daring as anything else I have ever read about, he and his men simply stole the galleon from under the noses of the English in Port Royal and sailed off with it, and it was never seen again.'

'That's quite an intriguing story,' observed Andrew.

'Yes,' said Fiona, 'but as I was researching this, I came across a recently uncovered journal that I think could provide a clue to this mystery. It was written by a French merchant named Eduard Leroux who lived on the island of Tortuga, and who was at a hilltop fort there in late 1714.'

'Tortuga,' said Andrew. 'That name sounds familiar.'

'It was the first real pirate haven in the Caribbean,' said Fiona. 'And the Leroux was there when a ship that was anchored in the harbour below suddenly exploded in the dead of night, creating a huge fireball and a boom that could be heard all the way to Hispaniola. According to his account, the ship was a pirate frigate called the Marauder, and that was Jack Flynn's ship. And I am convinced that somehow those two events are connected.'

'Holy cow,' said Andrew. 'Sounds interesting.'

'I know,' said Fiona excitedly. 'Now, I have been able to find other references to this explosion, but up until now, there have been conflicting reports about whether it even happened. At best, there were only third-hand accounts from various people, with some saying that the explosion was close to the harbour, others saying it was far away, and yet others claiming that it was either to the west, the south or southwest. So, no one really seemed to know if it actually happened, and even if it did, no one could say precisely where it was supposed to have taken place. So for anyone interested in finding the wreck of Jack Flynn's pirate ship, it would involve combing a vast area of seabed. But with this new information, I believe I might be able to narrow it down significantly.'

'How so?' said Andrew. 'And why?'

'Well,' said Fiona. 'Leroux, who was on that fort in Tortuga, noted his exact location at the top of one of the fort's towers when the explosion happened, and there are also written accounts from the island of

Hispaniola around five kilometres away, so I should be able to triangulate its location using other accounts of the incident from Tortuga's harbour. As for the why, it's simple. I think that perhaps the Marauder might have been carrying some, if not all, of the treasure from the Black Galleon. And if that is true, then that gold and silver could still be on the seabed somewhere off the coast of Tortuga.'

'That would be amazing,' said Andrew. 'And it would probably be worth billions in today's money.'

'That's right,' nodded Fiona. 'Those treasure ships were crammed full of valuables.'

'And you want to go and look for it?' said Andrew somewhat sceptically.

'Right again,' Fiona said. 'I know this is a bit outside my usual remit, to put it mildly, but I am just so fascinated by this story. Can you imagine actually locating the treasure from the Black Galleon? It would be an incredible find, not to mention the fact that the gold and silver could then be returned to their rightful owner.'

'Yes,' said Andrew hesitantly. 'But that sounds like a big job. And if I am not mistaken, these sorts of ventures usually cost a hell of a lot of money to carry out.'

'This one won't,' said Fiona confidently. 'If I can get to Tortuga and triangulate the location precisely, then it should be straightforward to find the remains of the wreck.'

'Right,' said Andrew, regarding her for a moment. 'I can see you're really fired up about this. Am I correct in thinking that you might want some help?'

'Yes,' said Fiona. 'Definitely. I'd like you to come along. But first, I really need to understand all this stuff much better. The whole story about piracy in the Caribbean is so rich and complicated that I need to talk to a real expert, and I think I know who to go and visit. He might even have heard the story about the Black Galleon and the Marauder.'

'Who then?' said Andrew.

'A chap named Marcus Tobin,' said Fiona. 'He's a professor and senior lecturer in maritime history and early modern piracy at King's College. But he has worked with the British Museum as an advisor before, so I am hoping I can pick his brains about this. I've already set up a meeting with him tomorrow. Hopefully, he can help me make sense of it all. I am really excited.'

'I can tell,' smiled Andrew affectionately, moving to get to his feet. 'Anyway, come on. Let's head out for dinner.'

'Good plan,' said Fiona. 'Let's have Thai food. I'm absolutely starving.'

Five

The petite and slightly built Laura Hartley was making her way across the central Great Court at the British Museum. The glass-covered interior space was enormous, and it seemed even more so now when it was completely empty of visitors, and all she could hear was the sound of her soft, black shoes on the marble floor as she padded along. At this hour, close to 2 a.m., when the huge building in central London was staffed only by a small security team, it felt like a very different place than during the day when throngs of visitors flowed through its galleries and exhibitions, marvelling at the thousands of ancient display items collected over centuries from all over the world.

Being here by herself, the young, petite and slightly built woman could almost allow herself to feel as if she owned it, and that she was its sole loving custodian. And in some ways, that was true. She had often come here with her father Fred as a child, and he had sparked in her a true fascination with ancient civilisations and the art they had produced. For a long time, growing up, she had imagined herself one day becoming a curator of this hallowed place. However, life had taken a different turn for her when her father had become gravely ill and she had taken on the role of his full-time caregiver. He had eventually passed away, and not long after that, Laura had seen a job advert online that had caused her to suddenly experience an epiphany. She might well have missed her chance at becoming a curator at the museum, but she could become part of the staff here nonetheless. The job advert had been for a role as a security officer with the prestigious museum's Visitor and Security Services Department. Requirements were minimal, and after a few months of on-the-job training, she had been given her official uniform and a name tag, and she had then been welcomed to the team.

As she signed the contract for a permanent position, Laura had thought only of her father. After walking out of the office of the head of HR wearing her smart, dark uniform, she had carried her copy of the contract to her father's favourite display items that were located in Room 6, which contained items from ancient Assyria. They were the two gigantic, winged and human-headed lions called the Lamassu, which almost three thousand years ago had flanked the grand entrance to the palace of King Ashurnasirpal II in the ancient city of Nimrud near the city of Mosul in present-day Iraq. There she had closed her eyes and whispered a few tender words to her father while holding the contract close to her chest, and for a brief moment, she had allowed herself to imagine standing there again as a little girl while he regaled her with stories about that ancient culture and how these two statues had been found and transported to Britain in 1852.

As Laura crossed the cavernous open courtyard and walked past the circular, central reading room, she peered up at the intricate curving patterns formed by thousands of triangular glass panes from which the roof had been constructed and which, through some miracle of modern engineering, was able to remain suspended up there despite weighing several hundred tonnes. She checked the time on her wristwatch and continued along her normal nightly route through the galleries, now heading for the extensive collection of items from ancient Greece. Extracting her phone from a pocket in her uniform jacket, she opened her messaging app and saw that there was a message from her friend Rosie, who was spending the night at her flat looking after her dog Wilbur. The excitable black labrador was only ten weeks old and needed someone in the house at all times, so Rosie had offered her services as a nighttime dogsitter for the first couple of weeks of the puppy's life.

Laura smiled as she opened the app and saw a picture of Wilbur sleeping in his wicker basket. She loved the little guy, and she was looking forward to seeing him and taking him for an early morning walk when she got home. In another half an hour or so, she would make her way to the staff rooms and help herself to a cup of coffee. After that, she would continue her night watch routine until the first of the museum's daytime staff arrived early the next morning, a couple of hours before its official opening hours began.

★ ★ ★

Wearing dark clothes and a black cap and carrying a small, slim backpack, Antonio Ortega turned the corner at Russell Square and began walking south along Montague Street. The tall, muscular former soldier and intelligence officer looked relaxed as he ambled along the pavement, glancing across to the other side of the street every few seconds. The row of exclusive white-fronted Edwardian townhouses on his right-hand side was among some of the most expensive real estate in London, and they were sandwiched between the street and the British Museum behind them. Each one of them had a small rear patio garden that backed directly onto the eastern exterior walls of the massive museum building. A narrow walled alley ran between the gardens and the 5-storey repository of ancient artefacts, but it was inaccessible through the tall CCTV-monitored gate on Montague Place, which ran along the northern side of the museum.

However, Ortega had devised a plan that did not require him to enter through any of the secure and alarm-fitted exterior doors. He had plenty of experience in this type of work, and he had done his share of covert work for Spanish military intelligence before taking his skills private and finding a lucrative job working for Count Carlos Roberto Velazquez de Toledo. In that capacity, he was now taking orders from that slightly pompous and self-important Englishman, Lawrence Blake. But Ortega had no problem with Blake's personality. He had experienced far worse from his superiors in the *Centro de Inteligencia de las Fuerzas Armadas*, and as long as he got paid, he didn't much care who gave the orders. That was simply the life of a soldier, whether working for the state or for the highest bidder in the private sector.

This night, he had been instructed to enter the British Museum unseen and make his way to Room 27 where the museum's Mesoamerican relics were displayed. Inside a glass-fronted display cabinet whose precise location he was already familiar with after his visit earlier that day, was located an item that Blake needed retrieved. Ortega understood that it was really the count who wanted that item, and that Blake was merely the treasure hunter who had located it after their joint trip to Panama. Apparently, the jade figurine, which was identical to the one they had taken back from Fort San Lorenzo, had come from a private collection owned by a minor Spanish royal who had sold it to the museum in 1876. If Ortega could complete tonight's assignment successfully and snatch the ancient figurine, the count's gratitude would invariably spill over to him as well in the form of a bonus paid in hard currency.

When he was directly opposite No. 43, he crossed the road, jumped adeptly over the low, black-painted wrought iron fence and moved down the metal stairs to a narrow lower-ground window below the townhouse's façade. Here, he extracted a set of glass cutters and quickly removed a small circular piece of one of the window panes. He knew that he was safe to do so because the house was currently listed on the market, and an inquiry to the gushing female estate agent trying to secure a sale had relayed that the townhouse was currently unoccupied and unfurnished.

Reaching inside, he lifted the metal latch on the window fastener and pulled gently to release the window from its frame. Opening it fully, he unslung his backpack, dropped it onto the floor inside and climbed through. He found himself in what passed as a bedroom, although he struggled to see how even a single bed would fit in there. He then made his way up the stairs to the ground floor and continued across the hardwood flooring through the hallway and the living room until he reached the patio doors at the back. The key was in the door, and he turned it smoothly, pushed open the door and then moved out onto the patio's flagstones where a number of small potted palm trees and two sun loungers had been neatly arranged. In front and above him rose the enormous, dark 5-storey museum building. He closed the patio doors behind him, moved silently across the flagstones and began scaling the property's rear wall. Climbing up and over it with speed and agility that seemed at odds with his size and bulk, he landed catlike in the narrow alley. He then rose slowly to his full height, listening out for any threats of being discovered, but everything was dark and quiet.

Glancing past a set of large rubbish bins towards a door that led into the museum's interior, he could see the brief, regular flashes of a red LED through the glass, indicating that the door was wired with alarms that were certain to trigger if he tried to enter that way. But that had never been his plan. Putting his head back and craning his neck, he gazed up along a thick metal drainpipe that ran all the way up to the roof. He extracted a set of climbing gloves with tiny rubber pads affixed to the palms and fingers, and then he began his ascent. Using his hands and his soft and grippy trainers, he quickly made headway up the wall. He didn't stop to look behind him to see if he was being watched. He was committed now, and any time spent looking over his shoulder would mean more time spent getting to the top. He simply focused on his hands and feet, which alternated smoothly as he made it all the way up to the gutter at the top. Taking a moment to inspect the gutter, he then found its nearest metal fixings, gripped them firmly and hauled himself up and onto the flat roof of the building.

Slightly out of breath, he rolled onto his back and lay there panting for a few moments as he allowed his blood to re-oxygenate. Then he got to his feet and moved hunched over to the skylight placed directly over the museum's east stairwell. Extracting a small but powerful handheld drill from his backpack, he then drilled into the wooden frame of the skylight and straight through the lock, which disintegrated as the hardened steel drill bit ground its way through it. He carefully opened the skylight, affixed a lightweight and flexible metal cable ladder to the outside frame and tossed the bulk of the ladder through the opening. The last thing he did before climbing down was to reach inside his jacket and pull out a black balaclava, which he donned with well-practised adeptness. Seconds later, his feet touched the stone floor on the landing at the top of the stairwell. Next to him was a sign that said 'Upper Floor', and another saying 'Ancient South Arabia, 53'. Before leaving for tonight's mission, he had studied the interior layout of the enormous building and knew exactly where he was.

Heading quietly down the stairs, he kept an ear out for sounds of patrolling nightshift guards. He was aware that there were a couple of them patrolling the museum at all times during the night, but the vastness of the building meant that they would only spend a small amount of time in each section before moving on. In addition, because of its acoustics and lack of any visitors at this hour, he should be able to hear them coming well before they would be able to spot him and raise the alarm.

Having descended to the main floor, he left the stairwell and stepped into the first room to his right. Fixed to the wall next to the doorway was a sign saying 'Mexico, 27'. The room's interior had been clad in sheets of plasterboard painted a dark charcoal grey, and the upper part of the walls was slanted inward, no doubt to mimic the pyramidal ideal of Aztec temples. On display in the large glass-fronted cabinets were stone stelae with intricately carved images and symbols, a 2700-year-old jade plaque depicting a powerful Mayan king, and a reproduction of a pictorial paper codex with images relating to astronomy, seasons, religious rituals and medicine.

Ortega had no interest in the cultural peculiarities of anything inside the room. He was here to do a job, and he wanted to do it as fast as possible and then return to Blake with the jade figurine. It only took him a few seconds to locate the artefact, and he wasted no time cutting through the glass. Having made a hole sufficiently large for the figurine to pass through, he reached inside and carefully extracted the priceless relic. He placed it inside a bubble wrap bag where it fitted snugly, and then he put the bag inside his backpack and zipped it up. As he did so, he thought he heard the sound of someone producing a brief whistling tune coming from the stairwell. Or was it from somewhere further inside the building?

He moved to the doorway to the adjacent room and managed to spot a glimpse of someone wearing a security guard uniform who was ambling along in his direction. He quickly moved to the side to stay out of sight and pressed himself against the wall, realising that he had managed to get himself trapped in a corner of the room from where he would be unable to exit without being seen. He winced at his mistake.

Standing perfectly still, he now heard the sound of soft footsteps as the guard approached. Then some more whistling. Cursing silently for allowing himself to be caught in this exposed position, he steadied his nerves and found himself switching from covert mode into something more akin to a combat mindset. There was no way he was going to let himself get caught, and unless the guard was built like a 200-pound gorilla, there was no chance of that happening. Without moving a muscle, he watched as the guard's shadow stretched across the floor and into the room, and he could now hear the soft rustling of clothes along with the gentle padding of footsteps.

*   *   *

When Laura Hartley entered Room 27, she only made it a few paces inside when she spotted the neat circular hole in the glass front of one of the display cabinets. Her eyes narrowed and her brow creased as she stared at it, and then she suddenly realised what she was looking at.

'What the hell?' she muttered.

There was a small, empty display platform directly underneath the hole in the glass. Someone had managed to get into the museum and steal whatever had been there. Without taking her eye off the hole, she reached down to the radio that was attached to her belt, gripped it and brought it up to her mouth. She pressed the button to speak, and her lips had barely parted before a massive dark shape came at her from the shadows. She almost managed to turn towards what proved to be a huge man with bulging muscles and dark, menacing eyes, but then he was on her. As he wrapped one of his arms around her neck, he somehow also managed to restrain both of hers with his other hand as the radio clattered to the floor. She tried to scream, but he was choking her, and no sound came out.

* * *

Moving with a predator-like economy of motion efficiency, Ortega had managed to close the distance to the small female guard in an instant, and he now had her in a tight chokehold that prevented her from making a sound. It also stopped her from breathing, and in a few seconds, she would pass out, and he would be able to place her down on the floor and then leave the museum quietly. He was surprised at how much she managed to struggle, and she was exceptionally feisty for her size. However, compared with her, he was a giant. It was such an uneven contest that it was almost unfair, but in his experience, that was the best way to win a fight.

She tried desperately to stamp on his feet in an attempt to force him to release his grip, but that only made him angry, and he tightened his grip around her neck. That usually did the trick when the victim realised that it was pointless to resist, and in this case, she would surely realise that fighting back was utterly futile.

To his surprise, she began to struggle even more furiously, and she wriggled wildly and attempted to free her restrained arms and slam her elbows into his sides. At this point, irritation began to overtake Ortega, and he tightened his vice-like grip around her neck even further, hoping that the spirited guard would finally pass out so he could get out of there. Suddenly, there was a snap and a brief, wet crunch that sounded much like someone crushing an ice cube between their teeth. From one instant to the next, the female guard's body went completely limp in his powerful arms.

'*Mierda,*' he muttered bemused to himself, the well-worn profanity escaping his lips as Laura's small frame became like a ragdoll.

Her arms flopped down along her sides, and her legs buckled underneath her. The only thing holding her up was Ortega's chokehold, and when he realised what had happened and began to release his grip, air wheezed gently from the young woman's lungs for the final time as her head lolled forward.

'*Dejame de joder!*' Ortega muttered in an exasperated phrase, imploring the world to give him a break.

There was a hint of surprise and even annoyance in Ortega's voice as he spoke, as if he couldn't quite believe just how frail the female guard's body had proven to be. He also knew that this wasn't supposed to have happened and that he would now have to provide a plausible explanation to both Blake and their common paymaster in Spain as to why he had ended up killing a guard when he had received strict instructions to harm no one. Gripping her collar and holding her entire weight in one hand, he then lowered her lifeless body quietly to the cold marble floor, shaking his head with a derisive grimace, as if to say. '*You shouldn't have taken this job.*'

Six

When Fiona emerged from Temple tube station on the Embankment, it was midmorning on a day of changeable and unpredictable weather. The autumn sun was shining brightly, but the streets and pavements were glistening in its light after a recent heavy rain shower. The fluttering leaves on the plane trees lining the Embankment as it stretched along the Thames were still clinging on to their branches, but they were now turning beautiful shades of yellow and pale orange, and a few wet clumps of them had gathered in places where they were safe from being scattered by the wind.

As Fiona flipped up the collar on her dark green leather jacket and began walking swiftly west along the pavement, her blonde shoulder-length hair moved lithely in the mild breeze. Reaching the end of the tube station building, and about to cross over Temple Place on her way to King's College University, she glanced to her right to see the oversized bronze statue of Isambard Kingdom Brunel. The early Victorian-era civil engineer was at the heart of some of the largest building projects during that time. Aside from working on the first tunnel under the Thames, various suspension bridges stretching over deep gorges, and the Great Western Railway linking London with much of the rest of the country, he was heavily involved in the building of transatlantic passenger ships, including the steam-powered SS Great Britain, which was the largest ship in the world during the middle of the 19th century. As she looked up at the statue, she reflected on what an impact a single person can have on history given the right set of circumstances. This was something she had observed countless times during her work as a historian, and more recently, it was something that she had discovered applied in spades to Queen Elizabeth I and also Sir Francis Drake. Without those two people at that precise time in history, London would most likely never have become the world's preeminent naval power and the centre of a global empire.

She was about to step out into the road when she both felt and heard her phone ring and vibrate in her jacket pocket. She stopped and extracted it, swiping across the screen to unlock it and read the message. It was a brief email from Emily Butler at the British Museum.

Hi Fiona. Just wanted to check if you heard about what happened here last night? I feel sick. E.

Fiona stared at the message for a moment, and instead of typing a reply, she decided to hit the call button. As the phone rang several times at the other end, she pressed it to her ear as she walked over to stand next to the bronze statue to get out of the way of other pedestrians. When Emily picked up the call, she sounded nothing like her usual cheerful self.

'Emily,' said Fiona anxiously. 'What's happened? Are you alright?'

'Hi Fiona. Yes, I'm fine,' said Emily, although she sounded anything but fine to Fiona. 'So you haven't heard yet?'

'No,' said Fiona, puzzled. 'Heard what? What's going on?'

'You remember Laura Hartley, right?' said Emily, her voice almost breaking.

'The new security guard?' said Fiona. 'Yes, of course. She's really nice. I've been chatting with her a few times about the exhibits. She was so thrilled to have got that job. Wait. Has something happened to her?'

'She's dead,' Emily sniffed. 'They found her early this morning. They said that her... neck had been snapped.'

'What?' Fiona breathed, suddenly feeling faint as her hand reached out to the base of the statue in an attempt to steady herself. 'How is that possible? Who did this?'

'Some intruder,' said Emily, her voice quivering. 'Someone who broke in and went straight for Room 27. He cut a hole in a display cabinet and stole a small jade statue. I don't know what, exactly. That's all I heard.'

'I can't believe it,' said Fiona, her mind flooding with images of the enthusiastic female security guard as a tear suddenly formed under her eyes and made its way slowly down her cheek. 'This is awful. Is the police there now?'

'Yes,' said Emily. 'They've closed the entire building for visitors for today. I expect it will be all over the news soon. It's just horrid. She was such a lovely person.'

'I don't know what to say,' said Fiona. 'Are you ok?'

'Yes,' said Emily. 'Well, no. Not really. I'd like to go home, but the police are interviewing everyone, so we all have to stay here for now.'

'I really hope they catch the bastard,' said Fiona. 'It's so senseless and just evil.'

'Me too,' said Emily. 'Anyway, I have to go. There's a staff meeting shortly.'

'Alright,' said Fiona, wiping her cheek dry. 'I'll let you go. We'll talk again when I am back.'

'Alright,' said Emily. 'Take care. Bye.'

Emily hung up, and Fiona put the phone back into her pocket and stood for a long moment in an eerie imitation of the immobile bronze statue that towered above her. Staring down onto the pavement, she felt cold and empty inside. Laura had seemed a kind soul with a genuine interest in the museum and its mission to educate and spread the love and fascination that she herself felt for the thousands of ancient items in its galleries. And now she was gone. Snuffed out and taken from this life. All so that someone could get their hands on some item from Room 27, which Fiona knew to contain artefacts from ancient Mexico. But why? Who would be prepared to kill to do that? And for just a single item. How could one artefact be deemed worth someone's life? It made no sense.

She shook her head and lifted her gaze to the four-storey university building in front of her. Her meeting with Professor Tobin suddenly seemed trivial and unimportant, and she was almost about to turn around and head back to Hampstead. But then she decided against it. Laura's murderer had already done great damage to that poor woman, her family and everyone who knew her, Fiona included. And there was no way she was going to let the killer stop her from going about her business. She took a deep breath and steeled herself. Then she crossed Temple Place, slipped through the ornate arch of the university's South West Block and into the open, elongated square in front of the main building. Pushing inside through the glass doors and reporting to the front desk, she soon found herself being escorted upstairs by a friendly receptionist who had offered to show her the way to Tobin's office. When she knocked on the dark hardwood door, a slightly hoarse but jaunty male voice sounded from inside.

'Come in,' it called. 'Door's open.'

Fiona walked inside and was greeted by an office that was everything she had imagined it to be. Apart from the wall directly opposite the door, which had three large windows, the office was bedecked with tall bookshelves crammed full of hundreds of tomes, old and new. There was a large, substantial-looking desk at one end of the room, and hanging in a clear wall space facing the desk was an oil painting. It depicted a redheaded, longhaired woman dressed in flowing and somewhat androgynous clothing. She was holding a cutlass in one hand and gazing steely-eyed out towards a large, square-rigged warship on the ocean behind her. Her light beige shirt was unbuttoned and open, revealing the curves of her breasts, and it was obvious that it had been left like that intentionally. Fiona couldn't help a faint smile spreading across her lips as she saw it, but then she turned towards the other side of the room.

On the large hardwood desk was an antique wooden globe, and on the wall behind it was a large, square-rigged, three-masted sailing ship from what Fiona thought might possibly be the 17th century. Sitting in discreet metal racks beneath it were what looked like two old flintlock pistols like the ones she had seen in pirate movies. Behind the desk sat the professor with his feet up and resting on its corner. As Fiona entered, he looked up from the large book he was reading. When he saw her, he put the book down, got to his feet and moved around the desk to greet her.

'Fiona Keane!' he said with a broad, friendly smile. 'How nice to see you again.'

Seemingly in his late fifties, he was tall and quite handsome and suave in a bookish sort of way with his chestnut-coloured tweed jacket and a navy waistcoat over a light blue shirt. He had brown, greying hair and a beard to match, both of which looked carefully trimmed and styled. The hair was mid-length and wavy, and it had been combed to flow neatly up and over the top of his head in something resembling a quiff. It gave him a very youthful appearance, betrayed only by the vague smile lines around his eyes. Although attractive, his hairstyle seemed to Fiona somehow to be at odds with his chosen profession. But as she immediately reminded herself as she entered his office, one should never judge a book by its cover.

'Yes,' she said, realising upon hearing her own voice that she sounded shaky and slightly dispirited.

Tobin immediately picked up on her demeanour, which was no doubt very different from when they had spoken on the phone the day before.

'Are you alright, dear?' he said sympathetically as he came over. 'I heard the news about that young woman who was murdered at the museum. What terrible business. Who would do such a thing? Did you know her?'

'A bit,' said Fiona, attempting to produce a brave smile but mostly failing. 'We'd met a few times. She seemed so nice.'

'It's shocking,' said Tobin, shaking his head with both revulsion and contempt. 'Absolutely shocking. What is the world coming to? Hopefully they'll catch whoever did it soon. Surely the museum has an extensive CCTV system, doesn't it?'

'Yes,' said Fiona, nodding. 'I am sure the whole thing was recorded on at least one camera, but that doesn't mean they are going to catch whoever did it.'

'Well, I do hope it hasn't been too upsetting for you,' said Tobin softly, placing a hand gently on her shoulder. 'I know what it's like to lose someone.'

'Thank you,' said Fiona with a nod, keen to move along and focus on why she had come to visit. 'Anyway, I really don't want to take up too much of your time today.'

'It's quite alright,' said Tobin amiably. 'Come sit.'

He gestured to the comfortable-looking upholstered leather chair across from his desk, and Fiona sat down as he returned to his own chair and reclined.

'Who's she?' said Fiona, glancing back at the oil painting of the woman as she sat down. 'Was she a pirate?'

'She was indeed,' said Tobin, pouring Fiona a cup of coffee, which she accepted with a smile. 'That was Anne Bonny.'

'I think I have heard of her,' said Fiona, taking a sip.

'I'm not surprised,' said Tobin. 'I must admit, I have a bit of a soft spot for her. There's something very powerful about a woman showing up the men and becoming one of the most well-known pirates of all time.'

'How did she manage to do that?' said Fiona.

'Grit, determination and probably a large dose of ruthlessness,' said Tobin. 'She was born in Ireland at the beginning of the 18th century as the lovechild of an attorney and one of his maids. She went to America as a young woman and married a sailor, and that led her to make the acquaintance of Jack Rackham, who is probably one of the most famous pirates of that time. She and another woman named Mary Reid joined Rackham's crew and took part in many of his raids against merchant ships. The two of them were known to fight alongside the male crew with their shirts open. The whole idea was to make a statement. Instead of hiding their supposed weak gender, they put it on open display and showed everyone that they were as tough as the men.'

'Interesting,' said Fiona. 'I imagine it might also have served to distract whoever they were fighting. You know. Men at sea for a long time without seeing a woman, and then suddenly coming face to face with one showing her breasts and holding a cutlass. It would have been quite a shock.'

'Yes,' chuckled Tobin. 'I suppose there's that too. Anyway, you said you would like to know more about Francis Drake and his lesser-known exploits, is that correct? Is this to do with the museum?'

'Yes,' said Fiona. 'I'd like to understand the link between him and how piracy in the Caribbean evolved. It seems to me there is a connection there.'

'Very much so,' nodded Tobin.

'He wasn't just an explorer, was he?' she said.

'He certainly wasn't,' said Tobin.

'And yes,' Fiona went on, 'I am considering proposing to the management that we do a section about Drake in an upcoming exhibition we're doing on Queen Elizabeth I.'

'That's an excellent idea,' said Tobin. 'He did play a major role in securing her power and that of the British Empire in the decades and centuries that followed, as well as sowing the seeds for what we call the Golden Age of Piracy.'

'When was that exactly?' said Fiona.

'Well,' said Tobin. 'As with all things academic, there's always a lively debate about every last detail, including the exact start and finish dates of that period. But it lasted for about a century from around the year 1630. Although there was a long chain of events leading from Drake's exploits to the sort of Caribbean piracy that most people would recognise today.'

'Yes, I thought there might be,' said Fiona, 'and I always found it quite intriguing how it all happened. I mean, we all know something about pirates, and most people probably have some sort of vague idea about what the pirates plying their trade in the Caribbean were all about.'

'That's very true,' said Tobin. 'Most people tend to think of it as just another period in world history, and they are so familiar with it in general terms that they treat it almost as if what happened was normal.'

'But it was anything but normal, right?' said Fiona. 'As far as I can tell, it was a completely chaotic time. And what those pirates managed to get away with decade after decade was pretty extreme when you think about it. Robbing ships at will. Plundering countless coastal towns throughout the Caribbean. Raping and pillaging their way through an entire region of the world. And it was allowed to go for such a long time.'

'That's right,' said Tobin. 'It is a remarkable story.'

'So how did it all start?' said Fiona. 'How did that part of the world end up as such a pirate paradise for so long?'

'Well,' said Tobin. 'Let's start at the beginning if you don't mind.'

'Great,' said Fiona, holding the coffee mug in both hands and looking at the professor expectantly.

'In many ways,' said Tobin pensively, 'piracy is as old as seafaring, which is to say that this most dastardly of phenomena has existed ever since it was possible for the crew of one ship to take over another ship by force and steal its cargo and valuables. Whether it was in the Indian Ocean, the South China Sea or in the Mediterranean, it has always been the scourge of peaceful merchants the world over. However, in the Caribbean, it has its own very unique backstory and one that is perhaps less than flattering for the English. And it is a story of kings and queens, global geopolitics and religion all coming together to create the perfect storm for the emergence of high-seas piracy. You see, these men, and they were almost exclusively men, didn't just suddenly appear out of nowhere and decide to plunder defenceless ships. The whole phenomenon sprang out of a complex tapestry of circumstances that conspired to create the Golden Age of Piracy, and it is fair to say that it all started right here in London.'

'Really?' said Fiona, raising one eyebrow. 'Caribbean piracy began in London? How?'

'Well,' said Tobin. 'The English, and specifically Queen Elizabeth I, didn't exactly invent piracy, but they did take it to a whole new level in the 16th and 17th centuries. You might even call it piracy on a genuinely industrial scale, although its instigators and the men who carried it out didn't refer to it as such at the time. Now, you may have come across several nicknames for Queen Elizabeth I, such as the Good Queen Bess because of her dogged survival skills. Or the Virgin Queen, because she vowed never to marry and said that she was married to England. And I am sure you have heard the name Gloriana because she had brought glory to England, and also because of her lavish coronation. But she also earned another name, which most people have never heard about. She was called The Pirate Queen.'

'Oh, this should be good,' said Fiona, smiling expectantly, shifting slightly in her chair and enjoying the company of the effusive professor.

'But,' said Tobin, holding up an index finger as if to underscore a point. 'In a roundabout sort of way, it was actually religion that was the proximate cause of the emergence of piracy.'

'Religion?' said Fiona, now looking mystified.

'I know,' said Tobin, holding up a hand placatingly. 'It sounds a bit odd, perhaps. But allow me to explain. I am not saying that piracy in the Caribbean was a religious venture. Far from it, although at times religion was used as justification, especially in the early days. But the best way to frame it is probably to say that religion and religious conflict during the 15th and 16th centuries in the Old World in Europe, including here in England, were ultimately the triggers for a whole series of events that eventually spawned the rise of Caribbean piracy as we think of it today. So, let me paint a rough picture for you.'

Tobin lifted his coffee cup and took a sip, his brow creasing while he collected his thoughts.

'Now,' he continued, clearly getting into the swing of things. 'As I am sure you know, the Italian explorer Christopher Columbus, who had sailed his small fleet of ships from Spain across the Atlantic, had discovered what he thought was India in 1492. Of course, it wasn't really India he had discovered, but it eventually proved to be an enormous boon for the Kingdom of Spain over the next several centuries. A kingdom that was very much Catholic.'

'Such arrogance,' scoffed Fiona with a wan smile. 'Imagine that you set out to find a part of the world that you already know exists under the name of India. Then you bump into a whole separate part, which you mistakenly think is India, and so you call the natives 'Indians'. But then you eventually realise that you were mistaken and had actually found the Americas, yet you *insist* on continuing to call the inhabitants of those lands 'Indians' from then on, even up until today. It's just ridiculous.'

'Well, yes,' said Tobin, smiling uncertainly. 'It's not really very sensitive, is it? But that's how things go sometimes, I suppose. Anyway, the treasures brought back to Spain from Central and South America over the next decades were of such enormity that it soon funded a huge expansion of the Spanish military, especially its navy. And that, in turn, made Spain the undisputed global superpower at that time. But there was another power that had a different kind of hold over the continent in those days, and that was the Catholic Church. The original church of Saint Peter, which had been co-opted by the Roman Emperor Constantine I around the year 325 BCE in an attempt to secure his own reign. And for a millennium after that, the Catholic Church was at the heart of power in Europe, mainly through old-fashioned power brokering and backroom deal-making, but also very often through familial relationships between popes, kings, dukes and what have you. It became a sort of dynasty. In that process, it also became obscenely wealthy, and I don't think it is an exaggeration to say that the organisation was run like a giant international corporation. You can think of the nations, monarchies and principalities of Europe as being subsidiaries of the parent company in Rome, where the pope acted as its CEO, and he and his extended family lived in lavish luxury and decadence. They owned vast amounts of land, and they effectively extorted money through tithing from the citizens across the continent, under threat of eternal damnation in hell if people didn't pay up, of course.

So in all honesty, it was not dissimilar from a mafia protection racket.'

'Nice soul you have there,' said Fiona sardonically. 'It would be a shame if something bad happened to it.'

'Something like that,' smiled Tobin, enjoying the analogy before continuing. 'Now, the church also had a near monopoly on education, so it was really able to insert itself into every aspect of society and profoundly shape life for almost everyone alive in Europe at that time. And eventually, it just became too suffocating for a great many people who longed for more personal freedom and the ability to live their lives as they wanted. This was especially the case in northern Europe, and it was especially true for a man named Martin Luther, who was a pious but disillusioned German monk. He had seen firsthand how the church had promised and encouraged a rich spiritual life dedicated to the service of God, only for it to then demand money from its followers to shorten their time in purgatory before going on to heaven. There were many other similar schemes that served only to enrich the Catholic Church, and eventually, Luther could no longer stomach the hypocrisy. Through his writings, including the seminal '95 Theses', he started the break with Rome that eventually became the process we now call the Protestant Reformation, beginning around the year 1517. A process that sowed the seeds for centuries of intense and often violent religious strife between Protestants and Catholics.'

'I am beginning to see how this ties in with Queen Elizabeth I,' said Fiona. 'She was about as staunch an anti-Catholic as they come, right?'

'That's exactly right,' nodded Tobin approvingly. 'And she truly was a remarkable woman, I have to say. Highly intelligent and shrewd, she quickly became such a thorn in the side of the pope that he decreed that any Catholic who assassinated her would be innocent of sin and would instead secure a place in heaven.'

'What a bastard,' said Fiona with a derisive chuckle.

'And unsurprisingly,' Tobin continued, 'this led to several assassination attempts. Obviously, none of them succeeded, but it is a pretty striking example of just how deep the rift between the English as well as other European Protestants and the Catholics in the southern part of the continent really was. Anyway, because of these religious tensions between north and south, Europe was going through quite a fraught time in this country too. It was felt as a menace that constantly hung over this nation. A foreign threat that might strike at any moment. Catholicism was seen as the great evil from abroad that was threatening the English civilisation and way of life. It is analogous to the time before the Second World War when the English were watching with trepidation as the Nazis rose to power in Germany and threatened to take over the continent and possibly the British Isles. In the 15th century too, at the beginning of Queen Elizabeth's reign, there was a real and not entirely unfounded fear that one day the Spanish Armada would show up and lay waste to English port towns and perhaps even London. There is a fort on the Thames built specifically to defend against the armada, should it one day show itself and threaten London.'

'Tilbury,' said Fiona. 'Where she gave that famous speech.'

'Very good,' nodded Tobin. 'As I think you know, the fort is still there to this day. And of course, in 1588, the Armada did in fact arrive and was dealt a severe blow by the English fleet in the famous battle off the coast of northern France. And on that day, Sir Francis Drake was second in command, serving as vice admiral aboard a galleon named Revenge as he captured the Spanish flagship Rosario.'

'Yes, I read about that battle,' said Fiona. 'They used some very different naval tactics than today. Essentially lining up and sailing past each other, firing guns until one side had won.'

'That's right,' said Tobin. 'The so-called line battle. In fact, this is where the term 'ships of the line' comes from. It was applied to the most powerful ships in a navy that would be able to take part in such a battle. Now, as I am sure you understand as well as anyone, during this time, Queen Elizabeth was very much the embodiment of English resistance against a Catholic empire that was threatening to consume all of Europe. And she certainly saw herself that way, hence the reference to her own body in that speech.'

'As I understand it from the primary sources,' said Fiona. 'That speech really galvanised the English ahead of the arrival of the armada.'

'I have no doubt of that being true,' said Tobin. 'But what followed was less straightforward to deal with. You see, because of the deep religious schism between England and Spain, which resulted in England being unable to trade freely in Europe or in the New World from around 1560, the coffers in the

English treasury were dwindling fast. Because of the threat of a Spanish invasion, Queen Elizabeth had to resort to some fairly unconventional tactics, and she did so with significant success. And this is where Francis Drake really began to shine. He was part of a group of young men who had won the favour of the young queen, and who had been engaging in smuggling goods out of European ports such as Antwerp across the Channel to England. She was young and pretty and unmarried, and they were resourceful and fearless and keen to win her esteem. And at that time, her kingdom needed a serious shot in the arm after the spigots had been turned off from Spain and the coffers were running dry.'

'Right,' nodded Fiona. 'I read that England had lost the treasure fleet income from Spain after Queen Mary had died and Elizabeth had become the new queen.'

'Exactly,' said Tobin, 'and Elizabeth's collaboration with these Sea Dogs, as they were known, proved a very fruitful joint venture for both England and these men. In essence, she issued several of them, including Drake, with letters of marque, which allowed them to go off and raid Spanish ships and towns in the Caribbean. So England was essentially employing guerrilla tactics against what was then a much more powerful adversary. And it paid off. Drake was the first Englishman to raid Panama City in 1572, and on one of his trips, he brought back in a single ship enough gold that he had stolen from the Spanish to fund the English Crown's budget for an entire year.'

'Crikey,' said Fiona. 'I think that probably qualifies as piracy.'

'Very much so,' said Tobin. 'And the Spanish were not exactly pleased.'

'I'm not surprised,' said Fiona. 'Hence the arrival of the Spanish Armada. Although, that was more than a decade later, right?'

'Yes,' said Tobin. 'Sixteen years later, in fact. Sixteen years during which the English, under Drake and others, raided countless Spanish ships and towns throughout the Caribbean.'

'Why did the Spanish put up with these raids for such a long time?' said Fiona. 'That seems really odd.'

'Yes,' said Tobin, nodding. 'But, you see, the Spanish Empire had begun to decline from around the middle to the late 16th century. This was mainly due to a combination of economic mismanagement, excessive wars against the French, and a gradual decline caused by the fact that gold and silver had been pouring in from New Spain for generations. On top of making those precious metals somewhat less precious, this had also bred a less than industrious and forward-looking mindset amongst the ruling classes back in the old country.'

'So they didn't have the resources to prevent the attacks?' said Fiona.

'They probably did,' said Tobin, 'because the treasure fleets from New Spain kept coming. But the Spanish had been so high on this seemingly inexhaustible source of wealth for so long that they lost the ability to govern effectively. And soon, that power vacuum in the New World across the Atlantic began to be filled by the English, the Dutch, the French and the Scandinavian countries who all managed to grab possessions there. Over the next several decades, all of those nations secured several smaller islands in the Lesser Antilles, which is that long, curved row of islands that sit like pearls on a string from north to south in the eastern Caribbean Sea. And this is where the story of proper swashbuckling piracy really begins to take shape.'

'Oh good,' said Fiona keenly. 'That was in Tortuga, wasn't it?'

'That's correct,' said Tobin. 'Now, back in 1492, when Columbus had first discovered and sailed along the north coast of the massive island that he had named Hispaniola, which today is split between Haiti and the Dominican Republic, he came across a small island just a handful of kilometres to the northwest. Observed from near the shores of Hispaniola, with its jagged and rocky contours, it apparently reminded him of the shape of a tortoise, which is why he named it Tortuga. It turned out to be a very wild and rugged place with dense forests of huge trees and many sheer rock faces, especially on the northern coastline, and this made it impossible to get onto the island from that side. However, its southern coast had a perfect natural harbour and plenty of wild animals, and the terrain was more conducive to habitation. But because Hispaniola was so much larger and richer in resources, the island of Tortuga was never of much interest to the Spanish Empire. At least not in the beginning. So, in 1625, when a French expedition to the Caribbean tried to settle on Hispaniola and found the Spanish there less than friendly to them, they decided instead to settle on Tortuga. These Frenchmen set about building homes and plantations, and they became highly skilled hunters, shooting mainly wild hogs with their long muskets. They then roasted the meat on a wooden frame called a '*Boucan*', and so they became known as '*Le Boucanier*', from which we now have the word 'buccaneer'.'

'How interesting,' said Fiona. 'I had no idea.'

'And the word buccaneer,' Tobin went on, 'soon became synonymous with the word pirate, because as time went on, more and more people settled on Tortuga, and these were mainly deserters from various nations as well as escaped slaves called maroons. And every so often, the buccaneers would see a lone merchant ship passing by in the narrow strait between Tortuga and Hispaniola, and they would sometimes sail out in their canoes, commandeer it and take its cargo.'

'So in a way,' said Fiona. 'You might say that these buccaneers were the first true pirates of the Caribbean.'

'You might say that,' said Tobin, 'but things had only just got started. Because they soon got their hands on bigger ships, such as the fast and very manoeuvrable sloops that were fitted with cannons. These vessels could run rings around much larger Spanish merchant ships, including those that were armed with their own guns. Of course, the Spanish were less than pleased with this, and they tried several times to send fleets to destroy the settlements and get rid of the pirates, but each time, the buccaneers would use guerilla tactics, simply melting away into the jungle and then picking off the Spanish soldiers with their excellent marksmanship skills. And in this way, over the next decades, Tortuga established itself to become the first real pirate haven, and the men who operated from there took to calling themselves the 'Brethren of the Coast'. They were the ones who came up with the famous Pirate Code that regulated payments to crewmembers, compensations for injuries and so on.'

'I see,' said Fiona, intrigued.

'Eventually, it became quite an organised place,' said Tobin. 'If you could go back there during the middle of the 17th century, you would have seen several large pirate ships and many sloops and other smaller vessels anchored in the harbour, and the town itself and its port would have been bustling with activity. Merchants, taverns, brothels and all the other types of businesses that would spring up to support this type of place.'

'I often wish I had a time machine,' said Fiona. 'I'd love to be able to go back and see that for myself.'

'Well,' chuckled Tobin. 'You're certainly not alone there. It would have been quite a sight. However, the Spanish represented a permanent threat to Tortuga, and eventually, the Brethren of the Coast asked the French for protection against the Spanish, and this prompted the arrival of a French engineer called Jean Le Vasseur. He arrived in 1640 with one hundred men and built a fort on a hill above the harbour called *Fort de Rocher* that had a gun battery with forty cannons.'

'Yes, I have read about that fort,' said Fiona. 'Is it still there now? I seem to remember that many of those old fortifications built throughout the Caribbean remain relatively intact.'

'I believe so,' nodded Tobin, 'although it is probably in quite a dilapidated and overgrown state by now. As I am sure you're aware, Haiti has been one of the poorest countries in the world for decades now, as well as being a fairly chaotic and lawless place. I imagine that maintaining or restoring old forts is probably not very high on their list of priorities.'

'Fair enough,' said Fiona.

'Anyway,' said Tobin. 'Le Vasseur became governor of the island and struck a deal with the Brethren of the Coast to give them legal protection to ply their trade in the waters around Hispaniola in exchange for them providing physical protection for the town and the fort. So, it was very much a mutually beneficial agreement, and it only served to cement Tortuga's position as a true pirate haven. Le Vasseur soon opened up the island to pirates from all nations, and in the roughly fifteen years that followed, the French buccaneers were joined mainly by British and Dutch men who were either deserters, criminals on the run, or freed indentured servants. But of course, nothing lasts forever, and eventually, the Spanish returned and launched two large invasions against Tortuga in 1653, the second of which succeeded. After sacking the town and the fort, instead of occupying the island, they then retreated back to Hispaniola once more, but Tortuga was never the same again after that.'

'So what happened next?' said Fiona. 'This was still early in the Golden Age of Piracy, wasn't it?'

'Very much so,' said Tobin. 'With Tortuga now permanently diminished as a base of operations for the pirates, they immediately sought out other locations to use. And once again, the English were instrumental in what happened next. You see, at the same time as these things had unfolded on Tortuga, the English Civil War had been raging back in England. And of course, Oliver Cromwell had now become Lord Protector after the execution of King Charles I. But Cromwell had inherited exactly the same problems faced by both Queen Elizabeth I and King Charles I, not least of which was the issue of how to finance the kingdom with the Spanish still holding a near-monopoly on the lucrative trade in the New World. So in 1654, he sent off an expedition tasked with nothing less than to capture both Hispaniola and the island of Cuba from the Spanish.'

'Seems ambitious,' said Fiona dubiously. 'The Spanish had been entrenched there for more than a century at that point.'

'That's one way to describe it,' said Tobin with a wry smile. 'I might use the word 'foolhardy'. It was never going to be a success. The English expeditionary force had brought nowhere near enough ships and men to succeed, even if they did make stops on the way at both Bermuda and St Kitts to take on more men, mainly criminals and vagrants. And of course, they did in fact end up failing spectacularly and having to run away after several engagements with Spanish forces on Hispaniola. But then something interesting happened. You see, instead of sailing defeated back to England and facing the wrath of Oliver Cromwell, they decided instead to attempt to take the island of Jamaica, which was large and had lots of potential for setting up sugar plantations and establishing it as an English trading hub. It was also perfectly situated right in the middle of the Caribbean Sea. Now, it was obviously held by the Spanish at that time, but only a few thousand people lived there, and it was very poorly defended. So the expedition succeeded in taking the island, and Port Royal soon became the main hub where a new fort named Fort Cromwell was built. This was later renamed Fort Charles after the restoration of the monarchy in 1660 and the ascension to the throne of Charles II.'

'This was where Henry Morgan operated from, right?' said Fiona.

'Indeed,' said Tobin. 'Morgan and a whole host of other privateers. You see, the English governors of Jamaica soon realised just how vulnerable they really were sitting there in the middle of what was still very much the Spanish New World, so they issued letters of marque to dozens of the former buccaneers from Tortuga. These pirates, now officially called privateers, would then provide protection for Port Royal in exchange for being given free rein to raid Spanish ships and towns wherever they could. Being based in Port Royal rather than Tortuga brought with it some obvious benefits. It gave them a screen of legitimacy since they were formally operating on behalf of the English Crown. It also provided them with a relatively large and well-connected base to operate from right in the very centre of the Caribbean. So pirate activity out of Port Royal really began to scale up during the following many years.'

'I see why the line between privateers and pirates would get quite blurry,' said Fiona. 'It all sounds very messy.'

'It was very messy indeed,' said Tobin. 'There was no real way of regulating precisely what these pirates were up to, and because both they and the English were almost exclusively Protestants, no one really had a problem with robbing from the Spanish Catholics, whether it was ships or towns and whether they were civilian or military targets. It was a virtual free-for-all.

Interestingly, Morgan might well have been among the young men brought over from England as part of Cromwell's expedition, and it's fair to say that he went on to make quite a name for himself.'

'Yes, I have read a bit about him too,' said Fiona. 'He raided Panama, right?'

'Yes,' said Tobin. 'That was probably one of his most successful raids, and the year before that he sacked a place called Fort San Lorenzo, which was one of the places from which the Spanish treasure fleets set sail for Spain. A quite spectacular fort that I have actually had the pleasure of visiting myself. It's very well preserved and sitting in a beautiful location.'

'So, for how long was Port Royal the main pirate hub?' said Fiona.

'Quite a number of years,' said Tobin, stroking his beard. 'But there were some ups and downs. As you know, Oliver Cromwell died in 1658, after which King Charles II took the throne. And importantly, this happened with the backing of various royals in Europe. Most notable among them was King Philip of Spain, who, after the end of the Anglo-Spanish War, had offered his support to Charles in exchange for a promise to hand Jamaica back to Spain. But King Charles soon changed his mind and decided to keep the large Caribbean island, which naturally incensed the Spanish. But there was very little they could do about it because of the numerous and well-armed privateers now operating out of Port Royal. However, Charles did perceive that continued piracy sanctioned by the Crown against Spanish ships and towns might eventually elicit a response from the weakened but still powerful Spanish Empire. And after the very tumultuous decade of the English

Republic, England was likely not in a position to deal with such an attack. So King Charles wrote to the governor of Jamaica and stated that the law was clear. The attacks by privateers from Port Royal were piracy, illegal and had to cease. The governor resisted this since kicking out the privateers, buccaneers and pirates would leave Port Royal with little to no defences. The governor was replaced in 1664 and succeeded by another man who also soon understood that the protection provided by the privateers was the only thing that kept Port Royal safe, and so he also continued issuing letters of marque. And I am sure that he personally received a cut from the pirate takings, so he probably had some personal financial incentives as well.'

'That seems to be a repeating pattern,' smiled Fiona.

'Yes, it was the Wild West before the American Wild West,' said Tobin. 'Everyone was looking for a way to get rich off the treasures of the New World. But in 1670, peace finally broke out with the signing of the so-called Treaty of Madrid, in which England and Spain agreed to cease disputes in the Caribbean and finally make piracy against ships and towns illegal once and for all. With ever more restrictions on the issuance of letters of marque and on privateering in general, Port Royal began to decline in importance as a pirate haven. Instead, many of the pirates relocated to the coastal town of Petit-Goave on the southern part of Hispaniola, and some converged on the relatively newly established town of Nassau some eight hundred kilometres north of Port Royal in the Bahamas off the coast of Florida.'

'Nassau,' said Fiona. 'I've read a bit about some of the pirates operating out of there too. That was during the last decades of the golden age, right?'

'Yes,' said Tobin. 'It was the time of Blackbeard, Jack Rackham, Charles Vane, Benjamin Hornigold and that lady in the painting behind you.'

He glanced past Fiona at the captivating oil painting of Anne Bonny, and Fiona noted that as he did so, he couldn't help an admiring smile playing on his lips.

'Nassau has its own interesting story,' he then said, returning his gaze to Fiona as he gathered his thoughts. 'The Bahamas, which it is part of, was first claimed by the English in 1629, and the island where it eventually sprang up was settled by a group of Puritans in 1666. The year of the Great Fire of London. They were all staunch Republicans who had lived in Bermuda, but soon after the coronation of Charles II, they had fled the English Crown due to its persecution of Republicans who had supported Oliver Cromwell. They believed very much in self-governance, the rule of law and equal rights. Many of the same values that we take for granted today. But this was centuries before any semblance of true democracy emerged back in the Old World. Of course, the new king would have none of this, and four years later, in 1670, which was the year Henry Morgan raided Panama, he sent a governor to take control of the island. Now, as it happened, his ship sank within sight of the harbour, but he managed to survive, and being convinced that this was clearly God's will, he named the island New Providence Island and he named the town Charlestown. But things didn't go exactly according to plan, because the island was raided by the Spanish who burnt it to the ground in 1684 because it had become a base for privateers and pirates. Eleven years later, the town was rebuilt under the new governor, Nicholas Trott, and renamed Nassau after the new King William III. Most people probably know him as William of Orange, who belonged to the House of Nassau. It also acquired a large fort overlooking the harbour with a battery of 28 large guns to protect the town against the Spanish. Now, in 1696, the pirate captain Henry Avery arrived there in the fledgling town with his powerful 46-gun warship, 'The Fancy', which he had commandeered after leading a mutiny. And similarly to what had happened in Tortuga half a century earlier, Governor Trott entered into a deal with Avery. Trott would allow Avery to operate out of Nassau in exchange for the town receiving protection from Avery and other pirates.'

'Same thing again,' smiled Fiona. 'But I guess the Caribbean was a pretty chaotic and dangerous place at that time, and these people had to be pragmatic.'

'That's a very good way of describing it,' said Tobin approvingly. 'And Avery soon became a living legend. In fact, it is likely that men like Blackbeard and Charles Vane were young boys when all this was happening, and they would have seen Avery as their role model. Anyway, Trott was eventually replaced, but his successors were weak and incompetent, and Nassau fell into decline, not least because it was sacked three times by the Spanish in the three years from 1703 to 1706. For the next decade or so, there was no legitimate English governor in Nassau, and this was when the town evolved into what has since been called the Pirate Republic.'

'That sounds grand,' said Fiona. 'What did that mean exactly?'

'Well,' said Tobin. 'With England having lost interest in trying to govern this tiny insignificant island with barely any resources, at least for a time, it left a power vacuum that was soon filled by the pirates. They established a new form of society with no governor, no king and no clergy to control them. It was more of a loose democratic collective, although there was a central figure who attempted to manage the town with the consent of the pirates, and this was Benjamin Hornigold. Now, all of these men were most certainly criminals, but they did manage to live more or less peacefully by the code that had been pioneered by the buccaneers of Tortuga almost a century earlier. And because they all faced the same external threat from the major European powers, it was in everyone's interest to at least try to work together.'

'So how did it all come to an end?' said Fiona.

'In a way,' said Tobin, 'Nassau became a victim of its own success. It began to become a real problem for the English merchant fleet, and in 1717 a proclamation was issued by King George I, which became known as the King's Pardon. It essentially said that for a period of one year, any pirate prepared to lay down their cutlass and take up a peaceful life outside of piracy would be given a full pardon and even be allowed to keep their ill-gotten gains.'

'Wow,' said Fiona. 'Quite a radical approach.'

'It was,' said Tobin, nodding, 'and there was plenty of opposition to it. After all, pirates operating out of Nassau had been a thorn in the side of the English

Crown for a long time at this point, and many influential people in London wanted to see them all hanged. But the plan worked. The king sent a former privateer named Woodes Rogers to Nassau, and with the pardon in his hands, he quickly turned things around. A new civil administration was established, legal commerce returned, and the vast majority of the pirates put behind them their former lives and became regular citizens. All except for a few famous characters such as Blackbeard, Rackham, Vane and others who continued plundering ships around the Bahamas, and they all ended up being killed in battle or hanged.'

'What a truly fascinating story,' said Fiona, smiling appreciatively at the professor.

'It certainly is,' said Tobin. 'And it is interesting to reflect on the fact that it was during this period that the foundations of the later British Empire were laid. So without Queen Elizabeth I and her Sea Dogs, and without the pirates in Tortuga, Port Royal and Nassau, the British Empire would never have materialised.'

'Amazing,' said Fiona. 'Sometimes I think I was born in the wrong era. I would love to be able to go back and experience all that for myself.'

'Me too,' said Tobin, regarding her with a look of approval as he paused for a moment before continuing in an almost dreamy manner. 'I have always been attracted to the fact that regardless of their past lives, these pirates, who had often fled tyranny and oppression in the Old World, were given an opportunity to completely start anew in the Caribbean. Just like on the plains of America in the middle of the 19th century, the Caribbean in the 17th and 18th centuries was often quite anarchic and lawless, so it was a place where men could strike out and forge a whole new life. For thousands of young men in England and the rest of Europe who either had no prospects or a past that made a good future impossible, it was a chance to start fresh. A chance to reinvent themselves. To become someone else and live a new life far away from whatever it was they were running from when they had first arrived. A life full of adventures and the freedom to do as they pleased. You have to admit, there's a certain charm to that idea.'

'Oh, I get it,' said Fiona. 'I think most people can see the appeal in that. Anyway, thank you for that very useful private lecture. I really appreciate it. But there's one final thing I'd like to talk to you about.'

'Certainly,' said Tobin amiably. 'What is it?'

'I was wondering,' she said, leaning forward slightly in her chair as she clutched the now tepid coffee cup in her hands. 'Have you ever heard of a Spanish galleon by the name El Castillo Negro?'

Tobin narrowed his eyes slightly and tilted his head for a moment as if rummaging through his no-doubt extensive cerebral library of facts about Caribbean piracy.

'I have heard of the Black Galleon, of course,' he finally said. 'The Spanish galleon that was taken from Port Royal and never seen again. But I can't say I am very familiar with the details of the story. Why do you ask?'

'Well, I was looking into the story,' said Fiona, 'and I came across a journal written by a French merchant who was on Tortuga a few weeks after the galleon was commandeered. He stated that he was up on the fort, the one you said was called Fort de Rocher, when he watched a ship called the Marauder suddenly explode in a giant fireball late at night. Have you ever heard of that ship?'

'No,' said Tobin. 'Not that I remember. What's the connection?'

'Well,' said Fiona, 'there were rumours that the captain of the Marauder, who was a man named Captain Flynn, had been responsible for the capture of the Black Galleon in Port Royal, and that its gold was on his ship when it exploded. But they were never more than rumours. And the wreck has never been found since it was so long ago, and there were wildly conflicting reports about what actually happened and precisely where it took place. Anyway, I found the story really fascinating, and I wondered if you might know something about it.'

'I'm sorry,' said Tobin genially. 'But I'm afraid that I can't tell you anything more than what you already know. Where did you come across that Frenchman's journal, if I may ask?'

'It was uncovered in some obscure archive in Paris,' said Fiona. 'It showed up in the results when I searched for references to the Marauder.'

'Interesting,' said Tobin, raising his eyebrows as a smile played on his lips. 'Very interesting. Especially if those rumours you mention turn out to be true. About the gold, I mean.'

'Well,' said Fiona with a shrug. 'It might be nothing, or it might be something. I am thinking about trying to find it myself.'

'Really?' said Tobin, his eyes seemingly lighting up with intrigue for a brief moment. 'Well, best of luck to you. Nothing like a treasure hunt, eh?'

'Well, yes,' said Fiona haltingly, suddenly feeling self-conscious at the notion of being perceived as one of the greedy treasure hunters that she had always loathed. 'I would give the treasure back, of course. To whoever could rightfully claim it after all these years.'

'That's very commendable,' said Tobin, giving a deep nod of approval. 'That's the right thing to do. I once dreamed of becoming a treasure hunter myself, but then I suppose I grew up. And I was never gifted at working in the field. So here I am instead. Buried in books and old maps.'

'There are worse fates,' said Fiona, giving him a quick smile. 'Anyway, thank you very much for your time. I should leave you in peace now.'

'Oh, but you are most welcome, Fiona,' he said. 'Let me know if there's anything else I can help you with. And I look forward to reading about you in the news once you've discovered that Spanish treasure.'

A few minutes later, Tobin was once more sitting in his office by himself, gazing across the room at the painting of Anne Bonny. After a brief moment of quiet reflection, he stroked his beard, rose to his feet and walked over to one of the large windows from which he could see the university courtyard below. Standing with his hands clasped behind his back, he stood up straight and watched the courtyard below as Fiona emerged from the building and turned left towards the exit to the Embankment.

'Captain Flynn,' he muttered pensively to himself as his fingers gently touched a small scar created by a recent cut on the palm of his left hand. 'Perhaps the stories were true after all.'

Seven

That evening, Fiona relayed her conversation with Professor Tobin to Andrew over a tasty and fortifying meal consisting of sausages and mash served with pints of ruby ale in one of Hampstead's characterful pubs. Her recap of the meeting was almost word for word, which for someone like Fiona, who had an eidetic memory, was about as easy as remembering the contents of a shopping list with three items written on it. However, time and again, she found herself circling back to the murder of Laura Hartley the night before.

'I still can't believe it,' she said glumly. 'It seems unreal somehow.'

'Did the police speak to you as well?' said Andrew, before taking a sip of his pint.

'They spoke to all of us,' said Fiona. 'Not that I think it will do much good. They didn't exactly inspire a lot of confidence, to be honest. And none of us were there, right? So I'm not sure how we could be of any help. And I just can't believe that anyone at the museum was complicit in her death. That would be too awful to even think about.'

'I guess they can't rule anything out at this stage,' said Andrew.

'I wish there was something I could do,' said Fiona, giving a weak shake of the head. 'And now I am sitting here wondering if we should go to Tortuga after all.'

'Whether we go or not will have no bearing on the police investigation,' said Andrew with a small shrug. 'Although…'

'What?' said Fiona.

'Would you be able to get your hands on the CCTV recordings from last night?' he said. 'Didn't you say you had a friend in the monitoring room?'

'Yes,' nodded Fiona musingly. 'I might be able to do that. The guys in charge of security are obviously not meant to hand those out, but I should be able to get hold of them if I ask nicely. But how will that help?'

'You just never know,' Andrew shrugged. 'I would be interested to see what the police actually have to work with. And maybe I can pull a favour from someone in the intelligence services. It's worth a shot.'

'Alright,' said Fiona. 'I'll do that.'

'I also wanted to talk to you again about going to Tortuga,' said Andrew. 'It involves flying into Port-au-Prince in Haiti and driving north for several hours through a pretty lawless place. I just wanted to make sure that you understand what you're getting yourself into.'

'Alright,' nodded Fiona as she waited for him to go on.

'You do realise that Haiti is no amusement park these days, right?' he said. 'It is an extremely unstable place, and it barely has a government. It is the poorest country in the Western Hemisphere, and it has been hit by several devastating earthquakes that they just don't have the resources to fully recover from before the next one hits. And that's before we're even talking about the rampant gang violence and the corruption.'

'I know,' said Fiona. 'I am completely aware that the country is a bit of a mess. But that doesn't mean it is going to be dangerous. I choose to believe that the vast majority of people on this Earth are good, decent people, even if they live in a troubled place. So I think I'll be fine. Either way, I am going, and you can't stop me. But, of course, if you're worried, you could just join me.'

As she finished speaking and lifted her pint glass from the table, she gave Andrew a playful wink. He regarded her for a moment, and as he did so, an affectionate smile played on his lips. He had once again come up against her obstinance and simple but razor-sharp logic. She was as clever and resourceful as they come, and despite being somewhat gun-shy on occasion, she had within her the same level of bravery that Andrew had seen in some of the hardest men in 22 SAS. On top of that, she was infuriatingly stubborn. And she was right, of course, but that didn't necessarily make him feel any less worried for her. However, at this point, he knew that there was no sense in arguing. Once a fire had been lit inside her and she had made up her mind, there was no stopping her. He could go on about the lack of security and the difficulty in going there and doing what she wanted to do, and he knew that she would listen and nod. But by the end of it, she was going to go and look for that wreck. Which only left one question. Was she going to go by herself and face those risks alone, or was he going to go with her and provide her with the protection that she very well might need? The answer to that question was simple. He was never going to let her set off by herself. They were going to Haiti.

★   ★   ★

Standing between two smooth Greek columns under the portico of an elegant townhouse in Mayfair, Marcus Tobin entered the six-digit security code on the alphanumeric keypad next to his heavy, black oak front door. On his way back from King's College on the tube, he had been pondering his meeting with Fiona Keane the whole way. It was a strange coincidence that she should show up and talk about pirate treasure just as he was about to conclude his latest venture and embark on a new research project centred on the man who had been named Edward Teach, known to most people simply as Captain Blackbeard. This most famous of pirates from the dying days of the Golden Age of Piracy was rumoured to have secretly buried substantial amounts of treasure in the Bahamas, but no one had ever found any of it. Or if they had, they had clearly never told anyone else, and Tobin had always been drawn to the idea that this treasure was out there just waiting for someone to find it. But as he knew from experience, sorting facts from fiction when it came to tales of treasure was never easy, and 'X' almost never marked the spot.

However, Fiona's story about Jack Flynn and the galleon named El Castillo Negro had once again rekindled his interest in what, as far as he knew, had up until now been little more than a barely supported myth. Despite the persistent rumours and anecdotes over the two centuries since the event, no hard evidence had ever been produced linking Flynn to the Black Galleon. Its disappearance from Port Royal had been one of the great capers of the pirate age, and it had almost certainly been laden with treasure when it happened. To Tobin, the spectacular and daring nature of its hijacking had been eclipsed only by the mysteriousness of its subsequent disappearance and the apparent complete lack of any trace as to what had happened to it next. But perhaps, just perhaps, the young Ms Keane was now really onto something. It was a highly compelling and almost irresistible prospect.

The electronic door panel beeped, and then the lock produced a metallic-sounding snap, allowing him to grip the handle and pull open the door that was polished to a high sheen. Wearing his shirt and tweed suit and carrying a slim, worn leather messenger bag, he entered the building and closed the door behind him. The raised ground floor hallway extended to the back of the house, and on either side were large, high-ceilinged and tastefully furnished living rooms with hardwood flooring, extensive cornicing and substantial ceiling roses some four metres above the floor. At the rear of the townhouse was a large open-plan kitchen with a conservatory backing onto a small but neat garden. Having hired an expensive interior designer to assist him, the entire house now looked just the way he wanted it, and he had poured substantial amounts of money into restoring and furnishing it after first buying it almost a decade earlier.

He was very selective about who he brought to his home, and he was always careful to make sure that no one connected to King's College ever set foot there. Anyone who entered would immediately be struck by the apparent mismatch between what a relatively lowly-paid professor could earn and the scale and expensive opulence of his residence. Not that this was terribly unusual in London, where there were plenty of people with inherited wealth who lived well beyond their own means on the back of fortunes that had been created during colonial times. These fortunes, managed by investment banks and private wealth managers, were often still alive and well after several centuries, and every year, they accrued interest and funded the lives of a select few descendants of various plantation owners, merchants and a long line of governors of dozens of far-flung British colonies and territories across the world. Tobin, however, was none of those. He did not grow up wealthy, and his family had no connection to those century-old fortunes. He was very much a self-made man, although he never discussed this with anyone outside of a small circle of associates who assisted him in his ventures.

Walking upstairs, he entered his large but cosy study. It looked more like a stuffy 19th-century library than anything else, and there was a substantial oak desk by the window and old maps and paintings hanging on every available bit of wall. The theme was very much one of exploration and adventure during a time when maps of the world still included many large white patches where no westerner had yet been.

Dropping the leather bag on the desk, he then proceeded into the bedroom where he took off his jacket and threw it over an expensive, upholstered Louis XIV armchair. Then he changed into a set of clothing in which he felt much more comfortable. Moments later he was wearing beige linen trousers with a wide black leather belt, a big brass buckle and an off-white open-collared shirt with rolled-up sleeves showing his tanned lower arms. After this quick transformation, he walked over to the tall, framed mirror that was leaning against the wall by one of the windows. He then adjusted his shirt and ran his fingers through his hair. Standing there with his feet slightly apart, his back straight and his bearded chin slightly raised, he regarded his own reflection contentedly. Looking back at him from the mirror with a thin smile was the adventurer, treasure hunter, as well as his alter ego, Lawrence Blake.

★ ★ ★

When the packed flight from Heathrow to Miami International Airport took off in the early afternoon on the next day, it was grey and overcast in London. Andrew and Fiona strapped in and made themselves as comfortable as they could for the almost ten-hour trip across the Atlantic. While Andrew tried to catch as much sleep as possible, Fiona immersed herself in research about Haiti. Whenever she went anywhere new in the world, she liked to get a better sense of the history and culture of the place she was going, and in the case of Haiti, she soon found herself falling down a rabbit hole that sounded stranger than fiction.

After the first inflight meal, Andrew glanced across to her as she stowed her tray table and resumed her reading.

'Discover anything interesting?' he said. 'You've been engrossed in that stuff for hours.'

Fiona lifted her head slowly from her tablet and then turned to look at him with slightly glazed-over eyes as if she had been off somewhere far away and long ago and had just been pulled back to the present moment.

'You could say that,' said Fiona. 'I had no idea just how tumultuous a history Haiti has. All I've really known about it up until now is its rough history during that time after Columbus when it was a Spanish colony and then later during what Tobin called the Golden Age of Piracy. But there is a lot more to it than that, and it is frankly a pretty depressing story.'

'Alright,' nodded Andrew. 'I'm not going anywhere. Tell me.'

'Right,' said Fiona, shifting in her seat to face him. 'I'll try to give you the short version. Basically, in 1697, after decades of fighting over the western part of Hispaniola, which had become home to several pirate havens, the Spanish ceded that part of the island to the French, who then renamed it Saint-Domingue. They immediately began bringing over huge numbers of slaves from West Africa to work on the sugar and coffee plantations, and at one point there were about a million slaves living there, roughly fifteen times as many as their colonial French masters. Over the next century or so, Saint-Domingue became the jewel in the French colonial crown, and the enormous profits from its plantations poured back into French banks in Paris.'

'Sounds familiar,' said Andrew. 'That happened all across Europe, right? Everyone was at it.'

'Yes,' said Fiona. 'Definitely not the continent's finest hour. Anyway, after the French Revolution in 1789, the slaves of Saint-Domingue got the crazy idea that the ideals of the revolution, which were freedom, equality and brotherhood between all men, should be universal and also extend to slaves.'

'Right,' said Andrew sarcastically. 'What an insane notion.'

'Yes, isn't it just,' said Fiona, mirroring his demeanour. 'Anyway, this resulted in several slave revolts in Saint-Domingue spanning a number of years. Napoleon Bonaparte eventually dispatched a massive invasion force to take back control of the restive colony, but his forces were defeated in a famous campaign fought by under-equipped but highly motivated former slaves, and Haiti declared itself independent in 1804 as the world's first nation made up of such people.'

'That's very impressive,' said Andrew. 'I had no idea.'

'Yes, but get this,' said Fiona with a small shake of the head. 'This is just about the most obscene thing I have ever read. After the French defeat, the government in Paris forced an agreement on the new nation of former slaves saying that they would be recognised as a country only if they compensated France for the loss of its property, meaning the slaves themselves.'

'Wow,' said Andrew. 'So the slaves were essentially allowed to buy their own independence and freedom by paying money to Paris?'

'Exactly,' said Fiona. 'Otherwise, the French navy would turn up and bombard its defenceless cities.'

'Those are some serious gangster tactics,' said Andrew. 'It was basically a demand for ransom under threat of violence.'

'That's not a bad way to describe it,' said Fiona. 'Of course, the Haitians had no choice but to comply. But they were a completely new and essentially penniless nation, so in order to pay that money, they had to take out a mountain of high-interest loans with French banks. And France then used these loans to suck the country dry over the next many decades. At certain points, up to eighty percent of the Haitian government budget went just on paying interest on the debt to those banks. This debt burden was obviously ruinous, and it crippled the country for the next 120 years and was only finally repaid after World War Two.'

'That's pretty despicable,' said Andrew.

'It got even worse,' said Fiona, 'because up until the American Civil War, the United States had refused to recognise Haiti, because it might induce the slaves in the US to revolt too. So Haiti was economically isolated and barred from international trade. But when the US finally opened up for trade, it soon became the largest trading partner by far, effectively taking control of much of Haiti's economy. And then in 1914, fearing German influence in the country on the eve of World War One, the US actually invaded. Using perfectly legal measures through Wall Street banks, they bought Haiti's central bank and then immediately stole the country's gold reserves.'

'Holy crap,' said Andrew, bemused. 'That sounds a lot like legal piracy to me.'

'Yes,' said Fiona. 'It really wasn't very different from what 17th-century pirates did when they raided Spanish coastal towns. Except the US actually took control of the country for about two decades, installed a puppet government, and once again forced its people to work on plantations.'

'That's astonishing,' said Andrew. 'The irony of it is pretty shocking. Depressing, even, given the history of that place.'

'I know,' said Fiona. 'Now, when the US finally left in 1957, François Duvalier, who was nicknamed *Papa Doc*, came to power on a platform of Black nationalism and reform, but he soon became just another corrupt and thieving autocrat himself. And in 1971 he was followed by his son Jean-Claude, who was aptly named *Baby Doc*, and he was at least as bad a kleptocrat as his father. He was eventually forced to flee the country, though, taking shelter in France, of all places.'

'Obviously,' said Andrew sardonically.

'In the aftermath of all this,' continued Fiona, 'during a period when the country was pretty unstable and completely dependent on US aid, it was then forced by the US government to slash tariffs, which until then had protected Haitian farmers from cheap foreign imports, especially rice. And in the US, rice production is heavily subsidised by the federal government, so virtually overnight, the Haitian market was flooded with American rice sold at huge profits, and this basically killed the domestic agriculture industry. And now, about one-third of the population relies on subsistence agriculture for their meals.'

'Just when I thought it couldn't get much worse,' said Andrew, struggling to take in the seemingly endless litany of tragic events. 'That was a low blow.'

'Yes, and as you can imagine,' said Fiona, 'by that point, the country was essentially completely broken, and what remained of its economy and government was controlled by a small number of oligarchs. And to top everything off, as I am sure you already know, Haiti has suffered several pretty devastating earthquakes that wiped out what was left of a functioning society. So since then, despite billions of dollars in foreign aid flowing into the country, things have only got worse. And one of the reasons seems to be that a lot of that money has often found itself into the hands of a few corrupt government officials.'

'Yes, I do know that it is virtually a lawless place at this point,' said Andrew. 'I had a word with someone in foreign intelligence before we left, and aside from strongly advising us not to go, he said that right now, most of the capital and much of the rest of the country is controlled by violent gangs who are fighting the government and each other practically every day of the week. Something like half of Port-au-Prince is under the control of various gangs armed to the teeth with modern weapons, so we really need to mind where we're going. In fact, we should hire a car and get out of Port-au-Prince as soon as possible. The

UN has sent an international intervention force to help the authorities stabilise things, but according to my contact, it has had very little effect, and in many cases, it has made things worse or simply created a whole new set of problems. Port-au-Prince basically makes Kabul look like a nice day out in the park, so I can't emphasise enough how vigilant we need to be. There are obviously pockets of the city that are still calm and under the control of the police or the military, but they are small, and the gang wars sometimes spill into those as well. So before we do anything, we need to find a way to buy weapons.'

'Weapons?' said Fiona dubiously. 'Are you sure? And how?'

'I'm absolutely sure,' said Andrew resolutely. 'There's no way I am escorting you through that country without a firearm. Preferably several. But don't worry. There are about as many guns in that place as there are people, so it shouldn't be too difficult. I'll sort it out when we get there.'

Eight

With the late afternoon sun seemingly resting on the horizon as they descended towards Miami International Airport, Andrew looked out of the window on the righthand side of the aircraft. Below them, the Atlantic Ocean became the shallow Biscayne Bay, beyond which lay the huge metropolis of Miami City. They passed over Miami Beach, which stretched for miles from north to south along the narrow barrier island by the same name. Soon they swept over the tops of tall, white residential high-rise buildings all laid out in neat square grids of city blocks, and then they finally touched down on the main runway. After a few minutes, the aircraft parked up on its designated apron, and the two of them disembarked along with roughly four hundred other passengers. The walk to passport control through the long, wide carpeted corridors of the sprawling airport complex seemed to take an age, and then they found themselves waiting in the transit area until the flight to Port-au-Prince came up on the boards.

The roughly one-thousand-kilometre-long flight southeast to the Haitian capital took just over two hours, and when the small, half-empty passenger plane flared out over Port-au-Prince Bay on its final approach towards the airport that was located just north of the capital's centre, the contrast between Miami and this place could hardly have been more stark. Instead of neat grids of roads through affluent areas crammed full of high-rise buildings, what slid past them down below as they approached the runway were neighbourhoods that reminded Andrew mostly of the infamous slums and favelas of Rio de Janeiro. There appeared to be no buildings taller than two storeys, and most of them were tiny, densely packed shacks, often with corrugated metal roofs that lined narrow and unpaved dirt roads. Even from the air, the squalor and lack of basic services such as sanitation were obvious. Most of the houses looked ramshackle, and there were huge piles of sometimes burning rubbish lying in the streets in several areas. In the distance, further towards the south, Andrew could see what appeared to be a somewhat more affluent part of the Haitian capital, and he knew that this was where the embassies and a handful of Western hotels were located. They were no more than about three kilometres away, but they might as well have been on a different planet. Between the parts of Port-au-Prince that surrounded the airport and those vaguely civilised neighbourhoods, there would be police roadblocks and private security teams watching all the roads leading in and out, and they would be there 24/7 to protect the diplomatic missions and the heads of the western companies still managing to operate in the country.

By the time the two of them exited Toussaint Louverture International Airport, it was almost dark, and they headed for a small hotel nearby. It was located across from the arrivals terminal's exit, not far from a small car rental hub, which, despite the state of the country and its capital, still somehow managed to operate all the major hire car brands.

As they exited the terminal, the first thing that met them was the muggy heat that immediately wrapped itself around them. Within moments, and despite the late hour and the fact that the sun had disappeared below the horizon almost an hour earlier, they both began to sweat. Walking across the large terminal concourse carrying backpacks packed with essentials and a few spare clothes, Fiona looked at the people milling around outside, and she noticed that there were hardly any other Caucasian faces in sight. There were the ever-present taxi drivers and a few people moving in and out of the arrivals hall, but it seemed as if the airport was winding down for the day, and Andrew thought that there were probably only a handful of flights per day now that the security situation was as dire as it had become.

'Come on,' he said. 'Let's get to that hotel. I think we both need some sleep to deal with our jet lag. Although, there's something else I need to do first.'

An hour later, Andrew left the clean but very basic hotel. On his way out, he stopped by a pair of its resident guards who were standing by the front doors looking large and mean.

'Evening, guys,' he said calmly but in slightly hushed tones, turning his back to the hotel entrance as if wanting to prevent anyone inside from hearing him. 'You wouldn't happen to know where I could find a drink and some friendly company?'

The two guards who had watched him and Fiona enter the hotel together earlier glanced at each other with a look of mild surprise.

'You mean… female company?' one of them asked with a cautious leer on his lips and a heavy French-Creole accent.

'That's right,' said Andrew, pulling a thick wad of US dollars from his back pocket. 'A nice place. Not one of those shitty ones.'

The guard shrugged and looked down along the virtually deserted road to his left. It ran through what looked like an increasingly dilapidated part of town, and at least every other streetlight was either out or flickering intermittently.

'There's a place about two kilometres that way,' the guard said, jerking his head east. 'It's called Madam Claire's. Old hotel building. Red lights all over the front. You can't miss it. Expensive but good quality. Nice girls.'

'Great,' said Andrew, pulling two banknotes from the wad and pressing them into the guard's hand. 'Thanks a lot.'

'You need some wheels?' said the guard. 'You can take my bike for a few more of those.'

He gestured towards a motorcycle parked off to one side, and then he nodded at the cash.

Andrew pulled out a few more notes from the wad and handed them to him.

'I will bring it back shortly,' he then said.

'Hey,' grinned the man as he stuffed the money into the inside pocket of his jacket. 'Take your time, man. Enjoy yourself.'

'I'm sure I will,' Andrew replied.

He mounted the motorcycle, turned the key and pressed the starter button, and its engine immediately sprang to life. With a quick salute to the guards, he then switched on the headlight and took off down the road while the two men grinned knowingly at each other as they returned to their guard duty.

About five minutes later, Andrew arrived at the brothel, and the guard's description turned out to have been accurate. This was definitely the place. It was an old colonial building with a wide, sweeping staircase leading up to a set of large double front doors, and they were flanked by two tall, muscular local men wearing jeans and white t-shirts. Despite the fact that it was now completely dark outside, they also wore sunglasses, and they carried pistols in shoulder holsters. Whether they were as dangerous as they made out to be was anyone's guess, but they certainly looked the part. Andrew dismounted the bike and walked up to them looking as if he didn't have a care in the world.

'What's up, fella's?' he said casually, putting on an American accent. 'I'm looking for some entertainment, and I heard this was the place to go.'

'You have money?' said one of the brutes in a slow, baritone voice while his eyes examined what was no doubt an unusual visitor standing in front of him. 'You need money.'

Andrew pulled the cash from his pocket and was once again amazed at how easily the sight of ready dollar bills could turn a situation in his favour. The guard nodded and placed a massive, fleshy hand on the door handle behind him.

'Welcome to Madam Claire's,' he said, pushing it open.

Spilling out from inside the building was purple light and a soundtrack that this place shared with thousands of similar places the world over. It was a mix of up-tempo dance music and the raucous laughter of men who had come for a boozy night out with female company that they were more than prepared to pay for. Andrew stepped inside, and the doors closed behind him. As he walked through a short hallway, another guard frisked him to make sure he wasn't carrying any weapons, and then he proceeded up to the bar where he ordered a drink.

Less than a minute after placing himself on the barstool and being served, a scantily clad young woman approached and slid onto the stool next to him. She had a pretty face and looked like someone who could easily have got a job as a swimsuit model. As she did so, she made a well-practised effort to attract his attention with a coy smile and a flick of one of her long, elegant legs.

'Good evening, mister,' she said sweetly. 'What's your name?'

'Andrew,' he replied, giving her a brief smile.

'Are you here for a good time?' she said, clearly following a script that had been played back a thousand times before, yet somehow still managing to sound sincere.

'Maybe,' said Andrew. 'Tell me. Who owns this place?'

She looked at him uncertainly for a moment before replying. This was clearly not part of the script.

'The boss,' she finally said, glancing furtively towards one of the heavies by the door. 'I'm not supposed to talk about him.'

'Does he have a name?' said Andrew. 'I've never been to Haiti before, so I'm just curious about this place.'

'Marcellus,' said the woman. 'He owns a lot of places like this here in Port-au-Prince.'

'Is he here now?' said Andrew.

'No,' said the woman. 'I never see him. He never comes here.'

As they spoke, Andrew noticed that the bulky guards by the door seemed to be looking in his direction and conferring amongst themselves about something. It seemed that his lack of interest in the gorgeous young woman beside him stood out in this place where every other guest appeared to be busy getting as friendly and handsy as they could with the female staff.

'Right,' nodded Andrew, taking a sip from his drink. 'Listen, I need the men's room. Could you point me to it?'

'It's that way,' said the woman. 'Through that door and downstairs.'

'Thanks,' said Andrew, getting off the barstool and leaving the drink on the counter. 'I'll be right back.'

He walked casually towards the door and pushed through it to find himself in a small rear foyer of the building. There was a set of steps leading downstairs and a yellow, pulsing neon sign saying 'Toilets'. Another set of steps led further up into the former hotel, no doubt giving access to the various rooms used by paying customers for their entertainment. But Andrew was not interested in those, and he had not come here to be entertained. He was here because certain things always come as a package. Where there are brothels, there are armed guards, and where there are armed guards, there is an armoury. And in a place like this, which was operating in an often lawless city, it was virtually guaranteed to be extremely well stocked. Not only was a place like this a real money spinner for whichever gang boss owned it, but it was likely that other gangs would try to take it over given half a chance during the Haitian capital's never-ending turf wars. For this reason, the team of burly guards who protected it and its roster of female assets needed to have ready access to some serious firepower.

He headed up the stairs past two floors of what were now former hotel rooms serving as sordid venues for extracting as much money from the paying customers as possible. When he arrived on the top floor, he knew that he was in the right place. The lurid purple carpets had been replaced with a simple light grey, and instead of a long, dimly lit corridor with multiple doors leading to small pleasure dens, he found two offices across from a larger open staff area that was furnished with black leather sofas, a glass-fronted minibar full of soft drinks, a jukebox and a Brazil-themed table football game. This was clearly where the male staff members spent their time during breaks or before the doors opened for another night of business.

He paused for a moment to listen out for voices, but all he could hear now was the muffled thumping of the music downstairs. The entire top floor of the building was empty at this hour, and he slipped into the nearest and largest office, which had an armoured door that seemed overkill for such a basic room. However, the door was the giveaway that he had been looking for, and as he entered the room, he immediately spotted what he had hoped to find there. Mounted on the back wall next to a window that had iron bars on the outside was a large gun cabinet, and even from the doorway it was clear that it wasn't locked. If this establishment suddenly came under attack, finding the keys and unlocking the cabinet might well mean the difference between successfully protecting this particular golden goose and losing it to a rival kingpin. So everything was easily accessible.

He walked across the room and opened the cabinet's metal doors to be greeted by a sight that, even after all these years of being around some of the most advanced weaponry ever devised, caused a contented smile to spread across his face. There were several varieties of pistols, two types of shotguns, a dozen AR-15 assault rifles and boxes of U.S. standard-issue M67 hand grenades plus several ballistics vests. Whoever owned this place was certainly not playing around when it came to ensuring that it had enough hardware to protect itself. How the gangs of Port-au-Prince managed to get their hands on this much firepower was a mystery to him, but he assumed it was simply a matter of money. And he had been in enough conflict zones across the world to know that guns and ammunition for local warlords often made their way to war-ravaged areas much more easily than food and water for the civilian population.

He ended up taking a matte black semiautomatic Smith & Wesson SD9 pistol with an under-mounted laser for himself and a small and compact SIG Sauer P365 for Fiona. He knew that he was going to have to convince her to carry it around with her, but if ever there was a time and a place where it was better to be safe than sorry, it was here. He reached around to the small of his back and tucked the loaded SD9 under his belt, and then he put the SIG Sauer into a large black holdall that was lying at the bottom of the cabinet. He then picked an AR-15 assault rifle off the rack along with two black ballistics vests. Finally, he grabbed three hand grenades, several boxes of 9mm bullets and four fully loaded spare 5.56mm magazines for the assault rifles. Glancing back at the cabinet as he was about to leave, he decided to help himself to another assault rifle and a pump-action shotgun with ammo boxes, just in case.

Placing everything inside the holdall and zipping it up, he slung it over his shoulder and turned towards the door, and that was when he heard the sound of heavy footsteps coming up the stairs, and it sounded like more than just one person. He shot a quick glance towards the barred-up window a couple of metres away. There was not a snowball's chance in hell of him getting out that way. Certainly not in the time it would take him to break past the thick iron rods outside. Then he looked back at the bottom of the gun cabinet where a handful of black spheres the size of small apples lay in a plastic basket.

'This way,' said a deep voice from outside the office, now less than five metres away. 'He must be up here.'

An instant later, a black non-lethal stun grenade rolled out from the main office and came to a stop at the feet of the two dumbfounded guards who had followed the suspicious *'blanc'* to the men's room only to find it empty. Frozen to the spot, they stared at the grenade and were about to turn and throw themselves clear when the explosive charge detonated with an ear-splitting crack.

Andrew was safely inside the office and well clear of the blast, but even he felt the effects of the stun grenade. It seemed as if the entire building was vibrating in the seconds after the blinding explosion, and as dense grey smoke filled the corridor outside the office, he could hear the sound of the two guards yelling and moaning in pain. Wasting no time, he bolted out of the office and down the corridor where he had spotted a sign for the fire exit next to a glass door to the outside. As he ran past the guards, he was able to make out the forms of the two guards lying on the floor and writhing in pain with their eyes squeezed tightly shut and their hands pressed against their ears. They grimaced and groaned like animals from the shock and pain of the stun grenade, and it was clear to Andrew that they would present no threat to anyone for the next several minutes. However, their colleagues downstairs were already coming up the stairs amid angry and confused shouting mixed with the unmistakable sounds of the slides on their pistols being racked.

Andrew bolted for the end of the corridor and pulled hard on the fire exit's door handle. It was locked. He ripped the SD9 from his belt, racked the slide and fired twice into the door. The tall pane of toughened glass disintegrated into a million small crystal cubes that fell into a heap on the floor like huge grains of sugar. They had barely settled before Andrew rushed through the doorway and punched the release handle for the telescopic, metal fire exit ladder. For a moment, it seemed as if the rusty ladder was stuck in place, and he was already glancing down to the side alley below to see if there was a way for him to jump and land safely on something, but the alley was empty apart from an overflowing trash container about ten metres further down. The shouting at the other end of the corridor inside the building had now grown much louder.

'*Sortie de secours!*', someone yelled, clearly realising that the intruder had run for the fire escape.

Andrew kicked the ladder, and it immediately released and slid down rapidly, coming to a loud, juddering stop that made the entire metal support structure attached to the side of the building shake. Without a second to lose, he leapt onto it and slid down to the ground using the sleeves of his shirt to protect himself against the rusty metal. The shirt's fabric was shredded, but it meant that he was able to get down with only minor grazes on his palms.

Once down, he sprinted for the street and didn't slow down as he tore around the corner of the building and approached the motorcycle. He jumped onto the seat and hit the ignition button before the two guards at the front door knew what was happening. They already had their weapons drawn, having been alerted by the muffled sound of the explosion on the top floor, but they were looking inside through the open doors when Andrew fired up the four-stroke engine and took off. One of them had enough wits about him to realise what was happening, and he raised his pistol and fired off three shots, but they all went wide, answering the question as to how well-trained they really were.

Racing away from the brothel, Andrew glanced down into one of the side mirrors, and to his relief, there were no headlights pursuing him. The whole thing had unfolded in just a couple of minutes, and the guards had clearly not had a car ready and waiting for just this type of eventuality. With the motorcycle engine screaming between his legs and the wind tearing at his clothes and making his eyes water, he peered up ahead and wondered for a moment if there might be police on the way. But then he immediately realised just how unlikely that was. One, and possibly the only, benefit to being in a city almost completely taken over by gang violence was that the sounds of gunfire and even explosions were a daily if not hourly occurrence, and there was effectively no chance of it resulting in the police turning up. They had no interest in preventing the gangs from battling each other, and they seemed to have given up entirely on protecting civilians a long time ago. Only if the interests of the oligarchs or the international organisations and diplomatic missions were threatened was there a likelihood of them making an appearance. When he arrived back at the hotel, he parked the bike and walked over to the guards by the door.

'Thanks,' he said calmly, dropping the keys in the owner's palm. 'That was just what I needed.'

Then he walked inside and up to the room where Fiona was waiting anxiously.

'Did you find what you were looking for?' she said.

'Yup,' he replied, letting the holdall drop onto the bed and unzipping it. 'We should be fine with this. I'll feel a lot safer now taking you up north.'

Fiona looked inside the bag and turned to face him, and for a moment, she looked like she was about to direct a barrage of questions at him, but then she seemed to change her mind.

'I'm not even going to ask,' she said, giving a shake of the head.

'This is for you,' said Andrew, extracting the small SIG Sauer from the holdall. 'It's a 9mm pistol, but it's about half the size of a Glock 19. I want you to carry it on you at all times, OK? This place is no playground.'

'Right,' said Fiona, taking the gun in her hands and feeling its weight. 'I guess.'

'No,' said Andrew calmly but insistently. 'Promise me you'll do as I ask. I will do whatever I can to keep us safe, but you'll need to have your own means of protection here. Alright?'

'Alright. Fine,' nodded Fiona as she flicked the safety off and on again and then pressed the magazine release catch to check the ammo. 'I promise. I won't let it leave my sight.'

'Thank you,' said Andrew, feeling like an overprotective parent, yet also feeling a sense of relief that Fiona would be armed as well, just in case.

'There's something I need to show you,' she said, suddenly more glum, sitting down on the end of the bed and placing the SIG Sauer next to her as she opened a messaging app on her phone. 'My colleague Emily says that they have heard nothing from the police so far. They came in and talked to everyone, and then they left. But it seems like they're not allocating a lot of people despite this being a high-profile case. They probably just don't have the resources for a huge manhunt. Anyway, a guy I know in the security monitoring room at the British Museum sent me this video file. It's a short clip of the intruder. The man who killed Laura. Apparently, it shows the whole thing, but I don't want to watch it. In fact, I don't want it on my phone, so I am going to send it to you and then delete it, OK? Then you can look at it and tell me if it might bring us any closer to finding out who he is.

'Alright,' said Andrew, placing a hand gently on her shoulder. 'I'll take a look.'

A few seconds later, the message from Fiona dinged in on his phone, and he opened the attachment. It began with black-and-white footage shot by a CCTV camera mounted in a stairwell. In the top right-hand corner, it said 'Cam 72. East Stairwell.'. The resolution wasn't the best, but it was perfectly adequate for Andrew to be able to see a metal rope ladder being dropped from above and a large man wearing black clothing and a balaclava climbing down it with considerable skill and speed. Once on the landing, he headed straight down the stairs as if he knew exactly where he was going. Then the video switched to a different camera. It was designated 'Cam 56. Mexico.'.

Andrew kept watching the video as the man moved purposefully to a glass-fronted display cabinet and cut a neat circular hole in the glass, extracting what looked like a small statue, which he wrapped and placed in his slim backpack. A few moments later, he seemed to sense that someone was approaching, because he moved swiftly to stand in the shadows next to a wall. Less than ten seconds later, Laura Hartley's petite form appeared in the doorway leading to the rest of the museum's interior. And then followed a scene that caused even Andrew's stomach to tighten into a knot, despite him having seen his share of death firsthand. The large man stepped out of the shadow and wrapped an arm around the much smaller woman. She struggled and kicked, but he held her tight, and then suddenly, her entire body went limp and her arms fell to her sides. Andrew clenched his jaw as he watched Laura's life being snuffed out from one moment to the next. It was a painful and upsetting scene, and he soon felt anger welling up inside him at the callousness of it all. Whatever that man had wanted, it was not worth killing a defenceless security guard over. However, there was nothing about the man that would allow anyone to identify him. Nothing except perhaps the fact that he moved with such smoothness and control despite his large bulk that Andrew had to assume that he was a well-trained operator, either ex-military or possibly part of the security services. But apart from that, there was nothing to help pin down who he might be.

'I'm sorry,' said Andrew, switching his phone off and looking at Fiona. 'About Laura. And about the fact that there's nothing here to provide a clue to his identity. His face was covered the whole time. I'm afraid I don't think the police are going to get very far unless they catch a lucky break somehow.'

Fiona nodded silently with a dejected look. Then she turned to look at him.

'Don't ever tell me what was on that video,' she said. 'I just don't want to know.'

'I won't,' said Andrew, reaching over to take her hand in his and giving it a gentle squeeze. 'You made the right choice not to watch it. Now, I think we should try to get some sleep. We have a busy day tomorrow.'

★   ★   ★

The next morning, Andrew and Fiona paid the hotel bill and left for the car rental hub. It was already very warm and sunny by the time they had walked the short distance across the airport concourse to the rental place, and within about half an hour, they had secured a grey and plain-looking Ford with a few dents and scratches. Although close, it was not quite the cheapest car they could find, but it served the purpose of ensuring that they drew as little attention to themselves as possible. They could have rented anything up to and including a massive and shiny champagne-coloured Range Rover, but there was unlikely to be a car capable of attracting more attention from potential carjackers than that one in the entire country.

When they left the airport complex and headed west to catch Highway 1 going north, they both felt relief at the prospect of leaving the city behind. However, in the thick and chaotic traffic of the Haitian capital, none of them noticed the two motorcycle riders behind them who threaded their way nimbly through the slow-moving lanes of traffic, following at a distance of about fifty metres as they went. And what they couldn't have known was that one of the most powerful crime bosses in Port-au-

Prince was at war with the gang that currently owned the brothel where Andrew had acquired his small arsenal the night before. A scout working for that particular kingpin had been staking out the brothel when Andrew had paid it a visit. Conferring with his superiors back at the HQ, the scout had been instructed to keep an eye on the foreigner and see where he was going. Anyone prepared and capable of going to such lengths to rob a brothel was clearly someone worth watching, and he might just be up to something that could present a business opportunity. If nothing else, he and his blonde female companion might turn out to be juicy kidnap targets. Now, the scout and his fellow gang member were following the shabby-looking Ford as it made its way west towards the commercial harbour.

'This is absolute chaos,' said Fiona, placing a hand anxiously on the dashboard as Andrew navigated speedily through the anarchic morning traffic. 'And here I was thinking that London traffic was bad.'

'We should be clear of it soon,' said Andrew, as they picked up speed along an almost straight avenue that cut west through the city centre. 'Look over there. That's the UN.'

Parked at one of the major intersections was a group of UN soldiers wearing light beige uniforms and blue helmets and standing around next to their tall, jeep-like MRAPs. The specially designed mine-resistant and ambush-protected vehicles had been built to operate in warzones such as Afghanistan, but they had been a prerequisite for the UN force deployed here, so dire was the situation in the Haitian capital. All of the gangs in Port-au-Prince had ready access to heavy assault rifles that could make mincemeat of the soldiers unless they wore heavy body armour, and weapons like those would be able to turn the bodywork of a regular passenger car into a sieve in a matter of seconds.

'Those guys can't be local, right?' said Fiona, nodding in the direction of the heavily armed black UN personnel who stood by their vehicles, casting nervous glances this way and that.

'No,' said Andrew. 'They are Kenyans. With the colonial history of this place, I think it was deemed better to have an African contingent come in and assist the authorities here. A bunch of tooled-up white guys would not have been received very favourably in these parts, even if they were wearing blue helmets.'

'Last night I also noticed that we almost seemed to be the only white people here,' she said.

'I know,' said Andrew. 'There is basically no tourism here anymore. This country has hundreds of miles of pristine, beautiful tropical beaches with azure-blue waters, but with the way things are at the moment, mass tourism is a non-starter. It could have been a huge source of income for this place, the way it is just over the border in the Dominican Republic, but the gangs here make that impossible.'

'Right,' said Fiona. 'It's really sad. I think I read that the average income over there is about ten times what it is here in Haiti. Can you believe that? One thousand percent. That's huge. And it is only about twenty miles from where we are now. It's surreal.'

'Once a country starts to fall apart,' said Andrew grimly, 'it can disintegrate very quickly, and then it's a long way down to the bottom from there. I've seen it before. And righting a ship like that is almost impossible without massive intervention from the outside. That might happen one day, but that's not what is happening right now. This place is essentially left to its own devices, and the result is pretty chaotic, as you can see.'

'Look over there!' said Fiona, suddenly pointing excitedly out of the windscreen at an equestrian statue on their left sitting atop a large horse and wearing an elaborate 19th-century military uniform. 'That's Jean-Jacques Dessalines.'

'Who?' said Andrew, glancing at the enormous statue before returning his gaze to the traffic in front of them.

'He was a black man who served as an officer in the French Army,' said Fiona. 'But he ended up as a commander of the revolution against the French here, and it was his army that defeated Napoleon's invasion force in 1803.'

'Interesting,' said Andrew. 'So I guess he's a big national hero.'

'You could say that,' said Fiona. 'Although, he also ordered the massacre of about five thousand of the white minority here, and then he pronounced himself emperor and pretty much became a dictator until he was assassinated a few years later.'

'Right,' said Andrew pensively. 'I guess that helped set the tone for a lot of what happened here after that.'

'It might have done,' said Fiona. 'A bit of a checkered history, to put it mildly.'

They eventually merged onto Highway 1 and curved north near Port-au-Prince Bay past a large container terminal. As far as Andrew could see, there were only two small freighters docked there, and only a small number of containers stacked on the quayside. After another few minutes, they drove across a large intersection with dilapidated, although functional housing on one side and some of the worst slums he had seen on the other.

'Down there is Cité Soleil,' said Andrew, jerking his head along the road stretching towards the bay and the slums. 'It's notorious for being one of the most deprived areas, and it's under the complete control of the gangs. The police never go in there for any reason.'

Fiona glanced along the road, and in the distance, she could see what appeared to be a makeshift roadblock made up of two regular cars blocking access to the neighbourhood. However, not far from it were several small children playing football in the middle of the otherwise deserted road.

'What a crazy place this is,' she said, and for the first time since they had arrived, Andrew sensed that she was truly beginning to appreciate just how unpredictable and often dangerous Haiti could be.

After exiting the city, they continued north through the increasingly rugged and mountainous terrain, and the settlements became smaller and, if possible, their inhabitants even more destitute-looking. They passed dozens of tiny homes that appeared to be owned by subsistence farmers, and as they made it ever further north, the amount of traffic on the roads dropped to next to nothing.

Finally, after almost six hours of strenuous driving through the intense heat and along the often badly maintained roads, they finally arrived in a small coastal town by the name of Saint-Louis-du-Nord. After parking up on what amounted to the town's beach promenade next to a sandy beach lined with palm trees, they felt as if they were now in a different world altogether. The houses were relatively neat and often painted in primary colours or pastel pinks and blues, which gave the place a cheerful look. There were still ramshackle buildings in some places, but the residents walking along the streets or standing by the roadside food stands looked calm and relaxed, and although clearly not an affluent place, it was far from as destitute as much of Port-au-Prince had been. All in all, the small coastal town managed to appear like a different planet compared with the menacing feel of the capital.

Getting out of the car by the curving, palm-lined promenade and stretching their legs, the fresh sea air blowing in from the ocean quickly cooled them down, and Fiona turned to Andrew with a smile.

'Check out the ocean,' she said, pointing at the clear, azure blue waters stretching along the beach. 'And look out that way.'

Andrew squinted under the bright midday sun as he followed her gaze out across the water, and through the shimmering heat, he could clearly see an elongated shape with tall, mostly tree-covered rocky hills some five kilometres away.

'That's Tortuga over there,' Fiona said excitedly. 'We finally made it.'

* * *

Carrying the holdall with the weapons and equipment they had brought with them over his shoulder, Andrew locked the car, and the two of them then began moving along the promenade towards a small group of buildings near the beach. Finding an inviting-looking beachfront eatery nestled under a group of palm trees, they sat down on its slightly raised concrete porch overlooking the beach and the ocean. Across the waves in the hazy distance, the almost forty-kilometre-long and roughly eight-kilometre-wide Tortuga Island beckoned to them as they ordered soft drinks and a couple of wraps with pork, vegetables and a type of dressing that tasted nothing like anything the two of them had tried before.

'This is all very pretty,' said Fiona brightly as the warm and gentle sea breeze played with her hair. 'I'm glad to see that the whole country isn't like Port-au-Prince. If it weren't for that long drive up here, this town could be a great place for tourists.'

'Yes, it's nice,' said Andrew, peering down along the beach where he noticed that some sort of building works were taking place.

He got out his binoculars and trained them on what turned out to be a group of about ten men working on building a boat. Sitting propped upright by long, thick pieces of timber directly on the beach about forty metres from the water's edge, the vessel looked to be about thirty feet long with a wide beam, and its curved wooden hull was yet to be painted.

'Looks like they're building a sloop down there,' he said. 'If I am not mistaken, those boats were the first real pirate ships. Small, fast and nimble with a single, large triangular sail that I think is called a Bermuda sail. There's no mast, though, so maybe they are planning to put an engine in this one.'

'Like the one out there?' said Fiona, pointing out to sea where a similar-looking brightly coloured vessel was making its way slowly along the coast amid the softly puttering noise of a two-stroke diesel engine.

'I guess so,' said Andrew, watching the sleek shape of the vessel as it cut smoothly through the crests of the small waves. 'We should see if we can hire one of those. That should be more than adequate for getting us across to Tortuga. And we also need to hire some diving gear.'

'I saw a sign for boat hire a bit further along the road,' said Fiona.

'Good,' said Andrew. 'What do you plan to do first once we get over there?'

'Well,' said Fiona, pulling a paper map from her backpack, spreading it out on the table and pointing to a location on the south coast of Tortuga. 'This spot here is where the old harbour at Tortuga used to be. It's such a useful natural harbour that the locals still use it today. But unlike in the 17th century, there isn't really a town there anymore. Just a few houses. Piracy made it a big hub back then, and it had a very sizable port, but now there are only a few fishermen living there. In fact, I think the whole island has no more than a couple of thousand inhabitants at this point. Anyway, we need to get up onto the hill above the harbour and find the ruins of Fort de Rocher.'

Her index finger tapped on a small area of the map that, judging by the elevation contours, seemed to be at the top of a steep rise several hundred metres inland.

'I've got Eduard Leroux's account with me,' she went on, 'so if we can find the precise spot at the fort where he was standing when he saw the Marauder blow up, then that should help us pinpoint where she was anchored when it happened.'

She then got out a pen and used one of the eatery's cardboard menus to trace a straight line from their location in Saint-Louis-du-Nord to a spot slightly east of where Tortuga's pirate port had once been.

'The explosion was also witnessed by several people on this side of the Tortuga Channel,' she continued, 'and most of them agree that the fireball was slightly to the left of what they knew to be the port. So that's west. All we need to do is climb that hill up to Fort de Rocher and then draw a line on this map that reflects what Leroux saw. And where those two lines intersect, that should be where it happened, give or take a couple of hundred metres in all directions.'

'You make it sound so simple,' said Andrew as he studied the map in front of them. 'But that's still a huge search area. It won't be easy, especially since we're looking for the remains of a ship that literally blew to pieces.'

'I know,' Fiona conceded. 'But the account from the merchant is the best clue anyone has had for a very long time, so I am feeling optimistic.'

'Alright,' nodded Andrew. 'Let's finish up here and then go and see about a boat.'

Nine

When Andrew and Fiona arrived at the boat rental shop by the water's edge a little way further along the road, they found themselves in the middle of a small but busy hub of various tiny shops and street vendors touting their wares. Off to one side was the open shopfront of a small wooden building facing the sea, and behind the counter stood a handsome young man of about twenty-five years of age. Lean and fit with a dark tan and black, short-cropped hair, he was wearing light blue jeans and a bright red sleeveless t-shirt with a capital 'R' printed in black on its front. Above him was a sign saying 'Ronil's Boat Hire' in red lettering on a white background. The sign was clearly hand-painted, but it got the message across just fine all the same.

'I feel like everyone's watching us,' said Fiona as she looked around and smiled nervously at the various groups of people milling around near the boats, several of whom had now stopped and were looking in their direction.

'I don't think it's every day they see a couple of tourists walking around here,' said Andrew as they made their way through the crowd of shoppers and vendors towards the shop counter. 'It's fine. These people are all just going about their normal lives.'

They walked over to the shop, and as they came up to the counter, the young man behind it broke into a wide smile as he welcomed them in a thick Creole accent.'

'Good afternoon,' he said amiably as he looked at both of them in turn. 'Do you need a boat today?'

'Good guess,' said Andrew, offering his hand across the counter in an attempt to establish a friendly rapport with the man. 'My name is Andrew. This is Fiona.'

'Very nice to meet you,' smiled the young man, shaking Andrew's hand. 'My name is Ronil. And this is my boat hire shop.'

As he introduced himself, Ronil made a vague gesture to the small shack around him, and it was obvious that he took some measure of pride in his modest business.

'Ah,' said Andrew affably. 'So we're speaking to the boss?'

'That's right, my friend,' grinned Ronil. 'And if you want to hire me and my boat, I will take you anywhere you want. It's that blue one out there.'

Ronil looked pleased as he pointed to a roughly twenty-five-foot boat of a similar design to the one they had just watched being constructed a bit further along the beach. It was bobbing gently in the clear, shallow waters about ten metres from shore, and it was painted sky blue with a bright yellow stripe running along its side. At the rear was mounted a large outboard motor that had been swivelled up so that its propeller was out of the water.

'Very good,' said Andrew. 'We'd like to take a trip over to Tortuga. But we need to find a place to rent some diving equipment first.'

'Scuba diving, eh?' said Ronil, nodding knowingly. 'Lots to see down there.'

'One set should be enough,' said Andrew.

'Alright, my friends,' said Ronil with a calm and genial familiarity that instantly made them feel both welcome and relaxed in the young man's company. 'I will get the boat ready for you now. This will be the price.'

He scribbled a number on a piece of paper, rotated it on the counter and pushed it across for them to see.

'That's fine,' said Andrew after glancing at the figure, reaching inside a pocket for his wallet.

'And I will also call my friend Samuel,' said Ronil. 'He has some diving equipment you can rent. One moment, please.'

'Great,' said Andrew, handing over the cash. 'Here you go.'

Ronil accepted the money without counting it, and then he reached under the shop counter and placed two chilled cans of Coke in front of them.

'On the house,' he said. 'While you wait.'

'Thank you,' smiled Fiona cheerfully, taking one of them and popping it open. 'That's very nice of you.'

Ronil shot her a smile and gave a courteous nod, and then he disappeared swiftly out of the shop's back door, leaving them to sip their drinks and watch the locals going about their business in the small commercial beachfront hub. A few minutes later, they watched as he waded out to his boat and then pulled it back to the shore and partially onto the beach. Moments later, another young man, who they assumed was Samuel, appeared carrying a mask, flippers and a regulator in one hand and a brushed metal oxygen tank in the other. He walked down to Ronil at the water's edge and loaded the equipment into the boat. The two young men gave each other a pally fist bump, and then Samuel disappeared back up into the town.

'Nice to see a couple of hard-working young men just getting on with things,' said Andrew to Fiona. 'I guess there's more to this place for someone like him than just the gangs.'

'He seems really nice,' said Fiona. 'Remember what I said about most people being perfectly decent?'

'Yes,' said Andrew pensively. 'You're probably right. Maybe I am overly suspicious of people. Comes with the job, I guess. Not much I can do about that.'

'It's alright,' said Fiona, placing a hand on his arm. 'Like you always say. Better safe than sorry.'

As they watched, Ronil moved the diving equipment into the back of the boat near the outboard motor. He then raised his head and looked in their direction with a bright smile, signalling them with a quick wave.

'I guess we're all set,' said Andrew. 'Let's go.'

They climbed into the sleek boat, got themselves comfortable on the central bench seat, and then Ronil lowered the propeller into the water and fired up the outboard motor. A few minutes later, with the balmy air in their hair and the occasional salty spray hitting their faces, the small town of Saint-Louis-du-Nord and the tree-covered mountainous island of Hispaniola quickly began to recede behind them. With Ronil steering the boat competently across the Tortuga Channel, they were soon well underway towards the island that once upon a time, for many decades, had been home to one of the most famous pirate havens in the Caribbean.

★ ★ ★

When they arrived on the beach on Tortuga Island, two things were immediately obvious. One was that the 17th-century pirates had picked a perfect place for a harbour and a base for their operations. The bay and natural harbour was shallow with a long stretch of sandy beach, and the terrain was virtually flat for a couple of hundred metres before then rising steeply towards the tall, rocky and partially overgrown hills above. The second obvious thing was that the island was significantly less developed and affluent than the town they had left behind on Hispaniola about half an hour earlier. What few scattered houses there were along the beach were all noticeably dilapidated, and the handful of small, barely seaworthy boats anchored in the harbour gave the place a decidedly down-at-heel vibe.

Fiona glanced back across the water towards Hispaniola, which was now framed by a few fluffy, white cumulus clouds on the otherwise clear blue sky. As Ronil steered the boat gently onto the beach and they jumped down onto the soft, wet sand, a group of young men were sitting under a bushy tree nearby. Next to them were a couple of small motorbikes, and the men were smoking and watching the new arrivals as they disembarked from the boat. Ronil gave them a wave and called out a quick, casual greeting in Creole.

'It's OK,' he said, lowering his voice as he spoke to Andrew and Fiona. 'They are just local boys waiting for the sun to go a bit lower in the sky. Then they'll go out in their boats and put out their fishing nets.'

'Right,' said Fiona as they walked across the beach to a dirt track that ran parallel to the beach through low palm trees and bushes. 'We've read a lot about gangs in Haiti. So, if you don't mind me asking. Is that a problem up in these parts of the country?'

Ronil shrugged as they paused in a shady spot under a tall palm tree whose large, wide fronds were rustling gently in the breeze above them.

'The gangs are everywhere,' he said, taking on a slightly dejected look. 'Sometimes they work with the police. Sometimes with businesses. We can't escape them. But it's not so bad here. Port-au-Prince is much worse.'

'Well, it seems like you're managing to run your business just fine, right?' said Fiona.

'Mostly,' said Ronil with a resigned shrug. 'We all have to pay some protection money to them. Otherwise, they will make life difficult. But it's like that everywhere. We are used to it.'

'Have they ever made life difficult for you?' asked Andrew.

Ronil seemed to hesitate for a brief moment before replying, and as he did so, Andrew thought he saw some unspoken pain briefly flash across the young man's usually cheerful face.

'I've done my best to stay out of all the gang business,' he finally said, taking on a stoic and somewhat philosophical expression. 'I just want to run my boat hire shop and live in peace. I try to treat everyone with respect, and I hope they will do the same for me. That's all I can say.'

'Alright,' said Andrew with a nod, sensing that this was not the time for trying to dig deeper into Ronil's past. 'Anyway, thanks for getting us over here. We're probably going to need a couple of hours, and then we might need to go out and perform a couple of dives just off the coast.'

'That's cool. I'll wait for you here,' said Ronil, jerking his head towards the boat. 'As long as we make it back to Saint-Louis-du-Nord by sunset.'

'We should be able to swing that, right?' said Andrew, turning to Fiona.

'Yes,' she nodded. 'With a bit of luck. But we need to get moving, then. We'll see you soon.'

'Alright,' said Ronil, flashing them a smile. 'I'll be right here when you get back. Take care, guys.'

Following the route indicated on a GPS app on Fiona's phone, she and Andrew headed off along the dry dirt road that ran along the beach. Soon they found themselves slightly further inland and shielded from the intense sun by palm trees, and along the way, there were a few small ramshackle breezeblock houses nestled between dense vegetation. Each one was fenced off by a makeshift picket fence constructed from strips of palm wood and thick, flexible metal wire. Behind them were what looked like small vegetable gardens where the locals appeared to grow a lot of their food. However, there were no residents in sight, and Andrew reckoned that they were probably very sensibly staying inside their relatively cool dwellings at this time of day. After about ten minutes of walking, a trail led north up towards a large rocky promontory above them some three hundred metres away.

'That must be it,' said Fiona, checking her paper map once again. 'This is where the road up to the fort used to be. It's barely there anymore, but it's definitely this way.'

They began the ascent of the dusty trail that wound its way through the undergrowth and past what appeared to be small plantations of banana trees. The final stretch up the escarpment to the top of the plateau above was steep and treacherous, and it was only possible because it appeared to have been a while since it last rained. If the ground had been wet and slippery, they would have struggled to get all the way up. However, they eventually managed to climb past the final rocky crest and then found themselves in a relatively flat, open area. It was almost as overgrown as the hillside they had just traversed, but there was now no doubt in their minds that they were in the right place. About twenty metres ahead of them were the ruined walls and foundations of Fort de Rocher, and only now did Fiona get a true appreciation for its significant size during its heyday. It was at least one hundred metres across, and there appeared to have been an inner fortified structure that had most likely served as both barracks and private residence for Jean Le Vasseur during his time as governor here after the fort's construction had been completed. Turning around to look down the hill and out over the Tortuga Channel, Fiona shielded her eyes with one hand and placed the other on her hip as she caught her breath after the strenuous climb.

'What a place,' she said, a smile spreading across her lips as she turned to Andrew. 'I can't believe we're here. Have a look at the view of Hispaniola. It would have looked pretty much the same when the pirates that lived on this island three or four centuries ago were here. Right where we are standing now, people like Henry Morgan would almost certainly have stood and looked out over the sea to spot passing Spanish merchant ships.'

'It's pretty spectacular,' said Andrew, wiping sweat from his brow as he looked out. 'And somewhere around here is the spot where Eduard Leroux would have stood.'

'Exactly,' said Fiona, turning back to face the ruins. 'We just need to find it. The fort had a very typical layout for that time with a vaguely star-shaped design. This would allow defenders to fire down at approaching enemies from any direction. And from the sketches I have seen of it, it had two towers, both facing the sea, and Leroux would have been on one of them when the Marauder exploded.'

'What did he actually write about it?' said Andrew.

'Have a look,' said Fiona, extracting a piece of paper from her bag with a copy of the text she had found in his journal.

September 12th, 1714.

On this late evening, I had most courteously been invited for dinner with the esteemed governor and protector of the island, along with several other merchants, and I was about to make my way back down to the town when I decided to climb to the top of the east tower to view Tortuga for myself. The tower was at least twenty yards tall, and I was able to see all the way to Hispaniola, where faint lights from the Spanish settlements were clearly visible to me.

In the harbour below were several ships, and I noted that one of them was anchored much further out than the others. I knew this to be the frigate called the Marauder, which belonged to Captain Flynn, and its anchorage seemed strange to me. I had noticed its unusual position on my way up to the fort, because it happened that the sun was setting directly behind it on that evening, and the vessel looked most impressive, framed as it was by the setting sun.

As I stood there on the tower by myself and marvelled at this bountiful new world that we had made ours, the Marauder was suddenly engulfed in a terrible inferno that seemed to rip it apart from within in the blink of an eye. Not two heartbeats later, I found myself rocked by the terrible noise of the explosion, and the entire bay was lit up by the fireball. I have never seen such a thing before, and I hope I never will again. Every soul on that ship was lost in that very moment, and I pray that those men may find peace in their watery grave.

'Crikey,' said Andrew. 'That merchant had a flair for the dramatic, although I am sure it would have been quite a shocking thing to witness.'

'Yes,' said Fiona, 'but there are several clues here that we can use. Firstly, he said he was on the east tower.'

She began walking towards a part of the ruins that was near the escarpment where the terrain fell away down towards the coast. After a few moments, she climbed on top of a partially overgrown heap of stone blocks and turned to face Andrew.

'This would have been the east tower,' she said, as Andrew joined her and they looked out over the water from their new vantage point. 'And there's more. He said that it took not even two heartbeats for the sound of the explosion to hit him. How long is a heartbeat for a grown man standing still? A second? Maybe a bit less?'

'That sounds about right,' nodded Andrew, suddenly realising what Fiona was getting at. 'So that means it would have taken somewhere between one and two seconds for the sound to reach him. And with the speed of sound being about 340 metres per second, that means that the Marauder was between, say, 500 and 700 metres from this exact spot when it exploded.'

'Alright,' said Fiona. 'And the final clue is the sunset, which he said happened directly behind where the Marauder had dropped anchor.'

'How is that useful?' said Andrew.

'Look,' said Fiona, firing up an astronomy app on her phone and allowing it to pinpoint their current location. 'This is the way the night sky is going to look tonight. You can see the positions of all the stars and the planets, and we know that they will be in these exact positions because the orbits of the planets around the sun are predictable down to a few metres. And because they remain virtually the same even over millions of years, it is easy to dial back the clock and see where our sun would have set in this exact spot on that particular evening in 1714. Look at this.'

Andrew watched as she orientated the image so that the app displayed the view from their current position towards the west. Then she tapped on the date and quickly changed it to the twelfth of September, 1714. The entire scene changed in an instant, and with the small orange disc of the virtual sun just sinking beneath the watery horizon on her phone, the indicator at the top of the screen showed the exact bearing.'

'258 degrees, viewed from this location,' said Fiona.

'Almost directly west-southwest,' said Andrew, raising his eyebrows. 'I'm very impressed. Well done.'

'Thanks,' she beamed. 'I told you that journal was a breakthrough.'

She then pulled the paper map from her back pocket and sat down on one of the large stone blocks. Spreading out the map, she then drew a straight line out over the water from the fort in the direction halfway between west and southwest. Where it intersected the line she had drawn previously in Saint-Louis-Du-Nord, she drew a small circle. Finally, she traced out two short arcs to indicate the ranges of 500 to 700 metres from the fort, and the circle she had drawn was sitting almost perfectly between them.

'If that wreck is still anywhere to be found,' she said, sitting up straight and looking at Andrew, 'it will be somewhere inside that circle.'

'That's probably only a couple of hundred metres across,' he said, studying the map and gauging the distances using the scale in the bottom left corner. 'I think you might have cracked it.'

'Now all we have to do is go and look for it,' she said. 'Let's head back down. I don't want to leave here today without having found that wreck.'

As they made their way back down the rocky, bush-covered escarpment towards the flat terrain below, Fiona suddenly stopped and placed a hand on Andrew's arm.

'Something has just occurred to me,' she said, looking pensive and slightly apprehensive as beads of sweat were forming on her forehead. 'If we find that wreck, and if things really happened the way Leroux wrote, then this isn't just a shipwreck we're trying to find. We're actually talking about something that is a gravesite for upwards of fifty people.'

'I suppose you're right,' said Andrew, finding himself glancing out over the water towards the likely location of the wreck. 'Although, I am pretty sure there is nothing left of those men now. In fact, there's probably little, if anything, left of the ship after all this time. All the wood and the other organic material will almost certainly have disintegrated over the years. We'll be lucky to find anything that isn't made of metal.'

'Good point,' nodded Fiona. 'I guess that should make looking for the treasure that much easier.'

'Come on,' said Andrew. 'The clock is ticking. It's almost three o'clock now.'

They returned to find Ronil chatting to the young men who were still sitting under the tree, looking no closer to heading out in their boats with their nets. When he saw them approach, he gave them a wave and his usual broad smile as he got to his feet.

'Everything alright?' he asked. 'Did you find the fort?'

'How did you know?' said Fiona.

'I figured that's what you were here for,' said Ronil with a smile and shrug. 'There isn't much else over here, and you're not the first people to go look for it.'

'Yes, we found it,' said Fiona. 'Have you been up there yourself?'

'Of course,' said Ronil. 'Nice view.'

'And some interesting history as well,' said Fiona. 'I guess you know about the pirates that used to be here a long time ago.'

'Oh yes, of course,' said Ronil, as if this was common knowledge. 'Captain Morgan. Jean Le Vasseur. Plenty of others. It was a crazy time, yes?'

'That's certainly one way of describing it,' said Fiona.

'Listen,' said Andrew, keen to get moving. 'We would like you to take us out to a spot a few hundred metres southwest of here. And if you could drop the anchor there, I want to dive down and have a look around.'

'Sure,' Ronil nodded reasonably. 'We can do that. What are you looking for?'

'An old shipwreck,' said Fiona. 'A ship that is supposed to have sunk close to the port a long time ago.'

'Alright,' he said with a wry smile as if he had heard this particular story a few times before. 'I'll do my best.'

'How deep do you think it might be out there?' said Andrew.

Ronil turned to look out over the bay as he rubbed his chin for a moment.

'I'd say about 15 metres,' he said. 'Maybe 20. Not too deep.'

'Perfect,' said Andrew. 'Let's get moving.'

Twenty minutes later, the three of them were right where Fiona's paper map and her GPS app said they needed to be. As it turned out, Ronil had been more or less right about the water depth at that location. Looking down towards the bottom, which appeared to be mostly sandy but with several large coral-covered areas in places, it appeared to be no less than twenty metres below them, and they could make out a fair amount of marine life down there. Fiona turned to look at Ronil who was gripping the outboard motor's tiller and steering them out over the tranquil and crystal-clear waters.

'This is it,' she said. 'Let's get that anchor down.'

Ronil killed the engine, moved deftly past her, and then lifted the heavy, vaguely spade-shaped metal anchor over the side and dropped it in. It splashed through the surface and quickly sank down towards the bottom, unspooling a rope lying in the front of the boat as it did so. Andrew had already begun strapping on the oxygen tank and the regulator.

Finally donning his flippers, weight belt and mask, he then strapped a large diving knife to his thigh and turned towards Fiona.

'Here goes nothing,' he said. 'Wish me luck.'

'Take care down there,' said Fiona, suddenly feeling slightly uncomfortable being left back on the boat while he went exploring without her. 'And try not to break anything if you find something that looks like a wreck. Technically speaking, this is an archaeological site.'

'If the wreck is even there,' said Andrew, holding up a hand. 'We don't know what's down there, so I am just going to have a look. If I find anything, I'll come back up, and then we can discuss what to do.'

'Alright,' said Fiona. 'Perfect. Good luck.'

Andrew put the regulator's mouthpiece into his mouth, sat down on the side of the boat with his back to the water and gave her a quick thumbs up. Then he let himself fall backwards into the water with a soft splash. As he descended towards the bottom, he was amazed at the visibility, which was at least fifty metres. Directly below him was a large, irregularly shaped piece of coral reef that stretched off to one side. On the other was an expanse of sand that was patterned with neat, wavy ripples created by the currents. Dozens of colourful tropical fish were swimming around directly beneath him, and as he used his flippers to propel himself downward, he soon found himself inside a school of what appeared to be some type of iridescent blue and red parrotfish. He continued his descent until he was a couple of metres above the coral, and there he spotted a large octopus that jetted smoothly across the reef to hide under a mottled rock, where it instantly changed its colours and patterns to emulate its new surroundings.

While keeping an eye out for anything that might appear man-made, Andrew began circling underneath the boat, spiralling ever further out from it. He quickly covered a large area this way, but he was unable to spot anything that looked out of place in this otherwise pristine natural environment. Then he thought back to when he and Fiona had been standing on top of the promontory looking out towards where he now was. Assuming that her astronomy app was correct, and there was no reason to doubt it, their direction was almost certainly accurate to within a few tens of metres. However, the precise distance from the fort was the main source of uncertainty in their estimate of the wreck's position. Leroux's assertion that the sound of the explosion had travelled for no more than a couple of heartbeats before reaching him was hardly an accurate measure of distance. So if they had got the location wrong in any way, it would be this. Either the wreck was closer than they thought, or it was further away, but it would almost certainly lie somewhere along a straight line from the fort to the point on the horizon where the sun had set on that fateful day in 1714. In the end, he decided to go with his instincts and proceeded across the reef and further out to sea.

As he pushed ahead through the water, he maintained the same distance to the jagged coral below him, but it was obvious that the sea floor was now dropping away from the relatively shallow natural harbour of Tortuga to the deep trench that separated the small island from Hispaniola. As he went, he could feel the pressure increase as the rising weight of the water above him was bearing down on his body. He glanced up towards the shimmering surface, and it was now noticeably further away than when he had first started his dive.

Pushing onwards, he soon found himself swimming out over a large open sandy area where there were significantly fewer fish. Only a few barracuda were gliding effortlessly across the seabed, but they appeared skittish and darted away as soon as they saw him approach. With very little in the way of reefs or rocks to orientate himself, Andrew began to lose track of the direction he intended to go in, so he glanced up to try to get a fix on the sun, which at this time of day would be close to a south-westerly direction. Satisfied that he had managed to reorientate himself, he continued on until he thought he noticed a dark shape moving off to the right in his peripheral vision. When he turned his head, he could have sworn that he saw something there, but then it was gone as quickly as it had appeared. A few seconds later, it happened again on his left-hand side, and this time he knew that he wasn't imagining things.

What he had spotted was a tiger shark, which was known to be one of the largest and most aggressive sharks in the Caribbean. The shark was about ten feet long, and it moved languidly through the water as it traced out a rough circle around his location. Seconds later, another shark appeared and began circling him in the opposite direction. He knew that these predators often hunted in packs, but the way these two were moving hinted at a disturbingly intelligent level of coordination. The two of them kept circling him in opposite directions at a distance of about fifteen metres, and it made it difficult for him to keep his eyes on both of them at the same time.

He glanced up towards the surface, but he was now so far away from the boat that he was unable to see it anymore. Sensing that he might well be in significant danger, he reached down to his thigh and was gratified to feel the hilt of the knife. He released the latch and pulled the knife from its sheath, and in that very moment, one of the two sleek marine hunters suddenly turned towards him, flicked its powerful tail and accelerated at a blinding speed towards him. He spun to face it, ready to slash it with the knife, but the shark veered off just a couple of metres from him and curved away. It had merely feigned an attack on its intended prey in order to gauge its capacity for defending itself. No sooner had it turned away than the other shark repeated the manoeuvre and raced towards him from a different direction. Once again, he faced it down with his knife in his hands, but this time the shark came much closer, and he could feel the turbulence in the water as it turned and flicked its tail violently to dart away from him again. Its companion, who initially appeared to have returned to its circling holding pattern, then suddenly curved back in towards him and came straight at him with blistering speed. Whipping its tail rapidly from side to side as it accelerated through the water, it opened its jaws, revealing a terrifying set of sharp, jagged teeth, and then it was on him.

Spinning and turning away, Andrew just managed to get clear of the razor-sharp teeth as the predator cut through the water a few inches from his chest. Seconds later, the other shark joined the fray and barreled towards him. But this time, Andrew was ready. He kicked hard with his flippers and twisted away just in time to avoid its jaws, and then he plunged the knife into the side of the shark as it barreled past him like a torpedo. Tensing every muscle in his right arm to avoid losing his grip on the knife, he held it in place as the shark scythed past him, and it cut a long, deep gash in the animal's side. As the panicked predator thrashed and sped away, it left behind a trail of blood that tinted the water a pale red.

Then, something happened that Andrew could never have foreseen. Triggered by a sudden bloodlust and perhaps a lack of food, the other shark suddenly turned on its injured companion, darting towards it and sinking its teeth into its bleeding side. Like flicking a switch, it was as if the shark had entered a feeding frenzy as soon as it sensed blood in the water, and it ripped and tore violently and mercilessly into the meat of its hapless hunting partner. Within seconds, the water was full of blood, flesh and the contents of ripped-open intestines, and Andrew watched in stunned fascination as nature showed itself at its most brutal, spelling out that most ancient tenet of survival on this planet. Kill or be killed. Eat or be eaten. It was all over in a matter of seconds, and when the surviving shark slinked off with a full stomach and disappeared into the haze of the water some fifty metres away, it left behind the mangled, skeletal remains of its erstwhile hunting partner on the sandy sea floor to be devoured by the smaller marine life near the reef.

As he watched the dark shape of the predator melt away into the distance, he realised that his heart was beating out of his chest and that he was breathing as if he had just run a marathon. His body had gone into fight-or-flight mode, but it was one that he knew only too well, and he quickly managed to take control of his breathing and calm himself down. As he did so, and his heart rate began to decrease, he spun slowly in place as he methodically scanned his surroundings for more threats.

Deciding that he ought to head back up, if nothing else then just to take a moment to compose himself fully before continuing the search, he was about to head upwards when he noticed a faint dark outline at the very edge of his vision. He kicked a couple of times with his flippers and allowed himself to drift closer to the murky shape ahead of him. It was about thirty metres long and rose about a metre from the sea floor. Its form looked like nothing he recognised, but it was clear that it was too small to have been the wreck of the Marauder. Except, of course, the Marauder had been torn to pieces in the explosion, so who was to say how large any remains of it might be after so many years.

Then he noticed something else. Protruding up from the dark shape at disparate angles were what looked like thin poles, and as he came closer, he could see that they appeared to be arranged roughly in two lines that extended off into the distance amongst the mass of dark material that he was now approaching. When he was about ten metres away, he suddenly realised what he was looking at. The dark, wide band along which he was now swimming was made up of rocks of virtually identical size, roughly as big as a basketball. These had once been the ballast of a large wooden ship, and they were all this size because it would have allowed them to be carried on and off the ship depending on the amount of cargo it was carrying at any given time. Large enough for a few hundred of them to weigh the ship down, but not so large as to be impossible for the average sailor to carry them to and from the bowels of the vessel.

The poles sticking up from the vessel's centreline took a moment longer for him to recognise, but he then realised that they were the metre-long bolts with which the ship's keel had once been constructed from multiple massive pieces of wood. These bolts were made of Muntz metal, which was a type of cheap brass selected for this purpose because, unlike iron poles, they did not rust and degrade over time in seawater. And even after three centuries, these metal poles were still standing up straight, virtually uncorroded and now held in place by the ballast rocks that had slumped down between them as the wooden hull of the wreck had eventually rotted away and disintegrated in the salty and unforgiving conditions on the seabed. This had to be it. This had to be the Marauder. Or what little was left of it.

Andrew moved slowly along the length of the strange, submerged vista, and as he looked across it, it appeared almost like the carcass of some ancient marine animal whose skeleton had fossilised in place through some underwater magic. He would be the first to admit that his knowledge of the intricacies of 17th-century ship construction was fairly limited, but it was clear to him that he had arrived at the wreck site near the ship's stern, and as he swam forward, he realised that he was now looking at what might be the clearest evidence for this being the ship they had been looking for.

Unlike near the stern, where whatever material was left of the vessel was clumped together in a footprint that roughly traced out the shape of the ship, the front of it was a very different story. Two-thirds of the way from the stern towards the bow, the area of debris and ballast rocks was increasingly spread out, hinting at the explosion having come from the front of the vessel. And since he knew that the gunpowder storage of these old sailing ships was always near the bow, it supported the theory that this was indeed the wreck of the Marauder. The explosion had ripped the front third of the ship to pieces, and the remainder had sunk to the bottom and slowly been degraded and eaten away by the elements over the centuries since then.

However, this left one overriding question in Andrew's mind. Where was the treasure? Even in an explosion like the one suffered by the Marauder, there would have been plenty of precious metals like gold and silver flung out in all directions, and the gold would have corroded very little since then, although both types of coins might now be encased in dirt and grime. As he approached the front of what used to be the hull of the ship, he noticed an even larger mound of material below him on the seabed. It soon became apparent that he was looking at more rocks, although these had a very different appearance. They were jagged, irregularly shaped and of varying sizes, and as he descended and used his knife to scrape the sediment from one of them, he could see that they were all of a much lighter colour than the ones that appeared to have constituted the ship's ballast. Looking closer, he found several heavily corroded articulated metal plates, which he soon realised were latches and hinges that could only have come from large wooden storage chests that had long since rotted away and disintegrated. He decided to pick up one of the hinges and store it in a small pouch attached to his weight belt.

He then spent the next ten minutes mapping out the perimeters of the wreck, and then he returned to comb through as much of the area around the front of the ship as he could. At one point near where he reckoned the foremast had once reached down through the hull to the keel, he found some bent metal implements that he realised were utensils that would have been used by the ship's resident cook, who would have been working in that exact area deep inside the vessel. Wafting away sediment near what would have been the side of the hull, he then made a grim discovery. Underneath thick deposits of sediment and some smaller rocks that had possibly been cracked into pieces during the explosion, he found fragments of bones and half a human skull. Almost all of its teeth were missing, and there was a gaping crater in the side of it allowing him to see into where the brain had once been. Whoever this person had been, he had been mangled beyond all recognition in the blast, and only fragments of his skeleton now remained. However, in the sediment nearby, Andrew found two large coins that this man might have had on his person when he died. He placed them inside his pouch, and then he was suddenly struck by an idea. Perhaps he had spent too much time around Fiona, but something made him take his knife back out, move over to one of the irregularly shaped rocks, and then prize off a piece by inserting the blade into a small crevice and wrenching hard. He had to put all his strength into it, and at one point he was worried that his only means of defending himself down here was about to snap, but he finally managed to break off a small piece of rock, which he stored away safely in the pouch in his belt. Then he glanced at his oxygen gauge and realised that he was running low.

Reluctantly leaving the wreck behind, he began his slow ascent towards the surface, making sure to slowly corkscrew his way upwards through the water so that he could keep a close eye on his surroundings the entire time. As he neared the surface, he felt the pressure on his chest diminish with every metre, and when he finally broke through, ripped off his mask and regulator and took a deep breath, the clean air and the warm afternoon sun on his face felt fresh and liberating after almost an hour down below. Within about a minute, Ronil and Fiona had spotted him, made their way over and helped him back onboard the vessel. With water dripping from his hair, he reached inside the pouch in the belt and extracted the items he had brought back up.

'I found it,' he said, panting slightly as he flashed an elated smile at Fiona. 'I found the Marauder.'

'You did? Really?' said Fiona, barely able to contain her excitement as she subjected him to a barrage of questions. 'That's incredible. Are you sure? How can you be certain? What did you find?'

'There's barely anything left of it,' he said, 'but what is still there bears all the hallmarks of having been ripped apart in an explosion. But there is no doubt that the remains down there are of a frigate like Captain Flynn's. And I found these.'

He rubbed some of the grime from one side of one of the coins, and then he handed it to Fiona. Despite its tarnished state, it still managed to glint in the sunlight, and Fiona instantly knew what she was looking at.

'Pieces of eight,' she said, captivated by the small metal discs in her palm.

'Wow,' said Ronil, sounding impressed as he eyed the coins with a big smile. 'Real pieces of eight. Cool, man.'

'That's amazing,' said Fiona. 'Were there more of them? There should be a lot of these down there.'

'There was no treasure,' said Andrew. 'Not that I could find. In fact, it seemed to me as if the ship was carrying nothing but rocks.'

'Rocks?' said Fiona. 'What on earth are you talking about?'

'It looks like the ship was carrying its usual amount of ballast rocks,' said Andrew, handing her the piece he had brought up with him. 'But it was also carrying a significant cargo of rocks that were clearly not of the same type as the ballast. This is a small piece of one of them. And there are several tonnes of the stuff down there.'

'I don't understand,' said Fiona, looking both puzzled and somewhat disappointed. 'Why would it be carrying rocks?'

'I don't know,' said Andrew. 'But that's what I found down there. Rocks, the remains of a skeleton, and those coins. There might be more, but there is no sign of a large treasure.'

'A treasure?' Ronil said, looking mystified. 'You didn't say anything about a treasure. This is all getting a bit too big for me. If there is gold and silver down there, it belongs to the people of Haiti. Not to treasure hunters.'

'You're right,' said Fiona earnestly, turning to face Ronil as she suddenly realised that for all he knew, she and Andrew were just another pair of chancers hoping to get rich by pillaging whatever they could find. 'We don't want to take it. I'm a historian, and all we are trying to do is to find it and hand it over to whoever has a rightful claim to it. And if possible, I wanted to include some of what we find in a museum exhibition back in London.'

'Right. I see,' said Ronil haltingly, still sounding somewhat unconvinced. 'As long as you're not here to steal things. We Haitians have had enough of that, if you know what I mean.'

'The independence debt to the French,' Fiona nodded sagely. 'Yes, we know about that, and we wouldn't dream of taking anything from here that doesn't belong to us. Trust me, we know that Haiti has already had its share of bad luck and exploitation.'

'Alright,' said Ronil, seemingly placated. 'Look, I am just a boat driver, but I am also proud of our history here. We are the first nation of free slaves. And if I thought you had come here to take things that do not belong to you, then I would try to stop you.'

Andrew regarded Ronil for a moment and felt a deep sense of empathy and respect well up inside him. Here was a young man who, despite the chaos in his country and the daily struggle to survive, still had it in him to stand up for his people and his history. Even if only in a small way by pitting himself against the people who were paying him for a boat trip.

'And you would be right to try to do that,' said Andrew, placing a hand on Ronil's shoulder and looking him straight in the eye. 'I have a lot of respect for people like you who are prepared to stand up for what they believe. You're a good man. And you have my word. We're not here to steal anything.'

'OK,' said Ronil, producing a nod and a small sigh of relief. 'Cool. So what are you here to do, then?'

'We're here to solve an old mystery,' said Fiona. 'A mystery of what happened to a pirate ship that went down here. The ship that Andrew has now found. I'm sorry. I guess we should have told you about it sooner. But now that we've found it, we're suddenly stuck with a bunch of new questions that we don't have answers to.'

'Well, whatever I can do to help,' said Ronil, 'I will do it.'

Ten

Count Carlos Roberto Velazquez de Toledo was taking his daily stroll through the expansive and carefully maintained gardens of his large rural estate. This personal domain of his, which had been handed down through generations of illustrious ancestors, was nestled in the rolling sun-kissed hills of the Castile-La Mancha region near the village of Esquivias, some thirty kilometres south of Madrid. It was comprised of several thousand acres of olive groves that produced a steady stream of revenue for the count, not that he needed it, and at its centre was the grand villa that had been built some four hundred years earlier. It had undergone several rounds of renovations since then, but each time, an effort had been made to preserve its unique character and history. With its thick cream-coloured masonry walls, red tile roofs and verdant, multi-tiered grounds that would be the envy of any major city's botanical gardens, it was his private haven far away from the decrepitude and decay that so obviously characterised and afflicted the modern world. Here, well away from the ugly struggles of regular people, everything was neat and controlled and just the way he wanted it.

De Toledo was in his early seventies, clean-shaven with a strong jaw, piercing grey eyes and black eyebrows, and his mid-length, slightly wavy and almost white hair was swept back over his head. He was wearing an elegant, white, tailored double-breasted suit with brass buttons, a silvery grey waistcoat and a white shirt and cravat. As a young man many moons ago, he had served as an officer in the Spanish armed forces, and with his upright posture and his shoulders back, he carried himself accordingly. Strolling slowly along the gravel paths that meandered through the manicured grounds, his hands were clasped together behind his back as he inspected the newly planted rose bushes near one of the water features. Spotting an imperfection in the way the bush had been trimmed, he reached inside a pocket of his suit jacket and extracted a pair of secateurs, which he then used to snip a red rose from the offending twig. He placed it carefully in a buttonhole high on his jacket and tucked the secateurs back into his pocket. Then he glanced at his gold wristwatch. It was almost time.

Returning to the villa past raised flowerbeds and lawns that would have been able to compete with the greens at the most exclusive golfing resorts, he made his way up several sets of short steps that connected the various tiers of the estate's gardens. He then proceeded across a wide patio into the main reception room through tall French doors that had been left open on this pleasantly warm and sunny day. Inside, his personal butler was waiting with a silver tray on which sat a glass and a small carafe with perfectly chilled spring water.

'*Los caballeros están aquí, señor*,' said the butler, deferentially announcing that the count's gentlemen visitors had arrived.

'*Muy bien*,' said de Toledo, lifting the glass from the tray, taking a sip and then instructing the butler to allow them to enter. '*Pueden entrar. Gracias.*'

The butler nodded obsequiously, waited for the count to replace the glass onto the tray, backed away a few steps and then turned to exit the grand, high-ceilinged reception room through tall, white and ornate double doors that were accented with gold trim. While he returned to the villa's foyer where the count's guests were waiting, Count de Toledo strode over to a cream-coloured upholstered armchair where he sat down and straightened a few creases in his suit. Then he leaned back and took a moment to enjoy the oil paintings on the walls as he waited. Each painting was several metres tall and sitting in ornately carved gilded frames, and they all depicted either castles and forts during famous battles, or stirring depictions of smoke-shrouded naval engagements between the ships of the famed late 16th-century Spanish armada and various other European adversaries, not least the English.

As he took in the beauty of the artwork, he couldn't help but reflect on how, centuries later, he himself was now collaborating with an Englishman to obtain some of the wealth that their two nations had been locked in mortal combat over so many years ago. He considered himself a keen historian, despite having no formal training, and he had now spent decades adding to his growing collection of artefacts from that most scintillating period that was generally known as the Age of Sail, specifically the 16th and 17th centuries when Spain had been at the pinnacle of her power, and all the other nations in Europe and beyond had trembled at the thought of a visit from her seaborne armada. Able to trace his lineage back to an esteemed ancestor who had served as captain and vice-admiral aboard one of those Spanish warships that had dominated the seas around the Americas, he was prepared to admit that he felt a sense of personal ownership over the artefacts that he had acquired over the years. The New World had been colonised and civilised, not by the people of Spain, but by a small, select group of intrepid individuals, mainly aristocrats, who had used their own resources, skill and cunning to build the Spanish Empire in the Americas. And so, in a manner of speaking, those many artefacts from that time were in fact rightfully his.

Employing a small but trusted number of resourceful professional treasure hunters, many of whom often had friends in low places to facilitate their ventures, he had now managed to gather enough relics to open a large museum. However, nothing could have been further from his mind. His collection of priceless relics was his and his alone, kept in his display rooms for his own pleasure and that of his closest friends. And today, he would be adding two exquisite Mayan jade figurines to it.

Bringing the two ancient relics to him today was Lawrence Blake. He had flown in from London for the day, accompanied by Antonio Ortega who was one of Count de Toledo's most capable men. The treasure hunter had been introduced to him several years ago through a mutual acquaintance who worked as a senior curator at Madrid's *Museo de América*, and Blake had proven highly adept at locating specific items that the count had desired, as well as finding dozens of other artefacts that he had been happy to pay for.

However, today was going to be about much more than the two figurines. Usually, the artefacts secured by Blake could be transported perfectly safely onboard the Spanish nobleman's own private jet, but Blake had requested an audience in person in order to discuss what he had called 'a very significant opportunity in the Caribbean.' Coming from almost anyone else, de Toledo would have been reticent or perhaps even outright dismissive, but coming from Blake, he knew that it was well worth his time and attention. And so, the count had dispatched his Gulfstream G550 business jet to London to ferry the treasure hunter and Ortega down to Madrid. From there, the two men had boarded a helicopter that took them to the small heliport near the villa.

When the butler returned, opened the doors and entered, he was followed by the smartly dressed and well-groomed Blake who was carrying a ribbed steel hard case in one hand. A few paces behind him was the hulking and usually monosyllabic Ortega, wearing dark blue jeans and a black t-shirt. Without getting up from his armchair, Count de Toledo extended a hand and gestured magnanimously towards the matching two-person sofa placed next to him. Blake approached and sat down nearest the count, but Ortega remained on his feet, evidently preferring to stand to attention a few feet away. Old habits die hard, as the count knew only too well.

As Blake set down the hard case and made himself comfortable, and Ortega silently clasped his hands in front of himself with his feet slightly apart, Count de Toledo regarded his English guest for a moment. As he did so, he looked aloof and almost expressionless, except for the fact that he also exuded a supreme self-confidence born of his sharp intellect combined with his conviction that someone of noble birth such as himself was simply a cut above the rest.

'Señor Blake,' he said calmly, now speaking in English with only a faint Spanish accent. 'Welcome back to Spain. I trust your trip went well?'

'Very well indeed,' said Blake, enjoying the VIP treatment and the surroundings as he embraced the character of his alter ego, locking the much less interesting and gregarious Professor Marcus Tobin away inside himself. 'It was a pleasant flight. Lovely flying weather today.'

'Very good,' said de Toledo. 'Now. To business.'

'Of course,' nodded Blake, reaching for the hard case, which he then placed on the sofa next to him.

Turning the case so that it would open towards the count, he snapped open the locks and lifted the lid. The interior of the case was foam, and sitting snugly in two tailored cutouts were the twin jade figurines.

'Here we are,' said Blake contentedly as he showed the relics to his paymaster. 'The two figurines from the Grand Temple in *Tenochtitlan*. Once the personal property of Moctezuma II himself. The one on the left is from Fort San Lorenzo in Panama. The one on the right was obtained by your man Ortega here.'

Blake glanced briefly up at Ortega and gave a nod of acknowledgement before returning his gaze to the count.

'You'll be glad to know that they are both in excellent condition,' he said. 'And I think you'll agree that they look much better as a pair.'

Count de Toledo was now leaning forward in his chair as he studied the two priceless artefacts. Even inside the hard case, they looked magnificent, and once they had been placed on the two pedestals that he had already reserved inside his private museum, they would be amongst his most prized possessions.

'*Excelente,*' he said. 'Very good. You did very well to acquire them. I am grateful, and you shall be paid in full later today. But tell me, was the death of the guard really necessary? I read about it in the news.'

As he spoke, he glanced up at Ortega who gave an almost imperceptible shrug as he clenched his jaw.

'Sometimes it happens,' he said in a deep, rumbling voice, seemingly unconcerned. 'It was just bad luck. But there's no need to worry. We're sure they can't trace it back to us.'

'Yes,' said Blake, looking slightly uncomfortable. 'I think we can all agree that it would have been better for that not to happen, but as we say where I come from. You can't make an omelette without breaking a few eggs. It was unfortunate, but sometimes these things can't be helped. The main thing is that we got what we came for, wouldn't you agree?'

'Of course,' nodded the count. 'Let's move on to the next item on the agenda. The opportunity you mentioned.'

'Right,' said Blake, closing the lid of the hard case and inching forward to sit almost on the edge of the seat. 'I have stumbled across something that I think you would be very interested in, and I would like to suggest another collaboration. It does not concern any specific relic this time, but it is possible that it might yield significant amounts of gold and silver from the treasure fleet.'

'Really?' said de Toledo, raising an eyebrow, which was about as much of an expression of excitement as anyone was ever going to get out of him. 'Go on.'

Blake proceeded to refresh the count's memory regarding the mysterious hijacking and disappearance of El Castillo Negro. He then went on to relay the contents of his meeting with a young woman by the name of Fiona Keane, who he knew to be a very capable historian and field archaeologist, and whose seemingly highly speculative theory about the missing treasure he had found himself unable to dismiss. He had already put together a basic plan for how to capitalise on this opportunity, and all he needed now was the funding and resources that Count de Toledo would be able to provide. Specifically, because of the current state of affairs at their intended destination, Blake asserted that he would need two highly trained men in addition to Ortega. Given the potential payoff from this particular venture, it didn't take long for de Toledo to agree.

'Very well,' he said, having contemplated the proposal for a moment. 'I will provide you with everything you need. Money, men and my private jet. I have two employees whose services I would be happy to lend to you. And I am sure that Ortega would vouch for them. Their names are Ignacio Gomez and Rafael Delgado.'

As he spoke the two names, the count glanced up at Ortega who produced a silent nod of approval. The two men were already on de Toledo's payroll, and like Ortega, they were both former members of the UEI. As the most elite unit of the *Guardia Civil*, which was the most militarised of the two branches of the Spanish police, the *Unidad Especial de Intervención*, or Special Intervention Unit, specialised in the protection of VIPs, counter-terrorism raids, hostage rescue, and capture and kill missions on behalf of the Ministry of the Interior as well as the Ministry of Defence. As such, all of its operatives were highly trained and experienced, and they had proven a perfect fit for Count de Toledo's personal protection team.

'They are both very capable,' said de Toledo. 'You shouldn't have any problems, even in Haiti.'

'I am sure I won't,' said Blake. 'With the help of your resources, we can no doubt establish fruitful relations with the gangs and even the police. To be blunt, with enough hard currency in my pocket, I can make just about anything happen in that part of the world. I've done it before.'

Blake was referring to a previous trip to Haiti, during which he had attempted to recover an artefact that had supposedly been buried and hidden away in the former pirate haven of Petit-Goave. The trip had not gone as well as he had hoped since he had failed to find the artefact. However, he had managed to recover a small hoard of pieces of eight. But more importantly, he had forged a useful relationship with a local gang boss nicknamed Jaws. The local criminal bigwig, who had acquired his name because of his shiny silver teeth implants, had provided protection for Blake and his team during their attempted recovery operation in return for a hefty fee.

Jaws was just one of many such friends in low places that Blake had made across the Caribbean over the years. His list of contacts now included drug smugglers in Panama, weapons traffickers in Havana, organised burglary gangs in Caracas, and the construction mafia in Vera Cruz in Mexico. Each group had its own unique ability to get things done outside of legal means, and Blake had found his relationships with them exceedingly beneficial. What was true everywhere else in the world was also true in the Caribbean. If you could buy your way to good relations with the local crime bosses, anything was possible, and they always cared a lot more for recently printed dollars than for ancient artefacts crafted centuries or even millennia ago. And in his experience, the only people who were capable of facilitating a treasure hunt better than a bunch of historians and archaeologists were a bunch of criminals. They seemed to have a knack for acquiring high-value items, old or new, and with a bit of luck, Jaws would be able to facilitate protection services for Blake inside Haiti, including in the chaotic capital of Port-au-Prince.

'Very well,' said de Toledo. 'Let us not waste any more time, then. My private plane is at your disposal, and Ortega here will make sure that Gomez and Delgado meet you back at the airport before your trip to Haiti. I assume you'll want to go straight there?'

'Absolutely,' nodded Blake. 'We shouldn't delay. This is bound to be quite an adventure.'

★ ★ ★

The skies to the west were glowing orange and red as Ronil steered his boat through the shallow waters at Saint-Louis-du-Nord and gently guided it onto the sandy beach. There was a light breeze that made the fronds on the palm trees rustle gently above them, and the water was calm with only small waves lapping at the sandy shore. Andrew was first to disembark from the front of the vessel carrying the diving equipment, and he then helped Fiona to jump down off onto the sand. After backing out again and anchoring the boat some fifty metres from the beach, Ronil slipped over the side and waded back in to join them. As the sun disappeared below the horizon, they returned to his small beachside boat hire shop, where he offered them another soft drink while he finished closing up the shop for the day.

'Thanks for your help today,' said Andrew. 'We really appreciate it.'

'That's alright,' said Ronil, producing his now-familiar broad smile. 'I'm glad you found what you were looking for.'

'Is there a nice place to have dinner nearby?' said Fiona. 'I'm starving.'

'Sure,' said Ronil. 'There are a few places.'

'Do you want to join us?' said Andrew. 'It would be nice if you could come along. Maybe show us the best dishes.'

'Why not?' said Ronil. 'I could do with some food.'

'What's the best place in town?' said Fiona.

'Well,' said Ronil. 'There's a very good meat place on the promenade called *Le Boukanye*.'

'As in 'Buccaneer'?' said Fiona.

'That's right,' nodded Ronil. 'It even has a skull and crossbones as its logo. It's very good, but it's a bit too expensive for me, so I don't go there unless there's a special occasion.'

'Well, we're buying,' said Andrew. 'And I think that today qualifies as a special occasion, wouldn't you agree, Fiona?'

'Absolutely,' Fiona smiled. 'Please, lead the way.'

Fifteen minutes later, two young men leaning against a nearby palm tree watched as the trio entered the open-air restaurant by the road just a stone's throw from the beach. They watched as the three of them were seated by a waiter, and as they placed their orders, one of the men extracted a phone from his pocket and typed a brief message to his superior in Port-au-Prince. Shortly thereafter, he received a response with new instructions.

'This all looks delicious,' said Fiona, glancing discretely around to see what the other guests in the busy restaurant were eating. 'What do you recommend?'

'You should try the *Cabrit Boukanye*,' said Ronil, glancing at the menu. 'It is the signature dish of this place. A typical Haitian dish. Chargrilled goat chops seasoned with Haitian spices and rice.'

'Sounds nice,' said Fiona. 'Exactly like the stuff the buccaneers used to make.'

'Done,' Andrew smiled as the mouthwatering smells from the kitchen reached him. 'I'll take your word for it. And for drinks?'

'Prestige lager,' said Ronil, seemingly not having to think about it. 'It's the most popular beer in Haiti. Very nice on a hot day.'

'Perfect,' said Andrew, giving the waiter a quick wave.

'So, what do you guys plan to do next?' said Ronil, after the meals had arrived and they had shared a toast to locating the Marauder.

'Well, we found the wreck,' said Fiona, 'even if it only seemed to carry a bunch of rocks.'

Andrew reached into his backpack and placed the three items he had recovered from the Marauder. The rock sample, the two pieces of eight, and the corroded metal hinge.

'Not exactly a treasure,' he said, taking a swig from his beer. 'But it's something.'

'Well, I think I might have an idea for what to do,' said Fiona, glancing at Ronil. 'Is there an international shipping office somewhere nearby?'

'There's a post office just a few streets away,' said Ronil. 'They have DHL services.'

'Perfect,' said Fiona.

'What's your plan?' said Andrew as he tucked into the richly flavoured grilled meat and moaned with pleasure. 'Man, that's good.'

'I want to send the rock sample you took back to London for analysis,' said Fiona.

'Why?' said Andrew.

'Because a rock isn't just a rock,' she said. 'All rocks are made of silicates. In fact, the whole planet is made of silicates. But each one has a different mineral signature depending on how and when it was formed, and you can sometimes pin down where they are from based on their composition. And I happen to know that the Natural History Museum in London has a mineral sample laboratory and a massive collection of rocks from around the world. Tens of thousands of them. So if they could perform an analysis of the sample you took, they might be able to point us to where it came from.'

'But how is that going to help us find the Black Galleon and whatever she was carrying?' said Andrew.

'Because I have a theory,' said Fiona. 'It came to me on the way back from Tortuga this afternoon. What if those jagged rocks you found were not simply part of the ballast? What if they had been carried aboard the Marauder inside a bunch of chests and placed deep inside her cargo hold?'

'Why would anyone want to do that?' said Andrew

'To pretend that they were full of gold and silver coins?' said Fiona.

'But why?' Andrew pressed on, still looking puzzled.

'Let's say you've just managed to steal a Spanish galleon loaded up with treasure,' said Fiona. 'You can't exactly take it to the bank, and you can't park the ship somewhere until you want the money. You need to hide it or transfer it to another ship.'

'Such as the Marauder,' said Andrew.

'Precisely,' nodded Fiona. 'And that is probably what Captain Flynn would have done. Except, what if he didn't? What if he only pretended to do that in an effort to deceive his men and take all the gold for himself?'

'Well, he was a pirate, after all,' said Andrew. 'So, you think he ordered the gold transferred from the

Black Galleon to the Marauder but then secretly made sure that what was brought over was just rocks?'

'It's possible,' said Fiona. 'Remember, no trace of the Black Galleon has ever been found after she left Port Royal on that night in 1714, so either she was sunk, in which case all the gold really had to be moved to the Marauder first, or she was taken somewhere and hidden along with her treasure. And then Flynn used rocks from that location to trick his own crew into believing that they still had the gold with them. And after docking in Tortuga, he blew up the ship, killing all of his crew, including anyone who might have helped him with this scheme who could have revealed what he had really done.'

'That's one hell of a diabolical scheme,' said Andrew. 'How did you come up with that?'

'Well, it's just speculation at this point,' said Fiona. 'But given what you found at the wreck site today, I think it's at least plausible. Imagine if you were Captain Flynn and you really wanted all that treasure for yourself, then a plan like that would certainly have worked if you could somehow pull it off. And it fits with what you saw down there.'

'I suppose you're right,' said Andrew, still trying to wrap his head around the sheer deviousness of the ploy. 'And you think the rock sample can help us pin down where Flynn hid the treasure?'

'Exactly,' said Fiona. 'It's certainly worth a shot.'

'True,' nodded Andrew. 'Nothing ventured, nothing gained.'

'Those Tortuga pirates were pretty ruthless,' said Ronil. 'Growing up here just across from the island, I used to imagine what it would be like to be a pirate back in those days. But now that I am older, I don't think I would have liked it. It was a very bloody and violent business.'

'Yes, I think Haiti has seen more than enough of that,' said Fiona. 'It's really nice to see someone like you doing well for yourself in this place.'

'I've tried my best,' said Ronil with a self-conscious shrug, a moment of glumness seemingly flashing briefly across his face. 'But it's not always easy.'

'How did you become the owner of a boat rental business?' said Andrew. 'There must be quite a few of those around.'

'Sure,' said Ronil, 'but I try to give people something extra. Good service with a smile. I also know a lot of interesting coves and reefs along these coasts, so I like to think I can give people something special. At least I hope so. Anyway, I bought my first boat when I was 14. Just a small one with a weak engine, but it worked. And I have worked my way up from there. The boat I have now is one of the best ones in this town.'

'Do you have any siblings?' asked Fiona.

'I have a younger sister,' said Ronil uncertainly, looking down into the palms of his hands as if unsure about how to proceed. 'Her name is Roseline. She also lives here in town. She works at the post office. And we had an older brother, Daniel. But… he died.'

A pained expression took over Ronil's face as he briefly pressed his lips together, clearly distressed by what he was relaying to them.

'I'm sorry,' Fiona quickly interjected. 'I didn't mean to pry. You don't have to talk about this if you don't want to.'

Ronil glanced briefly up at her and attempted a brave smile. Then he gave a small shake of the head.

'It's OK,' he said. 'You couldn't know. Daniel was the best. He took care of Roseline and me after our father left and our mother died when we were all young. He started a hardware store not far from here, and it was going well. But then one of the gangs from the south came and told him to pay protection money. Daniel refused. Told them to piss off and leave him alone.'

As he spoke, he made a dismissive hand gesture, emulating what his brother would have done when faced with the gang members trying to extort him.

'Sorry about my language,' he then said, glancing sheepishly at Fiona.

'No need,' said Fiona empathetically.

'Anyway,' said Ronil, looking downcast. 'One evening when Daniel was closing the store, they came in and used kerosene to set it on fire. He tried to fight them off, but they beat him up, and then they shot him several times in the stomach. He died. Right there on the floor in his own store. Everything burnt to the ground. They could barely find anything left of him for us to bury.'

'Gosh,' said Fiona with a distraught expression as she glanced apprehensively at Andrew. 'That's absolutely awful. I'm so sorry.'

'It was terrible,' said Ronil, shaking his head with his eyes closed as the memories washed over him. 'At least our mother was no longer here to live through it.'

'Did the police ever find the people who did it?' said Andrew.

'Police,' Ronil scoffed and shook his head. 'I don't think they even tried. As soon as they found out that it was gang-related, they stopped looking. I am sure of it. And in a way, I can understand. They don't want to put their own families in danger. Their own children. It's just what life is like here sometimes. Some things you just can't fight.'

'Damn,' said Andrew, placing a hand amiably on Ronil's shoulder. 'I'm really sorry to hear this, mate. When did all this happen?'

'Three years ago,' said Ronil, giving another resigned shrug. 'We're just trying to live in peace now, me and Roseline. And we've managed to stay out of trouble.'

'Have the gangs tried to extort you?' said Fiona.

'Yes,' said Ronil. 'I told them I have no money to pay them. I don't make a lot with my business. They said I had to give them a one-time payment to be left alone, so I did. I just hope they don't come back.'

'Bastards,' said Andrew bitterly, shaking his head. 'I'd like to get my hands on a few of those A-holes.'

'I don't think you should do that,' said Ronil, looking at Andrew hesitantly. 'They are dangerous.'

'So am I,' said Andrew darkly, before manufacturing a thin smile. 'But maybe you're right. Maybe it's better not to pick a fight with them. I don't want anything bad to happen to you or your sister.'

'Like I said,' Ronil sighed. 'We're just trying to live peacefully. And maybe one day, we can leave this place. Move to America. Many people have left already. I hope we can do that someday too.'

'I hope you both get everything you want,' said Fiona. 'You deserve it.'

'Thank you,' said Ronil, suddenly looking somewhat uncomfortable finding himself at the centre of the conversation and lifting his bottle of beer from the table. 'Anyway. To future happiness.'

'To future happiness,' Andrew said, lifting his own bottle. 'If we don't see you again after tonight, I hope everything works out for you. You're a good man.'

Eleven

In Port-au-Prince, roughly 160 kilometres south of Saint-Luis-du-Nord as the crow flies, darkness was falling. Teams of heavily armed guards were patrolling the perimeter of a property that had once served as the official residence of the ambassador of a small West African country whose tattered tricolour flag still hung from the top of the building. However, the embassy staff had fled several years ago, and the once elegant but now somewhat dilapidated French colonial-style building, with its pitched slate roofs and dormers, balustraded porches and Greek columns on the front façade, was now occupied by a very different resident.

The wooden, slatted shutters on the tall windows to what used to be the ambassador's personal office had been pulled almost shut, and only a small amount of light from the building's exterior floodlights penetrated through the gaps to the inside. The office was lit mainly by candlelight, some tall and thin and arranged in silver candleholders, others low and thick with heavy-duty wicks and large orange flames. Many had been spread out and placed directly on the varnished floorboard, causing vague shadows to dance across walls that were covered with ornate wood panels, and whose paint was now peeling.

Slumped back in a wide leather armchair arranged like a throne directly opposite the double doors leading inside from the foyer sat a large, burly man by the name of Marcellus Solomon. A proud descendent of his West African slave ancestors, he had long ago embraced their ancient religion of voodoo, whose rituals and practices he was convinced had ensured that the spirits protected him and even sometimes did his bidding, as well as making him mighty and invincible.

Now in his mid-fifties, but still as strong and physically imposing as he had always been, he was wearing black jeans and boots, a leather vest exposing his muscular arms, and a low leather top hat with metal studs. Around his neck hung several heavy gold chains, and the fingers on his powerful hands were bedecked with gold rings. Across the left side of his face, running from his ear along his jaw and almost up to his lower lip, was a deep and jagged scar from a knife fight during his youth in which he had almost been killed. But he had lived, his attackers had not, and the scar had become a daily reminder of the fact that, ultimately, he could trust only himself. Whenever he spoke, the scar tissue moved and flexed unnaturally, and whenever he smiled or grinned or otherwise showed his teeth, the result was a maniacal grimace that made his underlings back away in fear.

On the dark, wooden floorboards in front of him was a large, intricate circular pattern created with a white powder. Tracing out a voodoo design intended to facilitate communion with his ancestral spirits, this type of pattern was centuries old and usually created using special coloured powder. However, he had long since taken to creating the patterns with a white powder that could also be snorted and which had proven beneficial to both himself and the soldiers in his organisation whenever they were getting ready to fight the rival gangs, the police or paramilitary government forces.

Hanging above and behind him on the wall was a large painting of a black man wearing a dark grey pinstriped suit and a top hat with a white crucifix. He was holding a black, lacquered cane with an ornate silver pommel in one hand and a bottle of rum in the other, and he was wearing white face paint in the likeness of a human skull. This was Baron Samedi, who was one of the most powerful voodoo spirits. Known for his obscenities, debauchery and general disruption, as well as his smoking and drinking, he is the spirit of the dead, but he is also believed to have the power to prevent death if sufficiently placated by offerings. For this purpose, underneath the painting was a voodoo altar where Marcellus had placed such offerings in the form of rum, cigars, coffee beans, bullets and small bags of cocaine.

Leaning forward in his armchair, he reached for a bottle of rum sitting on a side table, pulled the cork out with his teeth and spat it onto the floor. Then he brought the bottle to his lips and drank a large gulp. Placing it back onto the side table, he then picked up a small bag of cocaine, created a thin line on his other hand and snorted it. Groaning as he tossed the bag back onto the side table, he then shook his head and leaned back into the armchair.

As he felt the rush of the drug flood through his body, he contemplated how far he had come in this life. From a powerless street orphan to one of the main kingpins in Port-au-Prince, he had clawed himself up through the chaos and death that characterised the capital city's gangland scene, and he had built a reputation for extreme violence, shrewdness in business, and an uncompromising attitude to disloyal members of his criminal clan. Marcellus despised the white men who had stripped the country of its wealth for centuries and humiliated its slave population, and as far as he was concerned, they were all legitimate prey. Taking everything from them, even their lives, could never make up for what they had done to the Haitians, and Marcellus had justified many of his attacks on businesses, private homes and various relief agencies by recounting these stories of racial oppression to his men.

However, to him, there was one type of person who was even more wicked than the white man, and that was the snitch. The gang member whom he had taken under his wing and given a life of relative luxury and safety amid the chaotic reality of the slums of Port-au-Prince, only for them to take money for providing information to rival gangs about his gang's activities, or worse still, to inform the police about his whereabouts during interrogation to save their own skin. And this evening, he was going to make a statement to those in his now large organisation who thought they could divide their loyalties and outsmart him. Marcellus had eyes and ears everywhere, and with a core of loyal lieutenants, he would always find out if someone had been disloyal and was playing more than one horse. Sometimes it was simply the case that punishment had to be meted out, and examples had to be made. And tonight was one of those occasions.

There was a familiar knock on the double doors to the foyer, and a moment later, they were opened by a tall and athletic woman who looked to be in her mid-twenties. Her short hair was arranged in a slicked-back bob, and her face was like that of a supermodel. Her full lips were glistening with a deep purple lipstick in the candlelight, and she was wearing skimpy denim shorts and a tight-fitting, cropped, multicoloured top that left very little to the imagination. As her long, lithe legs carried her inside the room, anyone watching the scene unfold, and who was unfamiliar with Marcellus and his entourage, could then have been forgiven for thinking that they were seeing double. Behind the woman strode forward what appeared to be her clone, and in some ways she was. The two stunning apparitions were identical twins, and they were some of Marcellus' most trusted and loyal followers, as well as being his late-night companions. Their names were Angelique and Celestine, and in accordance with their master's wishes, they dressed and arranged their makeup to evoke the appearance of Ezili Freda, the voodoo spirit of femininity, sexuality and prosperity. Since he had taken them under his wing when they were just teenagers, the two women had proven formidable weapons in his ongoing quest for power and wealth in the brutal underworld of Port-au-Prince. Whether it was by using their charms and setting honey traps for unwitting mid-level members of other rival gangs, or whether it was their affinity for sharp blades that they regularly put to use in eliminating threats to his rule,

Angelique and Celestine had become essential to Marcellus remaining in power.

Behind the two beautiful but lethal young women came a scrawny-looking man who was being pushed forward into the room by a large, burly guard carrying a baseball bat in his right hand and a pistol in a shoulder holster. The bound youngster, whose name was Junior, was in his early twenties and wearing pale blue jeans and a loose, yellow shirt. He had short, messy dreadlocks, and he looked terrified as he was being shunted into the office of the big boss whom he had never met before in person. The burly guard placed an enormous hand at the back of his neck, marched him forward until he was about three metres from the still-seated Marcellus, and then he was pushed down onto his knees. The guard then took a step back and gripped the baseball bat, ready to strike if Junior made any sudden moves.

As Marcellus sat up in his chair, he wiped the remnants of the cocaine from his nose and leaned forward to place his elbows on his knees as he regarded the petrified young man in front of him through the unnaturally dilated pupils of his eyes. As he did so, he ground his teeth in anger, and his face became an image of loathing and quiet fury. Junior had been caught fraternising with members of a rival gang, and when a recent raid on a money transport had been foiled by another gang hitting it first and running off with the cash, it had become clear that only this young man could have been the source of the leak.

'What is the most important thing in the world?' rumbled Marcellus in a deep and intimidating voice with a heavy Creole accent as his eyes bored into those of the prisoner. 'Tell me.'

'Loyalty,' stammered Junior, who knew that to the boss, only this quality mattered. 'Loyalty to the family.'

'That's right,' said Marcellus with a slow nod. 'Loyalty to the family. And you forgot that, didn't you?'

'I…,' began Junior nervously.

'Or maybe you did not forget,' said Marcellus, getting up from his chair to stand over the hapless young man. 'Maybe you got greedy. Right? Did you get greedy and tell our rivals about the hit on the van?'

'I was going to tell you,' attempted Junior. 'I was going to let you know what they were planning to do, and then you could have dealt with them.'

'No,' said Marcellus, reaching slowly around to the small of his back from where he then extracted his favourite pistol.

The gold-plated semiautomatic Desert Eagle, which sported a grip that was inlaid with pearl, fired .44 Magnum hollow-point rounds to devastating effect. As Marcellus brought it around to his front and racked the slide, Junior's terrified eyes locked onto the pistol that looked oversized even in the kingpin's large hand.

'You're lying, you filthy snake,' continued Marcellus, seemingly working himself up into a state of barely contained wrath that threatened to erupt like a volcano. 'We know what you did, and you're going to pay for it. Do you see who is behind me on the wall?'

With his lips quivering and a patch on the front of his jeans getting wet with urine, Junior looked up at the painting and immediately recognised the spirit baron. Then he nodded silently and swallowed hard.

'Baron Samedi has no tolerance for people like you who are disloyal to your own kind,' said Marcellus. 'And he will happily welcome you to the afterlife.'

'Please,' blurted a barely coherent Junior. 'I can make it up to you. Give me a chance.'

'No,' said Marcellus curtly. 'No more chances.'

He glanced briefly at each of the two twins in turn, and they moved forward in unison to stand on either side of the kneeling young man. They both turned their heads to look up at Marcellus, and as soon as he gave a brief nod, they suddenly moved like lightning. In a flash, they extracted a pair of identical concealed blades and threw themselves at Junior, plunging the knives into his chest and neck again and again in a furious and bloody frenzy that sent blood spatters flying through the air. The blades stabbed and thrust dozens of times in a matter of seconds, with Junior barely moving as his mouth opened and his eyes widened in terror. With blood oozing from multiple deep wounds, the two assassins suddenly pulled away and stepped back and to the side, and the guard also made sure to move clear. Taking two steps towards Junior, who was somehow still managing to sit upright on his knees, Marcellus gripped his hair and pulled his head back to look into his eyes.

'I will make you famous,' he sneered. 'You will be strung up at the crossroads to Cité Soleil, and everyone will know that you were disloyal to Marcellus. Everyone will know your name.'

Marcellus took a step back, raised the gold-plated weapon to point at Junior's face, and then he pulled the trigger. The hefty gun produced a deafening crack as it kicked in the kingpin's hand, and a brief muzzle flash illuminated the dark candlelit room. The heavy projectile exited the muzzle and tore through Junior's head in a split second, removing most of his brain as it exploded out of the back of his skull. The force of the bullet punched Junior's body back violently, and he fell onto the floor in a mangled heap where a pool of dark blood quickly formed around him. Moments later, there was a knock on the door, after which one of Marcellus's lieutenants opened it and poked his head inside.

'Boss,' he said. 'You'll want to know about this.'

Marcellus nodded, and the lieutenant walked inside, made his way around the pool of blood, and came up to lean close to his boss.

'One of the R9 gang's brothels was hit last night,' said the lieutenant.

'I heard about that,' said Marcellus irritably. 'So what?'

'We had one of our scouts watching the place when it happened,' continued the lieutenant. 'It was some *blanc*, and he took a bunch of their weapons and nothing else. Did it while the place was busy with customers.'

'Big balls,' said Marcellus, nodding and seeming impressed.

'So, we had two of our guys follow him and his woman,' said the lieutenant. 'And they drove up to Saint-Louis-du-Nord, where they hired a boat.'

'So what?' Marcellus repeated impatiently.

'We've just had a message back from one of the guys,' said the lieutenant. 'He said they overheard them talking to the boat driver, and they are looking for pirate gold. Some sort of big treasure in a wreck.'

'Pirate gold?' grinned Marcellus, clearly amused at the prospect. 'We should look into that. Have our guys talk to the boat driver.'

'Yes, boss,' nodded the lieutenant. 'I will send them a message now.'

The underling retreated past the dead Junior, exited the room and closed the double doors quietly behind him. Marcellus then looked at the guard who had not moved since the young man at his feet had been killed.

'Get this cleaned up,' Marcellus said to him, turning his attention to Angelique and Celestine. 'You two ladies come with me.'

Flicking the safety back on and placing the heavy Desert Eagle on the side table, Marcellus allowed his two female companions to sidle up next to him, and with an arm around each of their waists, he strode into the adjoining bedroom where the doors were closed behind him.

* * *

Night had fallen over Saint-Louis-du-Nord when the trio bid each other farewell in front of *Le Boukanye* on the promenade. The tempo had drained noticeably out of the town, and there were now only a few cars driving slowly along the beachfront. A few people were ambling casually along the footpaths and pavements as some shops closed up for the day, and the locals began congregating for late-night meals at eateries or for drinks in bars.

Watching his two customers for the past day head towards the small hotel where they had booked a room for the night, Ronil allowed himself a brief smile. He had appreciated their business and also enjoyed their company, and they seemed like thoroughly decent people. Perhaps they might come back again one day.

He turned and began walking back towards his small bedsit on the outskirts of town towards the east, and as he did so, he pulled his phone from his pocket to send a message to his sister. The two of them had arranged to meet up for lunch the next day, and Ronil wrote her a brief text to confirm the time. He also mentioned his two new acquaintances from London who he wrote might come into the post office the next morning to send a small package with a courier firm.

Less than ten minutes later he peeled off down a dark alley to the somewhat rundown two-storey concrete building where he lived. Crossing the street and heading for the front door, he spotted two small motorbikes turning down the alley from the main road and coming towards him. He picked up the pace to get out of the way, but it seemed as if they sped up as soon as he began to jog across the road. Before Ronil knew it, they had stopped right in front of him, and one of the two drivers had dismounted and come towards him holding a pistol, which he was pointing straight at his face. He was wearing jeans, a black T-shirt and expensive-looking trainers. He also had a thin gold necklace around his neck. His hair was in short dreadlocks, and his eyes were cold and hard. His companion wore similar clothes, but his head was clean-shaven, and he had a particularly reptilian look about him.

Ronil raised his hands disarmingly and tried to stay as calm as he could, despite being able to sense that the two assailants appeared to be high on drugs. However, this wasn't the first time he had been mugged, and as long as the muggers got whatever money he was carrying, there was no danger.

'Alright,' he said. 'Calm down. I have some money in my pocket. Let me take it out for you.'

'Shut up,' said the young man holding the gun as his companion dismounted his own bike and came towards him with a switchblade, which he flicked open with a flourish. 'Get over there.'

Using his gun, the mugger gestured to a dark area off to one side of the building. Reluctantly, Ronil complied and moved into the shadows away from the one weak streetlight in the alley.

'Brother, we gonna talk about those customers of yours,' the man with the blade said in a thick Creole accent. 'Who are they? What are they doing here?'

'They're just tourists,' said Ronil, confused. 'I don't know anything more about them. They wanted me to take them to Tortuga, so I did. That's it.'

'They are not just tourists,' sneered the man, placing the blade on one of Ronil's cheeks just below the eye. 'The guy. He robbed a brothel in Port-au-Prince and stole their weapons. So you tell me now. What kind of tourist does that?'

'What?' said Ronil nervously. 'Listen, man. I really don't know anything about that. They paid me for a boat trip. That's all I know. I didn't see any guns.'

'I don't believe you,' said the reptile, pressing the tip of the blade into Ronil's cheek and drawing blood.

'It's true,' said Ronil, his voice quivering as fear flooded his body and the fate of his older brother caused his knees to tremble. 'I don't know anything more about them. I swear.'

'What were they looking for over there?' said the knife-wielding gang member. 'They must have been after something, right?'

Ronil hesitated, and the two thugs immediately picked up on his uncertain demeanour.

'Don't make a mistake and lie to us now,' said the reptile. 'What were they looking for?'

'Nothing,' Ronil attempted, but he had always been a terrible liar, and the two thugs would have been able to spot it from a mile away. 'They just wanted to see the island.'

The reptile slashed the blade across Ronil's cheek, cutting a deep gash that instantly began to bleed profusely. Then he jammed a knee up into his victim's groin, causing him to double over and fall to the ground. The other youth, keen not to miss out on the action, lifted a foot and stamped down hard on Ronil's right hand, breaking at least one bone. Ronil cried out, but at that moment, all he could think about was whether he would be able to steer the boat with his left hand instead. The thug with the pistol knelt down next to Ronil's face and pressed the muzzle hard against his temple.

'We can do this all night, friend,' he said with a predatory grin.

For a moment, as Ronil clasped his broken hand, wheezing from the pain, he considered telling the thugs what Andrew and Fiona said they were looking for, but then he put it out of his mind. He wasn't going to debase himself and betray their trust, even in the face of these two violent bottom feeders. If he could just hang in there for a bit longer, they might believe him and go away. He grunted and panted as pain shot through his hand and up through his arm.

'I don't know anything,' he repeated. 'Please. Leave me alone.'

The reptile placed the tip of the knife on Ronil's earlobe and sliced right through it, causing blood to trickle steadily onto the ground. Ronil grunted from the pain, but he remained where he was for fear of the two thugs hurting him a lot worse than what they had already done. Whatever happened, he had to make sure that he got out of this alive, and with both of his attackers being pumped full of what might have been amphetamines, it might only take a small act of resistance to set them off.

'This is your last chance,' said the reptile. 'You tell us what they were doing over there and why they needed those weapons, or something very bad is going to happen. To your sister.'

Ronil felt the bottom of his stomach drop out of him as he broke into a cold sweat. How did these two know about Roseline? Had they already found her and intimidated her? Had they hurt her? He raised his head, and when the reptile saw the defeated and terrified look in his eyes, he tapped the bloodied tip of the knife against his own temple and gave Ronil a wink.

'OK,' he said with a malevolent, knowing smirk. 'Now, brother. Let's try this again.'

Twelve

The next morning, Andrew and Fiona checked out of their hotel and headed back to the beachfront for some breakfast. Picking up pastry and coffee from a bakery, they found a bench overlooking the Tortuga Channel and looked out over the waters as they ate their meal. The sun was now well clear of the forested hills to the east of Saint-Louis-du-Nord, and its rays were pleasantly warm and increasing in intensity as they sat there. Around them, the local townsfolk were getting into the swing of the daily commerce, and the place felt a world away from the oppressive tension, palpable fear and borderline anarchy of the capital. As they began tucking into their breakfast, Fiona's phone chimed with a new email. Pulling it from the back pocket of her jeans, she swiped across the screen to read it.

'Ooh...' she said, sounding intrigued.

'What is it?' Andrew said, glancing at her as he unwrapped another one of his pastries.

'I forgot to tell you something,' said Fiona after taking a bite of hers. 'I was in touch with Emily Butler yesterday via email. I had asked her to look into something for me, and she's just come back with some results.'

'Results about what?' said Andrew.

'Well, I asked her to do a general database search on the Marauder,' said Fiona. 'Everything she could find. Harbour records, trade logs, privateer rosters from around that time, reports of town raids or high seas piracy, and even crew lists and individual ship logbooks. Literally, anything she could get her hands on. It turns out that a surprising amount of that stuff has survived to this day, and there are a good number of active research projects actually digitising it all to make sure that it is retained even if the paper versions one day degrade or are lost to historians somehow. Anyway, she didn't find much about the Marauder specifically, but she did confirm that it was a privateer ship for a number of years under a certain Captain Jack Flynn. And during that period, she operated mainly out of Port Royal in Jamaica. So, this was obviously before Flynn turned to piracy. And interestingly, Flynn appeared to have had an older brother, James, who also joined the Royal Navy. But unlike Jack, who turned to piracy, James appeared to stay on the straight and narrow and continued his career with the navy while his younger brother became a privateer and then a fully fledged pirate.'

'Right,' said Andrew. 'That must have made for some pretty awkward Christmas dinners.'

'I doubt they saw much of each other,' said Fiona. 'Pirates were reviled as the worst of the worst in those days. And in fairness, they were generally a bunch of murderous thugs and thieves, so I don't imagine

James would have wanted to have anything to do with Jack after he turned to piracy.'

'Makes sense, I guess,' said Andrew.

'But there's a strange twist to this story,' said Fiona, 'because it seems as if the two brothers ended up having one final run-in with each other.'

'What happened?' said Andrew.

'When the Black Galleon was hijacked in Port Royal,' said Fiona, 'it was being guarded by a small group of Royal Navy redcoats, and they were commanded by none other than James Flynn.'

'Jack's brother was onboard the galleon when it was stolen?' said Andrew. 'What are the odds?'

'Yes, you almost couldn't make it up,' said Fiona. 'But we know this happened because the navy archives list James as the commanding officer and officially listed him as missing and presumed dead after the raid.'

'Jack killed his own brother to get his hands on some gold?' said Andrew, his head tilted slightly to one side as a disgusted look spread across his face. 'What an absolute scumbag.'

'That's how it appears,' said Fiona. 'James was never heard from or seen again, but there are indications that Jack somehow survived the explosion at Tortuga and continued his life of piracy. But that information is very patchy. He wasn't exactly one of the most famous pirates, and written accounts of acts of piracy from those days are few and far between as it is.'

'Interesting,' said Andrew, sipping his coffee. 'Is there anything else?'

'Yes and no,' said Fiona. 'Emily wasn't able to access anything more herself, but she discovered that there actually exists an extensive archive in Port Royal to this day. It is part of a collection belonging to the local maritime museum. But there's a catch.'

'There always is,' said Andrew. 'What is it this time?'

'The archives only exist in their original physical form,' she said. 'There are no digital records that have been organised into a database that could be searched quickly. In other words, we're literally talking about logbooks, harbour records, ledgers and other centuries-old pieces of paper that would need to be investigated manually. So, we would have to view them in person and hope to be able to find something useful.'

'But it would be possible, right?' said Andrew.

'Right,' said Fiona. 'It would be. But we would need to get ourselves to Port Royal and see what they've got. And who knows? There just might be some new and interesting information there about the Marauder and perhaps even Captain Flynn. Maybe we could use that to piece together some sort of clue as to what Flynn might have done with the treasure from the Black Galleon and perhaps even the ship itself.'

'Count me in,' said Andrew, finishing his pastry and licking his fingers. 'I'm up for it. I haven't been to Jamaica in years. But can we even get in to have a look at those records?'

'Emily has already put in a request,' said Fiona, 'and she is waiting for a response. Fingers crossed, they'll let us come and visit. But with my credentials from the British Museum, I think there's a good chance they'll allow us some time inside those archives.'

'Great,' said Andrew. 'We should drive back down to Port-au-Prince soon then. I say we just head straight for the airport and hang out there until we can catch the first flight to Jamaica.'

'Good plan,' Fiona nodded. 'First, though, I need to go to the post office to send off that rock sample.'

Leaving the bench, they crossed the road to a restaurant on the other side where they asked a waiter for directions to the local post office. After making their way along a set of narrow streets lined with colourful but somewhat dilapidated houses and shopfronts, they arrived at a corner where the post office was located. It was an old cream-coloured colonial building with a set of wide double doors that were painted bright red, and a few people were already walking in and out carrying letters and packages. Outside, a street vendor had set up his improvised shop to try to cater to the passing trade.

'So, this must be where Ronil's sister works,' said Fiona as the two of them crossed the street to the entrance. 'Roseline, right?'

'Yes,' said Andrew, glancing along the street out of old habit and making a note of who was around. 'I guess so. Let's see if we can spot her. They might look alike. Have you got the rock sample?'

'Right here,' said Fiona, extracting the sample, which she had wrapped inside a small plastic bag. 'Hopefully, they can make sense of it in London. It's probably our best clue to the treasure's location so far.'

They entered the building to discover a tiny room with one long counter and a couple of small kiosks with metal bars. Behind them sat two middle-aged and portly women who were wearing colourful dresses and half-moon reading glasses attached to lanyards hung around their necks. When Andrew and Fiona entered, the women appeared to finish a conversation, muttering something unintelligible in Creole and smiling meaningfully at each other, leaving Fiona wondering which salubrious topic of local gossip the two of them had been sharing when she and Andrew had entered the post office.

'Mm-hmm,' one of them smiled lazily at the other with one eyebrow raised and a knowing smirk.

As Andrew and Fiona walked up to the kiosk nearest to them, the woman behind it, who was wearing a name tag reading 'Sadia', regarded them over the top of her glasses before producing a cautious smile.

'Good morning,' she purred slowly in a heavy accent, correctly guessing that the two '*blancs*' in front of her were neither local nor French-speaking. 'How can I help you two?'

'I need to send this by international courier to London,' said Fiona, placing the plastic bag with the rock fragment on the counter and pushing a slip with the address of the Natural History Museum's rock analysis lab across the counter.

Sadia regarded the bag for a few moments, clearly puzzled by its contents, but then she shrugged, picked it up and placed it on a set of analogue weighing scales to her right.

'Alright,' she said unhurriedly. 'We can certainly do that for you, madam. Let me find the price for you.'

She punched in a figure on a table calculator and rotated it so that Fiona could see the display.

'That's fine,' said Fiona upon seeing the number and then glancing at Andrew, who pulled a wad of cash from his pocket and counted out the correct amount.

As he placed the money on the counter, Fiona made a show of glancing towards the other kiosk and then peering through the metal bars to the small office behind Sadia.

'Do you happen to have someone named Roseline working here?' she said, leaning forward and lowering her voice slightly. 'We met her brother yesterday, and we thought we might say hello to her. He told us that she works here.'

At the mention of Roseline's name, Sadia suddenly seemed to stiffen awkwardly as her gaze flicked to one side towards her colleague who had also heard what Fiona had just said.

'She's not working this morning,' said Sadia, suddenly looking uncomfortable. 'I am covering for her. Some sort of situation with her brother.'

'What situation?' said Fiona, sounding puzzled and a little concerned. 'Is he alright?'

'I can't say,' said Sadia, 'because I don't know. But Roseline called in this morning to say she couldn't come today. So here I am instead.'

'Do you know where she is?' said Andrew. 'We'd like to speak to her.'

'What about?' said Sadia with a hint of suspicion.

'We spent the day with Ronil yesterday,' said Andrew. 'He's a really good guy. So, if something has happened to him, we want to try to help.'

Sadia seemed to consider this for a moment as she looked alternately at Andrew, then Fiona, and then at Andrew again. Then she gave a slow nod, clearly led more by her intuition than anything else.

'Alright,' she finally said. 'Roseline said she wanted to go to the police station.'

'So something *did* happen to Ronil,' said Fiona, her concern now evident from her tense voice and anxious eyes.

'I don't know,' repeated Sadia. 'But she seemed very upset.'

'Shit,' said Fiona, glancing fretfully at Andrew, whose face had taken on a grim look.

'Listen,' Sadia said in a quiet voice, noticing Fiona's distress as she leaned forward towards them. 'I have a feeling this has to do with the gangs. I have seen it before. And those two have already lost their brother. If anything happened to Ronil, Roseline would be devastated. So, if you can do something, please help them.'

'Don't worry,' said Andrew with a steely expression as his left hand tightened around the holdall's carrying straps. 'We'll do everything we can to sort this out.'

About ten minutes later, Andrew and Fiona emerged onto a small square that had a couple of shops on one side and the local police station on the other. They were making their way across the square towards the station entrance when Fiona spotted a woman sitting on a bench under a tree with her head buried in her hands. As Fiona placed a hand on

Andrew's arm and stopped to look at her, she noticed that the woman's shoulders were trembling visibly. She was evidently crying, and they soon noticed the faint sobs reaching them from the bench.

'Do you think that's her?' whispered Fiona.

'There's only one way to find out,' he said, moving cautiously towards the bench. 'Come on.'

When they stepped closer to the distressed woman, she noticed their shadows on the pavement in front of her, and when she raised her head to look at them, Fiona's question was answered immediately. She was attractive with a slim face and large dark eyes, and her likeness to Ronil was striking. She was wearing stylish but now smeared makeup, light blue jeans and a pink t-shirt with a white floral motif printed on it, and her hair was done up in thick braids that had been arranged playfully on top of her head with pink hairclips and a ribbon. When she saw the two of them approach, it was as if she also realised who she was looking at. The two customers that Ronil had told her about the night before. Wiping away the tears that were streaming down her face, she sat up slowly and regarded them silently.

'Roseline?' said Fiona cautiously.

The young woman gave a quick nod, but she said nothing as she continued looking at the two new arrivals uncertainly.

'My name is Fiona. This is Andrew,' Fiona said, glancing briefly at Andrew before gesturing to a spot on the bench next to her. 'May I sit down?'

Roseline nodded again but remained silent except for a brief sniff as she wiped another tear from one of her cheeks.

'Your brother took us on a boat trip yesterday,' Fiona said. 'We went to the post office this morning to send something back to London, but Sadia told us something bad had happened. Can you tell us what it is?'

'He's been taken,' said Roseline, her voice thin and frail as she looked up at them with new tears welling up in her eyes. 'Last night after the dinner with you. He sent a message to me to say he had a good day and made decent money, but then he was taken by a gang.'

'A gang?' said Andrew. 'Who? Where to? And how do you know?'

Roseline hesitated for a moment as if trying to decide which questions to answer first.

'Someone saw it happen outside his building,' said Roseline. 'Two guys beat him up, and then a car came and took them all away. And they drove south.'

'Who were those men?' said Fiona, risking placing a hand comfortingly on Roseline's.

Clearly in need of support and reassurance, Roseline gripped Fiona's hand and squeezed it as she continued with a trembling voice.

'They are from Port-au-Prince,' said Roseline, 'and they wore red neck scarves. This means they belong to a gang boss called Marcellus Solomon. Everyone knows about him. They call him *'Il Sorcer'*. It means the Sorcerer. He uses voodoo to curse his enemies. He's a very bad man. And now he has Ronil.'

As the name of her remaining living brother escaped her lips, Roseline's voice caught in her throat, and she produced a small sob as her right hand found its way up to cup her mouth. She closed her eyes in a futile attempt to shut out the terrible reality that she and Ronil now faced, and more tears rolled down her cheeks. While she fought to keep her emotions under control, Fiona glanced briefly up at Andrew with a determined look that said, 'We need to do something!'. He gave her a small but firm nod, and then he sat down on the other side of the distressed young woman.

'Listen,' he said reassuringly. 'Roseline. What can you tell us about this Marcellus Solomon? What do you know about him and his gang, and where do you think they might have taken Ronil?'

THIRTEEN

It was mid-afternoon when Marcus Tobin's alter ego, the relaxed, cheerful and casually dressed Lawrence Blake, touched down at Port-au-Prince International Airport in Count de Toledo's private business jet. When the Gulfstream G550 rolled gently to a stop on its designated parking apron just outside the small VIP terminal, there was already a car there to meet him, and it wasn't a standard civilian car or even a limo. Blake's old contact, the Petit-Goave crime boss calling himself Jaws, had arranged for his personal silver Humvee to come and pick them up. The heavily armoured military vehicle, which had somehow found its way from the United States to the troubled Caribbean nation along with yet another shipment of hundreds of automatic weapons and tens of thousands of rounds of ammunition, had been sent to the airport from Petit-Goave, where Jaws had his headquarters. Driving it was one of his lieutenants, a large, brawny man wearing a somewhat comical outfit consisting of white jeans, a short-sleeved camouflage shirt and expensive red trainers.

'Welcome to Haiti,' he said after Blake had stepped off the plane, followed by Ortega, Gomez and Delgado who were both wearing black trousers and t-shirts, sunglasses, and looking very much like the guns-for-hire that they were. 'Jaws is waiting for you at a bar nearby. He has some news for you.'

'Excellent,' smiled Blake affably, keen to get moving.

Twenty minutes later, the group walked into a busy bar in one of the areas of the city controlled by the gangs. Inside the dark, neon-lit establishment, the music was playing, and the drinks were flowing despite it still being early in the day, and it was clear to Blake that only members of a select few gangs were allowed inside. Specifically, those who were not currently at war with the crime boss who owned it.

Their driver led them over to a booth where a large and heavily overweight man was reclining in his seat surrounded by young women wearing precious little clothes. The man's skin was unusually light, possibly hinting at some sort of encounter, forced or otherwise, between a female ancestor and one of the white French colonial masters who were once nearly omnipotent on this part of the island of Hispaniola. As he saw his driver approaching and then spotted Blake behind him, the corpulent man broke into a wide grin that put his silver teeth on full display. Blake had no idea how much this particular status symbol had cost his acquaintance, but Jaws seemed to think that it looked attractive, and Blake had to admit that, along with the silver Humvee, it made it plain to anyone and everyone that Jaws was something of a bigshot around here.

'Lawrence, my friend,' said Jaws in a heavy accent, struggling to get up and shake his visitor's hand. 'You're back.'

'I am,' Blake smiled, shaking the crime boss' sweaty palm and then surreptitiously wiping the wetness onto his trousers as he sat down opposite him. 'How are you?'

Jaws slumped back down heavily and once again revealed his silver teeth, spread out his fleshy arms and looked out over the bustling bar.

'I can't complain,' he grinned. 'Life is good, yes?'

'Clearly,' said Blake, picking up the cocktail that seemed to have magically appeared in front of him, courtesy of one of the scantily clad women. 'Although this city seems to have gone downhill a bit since I was here last.'

'No,' said Jaws, shaking his head and tutting. 'Not at all. We are taking back control of our country from the corrupt politicians and the foreign oligarchs.'

Oh Lord, thought Blake, making a heroic effort to hide his disdain for the overweight crime boss. *That old nonsense again. Anything to justify yourself, you fat bastard.*

'Of course,' Blake nodded musingly. 'I wonder who is going to lead this place once they are all gone?'

'We will!' said Jaws as if he had just stated the most obvious fact in the world. 'The bosses. We will create a grand coalition and rule this place properly.'

Right, thought Blake. *What could possibly go wrong?*

'I see,' he nodded thoughtfully. 'Well, best of luck to you. Anyway, you have something to tell me?'

'I do,' said Jaws, downing a drink and leaning forward with some difficulty as he raised his eyebrows slightly for dramatic effect and folded his hands on the table in front of him. 'As soon as I received your message, I put out the word and was able to discover that the two people you are looking for were spotted going to Saint-Louis-du-Nord. Your lady friend and her partner.'

'Really?' said Blake, who was more than familiar with Haiti's geography. 'They went to Tortuga.'

'That's right,' said Jaws. 'Apparently, they hired a boat and went on a little diving expedition.'

'Did they now?' said Blake, suddenly genuinely intrigued. 'And did they find anything?'

'I don't know,' said Jaws, leaning back. 'But I know a man who is trying to find out.'

'Who?' said Blake.

'Well,' said Jaws, inspecting and then picking his dirty fingernails. 'I would love to tell you, but maybe you could pay me for my trouble.'

Blake produced a knowing smile and shrugged. This was par for the course and a standard part of this type of meeting, and he deftly extracted a bundle of 100 dollar bills and peeled off twenty of them, which he pressed into Jaws' right hand. The crime boss grinned and nodded, and he then expended significant effort stuffing the money into a pocket in his trousers.

'You know of Marcellus Solomon?' he said.

'Of course,' said Blake. 'I have never met him, but I know his name.'

'Then you know that he's a major player here in Port-au-Prince,' said Jaws. 'He and I have a good business relationship. Cocaine import. I buy it in Colombia and transport it to Petit-Goave, and then I send it to him here in Port-au-Prince by truck. It's better than docking the ships in the port where it can be stolen by our rivals or even police officers.'

'I see,' said Blake, who was entirely disinterested in the criminal exploits of his host. 'So, what about Marcellus?'

'He has the boat driver,' said Jaws, conspiratorially. 'Brought him down to his mansion here in Port-au-Prince. And if the boat driver knows anything about what those two are doing, Marcellus also knows. Trust me. He will get the answers he needs.'

'I see,' said Blake. 'And would you be able to make an introduction? This issue is quite important to me, and there is a great deal of money riding on this whole venture of ours.'

'Is there?' said Jaws, his eyes glinting greedily at the prospect. 'I am sure I could make it happen. For a small fee.'

Without a word, Blake took his cash bundle back out and simply handed the whole thing to Jaws without counting it.7

'There's about ten thousand there,' Blake said, nodding towards the bundle. 'I take it that will do?'

'That will do,' grinned Jaws as he picked the money up and gripped it tightly in his hand. 'I will arrange it as soon as I can.'

He then lifted his drink from the table and held it forward towards Blake.

'Good to see you again,' he said. 'To old friends.'

'To old friends,' Blake repeated, picking up his own glass and downing it in one.

★   ★   ★

Andrew and Fiona ended up spending most of the day in their rental car. The long drive back down to Port-au-Prince felt even longer than when they had driven up to Saint-Louis-du-Nord. They had arrived in the small coastal town only yesterday, but it felt like several days since they had first laid eyes on Tortuga across the azure blue waters of the northern Caribbean. Before leaving town, they had urged Roseline to find somewhere safe to stay in case Marcellus decided to try to find her and use her as leverage. Eventually, and only very reluctantly, she had agreed to cross the border into the Dominican Republic and seek shelter with an aunt who lived there. With the border being about 100 kilometres due east along the coast, it could be reached by a fast boat in just under three hours, and Andrew and Fiona were happy to fund the trip. Roseline accepted going along with the plan only on the condition that she would be kept informed about the plan to get Ronil back.

Gripping the wheel tightly as he sped along, Andrew navigated the winding roads that meandered their way through the hilly central and northern part of the country, and in an attempt to save time, they made only one stop in a small village where they bought some water and a bit of food. Once back on the road, Andrew glanced over at Fiona, who had been silent for most of the trip and was now staring blankly out of the windscreen. When she spoke, she sounded weighed down by the sudden turn of events.

'If it hadn't been for us,' she said with a pained expression, 'Ronil and Roseline would never have ended up in this situation.'

'We couldn't have known,' said Andrew. 'The reach of those gangs clearly extends well beyond the capital. But all we can do now is try to get them out of it somehow. This obviously isn't why we came to this place, but there is no way we can leave them in the lurch. We simply have to help them.'

'What's your plan?' said Fiona. 'We can't just drive up to Marcellus' HQ and knock on the door.'

Before leaving Roseline in Saint-Louis-du-Nord, she had told them everything she knew about Marcellus Solomon, his organisation, his gang of violent thugs and their headquarters in what used to be a diplomatic area of Port-au-Prince before the gangs took over most of the city. Apparently, all of this was public knowledge, and Marcellus was evidently one of the most high-profile crime kingpins in the capital, not least because of his embrace of voodoo and his general affinity for publicity. Roseline had said that she couldn't be sure where Ronil would have been taken, but if he had been deemed important enough to kidnap and bring down to Port-au-Prince, then it was highly likely that he would have been brought straight to Marcellus himself.

'We find this Marcellus character's HQ, and then we wait for nightfall,' said Andrew. 'Then sneak in and search for Ronil.'

'That sounds really dangerous,' said Fiona, looking concerned. 'Are you sure this is a good idea?'

'There's no other way,' said Andrew evenly. 'But we might need a distraction at some point to take the attention away from me. And you'll need to make that happen.'

'A distraction?' Fiona said. 'Like what?'

'We'll think of something once we're there,' said Andrew. 'I am sure that these guys are tooled up and prepped for attacks from other gangs, but there's always a weak spot in any defence. All we have to do is find it.'

'That Marcellus sounds like a maniac,' said Fiona, recalling some of the gory details that a clearly petrified Roseline had relayed to them about the kingpin and his methods. 'I wonder if we can use that against him somehow. Someone like that doesn't get to where he is without being properly paranoid.'

'How much do you know about voodoo?' said Andrew. 'I thought it was an American thing. Down in the south of the country, like Alabama and places like that.'

'It is,' said Fiona. 'But what they have in America actually originally came from Haiti, where that religion was born. It is a strange mix of Christianity and ancient West African religion from places like Benin. This is where most of the slaves brought over to the French colony of Saint-Domingue originally came from, and they took their religion with them.'

'But what is it all about?' said Andrew. 'I get the impression it has to do with black magic, not that I believe that there is actually any such thing.'

'That's only part of it,' said Fiona. 'It revolves around the spirit world, mostly ancestral spirits who can supposedly be communicated with and even brought to life with the right types of rituals.'

'Sounds pretty far out there,' said Andrew.

'Well, there are millions of people around the world who believe it is very real,' said Fiona. 'But like you said, there is definitely also a dark side to it, which I suppose could be called black magic. But it is also a fact that voodoo has been demonised by white people for centuries, and not just because it was something strange and foreign that they didn't understand. As far as I understand it, there is a very powerful ancestral element to voodoo, in the sense that the ability to address dead ancestors ties into the notion of the African slaves having been taken by force from their homelands. It gave the slaves something to rally around, and in fact, the Haitian revolt in 1791 began during a voodoo ceremony and then evolved into a full-scale uprising throughout the colony.'

'Interesting,' said Andrew. 'So in some ways, voodoo created the spark that started the revolution that eventually created the first nation of freed slaves on Earth. That's fascinating.'

'Yes,' said Fiona. 'So, as you can imagine, slave owners in other colonies in different parts of the world, not least in America, were keen to demonise voodoo. And they did everything they could to make it out to be some sort of primitive and depraved religion involving things like human sacrifice. But that was never what it was really about. At least not in its original form. Of course, that doesn't mean that people like Marcellus can't use it and turn it into a tool for their own purposes. The former president Duvalier did exactly the same thing. Pretended to be some sort of voodoo master in order to scare the population into submission.'

'Well, whatever Marcellus has done,' said Andrew, 'he has managed to make himself into someone that everyone here seems to know about and fear. But he's just a man, and all men are mortal. None of them can stop a bullet, no matter how much damn black magic they try to conjure up.'

'You want to try to kill him?' said Fiona, looking at Andrew with an anxious expression.

'I am planning to use the Chicago mafia negotiation tactic,' said Andrew casually, trying to lighten the mood as he looked briefly over his shoulder to the backseat where the holdall full of weapons lay. 'They pull a knife, I pull a gun. They send one of us to the hospital, we send one of them to the morgue.'

'That's not funny,' said Fiona, unwilling to go along with his attempt at levity. 'Anyway, let's just hope it doesn't come to that.'

'Listen,' said Andrew, now more serious, glancing at her as he drove on. 'I am not going to set out to kill anyone. But if someone stands in the way of me getting Ronil out of there, then they'd better be prepared. They picked a fight with the wrong guy. And besides, I have an ace up my sleeve.'

'What sort of ace?' said Fiona, looking puzzled.

'One with a thick Scottish accent,' said Andrew with a grin. 'He's on his way as we speak.'

★   ★   ★

When the silver Humvee rolled through the gates of the former ambassadorial estate, Jaws was at the wheel, giving a quick wave to the heavily armed guard who was approaching the driver's side window. It had only been three hours since he had contacted Marcellus asking for permission to enter his fortified compound, but to Blake, who was sitting in the passenger seat next to him, that time had dragged on and felt like a century in the company of his perfectly affable but self-satisfied and somewhat dull host. Still, there was no other way to go about this, and it had been a stroke of luck that Fiona and her partner had already managed to make themselves known to the local crime bosses, so Blake was feeling confident that he was making progress.

After being given the OK to continue, Jaws drove the Humvee along the estate's tree-lined road to the colonial mansion where he parked in front of the main steps up to the front door. With considerable effort, he managed to get himself out from behind the steering wheel, and as soon as he left the air-conditioned interior of the customised military vehicle, beads of sweat began to form on his face. Blake opened the door and stepped down onto the gravel, followed by the bulky and grim-looking Ortega, Gomez and Delgado, none of whom had said barely a word since landing in the Haitian capital. All three heavies were carrying pistols in shoulder holsters, but as Jaws led them up the stairs, he asked them to unholster the weapons and give them to him. Ortega glanced at Blake with a displeased look, but when Blake nodded, he unclipped the straps and handed his gun to Jaws. Gomez and Delgado then followed suit, looking less than pleased about suddenly being unarmed.

'It's alright, chaps,' said Blake calmly. 'We're all friends here. It's just a precaution.'

With the three holsters dangling from his right hand, Jaws then led the quartet through the front doors, which were manned by two gang members carrying assault rifles and bandoliers with ammunition across their chests.

As they entered Marcellus' private lair at the back of the mansion, Blake noticed a strong smell of some sort of exotic incense in the air mixed with a hint of a sweet women's perfume. When the doors were opened and they were shown inside, even the usually confident and carefree Blake found himself slightly intimidated by what greeted them. Sitting in a throne-like armchair with a golden assault rifle across his lap and two stunning and barely dressed young women on either side was a tall and muscular man with leathery skin and eyes that seemed to bore straight through his guests as he regarded them from across the room. The large space was sparsely furnished and dimly lit by candlelight, and everything was arranged to make the seated kingpin the focal point. Everywhere he looked, Blake saw evidence of what appeared to be an obsession with voodoo. There was an altar with a crucifix draped with pearl chains and surrounded by what appeared to be various offerings, and above it was a huge painting of Baron Samedi, whom Blake was only too familiar with after his previous trips to Haiti in search of treasure. Privately, he felt nothing but scorn for this primitive African religion, but he had to admit that in this particular setting, it gave the place a certain sense of menace.

However, it wasn't just the imposing crime boss or the dark room with its superstitious paraphernalia and scattered candles that grabbed his attention. He found himself instantly captivated by the two young, lithe women who seemed to stand perfectly immobile with only their dark pools for eyes showing any sign of life as he and his companions approached.

'Marcellus,' said Jaws, attempting to sound casual and familiar, but the slight strain in his voice revealed the fact that the kingpin in the chair was placed much higher in the Haitian criminal pecking order. 'Thank you for taking the time to meet with me. I have my friend Lawrence with me.'

Marcellus regarded the suave and somewhat aloof-looking Blake for a moment, and then he glanced across to his three musclebound companions.

'They can wait outside,' he said, and at that, Jaws turned to look at Blake with a slightly anxious look that said that this wasn't merely a request.

'It's fine,' said Blake calmly, turning to Ortega.

The Spaniard hesitated for a moment but then shrugged and led the two other men back out towards the foyer, and as the doors were closed behind them, Jaws and Blake were left alone with Marcellus and his two beautiful female companions, who seemed to regard Blake the way a snake assesses its prey moments before striking.

Holding the gilded assault rifle by the barrel and placing the stock on the floor next to his chair, Marcellus raised his head slightly and regarded his European visitor suspiciously for a moment.

'Make it quick,' he then said.

'Certainly,' said Blake amiably, taking a cautious step forward and clearing his throat.

In broad strokes, he then proceeded to outline to Marcellus the story of the Black Galleon and the disappearance of its treasure, as well as relaying the efforts by his acquaintance Fiona Keane to find it. At the end of it, Marcellus nodded thoughtfully and pondered the issue for a moment before speaking again.

'I see,' he said. 'And you think this woman and her partner have found it?'

'It's possible,' said Blake. 'But even if they haven't, I happen to know that she is an exceptional researcher, so if anyone can find it, it will be her. All we have to do is make sure to watch them and see what they do next. Anyway, our friend Jaws here told me you had managed to get your hands on the boat driver.'

'That is correct,' said Marcellus. 'The one who took your *blanc* friends to Tortuga to look for the treasure.'

'Yes, Jaws here told me about that,' said Blake. 'Have you got anything from him yet?'

'I am about to go and have a little talk with him,' said Marcellus, his menacing eyes revealing that he was going to do a lot more than just talk. 'I am sure he will tell us what he knows.'

'Excellent,' said Blake, unperturbed by the prospect of violence being committed to achieve his ends. 'I am sure he will. Now, this is where I would like to propose a collaboration.'

'Go on,' said Marcellus, picking a long cigar from a chest pocket on his black leather vest, which he lit with a zippo lighter.

'Very simply,' began Blake. 'You provide me with some of your men, and also make sure that I and my three companions can travel safely here in Haiti, and in return, you get a cut of the treasure once Fiona has led us to it.'

'You seem very confident, Mr Blake,' said Marcellus as he puffed on the cigar and sent a cloud of smoke billowing up under the peeling ceiling high above them. 'What if she doesn't find it?'

'Nothing ventured, nothing gained,' smiled Blake disarmingly. 'But I think it's worth a shot.'

'And tell me,' said Marcellus, his brow creasing faintly. 'How much treasure are we talking about?'

As Blake looked up and to the right while making a show of estimating exactly how much the Black Galleon's treasure haul might be worth in present-day currency, Jaws glanced sideways at his old acquaintance, his interest clearly piqued at the prospect of gold from the Spanish treasure fleet.

'Several hundred million dollars,' Blake finally said, reflecting once again on the ease with which he was able to appeal to the greed of men such as these. 'Possibly more. It was a huge fortune then, and it is a huge fortune now. Enough for you to buy yourself full control of Port-au-Prince.'

As he spoke those words, Blake's thoughts returned momentarily to Count de Toledo, and he knew that he was here on his behalf and, as such, not in a position to give away any of the treasure. However, if dangling a carrot in front of this savage was what it took to secure his support in this endeavour, then so be it. There was nothing to stop him from double-crossing him later if that ended up seeming like the better option. That was one of the advantages of having an alter ego. At any time, Lawrence Blake could simply return to being Marcus Tobin and continue his quiet life in London until a new opportunity presented itself.

'Of course,' Blake continued reasonably. 'There's never any guarantee that this will prove successful, but even if it fails, you haven't lost anything. Think of it as a lottery ticket that costs you nothing. What could be better?'

Marcellus smiled, clearly impressed by the smooth-talking Englishman. Then he took another big puff on his cigar and exhaled through his nostrils as he looked straight at Blake.

'Alright, white man,' he eventually said. 'We have a deal.'

Fourteen

A purple and orange late-night dusk was falling over a deceptively pretty Port-au-Prince when the tall and well-built Colin McGregor walked out of the airport's VIP terminal carrying a large black holdall full of items that Andrew had requested in his message. With his beige slacks, black trainers and white shirt with rolled-up sleeves, McGregor could easily have been mistaken for a harmless tourist. However, he was anything but harmless, and that was precisely why Andrew had asked him to come to Haiti as soon as possible. Andrew was usually more than capable of handling a tight spot, but this time, facing off against one of the most hardened and violent gangs in the world, a team of two was many times better than just one man. And two highly trained and well-equipped members of 22 SAS should be more than a match for a dozen thugs.

Unlike Andrew and Fiona who had taken a flight to Haiti via Miami, McGregor had flown directly to Santo Domingo in the neighbouring Dominican Republic and then chartered an Airbus H135 helicopter and a pilot for the trip over the border to Port-au-Prince. This had ended up being a very expensive way of getting to the Haitian capital, but it had cut almost eight hours off his travel time. And with time being of the essence, Andrew had been more than happy to pay for the whole thing.

As soon as McGregor spotted Andrew and Fiona waiting for him outside, he lit up with a grin and gave them a wave.

'Fancy meeting you two here,' he said in his broad Scottish accent as he approached. 'Nice weather too. It's raining all kinds of pets back in the UK, as you'd expect.'

'Great to see you,' said Andrew, grabbing his friend's large hand. 'Good trip?'

'Aye,' McGregor grinned. 'Travelling like a prince, I was. I knew that trust fund of yours would come in handy one day.'

'Well,' Andrew smiled. 'It's worth the money. Glad to have you here.'

'Hi Colin,' said Fiona.

'Hello, Fiona,' McGregor said, flashing her a smile. 'Nice to see you. Everything alright?'

'More or less,' she said, stepping up to the Scot and giving him a quick hug. 'We could do with some help.'

'Thanks for dropping everything and coming out here so fast,' Andrew said. 'I assume you haven't told anyone at Hereford?'

'Nah,' said McGregor. 'This thing is off the books. I am doing this on my own time. I was about to go on a wee trip for the weekend with my new lass. But that'll have to wait.'

'Sorry about that,' said Andrew.

'No worries,' said McGregor. 'She'll understand. But I have to be back at Hereford Monday morning, so I only have about 24 hours here. Anyway, I take it you're in a spot of bother here with a friend of yours?'

'Yes,' said Andrew. 'Come on. Let's head to the car. I'll explain on the way.'

★ ★ ★

Three hours later, just after midnight, Fiona had taken up position in a half-finished office building whose construction seemed to have begun before the Haitian capital had descended into chaos, only to then be abandoned when the security situation had fallen apart. It was six stories tall, but it was nothing but a concrete skeleton with rusty metal reinforcement bars sticking out everywhere.

Wearing dark clothing and carrying only a pair of high-powered binoculars with night vision capabilities as well as her compact SIG Sauer P365 pistol, she had ensconced herself at the top of one of the stairwells from where she could see the entire ambassadorial estate where Marcellus Solomon had his headquarters. The estate was surrounded by a three-metre-tall barbed wire concrete wall that ran along its entire perimeter, and the grounds were dotted with trees and bushes. Once upon a time, these grounds had sported a perfectly cared-for lawn and lots of carefully arranged flowerbeds, but now it was a somewhat overgrown mess of tall grass and large bushes spilling out across the footpaths. From her vantage point, looking through the binoculars, Fiona could see three guards patrolling the expansive grounds, but there seemed to be no other movement anywhere in the compound. The main building was a three-storey mansion built in typical colonial style, and next to it, some thirty metres behind it, was a one-storey structure that might have been visitor's accommodation or perhaps staff quarters. There were also two minor structures on the estate, but they were much too small to be accommodation.

With a small boom mike attached to a lightweight headset, Fiona was able to wirelessly keep in touch with Andrew and McGregor, who were in the back of an abandoned restaurant just across the street from the estate's main gates. Andrew had explained the entire situation to his friend, and based on the reconnaissance that they had been able to conduct, the two of them had spent about an hour going over a tentative assault plan, knowing full well that it was unlikely to hold up once the shooting started.

'How's it looking up there?' said Andrew, keying his mike as he finished putting on the black tactical clothing that McGregor had brought, strapping on his ballistics vest and checking his weapons. 'See anything?'

'Just the same three guards as before,' said Fiona in a hushed voice, keen not to give her location away to anyone inside the compound or to random passersby. 'They seem to follow a set pattern, more or less. So I should be able to help you time your entry. There's no movement outside the perimeter. In fact, it seems like this whole part of the city is deserted.'

'Great,' said Andrew. 'Anything else?'

'Yes,' said Fiona, not quite able to believe what she had spotted in the large mansion's driveway. 'You'll never guess what's parked in the drive.'

'What?' said Andrew.

'Some sort of massive Jeep,' said Fiona. 'But I think this is one of those American Humvees, and it has a silver paint job. Actually, it looks more like chrome. Crikey. Someone paid a lot of money to have that done.'

'And who says crime doesn't pay?' said McGregor dryly.

'I guess it does around here,' said Andrew, slamming a mag into the magazine well and racking the bolt on his AR-15.

He then fed eight shells into the pump-action shotgun and strapped it to his back with the stock sticking up for easy access. Emptying the box of ammo into a pocket on the side of his combat trousers, he then glanced over to McGregor, who looked menacing wearing full kit and black face paint.

'Ready, mate?' he said.

'Aye,' nodded McGregor, now completely focused and no longer his usual jokey self. 'Let's do this, pal.'

Stopping briefly by the open main doorway of the ramshackle former restaurant, the two men made sure that the coast was clear, and then they jogged swiftly across the street and began moving along the perimeter wall away from the main gate. During their earlier reconnaissance using a small camera drone brought by McGregor, they had spotted a storm drain that ran under the wall on the compound's east side. With Port-au-Prince lying in a bowl surrounded by low mountains on three sides, heavy rainfall could lead to flash floods, so the estate's drainage system had been installed to direct excess water out and towards the River Grise, which ran from east to west through the entire city towards the bay.

The cylindrical concrete drain pipe was less than a metre across, so it would be a tight squeeze for the two fully kitted-out men, but with a bit of luck, they would be able to use it to penetrate into the compound and then launch their assault using the element of surprise. Staying low and pushing ahead swiftly but quietly, they were almost at the storm drain when the sound of a diesel engine reached them. A brief moment later, Fiona's voice came over the comms system.

'Stop!' she whispered, her voice tense as she peered through the binoculars. 'Car coming your way. It looks like one of those armoured vehicles.'

'MRAP?' said Andrew as he and McGregor went prone in the tall grass surrounding the estate.

'Yes,' said Fiona. 'One of those. That's the UN, right?'

'Yes,' said Andrew, staying completely still as the vehicle's headlights swept across their position and lit up the compound's perimeter wall right next to them.

'What the hell are they doing here at this hour?' Fiona said.

'Doesn't matter,' said Andrew. 'If they spot us, they'll shoot. They're known for being trigger-happy.'

The growling of the engine became louder as the MRAP approached, but then, as suddenly as the headlights had appeared, they then disappeared again as the vehicle made a right turn and headed back towards the centre of the city.

'OK,' said Fiona. 'You're clear to proceed.'

The two SAS men covered the remaining distance to the storm drain in less than a minute and got ready to enter.

'Fiona, we're heading inside,' Andrew whispered into the mike. 'Comms will be down for a bit.'

'Alright,' said Fiona, her voice already crackling as the signal began to break up. 'Good luck.'

The two men pushed inside, only to find that after about two metres they were blocked by a set of rusty metal bars. Having taken point on the way in, Andrew was in front and gripped two of the central bars and tried to wrestle them free. The corroded metal groaned slightly, and small bits of concrete came loose from where they connected to the storm drain's sides. However, it didn't budge.

'I think this is a two-person job,' he said, glancing back over his shoulder.

'Let me have a go,' said McGregor, who then squeezed past and gripped the metal bars tightly.

Gritting his teeth and groaning, the burly Scot put all his strength into pulling at the bars, and after a couple of seconds, they suddenly came loose on his righthand side, after which he was able to bend the entire grille inward and create an opening for them.

'I reckon driving a desk has made you go a bit soft,' he grinned as he panted and glanced back at Andrew. 'Or maybe you've not been taking your vitamins.'

'Alright. Very funny,' said Andrew, giving McGregor a friendly punch on the shoulder. 'Let's go.'

The two of them continued on through the cramped, damp and pungent storm drain, and they both soon found themselves sweating and panting from the effort. They passed under the perimeter wall above them and proceeded further through the long tunnel towards the middle of the estate until they came to a spot by a small concrete outbuilding that they had spotted earlier using the camera drone. The structure appeared to be some sort of storage or utility building once used by the estate's workers and gardeners, and it was partly hidden from view by tall and bulky bushes. Next to it on the ground, hinged on one side and set into a concrete slab, was a wide metal grille through which surface water could flow directly into the storm drain.

'This is it,' said Andrew quietly, looking up through the grille. 'Fiona, can you hear me?'

'Yes,' came Fiona's voice through the static, a note of relief in her voice after a couple of minutes with no word from the two men. 'Everything alright?'

'Yup,' Andrew whispered. 'We're at the outbuilding now. Any movement near us?'

'Two guards doing the perimeter wall patrol,' she said. 'I reckon they'll be back at your position in about two minutes. Maybe a bit less.'

'Alright,' said Andrew. 'Let's get out of here.'

Reaching up and gripping the metal grille tightly, he used his legs to push himself upwards, and the grille came loose with a brief metallic grating noise. Then Andrew rose to his full height, opening the grille and flipping it over onto the ground as quietly as he could manage. Within seconds, the two men were out.

'I see you,' said Fiona tensely as she watched them from afar through the binoculars. 'The guards are on their way. They haven't heard you, but they'll be there in less than one minute now.'

'Got it,' Andrew whispered as he lowered the grille back down and used his hand to smooth some dry soil over it to mask that it had just been opened.

'In here,' McGregor whispered as he moved to the outbuilding's door. 'We'll wait for them to pass.'

Andrew nodded, and McGregor then quietly opened the door and went inside. Doing a quick 360-degree turn to make sure no one was watching, Andrew then slipped in after him and closed the door. About half a minute later, the two roaming perimeter guards came into view from Fiona's vantage point as they cleared one of the tall bushes near the outbuilding, and she was then able to get a good look at them. With their red neckscarves and automatic weapons cradled in their hands, both men were obviously thugs belonging to Marcellus' gang, and they were well-built and mean-looking. One of them was smoking a cigarette whose ember glowed in the darkness, and they both appeared relaxed as they ambled along, seemingly without speaking to each other.

As they passed the outbuilding, the one smoking the cigarette glanced at the door for a long moment, at which point Fiona could have sworn that her heart stopped. However, he then continued on, and she breathed a sigh of relief. The two guards were about to leave the outbuilding and continue down one of the other footpaths when the smoker stopped and turned around. He glanced briefly at his companion and appeared to say something as he gestured towards the ground. He then took a step back towards the grille. Crouching down and resting on one knee, his hand touched the ground, and he then inspected something on his fingers. Getting back onto his feet, his gaze appeared to remain on the ground as he moved towards the outbuilding's door.

'Oh fuck,' Fiona whispered to herself, and as she keyed her mike, her hushed voice trembled with tension. 'The two guards. They're coming in.'

With no response from Andrew or McGregor, she watched helplessly as the two heavily armed men approached the door with their weapons gripped tightly in their hands, both of them now clearly suspicious about something they had seen. The smoker gripped the door handle and opened the door to what was a completely black and unlit interior. After briefly glancing back at his companion, the smoker moved inside, and a few seconds later, his buddy followed, and they both disappeared from view. Fiona watched breathlessly for what felt like several minutes, but then Andrew's voice suddenly came through her headset sounding somewhat out of breath.

'Alright,' he said. 'They're down.'

'Down?' said Fiona.

'They're dead,' said Andrew.

'Shit,' Fiona said, under her breath.

'Say again?' Andrew said, thinking that she might have spotted a new threat.

'It's just…' said Fiona haltingly. 'You said you would try not to kill anyone.'

'Well, that approach didn't work,' said Andrew matter-of-factly. 'It was either us or them. Do you see any other movement?'

'Hang on,' said Fiona, using her binoculars to scan the various parts of the estate. 'Not at the moment, but I can't see behind the mansion, so as you get closer, there might be guards there who could spot you.'

'Launch the drone,' said Andrew. 'You'll need to be our eyes for a bit as we push up.'

'OK,' said Fiona. 'Hang on.'

Opening the small grey plastic case containing the black, miniature quadcopter camera drone, she picked it up and switched it on, and then she paired its signal booster with her phone. Then she placed it on the lid of the case and used the controls on her phone screen to launch it. The drone immediately took off and lifted itself up to hover roughly ten metres above her.

'Drone up,' she said, glancing up at it. 'Good camera feed. Coming to you now.'

She used the virtual control pads on the phone screen to guide the mechanical insect forward across the street and over the ambassadorial estate, where she weaved through the trees towards Andrew and McGregor's position. When they saw it arrive, even they were amazed at how almost silent it was from the ground. Anyone not familiar with the faint whisper of its ultra-low-noise propulsion system would either not have noticed it or would have assumed that it was simply the wind in the trees. As it hovered perfectly still some twenty metres above the ground, she adjusted the exposure on the camera to enhance the image and allow her to see almost every detail of the surrounding area.

'Where do you want me?' she said as she looked at the image of the two SAS soldiers on her small screen.

'Curve around to the left and move towards the mansion,' said Andrew quietly, gesturing with his left hand while holding his AR-15 with the other. 'Call out any movement you see. We'll push up on the right and find the basement access. Ronil is almost certainly being kept down there.'

'Got it,' said Fiona, and then the drone zipped off and began moving away from the two men.

Andrew and McGregor moved onto the soft grass and followed one of the footpaths towards the mansion while making sure to stay low and remain in the shadows as much as possible. At one point, the view of the mansion was obscured by a cluster of thick bushes, and as the two men quietly pushed through them, they suddenly froze as they heard the sound of footsteps on the gravel path. Within seconds, they had both spotted another pair of patrolling guards through the foliage, and they were about twenty metres away and heading almost straight for them.

The two SAS soldiers didn't move a muscle as the pair approached, and for a moment it looked as if they were going to continue on their patrol, but then they stopped almost right in front of the bush where Andrew and McGregor were concealed at a distance of less than five metres. One of them lazily extracted a packet of cigarettes, offered one to his buddy and then stuck one into his own mouth. He lit both of them, and the two guards then turned to face the mansion, which was roughly a hundred metres away. As they stood there smoking and talking in Creole in low voices, Andrew was unable to make out what was being said, but he was sure that he heard the two names Angelique and Celestine, followed by knowing and lecherous laughter.

Andrew glanced at McGregor who tapped silently on his wristwatch, and his eyes said something like, 'We don't have time for this'. Andrew nodded and extracted his knife, which still had smudges of blood from the previous pair of guards on it. He looked meaningfully at McGregor who followed suit, and then Andrew indicated to the guard on the left and then jabbed at his chest with his thumb. McGregor nodded, and the two men began moving forward through the foliage as slowly and silently as two lions stalking their prey.

Twisting and turning their upper bodies to allow leaves to brush silently off their clothes as they placed each foot gingerly in front of the other on the soft soil, the two black, ghostlike figures seemed to drift inexorably forward through the foliage like black smoke. Emerging from the bush, they accelerated quietly towards their hapless targets, and by the time the two guards noticed movement behind them, it was already too late. Advancing in almost perfect unison, the SAS duo closed the final distance in a flash, wrapping one arm around the neck of their respective targets and plunging their knives into their chests once, twice, three times as they dragged the men backwards and into the thick, dark bushes where they disappeared. Seconds later, the leaves had stopped moving, and it was as if the two guards had never been there at all.

'Damn,' said McGregor as he released the dead guard he had just neutralised onto the ground. 'I would have liked to have a pistol with a suppressor right about now.'

'Yeah,' said Andrew, sheathing his knife. 'This got a bit messy. Let's keep going.'

Unaware of the takedown of two more of Marcellus Solomon's men, Fiona was focusing on the small screen on her phone as she steered the drone towards the mansion, keeping an eye out for more guards. As it approached the front of the mansion, she zoomed in on the silver Humvee. It might once have rolled off the assembly line somewhere in the United States as a top-of-the-line armoured vehicle complete with bulletproof glass and a camo paint job, but as she regarded it through the camera drone's artificial eyes, she struggled to think of a vehicle that was less inconspicuous than this. This was a car owned by someone who wanted to flaunt their wealth in what was now one of the poorest countries in the world.

As she zoomed back out, she noticed two guards standing under the porch by the front door. They weren't moving and did not appear to be talking, and if she had not been looking carefully at the screen, she might have missed them. She pulled back a couple of tens of metres from the mansion and made sure to keep her distance as she guided the drone along a curved path around the back of the mansion, which she had been unable to see yet from her vantage point on top of the abandoned construction site.

As the drone came around the back, she realised that the mansion had a large veranda facing south with views down across the urban terrain towards the city centre and the port. In times gone by, the resident ambassador would no doubt have entertained visiting dignitaries here as he showed off his opulent residence in what was once the jewel of the French colonial empire. It now looked somewhat dilapidated, but she saw that near the wooden railing were comfortable-looking garden chairs and a set of low tables with groups of bright burning candles. Adjacent to it and slightly further away from the mansion was a small swimming pool that was lit up by warm underwater lights. This was clearly a place where Marcellus enjoyed spending time during the evenings.

As she watched, the doors to the veranda suddenly opened, and a group of people emerged, along with the sounds of music and laughter spilling out of the mansion's interior and into the quiet night. Leading the group was a large and intimidating man wearing only trousers and a black leather vest that showed off his impressive physique. This had to be Marcellus. He was flanked by two gorgeous women wearing very little clothing, and behind them came an entourage of people that included some guards and a seriously obese man who not so much walked as waddled from inside the mansion and onto the veranda. Behind him came a group of four European-looking men. Three were black-clad, and the fourth was tall and in smart but casual clothing. Fiona zoomed in to get a better look. It took her a few seconds to realise exactly what she was seeing, but when she did, her mouth fell open and a cold shiver ran down her back.

'Tobin,' she whispered, barely able to believe her own eyes. 'What the hell are you doing here?'

As the words left her lips, a sudden and crushing realisation hit her, which instantly answered her own question. Tobin had somehow managed to follow her to Haiti, and there was only one reason why he would have done so. The treasure of the Black Galleon. He wanted it for himself. And here he was in the company of one of the worst gang bosses in the entire country. Her head was spinning, and she spent the next minute zooming in and gawping at the image, trying and failing to convince herself that perhaps this was someone else. He was dressed very differently from what Tobin usually wore, and his demeanour was somehow more carefree and jovial and much less that of a bookish academic. But there was no doubt in her mind. This was Marcus Tobin.

'You. Absolute. Bastard,' she whispered slowly as she watched him pick up one of the drinks and clink his glass against that of the kingpin. 'How could I have been so wrong about you?'

'Fiona,' came Andrew's voice over her headset. 'We've cleared a path on this side of the house, and we're about to move up. How's it looking on the other side? We can hear voices and music. What's going on?'

It took a moment for Fiona to compose herself and key the mike, and when she did, she still sounded somewhat confounded by what she had witnessed.

'It's Marcellus,' she finally said. 'He's throwing some sort of party with a bunch of guests.'

'Good,' Andrew's voice came back. 'That'll help us get in unnoticed.'

'Well,' said Fiona. 'There's more.'

'What's going on?' said Andrew.

'Marcus Tobin is here?' she said, producing an involuntary shake of the head.

'What?' said Andrew, sounding like he thought he might have misheard. 'Tobin? What the hell is he doing here?'

Using as few words as possible, Fiona explained the uncomfortable realisation that had just hit her, and there was pain and also a note of shame in her voice at having allowed herself to be taken in by what was clearly a conman masquerading as a serious academic.

'Bloody hell,' said Andrew, struggling to process what he had just been told. 'I can't believe it.'

'Me neither,' said Fiona.

'Who the hell is Tobin?' said McGregor, looking mystified.

'A friend of Fiona's,' said Andrew. 'Make that a former friend. The bastard tracked us here. He's trying to beat us to the treasure we're searching for.'

'What a sneaky bugger,' said McGregor disdainfully.

'What do we do?' said Fiona.

'We stay on mission,' said Andrew. 'This changes nothing right now. We came here to get Ronil out, and that's what we're going to do. We'll deal with Tobin later.'

'Right,' Fiona nodded slowly, gradually managing to mobilise some focus and composure again. 'OK. What do you need me to do?'

'Just keep an eye on them for now,' said Andrew. 'We're going to enter down into the basement through the exterior access hatches on the side of the mansion. And be ready to deploy the decoy device on my signal.'

'Alright,' said Fiona. 'I'll be ready.'

Having hidden the bodies of the two guards in the bushes, Andrew and McGregor used the available cover to advance towards the mansion, which sat on slightly raised ground at the centre of the ambassadorial estate. Moving swiftly but quietly, they covered the last few tens of metres in a crouched run and then hugged the exterior wall as they pushed up to the access hatches. The two small doors leading down into the basement under the mansion were installed at a 45-degree angle and hinged on the sides to open from the centre. Andrew and McGregor had expected them to be secured with a padlock, anticipating having to spend several precious seconds exposed there while they picked the lock, but to their surprise, they were able to simply lift them open and slip down a set of steps to another door.

Closing the hatches above them, they moved down a handful of steps to a metal door that led into the basement itself, and then they got themselves and their weapons ready to enter. So far, they had gone out of their way to remain stealthy, but there would come a point when that was no longer an option. When that happened, they intended to go loud in a big way, and two AR-15s suddenly firing on full auto was hopefully enough to cause chaos amongst Marcellus' remaining security guards. And if everything went according to plan, that would allow them to make their escape. However, as they both knew from hard-won experience, nothing ever went exactly according to plan, and they both realised that they had to be ready for anything, including finding Ronil already dead. Andrew had deliberately avoided discussing that eventuality with Fiona, but he was privately concerned that there might be a significant chance that Marcellus had already got what he wanted from the young boat driver, after which he would be of no further use to the gang leader.

Taking point, Andrew pressed the stock of his AR-15 into his shoulder and pushed open the metal door. Advancing swiftly while ready to engage, and in a movement pattern that mirrored what they had done countless times in the kill house during training at Hereford and in real-life breaching operations, the two men swept into the basement and quickly established that it appeared to be deserted. Finding themselves in a room that might once have served as storage for coal and firewood, they glanced silently at each other and then moved up towards the door on the other side of the subterranean room. While McGregor lowered his AR-15 and placed a hand on the round metal doorknob, Andrew moved up beside him, slung the bulky assault rifle onto his back, and extracted the Smith & Wesson SD9. He flicked the switch for the under-mounted laser, and a small red dot lit up on the door directly in front of him. Then he glanced at McGregor and nodded.

With perfect but unspoken timing, communicated only by the familiar movement of each man, McGregor twisted the doorknob and opened the door as Andrew pushed forward through the doorway with his pistol raised, ready to engage any hostiles stationed in the basement. He found himself in a dank corridor lit by a single light bulb, and there was a set of stairs at one end and a closed door at the other.

The walls were old brick with peeling paint, and there was a strange organic smell that Andrew couldn't place. And once again, there was no sign of any guards.

With a brief nod, Andrew signalled for McGregor to follow him into the corridor. Then with a quick hand gesture, he motioned towards the door at the far end, indicating for them to move up to it. Once again, the two men advanced silently together, this time side by side, as they approached the door in a combat stance with slightly bent knees and their weapons up. Halfway there, Andrew realised that there was another door on their right, and he stopped and leaned out past the doorframe just enough to see inside and bring the pistol around with him. The red dot danced across the small space on the other side of the doorway in tandem with his eyes as they scanned the room to make sure that there were no threats inside. It was unlit, but the lone light in the corridor was enough to reveal a disturbing sight. On the floor in the middle of the room was the body of what appeared to have been a young man wearing blue jeans and a yellow shirt with about a dozen bloody stab wounds across the chest. His matted dreadlocks and ghostly face were a bloodied mess, and much of the back of his head was missing.

'Jesus,' Andrew breathed, glancing back at McGregor whose jaw clenched at the gruesome sight.

Andrew composed himself and motioned for the two of them to exit the room and continue. They filed back out into the corridor and pushed up to the door at the far end. Here, they exchanged a quick look, having now seen what sort of people they were dealing with, and then Andrew gave the nod.

Moving rapidly, the two men burst inside the large, virtually empty room on the other side and immediately entered into a crouch as they scanned the space with their weapons ready to fire at anything that might be a threat. However, there was only one thing in the room that immediately stole all of their attention. It was the slim and completely limp figure of a young man hanging by the wrists from a metal chain attached to a large hook in the ceiling about five metres away. His wrists had been bound with rope, and a small winch had been used to lift him up. Almost directly above him was a single fluorescent tube that cast its cold light down onto the head of the lifeless figure, and below him was a puddle of blood that appeared almost black in the dim light of the room. Staring at the macabre vista, Andrew felt a sickening knot tighten in his stomach as he recognised Ronil's clothes. His blue jeans were dirty, and his red t-shirt was bloodied with large dark patches, but there was no question about it. This was the young man who just one day before had helped him and Fiona find the wreck of the Marauder.

'Shit,' said Andrew tensely, glancing at McGregor while nodding towards Ronil. 'It's him.'

'Dead?' asked McGregor, not taking his eyes off the young man.

Andrew didn't reply but began moving up towards the seemingly lifeless Ronil while he shoved the SD9 into its holster.

'Keep us covered,' he said. 'I'll get him down.'

While McGregor turned towards the open door to the corridor, resting on one knee and aiming his weapon towards the stairs at the other end, Andrew pushed up and rounded the immobile figure in front of him. Ronil's face was beaten and battered, with dark and swollen contusions everywhere and several knife cuts whose blood had left dark trails but had now stopped flowing. For a brief moment, Andrew thought the worst had happened, but then Ronil produced the weakest of moans as his body twitched.

'He's alive,' Andrew said with palpable relief, immediately stepping forward and wrapping an arm around Ronil's waist. He then reached down to pull his knife from its sheath, and within seconds, he had slashed through the rope, and Ronil's ragdoll body slumped down into his arms. He placed the young man gently on the floor and took his head in his hands, inspecting his injuries. They were serious but did not appear to be life-threatening unless there was internal bleeding that he couldn't see. He knew that those could be stealth killers within days if not operated on at a hospital, and the prospect of having that done in Port-au-Prince in the current environment was daunting. Still, Ronil was alive, and that was a lot more than he had dared to hope for.

'Ronil,' he said. 'Mate. It's Andrew. I'm here to get you out.'

Ronil moaned again and produced a small cough, and it then appeared to take considerable effort for him to open his bloodshot eyes. However, when he did, they widened at the sight of Andrew above him, and there was even a small attempt at a brave smile playing on his lips.

'I didn't think I would see you again,' he whispered.

'Well, you're not getting rid of me until I get you out of this place,' said Andrew.

'I'm sorry,' Ronil then said, his face changing into a pained mask of regret. 'I had to tell them about the wreck. They were going to kill me, and then Roseline too. I couldn't…'

'It's OK,' Andrew cut him off. 'Don't apologise. Fiona and I are the ones who got you and your sister into all of this. But don't worry. Roseline is safe with your aunt across the border.'

Relief swept visibly across Ronil's swollen face, and some of the tension seemed to suddenly leave his brutalised body.

'How many guards does Marcellus have here?' said Andrew. 'We took out four of them so far.'

'Many,' Ronil winced as pain appeared to suddenly shoot through the left side of his torso.

'Can you walk?' said Andrew, glancing down at Ronil's legs, which appeared beaten but with no obvious signs of fractures. 'We need to move.'

'I'll try,' said Ronil, grimacing as he tried and failed to sit up, groaning as he did so. 'I need some help.'

Andrew put an arm around him and hauled him to his feet, and after looking like he was about to fall over, Ronil finally managed to gain his balance while gripping Andrew's shoulder for support.

'I think I'm OK,' he said.

'Alright,' nodded Andrew as he turned his head towards McGregor who was glancing back at them. 'This is my buddy. He's going to help get you away from this place. Alright? Just stay behind us and keep low. We might have to shoot our way out.'

Ronil said nothing but simply nodded as he swallowed and appeared to muster whatever courage he had left after his violent ordeal in the basement under the mansion. As Andrew supported him towards the doorway, McGregor moved up in front of them with his assault rifle remaining fixed on the door at the far end. With Andrew by his side, Ronil limped along with gritted teeth as pain pulsed through most of his body. When they made it to the door leading to the room with the external hatches, Ronil suddenly yelped and fell to the floor, clutching his right knee and moaning.

'Argh shit,' he said through gritted teeth. 'I think it's broken.'

Andrew knelt down and helped him get back up again, but Ronil was now resting all his weight on his left leg and looked barely able to move.

'He can't make it all the way across those grounds,' said McGregor, jerking his head towards the hatches to the outside. 'There's no way. We need another exit.'

Andrew thought for a moment, and then he keyed his mike, relieved to find that the comms link was still up despite them being under the mansion.

'Fiona,' he said. 'We have him.'

'Oh, thank goodness,' came Fiona's voice, relief permeating every syllable. 'Is he alright?'

'No,' said Andrew. 'They did a real number on him. He can barely walk. But he's alive. Listen, is that Humvee still there?'

'Yes,' said Fiona. 'At least, it was a couple of minutes ago.'

'Alright,' said Andrew. 'That's our ticket out of here. We need to make our way to it, somehow. Any idea how many guards we need to get through?'

'I saw two outside the front door,' said Fiona. 'There are probably several more inside. And I am looking at four right here on the veranda with Marcellus and the rest of them, including Tobin, that arsehole.'

'Got it,' said Andrew. 'We will need to move up to the ground floor and then make it out of the front door. We just need to hope that the keys are still in the ignition. Keep me posted if you see movement.'

'OK,' said Fiona. 'Good luck.'

With McGregor leading the way and Andrew supporting most of the hobbling Ronil's weight, the trio made its way to the end of the corridor where a set of stairs continued up into the mansion above. Moving slowly and quietly, McGregor pushed up the stairwell, leaning and twisting his upper body to allow him to point the AR-15 up and around corners. Following close behind was Andrew who had to wait for a couple of seconds as Ronil struggled to take one step at a time, wincing and grunting quietly from the pain as he did so. As they approached the top of the stairwell, they began to pick up the music playing somewhere inside the mansion, and at one point, there was distant, raucous laughter coming through the door at the top.

McGregor gripped the doorknob and turned it as slowly and quietly as he could, and then he opened the door just enough to be able to see out. On the other side was a wide, well-lit hallway with polished wood flooring and rugs, wood panelling on both walls, as well as a couple of oil paintings. McGregor stopped and listened for a moment, but all he could hear was the noise of the gathering outside. He pushed the door open a bit more and stuck his head out to look around. It quickly became apparent that there was no one there, and it seemed that the hallway connected a large, brightly lit room at the back of the house with a similarly expansive but almost dark room near the front. As the trio moved quietly out of the stairwell and towards the front of the house, they realised that the large, gloomy room was lit by several sets of thick candles dotted around on the furniture and on the floor. When they moved inside, they saw a luxurious armchair placed like a throne in the middle of the room, surrounded by what Andrew assumed were various voodoo paraphernalia. On the wall behind it was a huge painting of the suited and skull-faced Baron Samedi wearing a top hat and glaring down at them menacingly with his empty eyes.

'Bloody hell,' whispered McGregor. 'This takes man cave to a whole new level.'

'It's creepy, alright,' said Andrew quietly, looking around as he supported Ronil. 'Come on. Let's just get the hell out of here.'

Moving across the large space, it became clear that there were two ways out of the bizarre throne room. One was through a set of double doors, which Andrew assumed led via a corridor to the foyer and then the front door. The other was through a single doorway that appeared to lead into an office of some kind. McGregor moved over to the double doors, thinking that this would be the more direct route, but they proved to be locked. He could easily have broken through them, but not without making a lot of noise.

'We have to go through here,' he whispered, moving swiftly towards the doorway to the office.

As the three men entered, they found themselves in what appeared to have once been the ambassador's private office near the front of the house. There was a door to the mansion's foyer on the other side of the room, and as Andrew looked around, he realised that it could easily have passed for an elaborate 19th-century film set. There was dark mahogany furniture and bookshelves, an elaborately carved and upholstered Louis XIV sofa and a pair of matching armchairs, and there was one of the largest antique office desks Andrew had ever seen. Several oil paintings hung on the walls, seemingly of spectacular Haitian natural vistas, and the bookcases were crammed full of leatherbound tomes.

'Seems Marcellus likes to pretend to be a scholar,' he said dryly.

'I need to sit down,' grunted Ronil, who was now in so much pain that tears were welling up in his eyes. 'Please. Just for a second.'

Against his better judgement, Andrew helped Ronil to slump down into an armchair for a brief rest, and when he stood back up, he glanced across Marcellus' desk and spotted various items seemingly related to the kingpin's voodoo practices, along with a couple of neat bunches of US dollars and what appeared to be small, clear plastic bags containing cocaine. However, next to those was something that Andrew had never seen with his own eyes before. A small leather pouch filled with what appeared to be raw, uncut diamonds.

They glinted in the light from the candles as he moved closer, and he estimated that there had to be at least twenty of them in the small pouch. Being raw rather than cut and polished, these gemstones, which no doubt originated from some African warzone, were less valuable than their cut version. However, the pouch on Marcellus' desk still represented an absolute fortune that made the bundles of cash pale in comparison, and the crime boss had no doubt converted some of his wealth into these gems in case he suddenly had to leave Port-au-Prince in a hurry.

'I don't think Marcellus is going to miss these,' Andrew said, picking up the cash and the pouch and feeling its weight in his hand. 'And I can come up with a better use for them.'

While Andrew shoved the pouch full of diamonds into a pocket, McGregor moved to one of the windows, which had its shutters closed. Peering out through a narrow gap, he could see the silver Humvee parked right outside.

'I see our wheels out there,' he whispered, glancing back at Ronil. 'Come on, lad. Not far to go now.'

Ronil nodded and placed his hands on the armrests as Andrew moved to help him up when suddenly the door to the foyer opened. In walked a lanky young guard wearing black jeans, a white t-shirt and the ubiquitous red scarf around his neck, and he was armed with a compact Uzi submachine gun. He looked shocked as he locked eyes with Andrew who had only just turned his head towards the door. However, before anyone could do anything else, McGregor was already moving at a pace that seemed unnatural for such a large man. Loath to fire his weapon now when they were so close to escaping undetected, he covered the distance to the guard in a couple of seconds. But before he could barge into him and disarm him, the young man managed to bring up his Uzi and pull the trigger. With his forward momentum carrying him straight at the guard, McGregor steeled himself for a barrage of 9mm bullets, which he hoped his ballistics vest would be able to stop most of. However, the barrage never came. All he heard was a metallic click as the Uzi jammed. A fraction of a second later, McGregor rammed into him, shunting him aside and slamming the door closed. As he did so, he gripped the Uzi with his left hand, yanked it clean out of his hand, and flung it aside and onto the floor while driving his meaty right fist up into a crushing uppercut that connected perfectly with the guard's jaw. The blow carried so much force that the gangly man's head snapped back and his feet almost lifted off the floor, and in the next instant, McGregor had moved past him and wrapped his right arm around his neck. Reaching over and across the guard's head with his left hand, he gripped it firmly and twisted hard. The guard's neck broke with a wet crunch, and his entire body went limp from one instant to the next. Hanging like a ragdoll from McGregor's arm, the Scot dragged him aside and lowered him silently to the floor. For a moment, the exhausted Ronil sat gawping at the terrifyingly efficient display of lethal hand-to-hand combat skills put on display by one of his rescuers, but then he snapped out of it and began to struggle back onto his feet, helped by Andrew.

'Help me,' he said. 'I think I am OK to go on.'

'Alright,' said Andrew, glancing at McGregor. 'Good job, mate. Now, let's just get out of here.'

While McGregor moved to the door that led out to the foyer, Andrew helped Ronil to cross the room from the armchair to the door. When all three men were ready, Andrew nodded to McGregor who then opened the door only to be faced with two heavily armed guards cradling assault rifles and looking stunned at what they were seeing. They had evidently heard the door to the office slam and had come to investigate.

Without a moment's hesitation, McGregor slammed the door shut again and threw himself aside just as a barrage of incoming fire erupted from the foyer and a hail of bullets began chewing up the wood. Andrew also flung himself down onto the floor, dragging Ronil with him. He then moved in front of the young man, using his ballistic vest to protect him, and a split second later, one of the badly aimed projectiles from the panicked spray of bullets smacked into his back. The vest ate it, but it left Andrew stunned for a brief moment.

By this time, McGregor had spun around on the floor and was pointing his AR-15 at it from a prone position lying on his back. Holding the trigger down, the assault rifle ate through the entire 30-round magazine in less than five seconds, and a scream cut through the deafening barrage as at least one of the guards was hit. McGregor released the spent magazine and let it clatter to the floor, and it had barely stopped moving before the Scot had slammed a fresh one in and yanked the charging handle back to chamber the first round.

By then, the chaos and gunfire had alerted Marcellus and his entourage on the veranda, and both he, his men, and Blake's three goons were running inside, and the two guards who had been standing outside by the front door had come into the foyer with their weapons drawn and ready to fire. There were frantic voices shouting and someone wailing in agony on the other side of the almost shredded door, and as soon as the two guards from outside saw it and realised that there were intruders in Marcellus' office, they opened up with their automatic weapons.

'The desk,' Andrew shouted, and while he dragged Ronil into cover, McGregor put his shoulder under the side of the huge mahogany desk and flipped it over onto its side.

As Andrew, McGregor and Ronil took cover, bullets were ripping through the door, which had now almost been reduced to kindling, but they were stopped dead by the massive bulk of the hardwood desk. This didn't stop the guards from firing, and they emptied magazine after magazine into the office as bullets peppered the walls and the desk and began chewing it up. Through the open doorway into the throne room, Andrew suddenly spotted a large man clad in black and carrying a pistol. He was moving from the far side of the mansion and into the room where the deranged wannabe monarch Marcellus would allow his subjects an audience. Andrew immediately sent a three-round burst through the doorway as the man sprinted into cover and out of view, and there was something about the way he moved that sparked a memory in Andrew's brain, even through the noise and the chaos of the firefight. And then it hit him. He could have sworn that this man looked and moved exactly the same as the one he had watched on the CCTV footage killing Laura Hartley inside the British Museum. And then it all suddenly clicked. Blake was behind that robbery too, and this man was one of his goons.

Andrew had barely finished this thought when the man suddenly reappeared and fired two quick rounds from his pistol. The bullets slammed into the wall directly behind Andrew's head, and he could hear them zip past uncomfortably close. This man was not only brave going up against an assault rifle with only a pistol, but he was also a good shot, and there was every chance that he might get lucky next time. Reaching up to his headset, Andrew keyed his mike and shouted through the noise of the gunfire.

'Fiona, can you hear me?' he roared, and Fiona's panicked voice immediately came back over the airwaves.

'Yes,' she yelled. 'What the hell is happening?'

'We're pinned down,' Andrew shouted. 'We could really use that decoy right about now.'

'On it,' Fiona shouted, and then the comms link was cut.

From several hundred metres away, Fiona had been able to hear the gunfire erupt, and on the feed provided by the small camera drone, she had seen an instant reaction from Marcellus and the rest of the people on the veranda. They had all jumped to their feet, except for the obese man who had dropped his drink on the floor and scrambled along the sofa to cower behind one of Blake's three large goons.

As soon as her conversation with Andrew had ended, she immediately guided the drone back around to the other side of the house where a large cylindrical fuel tank was located next to a garage. She primed the release mechanism on the drone and prepared for its last hurrah in the form of a suicide mission to cause maximum chaos inside the compound. The drone had been fitted with one of the hand grenades that Andrew had taken from the Port-au-Prince brothel, and it had been rigged up to the drone's inbuilt release catch. Swooping around the mansion, she set the drone down on top of the fuel tank near the main refilling valve, and then she hit the activation button. An instant later, a massive explosion ripped open an entire side of the mansion, and a blinding light emanated from the giant fireball that rose up from the tank as black smoke billowed up into the night sky. About a third of the mansion was now on fire, and flaming debris was falling all over the estate, some of which almost reached the perimeter where she was positioned. The blast was much larger and more ferocious than she had anticipated, and she instantly broke into a cold sweat at the thought of Andrew, McGregor and Ronil being so close to it.

'Andrew!' she shouted into the mike. 'Are you alright?'

There was no reply.

'Andrew, damn it!' she yelled. 'Are you guys OK?'

'We're OK,' said Andrew, who was still in cover behind the desk in Marcellus' office.

'Get the hell out!' Fiona shouted. 'Right now.'

'Moving,' said Andrew.

He grabbed Ronil around the waist and hauled him up onto his feet while McGregor advanced as if invulnerable to gunfire, shooting at anyone he could see in short, controlled three-round bursts. One guard, who had barely recovered from the blast and was looking confused and shocked, took all three bullets in the chest and was flung backwards into a wall. Another guard saw it happen and was so shocked that he failed to pull the trigger after aiming his weapon. The burst from McGregor's AR-15 removed most of his head, and he slumped to the floor in a crumpled heap of limbs.

As the trio moved from the office and into the foyer, gunfire erupted from their left side, and it came from the three black-clad men that Fiona had spotted on the veranda, almost certainly Tobin's personal security squad. While still half-carrying and half-dragging Ronil, Andrew managed to swing his own assault rifle around to release a long full-auto burst that consumed about a third of the magazine. Bullets peppered the doorway behind which the three men had been taking cover, and one of the projectiles smacked into the forehead of one of them. His head was jerked back and to one side as the bullet tore through his skull, and most of his brain matter was splattered onto the wall behind him. He then fell forward limply, and his mangled head slapped onto the floorboards with a wet thud.

While McGregor continued firing and clearing a path for them ahead, Andrew took the opportunity that the Scot's suppressing fire had created and put all his strength and focus into getting Ronil out of the foyer and into the driveway where the Humvee was parked. As they passed over the threshold, McGregor stopped, turned and crouched in an effort to cover their retreat until Andrew and Ronil were safely inside the vehicle. Outside, the entire estate seemed to be lit up by the roaring blaze on the other side of the mansion, and Andrew went as fast as he could down the steps towards the military vehicle with the silver paint job.

To his immense relief, the driver's side door was unlocked, and he yanked it open and then opened the door to the passenger seat behind it. Helping Ronil inside, he then slammed the door shut and turned to shout back to McGregor who was now firing controlled bursts in an attempt to conserve ammo. As Andrew turned, a bullet went right past McGregor's head and ripped through the doorframe, and an instant later, McGregor's body seemed to jerk back as if he had been punched in the chest, and he lost his balance and fell onto his back.

Without a thought for his own safety, Andrew sprinted back up the steps, emptying his magazine inside the mansion as soon as he could bring his weapon to bear. Then he tossed the AR-15 aside and grabbed hold of McGregor's ballistics vest. At that moment, a heavily obese man with a crazed, metallic grin appeared through a doorway into the foyer holding a sawn-off shotgun. As soon as he saw the two intruders, he brought up his weapon, but Andrew beat him to it. Ripping the SD9 from its holster, he brought it up, aimed and fired twice in quick succession before the huge man had time to pull the trigger. One of Andrew's bullets punched into his chest, and the other tore through his neck, ripping open his left jugular vein. Dropping to his knees as his weapon clattered to the floor, the flesh mountain gripped his jowly neck with a crazed, wide-eyed look on his face, and as he dropped backwards and thudded heavily onto the floor, blood sprayed up and out between his fingers in powerful spurts. Andrew knew immediately that this was not a survivable injury, but it might take several minutes for him to die, voodoo or no voodoo.

Andrew had barely stopped moving to take the shots, and he now continued dragging McGregor clear of the doorway. They were halfway down the steps by the time he realised that his friend was unhurt and heard him produce a stream of swear words.

'Come on!' Andrew shouted. 'We are leaving!'

McGregor staggered to his feet, and the two men scrambled inside the Humvee just as Marcellus emerged in the doorway. He was holding a golden assault rifle and was flanked by three of his men and Tobin's two remaining goons. Almost in unison, they raised their weapons and opened up on the armoured vehicle, and bullets began peppering the bodywork and the inch-thick glass of the windscreen.

'Fuck me!' said McGregor, watching the impact points on the windscreen as the incoming bullets connected. 'That was close. I think we've overstayed our welcome here.'

'No kidding,' said Andrew, reaching down to the ignition, only to find that there was no key. 'Shit. I can't start the engine.'

Without a word, McGregor extracted his knife from its sheath and slammed its tip into the hard plastic that surrounded the steering column. Twisting the knife hard to one side, the plastic cracked, allowing him to put his fingers into a gap and tear most of it off to reveal a set of wires.

'There,' he said, as more bullets continued smacking into the vehicle's windscreen and armour plating. 'Now over to you.'

Andrew reached down and tore the wires, and within seconds, he had short-circuited the starter motor, and the large diesel engine had sprung into life with a roar. With the gunfire abating as their adversaries began to run out of bullets, Andrew yanked the gear lever down into reverse. Then he gunned the engine and released the clutch, and the heavy vehicle leapt backwards as its wide tyres spun, spraying curtains of gravel across the driveway. The last thing Andrew saw out of the driver's side window through the partially cracked bulletproof glass was Marcellus' two female companions emerging next to the other shooters at the top of the stairs. They each held a pistol and fired them repeatedly, but it was their faces that he ended up remembering. They were both tall, slim and extremely attractive, but their eyes burnt with barely contained fury and hatred as they kept firing round after ineffective round at the heavily armoured vehicle. Seconds later, the Humvee was tearing along the tree-lined road towards the gate leading out into the city, and Andrew didn't slow down as they approached.

'Hang on!' he shouted, and moments later, the Humvee barreled into the gates, causing them to be ripped off their hinges, fly through the air and skid across the road on the other side of the perimeter walls.

Less than two minutes after that, Fiona hopped inside the back next to Ronil as Andrew stopped the car at the designated meeting point. Her eyes were wild, she was sweating profusely after her run to the rendezvous, and she was still holding the SIG Sauer P365 in her hand.

'You can put that down now,' said McGregor with a wry smile as Andrew raced off.

'Oh right,' said Fiona self-consciously before turning her attention to Ronil. 'Are you alright? I feel terrible about this whole thing. It's my fault.'

Ronil lifted a hand to stop her talking, and then he forced a thin smile as he looked at her.

'Thank you,' he said. 'I would be dead without you guys.'

'We're going to get you out of here,' said Andrew from the driver's seat as he tore along the deserted road of the tortured city towards the international airport. 'We're all leaving on a chopper and flying to the Dominican Republic. We're taking you to your sister.'

'Thank you,' Ronil repeated, his strength suddenly seeming to leave him as the adrenaline of the escape began to fade. 'I owe you my life.'

'You don't owe us anything,' said Fiona.

'She's right,' said Andrew, glancing back at him. 'But I grabbed something from Marcellus that will be able to give you and Roseline a fresh start.'

He reached into a pocket and extracted the pouch with uncut diamonds, handing it back to an amazed Fiona who showed its contents to Ronil.

'Oh man,' he breathed as the familiar broad smile passed across his lips despite his pain. 'I don't know what to say.'

'Don't say anything,' Fiona smiled sympathetically. 'Just try to relax, and we will take care of everything.'

'Are you alright?' Andrew said, glancing across to McGregor. 'I thought they got you there for a moment.'

'Nah,' said McGregor. 'It'll take more than that to take down a McGregor. I'm just happy that Uzi jammed when it did.'

'What happened?' said Fiona.

McGregor proceeded to tell her about his brush with death at the hands of the guard holding the Israeli-made rapid-fire submachinegun that ended up jamming.

'Oh crikey,' said Fiona. 'That was lucky.'

'Aye,' shrugged McGregor, seemingly unperturbed by the close call. 'The stupid bastard dinnae keep his gun clean. Had himself a wee L85 moment there.'

'A what?' said Fiona.

Andrew and McGregor exchanged a knowing grin before the Scotsman went on.

'A good while ago,' McGregor said, 'the British army started issuing its soldiers with a new rifle called the L85. It was meant to be this great replacement for the old standard-issue weapon. But it soon turned out to be a bit of a nightmare with all sorts of issues that made it almost impossible to use. So it got the nickname 'the civil servant'.'

'The civil servant?' Fiona repeated. 'Why?'

'Well?' said McGregor with a wide grin. 'Because you couldn't make it work, and you couldn't fire it.'

Fiona laughed despite herself, and as she did so, she felt the tension of the last couple of hours lift from her shoulders, and suddenly it was as if she was able to breathe freely again.

'That was a bit more excitement than I would have liked,' she said.

'You did well,' said Andrew. 'In fact, really well. You saved our arses back there.'

'What do we do about Tobin?' said Fiona as her mind flashed back to the image of the academic on her phone screen sharing drinks with the crime boss. 'He bloody tricked me. And he was working with Marcellus to grab the Spanish treasure for himself. I'm going to bury him when we get back to London. He'll never work in academia again.'

'Not if his goons get to you first,' said McGregor dryly. 'You can bet your bottom dollar that he is gunning for you now.'

At that, Fiona fell silent and stared out of the windows at the urban scenery that flashed past in a blur as they raced towards the airport.

'He's right,' said Andrew. 'This just got serious, and it's not over yet.'

'Shit,' Fiona said anxiously. 'This whole thing got out of control quickly.'

'It can happen,' McGregor shrugged. 'What we need to do now is make sure we get to my chopper and then safely into the Dominican Republic. And then we take it from there.'

'Good plan,' said Andrew. 'I assume the pilot is on permanent standby?'

'Of course,' said McGregor with a wink. 'Knowing I was meeting you here, I assumed the worst. And that's pretty much what happened.'

'Sorry,' said Andrew with a wry smile. 'Thank you for showing up. I knew I could count on you.'

'Not a problem,' said McGregor. 'I know you'd do the same for me.'

A little less than ten minutes later, the few onlookers present at the airport witnessed the bizarre sight of a bullet-riddled silver Humvee pulling up in front of the departure hall and four people spilling out and heading inside while leaving the battered vehicle's doors open. Shortly after that, the quartet sailed through the VIP passport control courtesy of a large bundle of cash surreptitiously changing hands. About half an hour later, the helicopter pilot received takeoff clearance, and the chopper lifted into the air and headed northeast across the Haitian capital towards the border with the Dominican Republic.

The next morning, Ronil had been checked into a modern hospital in the northern city of Pepillo Salcedo, just across the border from Haiti, where his and Roseline's aunt lived. He was dehydrated and exhausted and had suffered a number of serious injuries, although none of them life-threatening, and the doctors advised that he would need to stay there for several days before they could consider letting him go.

Within minutes of being placed in a comfortable bed in a large and airy room and saying goodbye to Andrew, Fiona and the tall Scot who had helped rescue him, he was placed into a medically induced coma to safeguard his recovery over the next several days. Standing over the unconscious youngster for a moment, Andrew then placed the two silver pieces of eight coins from the wreck of the Marauder into Ronil's hand and closed his fingers around them, knowing that he would take good care of them and neither sell them nor go back for more. Roseline then accompanied her three rescuers outside where they said their final goodbyes. She gave them each a tight hug and promised to put the diamonds to good use. She and Ronil would buy a new and bigger house for their aunt, who lived in a modest apartment, and then they would pursue their childhood dream of opening their own restaurant. And it was going to happen right here on the beachfront in the sleepy but neat and affluent Pepillo Salcedo.

'Good luck,' said Fiona, clasping Roseline's hands in hers. 'With everything. Perhaps we can come and visit you and your restaurant when it's up and running.'

'I would like that,' said Roseline. 'And I am sure Ronil would too.'

'You could call it R&R,' suggested McGregor. 'Rest and relaxation. I reckon you both need a few years of that after the week you've had.'

'I will ask Ronil when he wakes,' she nodded with a smile. 'He might like that name.'

'Give him our best when he wakes up,' said Andrew. 'Hopefully, we'll see him again one day. Take care of yourselves.'

They left Roseline standing outside the hospital as they drove off in a taxi and headed for the small airstrip outside of town. The final leg of their nocturnal journey went from Pepillo Salcedo and southeast across the central Dominican Republic to the capital city of Santo Domingo, where they touched down at the international airport just as the rising sun began to light up the eastern skies. Once there, Andrew and Fiona bid farewell to McGregor who disappeared into the departure terminal, strolling along casually with his holdall slung over his shoulder as if he didn't have a care in the world and looking for all the world like someone returning from a calm and restorative holiday in one of the Dominican Republic's many picturesque and idyllic beach resorts.

'Right,' said Andrew as he turned to face Fiona. 'Now that that's all settled, we still have Captain Flynn's treasure to find. So, what do we do now?'

'Port Royal,' Fiona said. 'We go to Port Royal and see what's in those old maritime archives.'

Fifteen

The fire at Marcellus Solomon's mansion had finally been put out by his remaining guards, but some of the surrounding trees that had been sprayed with burning kerosene during the explosion of the fuel tank were still smouldering, sending dark tendrils of smoke up into the pale blue morning sky and telling the surrounding city what had happened. A large part of the mansion had been gutted by the fire, but it was nothing compared to the gaping hole of burning anger and resentment that the Haitian kingpin now felt as he brooded in his chair inside his shot-up office. He was hunched over and staring blankly into space with furious, bloodshot eyes and a clenched jaw.

Within a single evening, he appeared to have gone from being an untouchable crime boss freely wielding his power in Port-au-Prince, to a wounded animal whose hiding place had been ravaged by an enemy that he had completely underestimated. And this was partly because Lawrence Blake had failed to make sure he understood who Fiona had been travelling with. An unforgivable mistake. On top of that, the bloated corpse of Jaws was now lying in the foyer. Not that Marcellus thought that to be a great loss to anyone. The fat bastard was a bloviating buffoon as far as he was concerned, and with him now dead, Marcellus would be able to swoop in and take over his territory and drug smuggling business down south in Petit-Goave. But the violent death of Jaws at Marcellus' supposedly well-fortified and heavily guarded mansion was an ugly testament to the sudden apparent collapse of his power, and everyone in the capital city would know about it within a day. Marcellus was fuming. The humiliation was intolerable, and it simply could not be allowed to stand. It could not go unanswered.

Blake and the remaining two members of his security team were now standing outside in the driveway waiting for a transport to take them out of the estate. Before returning to his office and slumping into his chair, Marcellus had spoken to the treasure hunter, and the two of them had agreed to continue with the plan to let Andrew and Fiona lead them to the Spanish treasure. Through his connections in what was left of the corrupt Haitian government, Marcellus had managed to discover that the chopper carrying the attackers, which had taken off from Port-au-Prince's international airport, had landed in Santo Domingo in the Dominican Republic only a few hours earlier, where it still remained. Where it had been in the interim was unclear, but that was of no interest to Marcellus. What mattered to him and Blake was where it was going next, and according to the flight plan already logged with Santo Domingo air traffic control, it was soon to take off for Kingston in

Jamaica. It had not taken Blake long to work out precisely where Andrew and Fiona were planning to go, and he had seemed confident that the two of them were on track to find the treasure.

Once it had been located, the agreement was for Marcellus to have a free hand to kill them. But before that happened, he would make sure that they suffered. Perhaps he would make the SAS soldier watch as Fiona was cut into pieces. Or perhaps he would feed them to his pet crocodiles in the pond by the perimeter wall. Or perhaps he would simply set Angelique and Celestine loose on them and let the two blade aficionados do their worst.

However, after having contemplated the situation for a while, Marcellus made a different decision. He had no intention of keeping his word to Blake. The Englishman had essentially been the cause of this entire debacle, and Marcellus wanted Andrew and Fiona dead more than he wanted his cut of the treasure. And at any rate, as soon as they were both dead, he could simply put a gun to Blake's head and force him to find the treasure instead.

With the plan coming together in his mind, Marcellus finally looked up at his two murderously gorgeous female bodyguards, both of whom looked hungry for action and eager to please.

'I have decided,' he said slowly as he regarded them from under his brow. 'I want them dead. Find them. Kill them.'

The two acolytes nodded silently and glanced at each other with reptilian smiles in anticipation of what they were about to set out to do. Marcellus turned in his chair to reach for a pair of small wooden boxes, which he handed to the two women.

'These will make you strong,' he said.

Engraved into the lids of the boxes were simple geometric voodoo symbols designed to imbue the user with power over death. Inside them was a sticky, gloopy substance made from white pigment, cocaine and plant extracts. The two women took the boxes in their hands, knowing what they contained since they had used similar substances in the past during various voodoo rituals.

'But if you think they might escape,' said Marcellus, 'I want you to use this.'

He reached down to the side of his chair and picked up a leather satchel. Opening one of its small front pockets, he extracted a circular electronic device the size of a large, thick coin. He held it up for the two women to see and turned it around slowly in his hand. On one side was a magnetic metal disc, and from the other protruded a tiny metal spike.

'With this,' he said, 'they won't be able to get away.'

★   ★   ★

Before McGregor had said goodbye to Andrew and Fiona and left on a flight for London, he had handed over to Andrew all of the kit and equipment he had brought with him. In addition, his helicopter rental had been extended so that Andrew and Fiona could get to Port Royal without first having to secure passage on a commercial airliner. This would also allow them much more flexibility once there, and the best part was that Marcellus was paying for the rental, courtesy of the bundles of cash that Andrew had taken from the kingpin's office desk.

After grabbing a handful of hours of sleep in the specially designed pods inside the VIP terminal, and as the sun began to rise in the sky, the pair boarded the chopper. This time Andrew was at the controls since he had flown a whole raft of different aircraft in the past, both fixed-wing and rotary. The Airbus H135 covered the almost 700-kilometre distance back to the border and then across southern Haiti and the open Caribbean Sea to Jamaica in just under 3 hours.

They landed at Norman Manley International Airport, which was located on the artificially enlarged isthmus just across the bay from Kingston a few minutes after midday. Here, they rented a white Ford Ranger pickup truck and joined the highway that ran along the four-kilometre-long causeway to the small town of Harbour View. From there, they continued on to the sprawling capital of Jamaica, which covered a roughly ten by ten kilometre area on the south coast of the island. Bypassing the city centre with its waterfront hotels, central business district, extensive docks, wharves, and huge freeport area, they continued on through the capital to emerge on its western side. They then followed the highway to Spanish Town, whose centre lay nestled near forested hills about ten kilometres from the sea, just as it had done centuries earlier when it had been the main settlement on the island, founded by the Spanish as Santiago de la Vega in 1534. When the English conquered Jamaica in 1655, the town was badly damaged, and Port Royal then became a temporary administrative centre. However, when an earthquake devastated much of Port Royal in 1692, Spanish Town again became the main location for the colony's government administration, and that was why Andrew and Fiona had come.

'It must be just up ahead,' said Fiona, pointing out of the windscreen.

They were driving along one of Spanish Town's streets, which were all arranged in a grid that covered most of the settlement. Most of them were lined with old colonial buildings whose white, colonnaded facades gave a clear nod to that bygone period.

'This is King Street,' she continued. 'It should be up here on the corner.'

'Alright,' said Andrew as he reduced speed and peered ahead for a place to park.

In the end, they managed to find a spot in the shade under a large sycamore tree on Parade Square, which was located in the centre of the town. On the west side of the lawn-covered square was what had once been the Jamaica Colony's governor's mansion, and at its centre was a water feature that produced a calm trickling noise. As they stepped out of the pickup truck, the dry heat hit them like a sledgehammer after having spent just under an hour inside the cool, air-conditioned car. There were only a few cars and a couple of pedestrians around, most likely because the locals were inside having lunch and trying to avoid the midday heat.

'Crikey,' said Fiona, glancing at Andrew with a smile. 'Why don't we have weather like this at home?'

'It certainly beats London right now,' said Andrew as he closed the car door and pressed the lock button on the key fob. 'So, where are we going?'

'This way,' said Fiona, pointing across the street towards the colonnaded, crescent-shaped façade of a wide building that had a large statue placed inside a chapel-like pavilion with a domed roof.

As they approached, Andrew noticed that there were two heavily corroded bronze cannons placed just inside the fence and pointing out over the square. He looked up at the statue and was surprised to see that the man it depicted appeared to be wearing a Roman general's outfit.

'Who's that guy?' he said, gesturing at the statue. 'Strange clothes.'

Fiona peered at the statue's base, which had a marble plaque set into its side with text chiselled neatly into it.

'George Brydges Rodney,' she read, before lifting her eyebrows. 'Oh, I think I know who that was. He was a Royal Navy admiral in the late 18th century. Fought the French in a famous naval engagement near the Lesser Antilles. Apparently, it prevented a French and Spanish invasion of Jamaica. I think it was in 1782.'

'Right,' said Andrew as he shook his head with amusement and glanced at her affectionately. 'I see. How you find space for all that information inside that pretty head of yours, I will never understand.'

'I can't help it,' she replied with a good-natured shrug. 'Trust me. There are things in there I'd rather forget. Anyway, let's go and find what we came here for. It should be on the other side of this pavilion.'

They walked past the statue, turned the corner and continued a short distance along King Street until they came to the next corner. Here, there was a large polished brass plaque on a light orange brick building saying 'The Jamaica Archives & Records Department'.

'Here we are,' said Fiona happily. 'This is it. Let's just hope they haven't forgotten Emily's request. I checked with her earlier, and she said that they are expecting us.'

'Good,' said Andrew. 'Let's go inside and see what we can find.'

They entered the air-conditioned building through a set of glass double doors and proceeded across the polished marble floor of the foyer to a reception desk. Behind it sat a large woman wearing a black, full-length silk dress with a geometric red, green and yellow pattern as well as a yellow headwrap. Around her neck was a necklace with chunky faux pearls, and she had large earrings to match. As they approached, she looked up unhurriedly and lit up in a big friendly smile, exuding a sunny and unflappable disposition that immediately made them both feel welcome.

'Good afternoon,' she purred in a broad and cheerful Jamaican accent. 'My name is Martisha. How may I help you today?'

'Hello,' smiled Fiona. 'We have an appointment. My name is Fiona Keane, and this is Andrew. I have requested access to your archives through Emily Butler at the British Museum in London.'

'Fiona Keane,' said Martisha, nodding and glancing down at a notepad, after which she looked up at the two visitors. 'Certainly. I have your details here. I have been corresponding with Ms Butler. Everything is in order. And welcome to Jamaica.'

'Thanks,' said Fiona. 'Nice climate you have here. And Spanish Town is very pretty.'

'Yes,' chuckled Martisha. 'I think it is too hot here, but I guess you can't have everything. Let me take you down to the archives. Please follow me.'

The large lady got up from her chair and walked slowly out from behind the reception desk and continued to a doorway beyond which was a corridor. At the end of the corridor was a metal door which she unlocked with a key and opened. They descended two flights of stairs inside a concrete stairwell and emerged into a large, high-ceilinged underground space with several separate sections divided by movable screens. Overhead, plastic fluorescent lamps cast a pale light across the expansive archive room, and the worn and scuffed linoleum floor looked like it might have been put down many decades ago. Along the walls and arranged into two rows in the centre of the room were various types of metal storage units containing thousands of official documents and records.

'Now,' said Martisha over her shoulder as she ambled along. 'As you know, we only have original paper archives here, so I must ask you to be extremely careful with the documents. We have applied for funding to have them scanned and digitised, but we are still waiting.'

'Of course,' nodded Fiona. 'We will be as gentle as possible.'

'Alright,' said Martisha as they reached a large wall-mounted storage cabinet with drawers about half a metre tall and almost two metres wide. 'Here we are. Let me find the relevant documents for you.'

Martisha pulled out one of the drawers and began leafing through the contents of its vertically hung binders. After a few moments, she had extracted three of them and carried them leisurely to a long wooden table nearby. They were each several inches thick, and they looked to be heavy.

'These are the Maritime Archives of Port Royal from the entire 17th and 18th centuries,' said Martisha. 'They contain all records of ships docking in the harbour there during that period. As you requested.'

'That's great,' said Fiona. 'Thank you very much.'

'Now, please wear these,' said Martisha, handing Fiona a pair of thin, white fabric gloves. 'To make sure we protect the documents.'

'Of course,' said Fiona, donning the gloves and sitting down on one of the tall stools next to the table. 'I will be very careful.'

'OK,' nodded Martisha, gesturing to a PC sitting on a nearby table. 'There's a computer over there with an index of our entire collection in case you want to use it. It is also connected to the internet. How long do you think you'll need here?'

'I'm not sure,' said Fiona uncertainly as she glanced at Andrew. 'Maybe an hour? Perhaps a bit more?'

'That's fine,' said Martisha. 'I will leave you to it and come back in an hour to see how you are doing. Alright?'

'Perfect,' said Fiona. 'Thanks again.'

With that, Martisha left the two visitors to pore over the many old and delicate documents from Port Royal. Fiona took the first binder reverently in her hands and placed it in front of herself. She opened it carefully and began gently leafing through the delicate, yellowed documents one by one and placing them in a neat pile next to herself once she had determined whether it contained any information related to the Marauder. Once done, she proceeded to do the same with the next binder. It took her less than half an hour to find all the entries for the pirate frigate. She copied all the entries onto a notepad, and very soon a pattern began to emerge.

'Look at this,' she said, turning to Andrew who had been sitting next to her and watching her work. 'For several years during the very early 1700s, the Marauder was a privateer ship operating out of Port Royal. And every time she returned to dock in the harbour, it was logged here in these documents. And in each instance, Jack Flynn was listed as her captain.'

'So that all fits with what we already know,' said Andrew.

'Yes,' nodded Fiona. 'But the last entry was in March of 1709, after which there is no trace of the Marauder anywhere in these pages. In other words, she never returned to Port Royal after that, which means that Captain Flynn turned to piracy at that time and so was never allowed to enter the port again.'

'Right,' said Andrew. 'So Flynn ended up as *persona non grata* at that point.'

'Exactly,' said Fiona. 'No doubt to be apprehended and hanged if he was ever caught. Now, in all of my research, I have never been able to discover what he did or where he was based after 1709, but it is likely that he would have used either Tortuga, Petite-Goave or Nassau as his base of operations. The only firm lead we have is the explosion in Tortuga. But anyway, there's another very interesting detail in these documents.'

'What?' said Andrew, leaning in to peer closely at the century-old handwritten pages.

'This man,' said Fiona, pointing to a name on her notepad that kept showing up, and then to an example of the name written in one of the original harbour records from Port Royal.

'Elijah Frasier,' Andrew read, glancing at Fiona. 'Who was he?'

'From these documents,' said Fiona, 'it appears that Frasier was Flynn's bookkeeper, and in every instance when the Marauder was docked in Port Royal, his name was always noted as the person liaising with the local harbour master.'

'But where does that get us?' said Andrew.

'Well, it means that he was serving with Flynn in a trusted position for a very long time,' said Fiona. 'And so there is at least a chance that we might be able to find out more about him and possibly also Captain Flynn.'

Fiona got up and went over to the PC where she sat down and began navigating the various menus in the archive's computer system. After a few moments, she opened a web browser and logged into her account at the British Museum. This then gave her access to a much more comprehensive research portal with options for retrieving digitised documents from all the British research archives. Within a few minutes, she had found something.

'Bingo,' she declared, glancing excitedly at Andrew. 'Look what I've discovered.'

Andrew had been studying the almost 500-year-old documents and marvelling at the fact that those very pages in front of him had once been inked with a quill just a few miles away by successive harbourmasters to whom the modern world would have appeared utterly baffling and incomprehensible.

'What have you got?' he asked as he came over to join her.

'Elijah Frasier,' said Fiona, pointing to the screen with a contented smile. 'He's listed here in the research database as the bookkeeper aboard the privateer ship the Marauder. But guess what he did later?'

'Later?' said Andrew, looking puzzled. 'I thought that all of the Marauder's crew died in the explosion at Tortuga?'

'Apparently not,' said Fiona with a small shake of the head, gesturing to the computer screen. 'Because Elijah Frasier ended up writing his own memoirs several decades later. And they're right here.'

Andrew peered at the screen to see digital scans of a large number of old handwritten pages, some of which were missing small bits of paper but which appeared mostly intact and legible.

'Wow,' he said. 'That's amazing. The wonders of modern technology. Can we get a copy of those?'

'I can send one to my own email account,' said Fiona, clicking a few buttons on the interface. 'There's also a typed-up transcript if you prefer that. I think I like the original.'

'Let's get both,' said Andrew. 'Just in case there are small discrepancies between them that we need to be aware of.'

'Good plan,' said Fiona as she clicked a few times with the mouse to make the transfer happen. 'Done. This should be interesting. Let's get out of here.'

* * *

The Marriott Hotel in Port-au-Prince was a small and almost surreal oasis of civilisation and calm in the otherwise chaotic and often dangerous Haitian capital. The white 12-storey building with some two hundred rooms was located on Avenue Jean-Paul II in the relatively affluent and therefore well-protected Bois Patate district, some six kilometres southwest of the international airport. In the leafy neighbourhood that surrounded the hotel were various United Nations missions, embassies and consulates, and there was a heavy presence of both local police and heavily armed private security personnel on the streets and stationed in front of most major buildings housing offices and businesses.

Lawrence Blake was sitting in a comfortable wicker chair by the swimming pool where a pair of Caucasian women wearing brightly coloured swimsuits were doing lengths under the hot sun. The occasional faint cracks of distant gunfire did not appear to faze them in the slightest as they enjoyed their day in surroundings that most local Haitians could barely even imagine, much less dream of ever experiencing for themselves.

Wearing his signature white shirt with an open collar, beige slacks and walking boots, Blake was sipping a sugary cocktail and reflecting on the violent events of the previous night. And despite the chaos, the death, the explosion and the gunfire, he found himself oddly calm and content. If there was such a thing as being gun-shy, Blake had long since discovered that he was the opposite of that. He had felt no fear during the firefight, although he had sensibly hidden and stayed out of the way of flying bullets, but what he had experienced was more akin to excitement than anything else. Being in close proximity to lethal danger was exhilarating, and he felt more alive now sitting by the pool and contemplating last night's incident than he ever did at home in London, where he was back to being Marcus Tobin.

He glanced over at the two women in the pool, and as one of them finished her length, slipped her toned arms up onto the edge of the pool and panted slightly, she shot him a smile, which he returned, giving a tip of an imaginary hat. Enjoying the attention, her smile widened and her eyes lingered on him for a moment, and then she slipped back into the water and resumed her leisurely swim.

At that moment, Antonio Ortega emerged from the main hotel building with Delgado at his side. The two men were wearing tan combat trousers and white t-shirts, and they both carried a grim expression as they walked towards where Blake was sitting. Ortega in particular appeared to have a dark, menacing shadow across his face. Blake knew what was coming, and he had already anticipated the talk they were about to have and how to deal with it.

'Señor Blake,' said Ortega as he lowered his tall, muscular frame into the chair opposite the treasure hunter, and Delgado sat down beside him. 'I want to show you something.'

'Alright,' said Blake calmly, taking another sip and placing the cocktail back on the table in front of him. 'What is it?'

Ortega fished a phone protected by a metal hard case out of one of the pockets of his trousers and placed it on the table. He tapped and swiped a few times and then spun it around and pushed it across for Blake to see. The Englishman leaned forward and found himself having to make an effort not to turn away from the image displayed on the phone screen. It showed a middle-aged man wearing a suit and tie lying on the concrete floor inside a parking garage. He was on his back, and there were four neat bullet holes in his white blood-soaked shirt, and a pool of dark blood had spread out from his body.

Blake glanced up at Ortega, but the Spaniard ignored the dubious look he gave him and instead swiped once on the phone screen to show another picture. It showed another dead man. He appeared to be lying on a neatly trimmed lawn with a terrace and a large house in the background, although the latter two were slightly out of focus. However, the thing that attracted Blake's attention and revulsion was the man's head, or rather, the fact that he barely had one. A large part of his face was missing, and most of his bloody and mangled skull appeared to have been removed, possibly as a result of a powerful shotgun blast. It was a truly gruesome sight, but Ortega remained impassive as he swiped again. This time, the phone screen displayed a photo of another man who appeared to be wearing jeans and a t-shirt, although it was difficult to tell from the blood and the dirt as well as the fact that the unfortunate individual was hanging upside down by his ankles with his arms flopped down towards the ground. Worse than that, however, was the fact that there was a gaping hole right through him where his chest and stomach should have been. From the angle the photo had been taken, it was possible to see straight through his corpse, and what was left of him was soaked in blood, guts and every other conceivable bodily fluid.

Ortega swiped once more, and Blake just caught sight of someone sitting decapitated in a chair when he finally decided that he had had enough of this display of abject barbarism.

'Alright,' he said with mild irritation as he leaned back and regarded the expressionless Ortega. 'What the hell is this supposed to be? The hitman top 10 for the year? Why are you showing me this?'

Ortega glanced up at Blake with a dark look, then he clenched his jaw for a moment before switching off the phone and putting it back inside his pocket.

'These men,' he said in a husky voice as his steely eyes looked straight at Blake. 'I killed them.'

'Wonderful,' said Blake sardonically. 'Well done. And very thoroughly too, by the looks of it. What does that have to do with me?'

'I killed them,' continued Ortega as if Blake had not spoken at all, 'because they killed my friends. Someone kills my friend, I find them, and I kill them. All of them.'

'Right,' said Blake, giving a faint nod and making an effort to look like he understood. 'Revenge, I take it?'

'Justice,' said Ortega. 'An eye for an eye.'

'Well, I'm not much of a religious person myself,' said Blake, 'but I think I know where this is going. This is about your friend Ignacio Gomez, am I right?'

'*Si*,' said Ortega coldly, leaning back in his chair and regarding Blake. 'It is about justice for Ignacio.'

'And you want to get your hands on the men who killed him,' Blake observed.

'*Si*,' Ortega repeated. 'The *hijo de puta*, his *amigo* and the woman.'

'I do understand,' said Blake reasonably, yet also with a small hint of aloofness, 'and you will have your chance once we have located the treasure. But only then. Is that clear? We can't jeopardise finding the treasure for some personal vendetta, much as I appreciate that you want this very badly. But I promise you, once the mission is complete, you can do whatever you want to both Fiona and her man Andrew. In fact, you'd be doing me a huge favour if you got rid of the girl. She's going to be a bit of a thorn in my side if she isn't removed, so please do make sure that she never returns to the UK. But only after the treasure has been found and Count de Toledo has received his share. Alright?'

At the mention of the Spanish count, who was in effect the Spaniard's real paymaster, Ortega seemed to contemplate the situation once more, and after a few moments, he finally nodded.

'Deal,' he nodded, somewhat reluctantly. 'We will wait.'

'Excellent,' Blake smiled magnanimously as he spread out his arms. 'Now, why don't you chaps get ready to move out? The car will be here in half an hour. I already know where our two friends are. In short order, I will be able to find out what they have discovered. And as soon as they make their next move, we need to get into the air. So be ready.'

Sixteen

From the computer in the basement under the archives building, Fiona had sent the digitised memoirs of Elijah Frasier to her own email account, and fifteen minutes later, she and Andrew had bid farewell to Martisha and were sitting on a bench near their pickup truck on Parade Square. The pretty and tranquil square had a number of tall palm trees spaced equidistantly from the water feature, which gave the place an exotic and undeniably tropical feel. The bench was in the shade under one of the trees, and the frond-shaped shadows danced gently on the ground where they sat as they began to pore over Frasier's memoirs written more than three centuries earlier.

After a while, Andrew left Fiona to continue reading while he walked to a small convenience store a couple of hundred metres along Adelaide Street, which cut west through the centre of the original parts of Spanish Town. Roughly half an hour later, he was back with sandwiches and two cold soft drinks.

'These memoirs are amazing,' said Fiona when he returned, sat down next to her and dug into the brown paper bag for the food and drink. 'The entries are fairly brief for this sort of thing, but there are some extremely interesting sections in here. It turns out that Elijah Frasier was not onboard the Marauder on the night of the explosion.'

'Well, that certainly explains how he survived,' said Andrew, popping open the soft drink cans.

'Exactly,' said Fiona, and then she began reading her own notes on the bookkeeper's century-old chronicle. 'Frasier spends a good deal of his memoirs talking about his time aboard the Marauder with Captain Flynn, and it is all pretty standard stuff. He describes a long period of years when the vessel was a privateer ship and Flynn was a respected captain. Then followed a handful of years after Flynn had turned to piracy. Frasier was apparently a willing participant in this transformation, and it seems as if he was paid several full shares after the taking of every prize, and that would have made him a man of decent means. He also describes how he and most of the crew were waiting aboard the Marauder that night when Flynn and a small group of his men hijacked El Castillo Negro in Port Royal's harbour. But it is all pretty vague, and he mentions how he and everyone else were sworn to secrecy about what happened to the galleon and her treasure after that.'

'That's a shame,' said Andrew. 'So this is a dead end?'

'Not quite,' said Fiona, 'because it seems that Frasier couldn't resist providing a hint, possibly to stroke his own ego at having participated in this very famous heist.'

'What did he say?' Andrew said, biting into his sandwich.

'There's really nothing very specific,' said Fiona, 'except that he alludes to the treasure being hidden on something that he calls Lizard Island. But there is no such place in the Caribbean. I checked. And he says that it was buried in what he refers to as the Cave of Skulls.'

'Well, those sound exactly like names a pirate would come up with,' said Andrew dubiously.

'I agree,' said Fiona. 'Especially in memoirs where Frasier might be trying to make himself sound like some swashbuckling adventurer.'

'So, how do we even know that this isn't just an elaborate fabrication designed to send treasure hunters down the wrong path?' said Andrew. 'That's what I would do if I were trying to keep something like that hidden.'

'Well, we don't,' conceded Fiona reluctantly. 'But at the moment, this is all we have to go on. And if Frasier really wanted to keep the whole thing under wraps and reveal nothing about the location of the treasure, then why even write anything in here about it? I think he just couldn't help himself, and this might actually be a true account. But unfortunately, it leads us nowhere if there isn't actually a place called Lizard Island. And apparently there isn't.'

'What else does he write?' said Andrew, handing Fiona the other sandwich.

'The next thing in here is the account of the explosion in September of 1714,' said Fiona. 'This is what he says about it. Let me read this passage to you.'

Having thus made our way to Tortuga, little did we know that this would be the end of our adventures with Captain Flynn and the end of the Marauder. I do not remember the precise date, but very late during a September evening, mere weeks after capturing The Black Galleon, Flynn had ordered all hands back to the ship at midnight. I too was in Tortuga town with the men, but I am ashamed to say that I was distracted by a most beguiling whore named Betty at a local bawdy house, and so I entirely lost track of time. When I realised my mistake, I flung on my clothes and ran to the harbour. However, just as I set foot on the jetty and was headed for the last remaining yawl to row out to the Marauder, the proud ship was consumed by a ferocious blast that tore the vessel apart. I knew then that no one could have survived, and I thanked the gods for sparing me, and Betty for keeping me from returning to the ship any earlier that night.

'Saved by a visit to a brothel,' said Andrew with a chuckle. 'Amazing. But it all seems to jibe with what that French merchant Eduard Leroux wrote.'

'Yes,' nodded Fiona. 'Quite the narrow escape, by the sounds of things.'

'What happened next?' said Andrew. 'I guess that must have been the end of Frasier's pirating days.'

'Yes, it was,' said Fiona. 'It seems that he eventually made his way back to Port Royal, where he somehow managed to become a respectable citizen working as an accountant for a local trading house.

Maybe he bribed some officials to ignore his past. Anyway, he had Betty brought down from Tortuga and married her. And then he settled in the town and continued working there until he retired some twenty years later.'

'Right,' said Andrew pensively, taking a swig of his drink. 'Interesting. But I'm not sure that brings us any closer to the location of the treasure.'

'Well,' said Fiona, raising an index finger and consulting her notes once again. 'This is where a really fascinating clue appears in these memoirs. The rest of the text holds little of value for us since it deals mainly with his very comfortable but ordinary life in Port Royal, but there is one section that sent a shiver down my spine when I read it.'

'Let's hear it,' said Andrew.

'Ok,' said Fiona. 'Listen to this. This next bit is remarkable.'

Some years later, during the summer of the year of our Lord 1724, having put my seafaring days firmly behind me and become at peace with being a landlubber no longer on the open seas, I one day suddenly found myself face to face with someone I never thought I would see again.

I was on my way home from the offices of my employer in Port Royal when I decided to take a stroll along the harbour to look at the ships and reminisce about my younger years. As I passed the third jetty and looked out towards a merchantman that had come into port from Nassau, I saw a sight so strange and bizarre that I thought I must be dreaming, and it left me frozen to the spot and feeling utterly numb as I watched from behind some wooden crates. Walking along the jetty towards the town wearing the clothes of a vicar, I saw none other than Captain Jack Flynn. He had the same strong physical presence, the same gait and the same face, except that it appeared to have been badly burnt on the left side. And yet, I struggled to make sense of it. It could not possibly be him. He and everyone on the Marauder had died years before in Tortuga. I had seen it with my own eyes. Nothing but dead and mutilated bodies of sailors had washed up in the shallow waters of the bay.

From my hiding place behind the crates, I watched as the clergyman approached and walked right past me, taking no notice of me as I stood there, and the resemblance was so strong that I felt the urge to step forward and greet him. However, for some reason, I found myself unable to move and remained where I was, and I soon convinced myself that the man was not Captain Flynn. It simply could not be true. For a long time thereafter, I questioned my own sanity, and on occasion, I wondered if I had imagined the whole thing.

However, a few months later, unable to forget my encounter on the docks, I sought out a friend in the Admiralty Records of Port Royal. He was able to deliver to me a copy of the list of pirates who had taken the King's Pardon and surrendered to His Majesty's Navy in Nassau in 1718. To my astonishment, amongst more than two hundred other names was that of my old captain. Jack Flynn.

These events are now many years in the past, but I still remember them as if they happened yesterday. However, to this day, I cannot fathom how Flynn could have survived the demise of the Marauder, much less how he ended up a vicar. But I am now old and have no desire to seek out the answers to those questions, or indeed to seek out the man himself in Nassau. Some things are best left in the past.

'Wow,' said Andrew. 'That's quite a story.'

'Amazing, isn't it?' smiled Fiona, glancing up at him. 'Frasier believed that he actually saw Captain Flynn come into Port Royal from Nassau about ten years later, dressed as a vicar.'

'He might have been in disguise,' said Andrew. 'Or perhaps he really did become a clergyman.'

'I suppose it's possible,' said Fiona. 'And now that I think about it, I have an idea for how to find this out.'

'How?' said Andrew.

'The British Admiralty is famous for its extensive recordkeeping,' said Fiona. 'Virtually everything that has ever happened on any ship flying its colours was recorded and kept for posterity. All of it has now been digitised and is stored in their research databases. I could access them and find out if Flynn really did take the King's Pardon, as Frasier says he did.'

'What exactly was this King's Pardon?' said Andrew.

'It was a royal proclamation issued by King George I in September of 1717,' said Fiona. 'At this point, because of the decline of Tortuga and then of Port Royal as pirate havens, Nassau had become the main base from which pirates operated. This was towards the end of the Golden Age of Piracy. The time of Blackbeard, Jack Rackham and Charles Vane, as well as a couple of famous female pirates. Piracy had become such a nuisance for merchant ships in the Bahamas and along the Eastern Seaboard and the American colonies there that the king had finally had enough. So, he issued the so-called 'Act of Grace'. Let me just find it for you.'

She quickly accessed a research database and typed the name into it, and a few seconds later, a text document appeared.

'Here we are,' she said, scrolling through the text. 'It was titled "A Proclamation for the Suppressing of Pyrates", and it was issued at Hampton Court and published in the London Gazette on the 5th of September, 1717. Let me just read you the relevant bits.'

Pyrates shall on or before the 5th of September in the year of our Lord 1718, surrender him or themselves to one of our Principal Secretaries of State in Great Britain or Ireland, or to any Governor or Deputy Governor of any of our Plantations beyond the Seas. Every such Pyrate and Pyrates so surrendering him or themselves as aforesaid, shall have our gracious Pardon of and for such his or their Pyracy or Piracies by him or them committed, before the fifth of January next ensuing. And we do hereby strictly charge and command all our Admirals, Captains, and other Officers at Sea, and all our Governors and Commanders of any Forts, Castles, or other Places in our Plantations, and all other our Officers Civil and Military, to seize and take such of the Pyrates who shall refuse or neglect to surrender themselves accordingly.

'I think I got most of that,' said Andrew. 'It sounds very stiff and legalistic.'

'Yes, I suppose it comes across as a bit clunky by today's standards,' said Fiona. 'But the meaning is clear enough. King George I offered a one-time deal for the pirates. Surrender themselves and be pardoned within the next year, or be hunted down by the Crown, most likely to be imprisoned or hanged. And later in the proclamation, the king actually orders the treasury to pay out specific rewards for anyone apprehending pirates after that year has expired. £100 for pirate captains. £40 for lieutenants, masters, boatswains, carpenters and gunners. £30 for lesser officers and £20 for regular sailors on pirate ships.'

'Those were huge amounts of money in those days,' said Andrew. 'They really meant it. With rewards like that, anyone not surrendering would have had the entire Caribbean looking for them to try to claim the reward.'

'Very much so,' said Fiona. 'It was hoped that the combination of the pardon and the promised rewards would be enough to finally rid the colonies of piracy once and for all. And it essentially worked. Hundreds of pirates surrendered, and only a handful refused, most notably Blackbeard, Rackham and Vane. And as a result, Nassau came back under the control of the Crown. So, it was basically a huge success. Anyway, let me just see if I can access the list of surrendering pirates in Nassau.'

Her thumbs flew across the phone screen, tapping and typing in a blur of motion, and soon after, she inched closer to Andrew to allow him to see.

'Here we go,' she said. 'Look at this. This is the entire list of pirates surrendering in Nassau during the year following the 5th of September, 1717. And look at the entry down here. March 8th, 1718.'

Fiona pointed at one of the names, and Andrew leaned forward to peer at it.

'Jack Flynn,' said Andrew, leaning back and looking at her. 'Holy crap. So Frasier was right. Flynn really did take the pardon. And then he became a vicar in Nassau?'

'Give me a second,' Fiona said.

She continued her tapping and swiping, and after a couple of minutes, her eyes narrowed and she produced a cautious smile.

'I think I might have something,' she said. 'I managed to access some of the records kept by the Diocese of Nassau, and they list a Reverend Flynn as having served as the local vicar at a church called Trinity Chapel from June 1721 until his death in December 1747.'

'Wow,' said Andrew. 'That's fascinating.'

'And it looks like the good reverend was buried in the church cemetery,' Fiona added.

'Where is this place exactly?' said Andrew.

'The chapel was located on Mount Royal Avenue in downtown Nassau,' said Fiona.

'Is it still there?' said Andrew.

'It looks like it,' said Fiona. 'Its address is listed here on the diocese's website.'

Having been hunched over and looking at the small phone screen, the two of them sat up, leaned back on the bench and looked at each other for a long moment before Fiona finally spoke.

'Are you thinking what I am thinking?' she said.

'Yup,' nodded Andrew. 'We need to pay a visit to Trinity Chapel in Nassau and find out who this Reverend Flynn really was.'

Seventeen

When Andrew and Fiona climbed back up into the cab of the pickup truck, it was late afternoon, and the sun was inching lower in the western skies beyond the distant hills of Jamaica's forested interior. The temperature outside was now pleasant as opposed to oppressive, and instead of running the car's aircon, they rolled down the windows and allowed the balmy air to flow inside and cool them down the old-fashioned way.

'Since we're here,' said Fiona, turning her head to look at Andrew as the wind played with her hair. 'We should drive over to Port Royal.'

'Sure,' said Andrew. 'I think it's about another eight kilometres further along the isthmus from the airport.'

'I'd really like to visit there and see Fort Charles for myself,' said Fiona. 'Apparently, the gun batteries and the walls are mostly intact.'

'Sounds good,' said Andrew. 'I guess we're in no rush to get to Nassau just yet.'

They headed out of Spanish Town and followed the highway back the way they had come through Kingston and Harbour View, and then they continued on past the international airport and along the isthmus towards Port Royal. The causeway leading out to what had once been the main hub for privateers and pirates in the Caribbean curved its way left and right for several kilometres, and being as little as a hundred metres across in some places, it afforded views north across the water to Kingston on one side and the open ocean to the south on the other.

As they reached the end of the causeway and entered Port Royal, they passed a small cruise ship port on their right-hand side and soon found themselves in the middle of what appeared to be a small coastal village. The houses were basic one-storey structures built mainly of wood, and many of them had a somewhat worn and tired look about them. As they drove through it, it became clear that unlike during its heyday when it had been one of the wealthiest towns in the whole of the Caribbean, it was now a fairly down-at-heel settlement with only a tiny population and very little going for it except for a small fishing harbour. They continued west through the modest town and passed a redbrick portal that appeared to once have been part of the outer perimeter walls of the Fort Charles complex, and then Fiona suddenly pointed ahead out of the windscreen.

'There it is,' she said excitedly. 'Wow. Look at that.'

Partly hidden by a clump of trees beside the narrow road, the roughly five-metre-tall redbrick walls of the fort came into view. Spaced roughly every ten metres there were gunports with the muzzles of large bronze cannons sticking out of them.

'This looks interesting,' said Andrew. 'Let's park up and get out.'

He pulled into a small gravel carpark and came to a stop, turning off the pickup truck's engine and pulling the handbrake. Looking out to one side, his eye caught a sign reading 'HMJS Cagway', behind which were a couple of buildings and a large parking lot.

'There's a Jamaican coast guard base right here,' he said, surprised.

'So there is,' said Fiona, peering past the buildings to see a pier where a small coastguard patrol boat was moored. 'It's nice to see that the maritime legacy of this place hasn't completely disappeared. And check out the name Cagway on that sign.'

'Who or what was Cagway?' said Andrew.

'Cagway,' said Fiona, 'is a corruption of the word *Caguaya*. It was the original native Taino word for this place. It means 'reef'. So when the first Spanish settlers arrived, they called it Punta Caguaya, and after the British invasion of Jamaica in 1655, it was renamed Point Cagway and then later renamed again to Port Royal.'

'What's in a name, huh?' said Andrew musingly, looking at the sign and then at Fiona.

'Yes,' she smiled. 'Names can offer great clues to the history of a place. Anyway, come on. Let's get out and have a look around.'

They stepped out of the car and walked along one of the fort's exterior walls for about thirty metres. The muzzles of the many bronze cannons sticking out of the gunports were as large as a grown man's head, and it hinted at the firepower this place had once been able to put to bear on threats from the ocean.

The main walls of the fort met at corners that appeared to alternate between obtuse and acute angles, and the entire layout appeared irregular, but it ensured that there were cannons pointing in all directions. Coming to the end of a section of wall, the two of them walked past a couple of mobile metal barriers that had been erected ineffectually across the gravel footpath leading up to the fort's main entrance.

'Oh, no,' said Fiona disappointedly, frowning as she gazed at the gates up ahead. 'It looks like it's closed for today.'

'I wonder why,' said Andrew. 'Maybe it is some sort of public holiday here.'

'Damn it,' sighed Fiona. 'I was really looking forward to this.'

'Well,' said Andrew, glancing around and noting that there was not a single human being anywhere in sight. 'There are ways around problems like this.'

Fiona glanced dubiously at him.

'Are you proposing we break in?' she said, her eyes narrowing slightly.

'No, we're not breaking in, as such,' said Andrew. 'We're just hopping over the walls and having a quick look. No harm done.'

Fiona looked at him for a brief moment, and then she glanced towards the fort. After a couple of seconds, she gave a nod and a shrug.

'Alright, fine,' she said. 'Let's just do it. It's not like we're going to break anything.'

A couple of minutes later, they had found the main entrance and realised that anyone could easily climb in through one of the adjacent gunports and enter the site, so that's what they did. Walking to the centre of the large courtyard on the other side, they stopped and looked around. There were high walls with ramparts and cannons on all sides, and at one end of the courtyard were a couple of whitewashed two-story buildings with grey slate roofs where the fort's administration might once have been. Fiona walked over to a nearby placard that had been mounted on a wall.

'104 cannons and 500 soldiers,' she said. 'That was the typical contingent here at the time. Quite a force.'

'Enough to keep the Spanish away, I guess,' said Andrew. 'Can we get inside there?'

Fiona walked over to one of the buildings and tried the door handle. To her surprise, it turned out to be open, and the two of them headed inside to look around. The interior had been fitted out as a living museum of what it looked like centuries ago when the fort had been part of Port Royal's defences. There were sleeping quarters with bunks for regular soldiers, storage rooms and administrative offices, as well as several fully furnished and much more luxurious and comfortable officers' rooms complete with large beds, wood panelling and paintings.

'Let's head up onto the walls,' said Andrew. 'I'd like to know what you can see from up there.'

They exited the main administrative building and walked up a set of steps to the top rampart, where parapets allowed for yet more cannons to point out across the harbour to the west as well as straight towards the headland to the south where the harbour met the open sea beyond the reefs.

'Amazing, isn't it,' said Fiona as she shielded her eyes from the sun and looked west across the harbour. 'Three hundred years ago, out there in that harbour, the Black Galleon lay anchored. And then Jack Flynn and his band of cutthroats turned up and simply stole her right from under the guns of this fort. Even standing here, it's hard to imagine that this actually happened.'

'And all that gold and silver just sailed right out of this harbour,' said Andrew, following her gaze, 'never to be seen again.'

'Hopefully, we can find something in Nassau that will help us,' said Fiona. 'Anyway, I spotted the restrooms down there, so I am going to go down and fill up my water bottle.'

'Alright,' said Andrew, sitting down inside one of the parapets and taking in the unobstructed view of the harbour, the azure blue Caribbean and the handful of small reefs just south of the Port Royal isthmus. 'I'll wait here.'

Fiona walked down the two sets of steps from the rampart and once again crossed the courtyard to the main administrative building. Following the sign on the exterior wall, she turned a corner and saw the open doorway to the restrooms, which were located in a smaller, separate building towards the far end of the fort's interior near the northern wall. She proceeded inside and began filling up her water bottle from the tap when, out of the corner of her eye, she saw a shadow move across the floor by the doorway. Puzzled, since she had neither seen nor heard anyone else inside the fort since their arrival, she turned her head to look and listen, and then she called out as her bottle became full and began to overflow.

'Andrew?' she said. 'Is that you?'

There was no reply as the shadow of what appeared to be a tall and lean person took form on the floor of the restroom. This was not Andrew. This was a female. But who?

The answer came almost immediately as a figure passed through the doorway and emerged into the small restroom. It was a young Caribbean woman with a body like an athlete and a face like a supermodel, but her eyes burned with malice, and as she stopped and regarded Fiona, a malevolent smile slowly spread across her face. For a brief moment, Fiona stood nailed to the ground, stunned by the unnerving apparition, and only then did it occur to her where she had seen the woman before. This was one of the two female companions she had observed on the drone feed at Marcellus' mansion.

As if this sight wasn't disturbing enough, what really unsettled Fiona was the woman's face paint. It appeared that she had smeared some sort of sticky, white substance over her face in a pattern that gave the vague appearance of a human skull, and Fiona was immediately reminded of the oil painting hanging in Marcellus' throne room depicting the disturbing Baron Samedi. Whatever the face paint meant, it clearly had something to do with voodoo, and it made the spectre of the woman even more intimidating.

'Hello, Fiona,' she said with a heavy accent, her voice like a whisper in the dark. 'Nice to see you again.'

'How the hell…' began Fiona nervously, but then she realised that Blake had probably told the woman everything about her, including her name. 'Get away from me.'

'No,' said Angelique as she shook her head with faux regret and extracted a long, thin knife from a sheath that appeared to have been hidden in the small of her back. 'You are not getting away this time.'

Fiona felt the blood drain from her face and her entire body break out in a cold sweat, and she was about to scream for Andrew when she remembered that she still had the compact SIG Sauer P365 pistol in the small handbag that was slung over her shoulder. Without hesitating, she reached inside the bag, pulled out the weapon and brought it up.

'I said,' she repeated, this time with a hard edge to her voice. 'Get the hell away from me, or I will shoot.'

Angelique didn't move or show any sign of fear despite the loaded weapon being pointed at her, and as she stood there breathing with an unnatural tightness and intensity, her smile began to morph disturbingly into a crazed grin. Only then did Fiona notice her eyes, and then it all made sense. Her pupils were dilated to the point where she appeared to have no irises at all, instead showing only two shining pools of pitch black that were staring straight at her intended victim. It was clear that she was so high on cocaine that Fiona could have pointed an artillery piece in her direction, and she still wouldn't have budged an inch.

'Last chance,' attempted Fiona feebly with a trembling voice, even though she knew it was pointless. 'Move and let me out, or I pull the trigger.'

Fiona had barely finished her sentence before the diabolically gorgeous woman suddenly launched herself forward with a shriek, her thin but razor-sharp blade scything through the air towards Fiona's neck. Fiona instinctively pulled back her head, and as the knife sliced through the air less than an inch from her throat, her index finger flexed involuntarily, and the gun went off. Inside the small, tiled restroom, it sounded like a hand grenade going off, and Fiona felt the gun kick in her hand as the recoil travelled up her lower arm.

The bullet left the barrel at just under the speed of sound, smacked into Angelique's lower left torso, punched through a rib and exited out the other side. It then slammed into one of the white tiles behind her, breaking as the mangled bullet hit it, and an instant later a small spray of blood slapped across its cracked face.

Somehow, Angelique seemed to take no notice, and her momentum carried her forward until she barged into Fiona, and the two of them fell onto the floor. Fiona screamed and tried frantically to wriggle free from under the crazed assassin, but she was unable to shift the woman's weight. Angelique raised the knife above her head to plunge it down into Fiona's head, but before she could deal the killer blow, Fiona managed to bring the pistol around in front of herself and fire a panicked and badly aimed shot at her would-be killer's head. This time, the bullet grazed the drug-crazed woman's left chin, carving a deep, bloody trail across it, and then it ripped through her earlobe, tearing most of it off in a mist of red.

Angelique screamed in fury and shock at the way her target was fighting back and inflicting pain on her, and she involuntarily gripped the left side of her head as she fell back against the wall with a furious scream.

Wasting no time, Fiona immediately jumped to her feet and bolted for the doorway, thinking only of putting as much distance between herself and Marcellus's assassin as possible. As she ran into the courtyard, she saw Andrew sprinting towards her, gripping his SD9 pistol, and only then did she suddenly wonder where the second of the two virtually identical supermodels was.

A split second later, the answer came in the form of a hail of bullets being sprayed from behind the corner of one of the administrative buildings, and Fiona felt projectiles zip through the air unnervingly close to her. She was no gun expert, but it sounded to her like some sort of fully automatic weapon. Realising instinctively that if she stopped, she would be dead, Fiona ran even faster towards Andrew, and she watched as he reacted almost immediately to the incoming fire. He came to a halt, entered into a low combat stance, raised his weapon and fired a volley of four or five shots towards what Fiona could now see was the second of Marcellus' two female assassins. The woman was leaning out from cover and appeared to be clutching what had to be one of the smallest submachine guns Fiona had ever seen. She also noticed that the shooter was wearing the same disturbing voodoo face paint as her apparent double. As Andrew's shots rang out in quick succession across the courtyard, she ducked behind the corner of the building as the bullets smacked into the masonry mere inches from her face, chewing up the white render and causing dust and debris to explode out into the air.

'Get to the car, now!' Andrew roared, keeping his gun trained on the corner where the woman had disappeared.

Fiona immediately veered off towards the entrance to the fort complex, only then realising that the main gates were still closed and that she would have to exit the way they had come in. Sensing Fiona's position out of the corner of his eye, Andrew began to step sideways towards the exit while still covering the last known position of the shooter, but when he glanced over and saw Fiona disappear through the gunport next to one of the enormous bronze cannons, he quickened his step and then broke into a full sprint towards her.

Whether it was just blind luck or whether the shooter had been watching him from a concealed position, he would never know, but as soon as he began running, more incoming fire erupted behind him. While still running, Andrew pointed the SD9 behind him and squeezed off another couple of rounds, but they were badly aimed and did nothing to deter the woman with the white face paint. She was firing bursts in his direction, and based purely on the rapid, dry staccato profile of the muzzle reports, Andrew recognised her weapon as being the tiny, compact Mini Uzi submachine gun. It was capable of spitting out 950 rounds per minute, sending a deadly torrent of lead towards a target, but its main downside was that the magazine would run dry after just a couple of seconds of firing unless the shooter was highly disciplined.

As it turned out, the woman was neither disciplined nor a firearms expert, and her long volley went wide and ended up peppering a redbrick wall some twenty metres off to Andrew's side. He had almost reached the gunport through which Fiona had disappeared when a second volley erupted behind him, and several of the 9mm projectiles hit the ground a couple of feet from him. A few more struck the massive cannon sitting in the gunport and making it ring dully like a bell. The sound was still reverberating through the massive, century-old cast bronze weapon when Andrew threw himself through the gunport and onto the soft grass on the other side of the fortification.

Fiona was pressed up against the wall with her back against the masonry and holding her SD9 pistol in her hand, and her wide, panicked eyes told Andrew everything he needed to know. Under similar circumstances, he would normally have taken up a defensive position here and put down suppressing fire on the attackers, but with Fiona by his side and less than a handful of bullets left in the SD9's magazine, there was only one option left. Run, and get the hell out of there before they ended up cornered by the two frenzied assassins.

'Move!' he shouted. 'To the car.'

Without hesitation, Fiona took off towards the pickup truck some fifty metres away, and Andrew bolted from the wall and followed her while casting glances over his shoulder to make sure the Uzi-wielding attacker wasn't lining up to fire another volley at them. As he ran, he spotted another figure out of the corner of his eye, and for a moment, he thought he was seeing things. Running almost parallel to him and Fiona inside the fort complex was a woman who looked identical to the one who had been shooting at him, but she was wearing different-coloured clothing. He was only able to glimpse her for brief moments as she became visible through the gunports in the fort's exterior walls, but she appeared to be clutching her bloodied side as she ran. She was clearly injured, and Andrew realised that this had to have been a result of Fiona firing her own weapon. In other words, there were two of them, and this one, despite her injury, appeared hell-bent on flanking them on their way to the carpark.

'Faster!' Andrew shouted, and Fiona panted as she pushed her legs to their limits.

When they reached the pickup truck, they threw themselves inside, and just as Andrew started the engine, the unnerving white skull of the injured attacker appeared above the parapet nearest the carpark, and then she brought up her Uzi to take aim.

Andrew rammed the gear lever into reverse, hit the throttle and released the clutch, and the meaty wheels of the 4x4 spun on the gravel and sent clouds of dust and pebbles flying up in the air as it lurched backwards. Spinning the steering wheel to line the car up with the road ahead, Andrew revved the engine and pushed the gear lever into first, and then the pickup truck lurched forward just as the shooter on the wall opened up with her submachine gun.

Bullets cut through the dust-filled air, and the car's powerful engine roared as the pickup accelerated violently along the gravel and onto the tarred road. The shooter held down the trigger and emptied the magazine in just over three seconds. In that time, fifty rounds of 9mm projectiles left the muzzle of the small weapon and sprayed down in a wide arc towards the carpark and the escaping pickup truck. However, the distance was now close to a hundred metres, which was well outside the maximum effective range of the Uzi, and most of the bullets went wide by tens of metres. However, a handful smacked into the bodywork of the car, and one shattered the cab's small rear window. Fiona screamed as the window exploded and thousands of tiny, cube-shaped shards of broken glass burst from the shattered glass and rained down onto the floor inside the cab.

'Are you alright?' shouted Andrew over the rush of wind inside the cab, flooring the accelerator as he glanced sideways to try to inspect Fiona's clothes for signs of blood. 'Are you hit?'

Fiona's hands fumbled clumsily across her arms, torso and legs in an attempt to make sure she was uninjured.

'You're bleeding,' said Andrew, an uncharacteristic stab of anxiety coming through in his voice as he pointed to the left side of her shirt.

'It's not mine,' said Fiona. 'I shot the one on the wall when she jumped me inside the restroom. She fell on me.'

'Who the hell were those two lunatics?' Andrew said, glancing up into the rearview mirror to make sure they weren't being followed as they raced along the road out of Port Royal. 'I think I saw them with Marcellus.'

'Yes,' said Fiona. 'I spotted them on the drone feed, but I figured they were just a couple of bimbos hanging out with the big man. I couldn't have been more wrong. They are like two crazy attack dogs.'

'Well,' said Andrew. 'They are either riddled with rabies or high on drugs. I've never seen anyone run like that after being shot.'

'Cocaine,' said Fiona. 'The eyes of the one I shot were like black marbles when she cornered me with a knife. Without this gun, I would have been dead.'

She looked down at the small SIG Sauer P365 that she was still gripping tightly in her right hand, and then she pressed the magazine release catch to eject the mag.

'How many left?' said Andrew as he raced the pickup truck along the causeway back towards the airport at several times the speed limit.

'Five,' said Fiona, clicking the mag back into the magazine well.

'Oh shit,' he said as he looked first in the side mirror and then glanced up into the rearview mirror again. 'We have company.'

★   ★   ★

Fiona's head spun around to look behind them, and as she watched, a black BMW sedan came tearing around the bend on the highway a couple of hundred metres behind them.

'It's them,' she said. 'It has to be. What do we do?'

Andrew felt for the SD9 next to him, but he knew that it now had less than ten rounds left in the magazine, and he cursed himself for leaving the rest of the weapons and ammunition in the helicopter.

'The only thing we *can* do,' he said, gripping the wheel tightly as he focused on the road ahead. 'Get to the chopper as fast as possible, and use whatever ammo we have to hold them off until then. Get ready to shoot. Wait until they are close.'

Andrew used the rearview mirror to keep tabs on their pursuers, and he didn't slow down since the BMW would easily be able to outpace the pickup truck, especially on a highway such as this. With the Ford Ranger's engine roaring under the bonnet, he placed the large vehicle in the middle of the road, signalling to whichever of the two homicidal supermodels was driving the car that he had no intention of allowing them to get too close or overtake. Within seconds, the BMW had caught up with them and was now less than thirty metres behind them. When Fiona turned around in her seat to look out of the back of the shattered window, she could see both of the two women with their skull-like faces glaring at her through the tinted windscreen. The one in the passenger seat next to the driver was baring her teeth, probably from the pain of the gunshot wound to her torso.

'Hold them off,' Andrew shouted over the noise of the engine and the wind inside the pickup's cab. 'But make those bullets count. We only have a few left.'

'No kidding,' said Fiona as she brought up the pistol and pointed it through the gaping window at the back of the cab. 'I'll try to hit the tyres.'

As soon as the driver of the BMW spotted the pistol, she began swerving unpredictably left and right to throw off Fiona's aim, and it worked, at least for the first couple of shots. Twice, Fiona aimed and fired, but somehow the driver seemed to be able to tell when she was about to shoot. And every time she did, the BMW lurched to one side or the other, causing Fiona to miss.

'Damn it!' Fiona yelled. 'I can't hit them.'

'Go for the windscreen,' shouted Andrew, glancing over his shoulder to get a better sense of the distance to the BMW. 'I am going to hit the brakes and reel them in. Then you shoot them. Alright?'

'Got it,' said Fiona, shifting in her seat and getting herself ready.

'In three. Two. One. Now!' Andrew called out as he lifted his foot off the accelerator and pushed down firmly enough on the brake to slow them down rapidly but without ending up skidding along the highway.

The distance between the two vehicles closed quickly as the pickup truck decelerated, and before the driver of the BMW could react, there were suddenly less than ten metres between Andrew and Fiona and their pursuers. Then Fiona began firing her remaining three shots straight at the BMW's windscreen. One missed, but the other two found their mark, shattering the glass and punching through the BMW's interior. Hundreds of cracks instantly appeared in a chaotic pattern that crisscrossed the windscreen and left it looking like a barely transparent sheet of ice. Only then did the female driver hit the brakes, but at that very moment, Andrew slammed his right foot down on the accelerator, and the muscly pickup truck leapt forward. What the 4x4 lacked in top speed, it made up for in raw power, and it quickly accelerated away from the slowing BMW, which was now swerving as the driver attempted to avoid going off the road. Her visibility was severely compromised, and there was no way the two attackers would be able to continue the chase. However, as Andrew was able to observe in the rearview mirror a few seconds later, the passenger, despite her gunshot injuries, managed to lift herself up and out of her seat and kick the shattered windscreen free of its frame. It bulged out and came loose, and then it slid off the bonnet and skidded along the road as the BMW accelerated and gave chase once more.

'They're still coming,' he shouted.

'Shit!' Fiona winced. 'What now?'

'You steer,' said Andrew, reaching for his SD9 and racking the slide.

'What?' said Fiona incredulously.

'Grab the wheel,' Andrew said. 'I'll manage the speed, you make sure we stay on the road.'

'This is a bad idea,' muttered Fiona nervously as she leaned over and reluctantly gripped the wheel with both hands. 'Alright. Whatever you're planning to do, make sure it works. I don't want to die today.'

'Me neither,' said Andrew dryly as he twisted around in his seat and rolled down the window next to him. 'Just keep us steady. Help me aim.'

'Got it,' said Fiona, her knuckles white as she gripped the wheel and turned her head to watch the road up ahead.

Andrew leaned out of the pickup truck with most of his upper body and was able to use both hands to grip the SD9 for a more stable aim. The wind was tearing at his clothes and ruffling his hair, but he had fired a weapon in more extreme conditions than this and felt confident that he could land a killer blow if only Fiona could keep the pickup steady on the road. As the BMW roared towards them and caught up, he tilted his head to one side and aimed down the iron sights at the driver. She immediately spotted him as he emerged and began swerving again, but Andrew used the regular motion of the car from left to right to attempt to predict where it was going to be, and then he pulled the trigger. The pistol kicked in his hand, and a fraction of a second later, he saw the BMW's rearview mirror explode in a cloud of glass and shards of black plastic fragments. He heard the driver scream in shock, but it was followed almost immediately by a shriek of fury, and then the BMW accelerated rapidly to slam into the back of the pickup truck. The impact was violent, and Andrew almost lost his grip on the SD9 as Fiona yelped and the pickup swerved from one side of the highway to the other.

'Keep us steady!' Andrew shouted, bringing his pistol back up as the BMW fell back, now with a crushed front grille and a broken headlight.

'I'm trying!' Fiona shouted.

Andrew jammed his right foot down onto the accelerator as hard as he could, but it was already as far as it could go, and the pickup was unable to go any faster. He aimed his pistol again and was about to fire when the other skull-adorned maniac in the BMW suddenly opened up with her reloaded Uzi. The submachine gun's angry staccato growl was clearly audible amid the roaring of engines, the howling of wind and the loud metallic pattering of dozens of bullets hitting the bodywork of the pickup truck. Andrew pulled himself back into the cab and somehow managed to avoid getting hit, and then another volley peppered the pickup's rear. Most of them punched into the tailgate whose lock splintered, causing it to flap down and begin bouncing and rattling as the vehicle roared ahead along the highway, but a couple of them tore through the cab's open rear window and sliced right through the metal roof and continued out and up into the air ahead of them. Fiona cried out in panic, and Andrew had to take the wheel to avoid them driving off the highway and crashing into the boggy undergrowth that flanked both sides. The driver of the BMW was still swerving from side to side behind them, looking for an opportunity to pull alongside and finish the job, but Andrew mirrored the car's movement and forced the driver to brake and abort her manoeuvre.

'I've got it!' Fiona shouted as she reached over to grip the wheel once again, and Andrew then risked a look out of the window and back towards their pursuers.

To his relief, he spotted the woman in the passenger seat struggling with the reload of the submachine gun, and he took the opportunity to fire two barely aimed shots down into the engine compartment, hoping to hit something vital. A couple of seconds later, he was rewarded with a plume of black smoke suddenly erupting behind the BMW, but it appeared to make no difference to the performance of the vehicle.

'Truck!' Fiona suddenly yelled, her voice panicked.

'What?' said Andrew, turning his head.

When he looked up ahead, he saw an enormous eighteen-wheeler coming barreling around a wide curve in the highway as it followed the natural topography of the isthmus. 'Oh shit!'

He spun around, grabbed the wheel just as Fiona let go, and then he wrestled it to one side just in time to avoid a head-on collision with the massive truck that would have left them both turned into mincemeat somewhere on the wrong side of its front grille. By the looks of it, the truck driver was as surprised to see the two vehicles on the road in front of him as they were to see him, and the truck swerved uncertainly just as it roared safely past the pickup truck. However, because the BMW was much lower than the pickup, the driver had not been able to see the truck coming until it was too late, and as the massive metal beast tore past, the BMW sideswiped the eighteen-wheeler, causing windows to shatter and bits of metal to be ripped from its bodywork.

Looking up into the rearview mirror, Andrew watched as the BMW was shunted to the opposite side of the road and then spun end over end as clouds of white smoke billowed from its screeching tyres. It somehow managed to stay upright and avoid flipping over into a deadly tumble, but it soon came to a stop at an angle across the two highway lanes, smoke and steam billowing up from under the bonnet. But then, unbelievably, it began moving forward again and resuming the chase.

'What the hell?' Andrew muttered incredulously. 'They are still coming.'

'Go!' shouted Fiona. 'Just go. We're almost at the airport. How many shots do you have left?'

'Three,' said Andrew after doing a quick mental tally of his shots fired so far. 'Whatever these two lunatics are on, I think I want some.'

'Enough with the jokes!' yelled Fiona. 'Let's just get the hell out of here.'

Andrew slammed his right foot down on the accelerator again, and the tortured engine roared violently under the bonnet in front of them. As Fiona turned and looked out of the gaping hole where the rear window had been, she could see that the BMW was trailing a huge plume of smoke, and there were sparks coming from the front left tire, indicating that it had been blown in the collision with the truck. Somehow, however, the mangled German car managed to begin to close the distance once more, and when it was about fifty metres behind them, the passenger opened up with her Uzi once more. Bullets sprayed out from inside the BMW, but hardly any of them hit their mark, and none of them did any damage to either the pickup truck or its two occupants.

'Almost there,' said Andrew, handing Fiona his pistol. 'About a kilometre left. Fire the last three rounds. We just need enough time to get into the chopper and take off, so try to push them back.'

'Right,' said Fiona, unsure of how exactly to accomplish that as she took the pistol in her hands.

She aimed again, lined up the iron sights with the driver of the BMW and fired. The car swerved, and then Fiona fired again, seemingly hitting nothing. Once more, the driver attempted to swerve erratically to throw off Fiona's aim, but there was no sign of her slowing down. Fiona fired the third and final round, which slammed into the remaining headlight, shattering it and sending a small shower of glass flying up and over the bonnet and into the BMW's interior. Fiona made sure that the magazine was completely empty by squeezing the trigger again, but as Andrew had predicted, the pistol now simply clicked empty. They were out of ammo.

However, to her immense relief, the BMW now fell back, and the distance between the two vehicles opened up slightly again. There was no indication that the two assassins were giving up, but with Fiona still pointing the pistol out of the back of the pickup, they had no idea how much ammo their quarry might still have left.

'Get ready to go off-road,' said Andrew. 'We're taking a shortcut.'

Fiona turned her head just in time to see Andrew wrestle the wheel to one side, and then the 4x4 ploughed through the vegetation and onto the relatively flat and open terrain surrounding the international airport. As they bounced along with the car's suspension system working overtime to keep the chassis level, Andrew steered the pickup in a wide arc towards the VIP terminal and the heliport where their chopper was parked. Behind them, the BMW had followed them off the highway and was now crashing across the stony ground, bouncing violently as it did so. There was every chance that the German car was about to expire in a burning heap, but if it could just hang on for another couple of minutes, the two assassins might be able to reach the heliport and finish off their targets once and for all.

'I can't believe those two psychos,' said Andrew, and he glanced over his shoulder at the pursuing vehicle. 'They just won't quit.'

'Fence up ahead,' said Fiona, pointing out through the windscreen.

'I see it,' said Andrew, pushing the pickup's speed even higher. 'We'll drive right through it. Hang on.'

Fiona lowered herself down into her seat and gripped the handle inside the passenger side door, bracing for the impact, but when it came, it was barely noticeable. The sheer momentum of the heavy 4x4 caused the pickup truck to cut right through the chain-link fence, ripping it to shreds as they barreled straight through it.

However, the newly created hole in the fence also allowed the BMW to follow them inside the airport complex, although the distance between the two vehicles was now a couple of hundred metres. The once sleek car was now a mangled mess, and so much smoke billowed from it that it appeared from a distance like an armoured personnel carrier that had activated its smokescreen to mask the deployment of a batch of soldiers.

'There it is!' Fiona called out when she spotted the gleaming Airbus H135 helicopter sitting on the tarmac near the VIP terminal.

Andrew pushed the tortured pickup to the limit as he navigated a couple of vans and a small warehouse building to then head straight for the chopper. The tyres screeched as he slammed the brakes, and the 4x4 came to a shuddering halt some twenty metres from the aircraft. Without a word, they both bolted from the vehicle and sprinted towards the helicopter, but Andrew took a moment to glance over his shoulder as he ran, and he spotted the BMW entering the VIP area and heading straight for them. They would only have a few seconds to get airborne. They just had to hope that the two crazed assassins were also running low on ammo.

Ripping open the door to the pilot's seat, Andrew climbed up into the cockpit and immediately began flipping all the switches required for engine start and takeoff. As Fiona climbed up into the seat next to him and slammed the door, the two turboshaft engines spun up with the characteristic whine of their jet turbines. Soon after, the main rotor began moving, and then the tail rotor began to spin.

However, it was not going to be enough. Racing towards them outside was the BMW, looking like a vision from a post-apocalyptic world of vehicles cobbled together from pieces of barely functional scrap. It was mangled almost beyond recognition and covered in dust, and thick smoke was pouring out from the engine and the exhaust. But it was still moving, and as it came right up next to the pickup truck, the wounded assassin in the passenger seat opened the door and bolted out before the car had come to a complete stop. Despite her injury, which had now soaked her entire left side in dark red blood, she managed something between a run and a hobble towards the chopper. Shuffling along with a wild and furious grimace on her face, she had only a blade in her hand, immediately answering the question as to how much ammo the two had left.

The chopper's engines were now almost spun up to takeoff revolutions, but it was clear to Andrew that the first of the two assassins was going to reach his side of the helicopter before he could take off. Jamming the engine power to full throttle, he yanked the collective back for a forced takeoff and simultaneously used his foot to apply full right rudder. The chopper barely lifted from the tarmac, but it was enough for the extreme rudder input to immediately take effect. As soon as the helicopter skids left the concrete, the chopper began to spin to one side around the axis of its main rotor, and the effect was deadly. The injured assassin was about five metres from the cockpit when it happened, and she had no time to react when the chopper's tail boom suddenly lurched in an arc towards her. Just as she turned her head in surprise, the tail rotor scythed across the tarmac and tore straight through her, turning the formerly gorgeous assassin into a mangled mess of gory flesh and bone that was flung in all directions as the rotor cut her into strips in a cloud of flying blood and tissue.

'Oh, Jesus!' Fiona yelled, holding up a hand to cup her mouth in disgust. 'That was awful.'

'Yeah,' said Andrew flatly. 'Good riddance.'

Outside, the other woman was exiting the car, and she produced a shriek that was somewhere between the furious roar of a deranged psychopath and the pained wail of an injured animal. Then she began sprinting for the chopper, but it was now in motion and lifting from the tarmac. However, the woman, having seen her twin turned into mincemeat, did not give up, and within a couple of seconds, she was almost there. In a final effort to reach the chopper, she launched herself through the air with a shriek as it rose from the ground, and she managed to grab onto one of the skids. As the shopper kept rising up into the air, Andrew leaned out to one side and was able to see the woman hanging on with both arms and legs wrapped up and over the skid.

'I don't believe this!' Andrew exclaimed, watching in amazement as the assassin clung on for dear life while the chopper rose higher and higher up into the air. 'She just won't quit. But she can't hang on forever.'

'We're going to let her fall?' said Fiona, looking aghast, despite everything that had just happened.

'You want to open the door and invite her inside?' said Andrew, glancing at her. 'Not a chance. One way or another, she's dead.'

He pushed the control stick forward as the chopper's nose immediately pitched down, and the aircraft swiftly began to gain speed. Within a few seconds, they were travelling about as fast as they had done in the pickup truck on the highway. Then, as the chopper swept across Kingston Harbour towards the capital at an altitude of a couple of hundred metres, they both suddenly heard a loud pop, and a bullet hole appeared in the cockpit's floor. Leaning out to his side again, Andrew looked down to see the woman holding a small pistol in her hand and trying to aim it up at the chopper's two occupants while the onrushing wind tore at her arm. She spotted Andrew looking down at her, and her face instantly curled up into a grimace of fury and hatred, and then she fired again. This time, the badly aimed bullet glanced off the aircraft's glass bubble canopy and somehow managed to avoid hitting the rotors as it cut up through the spinning blades.

'Enough of this shit,' Andrew growled. 'This is the end of the road for you.'

He then began applying full stick left and right, causing the chopper to roll from side to side in an attempt to make the assassin lose her grip and fall into the bay below. However, the drugged-up and seemingly superhuman attacker kept clinging to the skid underneath the chopper, and she even managed to get another shot off as she did so. Then Andrew had an idea.

'Hold onto something,' he said, and Fiona immediately gripped the handlebars on the inside of the cockpit.

Andrew pulled back hard on the stick, and the helicopter responded by raising its nose and entering a steep climb. When it was in an almost vertical ascent and slowing rapidly, he rammed the control stick all the way to the left, and the helicopter then began to spin around its own forward axis as it ascended. Andrew and Fiona were both being pressed into their seats by the centrifugal force of the manoeuvre, but down below by the skid, those forces were much stronger. The remaining assassin's legs soon lost their grip, and she ended up fully extended from the skid and desperately holding on with only her hands as the chopper kept spinning and gaining altitude. However, after a few seconds, she could no longer hold on and lost her grip. She was immediately flung out and away from the chopper, but not fast enough to avoid the main rotor, whose rapidly spinning blades swept through a wide arc as the aircraft spun higher. The blur of the heavy carbon fibre blades connected with the woman's body, and from one instant to the next, she was transformed from a living human being into a mist of red. The turboshaft engines seemed to slow almost imperceptibly as it happened, but then they were back to their regular RPMs.

'There,' said Andrew icily as he stopped the spin and brought the nose of the chopper back down to level flight. 'Problem solved.'

'Holy crap,' said Fiona, sounding out of breath and looking queasy from the manoeuvre and the gory end to the chase. 'I can't believe that just happened. That was so awful.'

'I won't lose any sleep over it,' said Andrew as he peered out through the windscreen at Kingston Harbour, which now stretched out in front of them. 'She's going to become fish food, and that's probably the most use she's ever going to be. It was probably those two psychos who tortured and almost killed Ronil. So they got what they deserved.'

'I guess you're right,' Fiona said pensively after a beat. 'Like you said. Good riddance.'

'Alright,' Andrew said, checking the fuel gauge and then consulting the moving map display on the control panel in front of him. 'Next stop, Nassau.'

Eighteen

It was becoming dark outside, and Lawrence Blake was standing in front of the full-length mirror in his 12th-floor luxury hotel room in downtown Port-au-Prince. He regarded himself carefully and wondered if he should give up entirely on Marcus Tobin and somehow stage the professor's death. With a bit of imagination, he might even be able to engineer a payout to himself from his own life insurance policy. And it would leave him free to fully embrace his swashbuckling alter ego and spend all of his time hunting treasure in the Caribbean. Lord knew it was a damn sight more interesting than sitting in a dusty old office in London writing papers and giving the odd lecture to a bunch of dweeby, snot-nosed university students. However, sending Tobin on early and permanent retirement would also hamper his ability to find and cultivate leads to hidden treasures, since his entire network of scholars and researchers would suddenly vanish like dew before the morning sun.

Blake stroked his beard and straightened his back, pleased with the reflection of the handsome and relatively youthful man looking back at him. Perhaps he should let Tobin live for a bit longer. After all, he could slip into his alternate persona almost at will now, and there would be plenty of opportunity for him to go on more adventures as Lawrence Blake in the future.

He was about to head down to the restaurant and order a meal from the à la carte menu when his phone produced a tinkling sound reminiscent of ice crystals shattering. When he picked it up, he saw that there was a message from Marcellus Solomon in which the Haitian kingpin suggested a phone call urgently, but without giving a reason. He raised his eyebrows and looked at the message for a moment, and then he shrugged and hit the speed dial to call Marcellus back immediately. It rang only once before being picked up, and then the gravelly voice of the kingpin came on the line. He sounded tired, angry and tense all at the same time.

'Blake,' he said, as the Englishman noticed reggae music playing in the background.

'Marcellus!' said Blake cheerfully. 'What news do you have?'

There was a long pause during which Blake could only hear the crime boss breathing heavily, and then there was the sound of him taking what seemed like a dangerously large gulp of a liquid, which Blake assumed had to be rum. Marcellus smacked his lips, and then he spoke again.

'We have a problem,' he said, sniffing twice as if trying to clear his nose.

'We do?' said Blake, unperturbed. 'What sort of problem?'

'Your little female friend and her soldier boy,' said Marcellus.

'Oh?' said Blake, now beginning to worry slightly. 'What's going on?'

'You and I agreed to make them find the treasure and then steal it,' said Marcellus. 'But I was angry. And I sent my girls to kill them.'

'You sneaky bastard,' Blake said slowly, in equal measure annoyed and impressed with the kingpin's deviousness. 'We made a deal to leave them and have them find the treasure for us.'

'I know,' rasped Marcellus, taking another hefty swig of the rum. 'Those *crétin*s blew up my house, so I decided that I wanted them dead.'

'I'm sorry,' said Blake. 'I don't quite follow. What exactly are you calling me about?'

'My girls are dead,' said Marcellus, his voice now cold and slightly husky. 'They were killed at the airport in Jamaica. You can see it online. Someone from the VIP terminal recorded it on his phone.'

'Right,' said Blake hesitantly. 'But what do you want me to do about it? As far as I am concerned, I am the one who should be angry at you. After all, you went back on our deal.'

'I know,' said Marcellus. 'But I have changed my mind. I just want my cut of the treasure when we find it. And then we can kill your two friends.'

'And how do you propose to do that?' said Blake, silently baulking at the notion of "*we*". 'Especially now that they know someone is out to get them?'

'Well, I know where they are going,' said Marcellus.

'Really?' said Blake. 'How?'

'I told Celestine to place a magnetic tracking device on their helicopter,' said Marcellus, 'and I can see that she managed to do it before she was killed. The device is military grade. Very accurate. And it is moving northwest from the airport across Jamaica as we speak.'

'I see,' said Blake. 'That was very resourceful of you. Any idea where they might be headed?'

'No,' said Marcellus, 'but we will know soon enough. The tracking device uses satellites to communicate, so I will know where it is anywhere on the planet to within ten metres.'

'Impressive,' said Blake. 'So, what do you need from me?'

'I want to give you the tracker and find the gold,' said Marcellus. 'And when we have it, I get my cut, and then I kill your two friends.'

Blake pondered the suggestion for a moment before nodding.

'Alright,' he finally said. 'I suppose that is our best option, given where we are. I suggest we meet up later this evening, and you can then hand the tracker to me in person. How about that?'

'OK,' said Marcellus. 'I will send you a location for a meeting at midnight.'

'Fine,' said Blake. 'And let's make sure we stick to the plan this time.'

Marcellus didn't reply but simply grunted and hung up, leaving Blake to stare at his phone with a frown. As he did so, a new plan began to form in his mind. One that would give him control over proceedings from now on and remove the erratic and unpredictable Marcellus Solomon from the equation once and for all.

★   ★   ★

With a cruising speed of 250 kilometres per hour, the Airbus H135 sped north across the terrain, leaving Kingston and the southern coast of Jamaica behind as the sun seemed to balance on the western horizon. A few minutes later, they would be sweeping back out over the ocean on their way to Cuba, after which they had just over an hour to go before reaching New Providence Island in the Bahamas and the city of Nassau.

After entering their flight path into the onboard flight computer, Andrew had disabled the transponder to make sure that they couldn't be tracked and identified by civilian air traffic control centres in Jamaica or anywhere else en route to their destination. He was also planning to fly low and fast across Cuba so that no radar systems would be able to detect them during their roughly one-hour presence inside the airspace of the authoritarian communist country. The last thing they needed now was to tangle with that country's air force.

'What an absolutely deranged pair of drugged-up lunatics those two women were,' said Fiona, gazing ahead through the chopper's windscreen as they cut across Jamaica's wooded interior on a heading that would take them some 700 kilometres northwest to Nassau.

'I've never seen anything like it,' said Andrew, looking down at the rolling tree-covered hills bathed in the golden light of the sunset. 'Drugs or no drugs. Voodoo or no voodoo. They were hands down the craziest people I have ever been up against.'

'The painted-on skulls were really disturbing,' said Fiona, 'but somehow they reminded me a bit of someone called Anne Bonny.'

'Who is she?' said Andrew.

'She was one of the most famous female pirates during the golden age,' said Fiona. 'It was actually Tobin who first told me about her. That absolute bastard. Anyway, Anne used the same sorts of tactics in battle to shock her enemies, most famously fighting bare-chested.'

'Crikey,' said Andrew, raising his eyebrows. 'I bet it worked too.'

'Probably, said Fiona, producing a faint smile. 'But her story is actually really interesting. She was an illegitimate child of a lawyer, whose name we don't know, and a maid called Mary, somewhere in Ireland in the late 17th century. Apparently, she was raised as a boy since the locals knew that the maid had given birth to a girl. But the deceit was eventually found out, and the lawyer and his maid then went off to America to escape the stigma of the affair. And they brought Anne along with them and settled in the colony of Carolina. By all accounts, her father became quite successful there, and the attractive young Anne's future looked to be shaping up to one where she would marry well and settle down and have lots of children. But there was just one small problem with that.'

'Which was?' said Andrew, glancing at Fiona.

'Anne didn't want any of those things,' said Fiona. 'Whether it was because she had been brought up as a boy or if she just had a rebellious streak and a free spirit, she broke with her family and married a sailor named James Bonny. Now, you might think that this was a case of young love, but by all accounts, Anne was just using James to get her away from her father. Either way, the two of them ended up in Nassau, which had become the prime spot for Caribbean piracy back in the very early 18th century. In fact, it was more or less at the same time as Jack Flynn was causing havoc on the high seas in these parts. Of course, by the time Anne Bonny entered the scene, the new Nassau governor, Woodes Rogers, had taken over, and the royal pardon had come into effect, so piracy was dying out. But as I've mentioned before, there were still some famous holdouts who didn't want to quit piracy just yet.'

'So Anne Bonny might have heard of Jack Flynn?' said Andrew, as he peered ahead to see the northern coast of Jamaica and the open sea behind it in the distance.

'It's possible,' said Fiona. 'But one person that she had definitely heard of was Jack Rackham, and according to the stories, the two of them were romantically involved. What we know is that by 1720, Anne was part of Rackham's crew along with another female pirate called Mary Read, and their first caper was the theft of a sloop that was anchored in Nassau Harbour. Along with about a dozen other pirates, they set to sea and spent several months hunting down merchant prizes in the waters around the Bahamas.'

'Without being caught?' said Andrew.

'The ocean is a really big place,' said Fiona. 'The Caribbean Sea covers several million square kilometres, and with Rackham and his crew sailing a small, fast sloop, it wouldn't have been too difficult for them to conduct hit-and-run tactics against merchant vessels and then disappear.'

'How do we know all this stuff?' said Andrew. 'It happened more than three centuries ago.'

'Mainly stories and legends from that time,' said Fiona, 'but there are also some more tangible bits of evidence available. For example, we know that Governor Rodgers put out a proclamation in 1720 ordering the arrest of a bunch of named pirates, and the list includes Rackham, Bonny and Read. You can find a copy of it online if you want to read it for yourself.'

'Interesting,' said Andrew. 'So, did they just carry on with their piracy after that?'

'For a while,' said Fiona. 'A couple of months later, they were attacked by a privateer ship commissioned by the governor of Jamaica. There was a fight where Bonny and Read were doing their bare-chested routine, but in the end, all of the pirates surrendered. They were then brought to Port Royal where they were sentenced to death. Rackham was hanged there in late November of 1720, but both Bonny and Read claimed to be pregnant, and so their sentences were not carried out immediately. The idea was to allow them to give birth and then hang them.'

'Brutal,' Andrew observed. 'Although, I suppose the governor didn't really have much of a choice, given the circumstances.'

'That's right,' said Fiona. 'It might have been a pretty ruthless period in history back then, but even they weren't prepared to execute a pregnant woman.'

'So, what happened to them?' said Andrew.

'Read died in prison the following April,' said Fiona, 'but interestingly, there is no record of Bonny either dying in prison, being executed or being released from prison. She seemed to have just vanished from history.'

'Well, that's quite an intriguing notion, isn't it?' said Andrew. 'Imagine if she somehow managed to escape prison and went on to give birth. Then there's a decent chance that her descendants are walking around somewhere in this part of the world right now.'

'Funny you should say that,' said Fiona, 'because there has been some speculation that she managed to use her family connections in the Carolina colony to be set free, and that she then travelled to America and settled there. But if I remember correctly, there's also an entry in a burial register in Spanish Town from a couple of years later that includes her name, so it is all a bit mysterious what really happened to her. But that's part of what makes history so interesting. Sometimes, you have to allow your imagination to fill in the gaps.'

'I suppose that's true,' said Andrew. 'And as you have proven, once in a while it is possible to guess correctly, like with the location of the wreck of the Marauder. I'm still impressed by how you managed to pin that down.'

'Sometimes you have to just let your imagination run wild,' said Fiona wistfully. 'You never know where it might take you.'

A couple of hours later, they had cleared Cuban airspace and were safe to climb to a more relaxed altitude of several hundred metres above the sea around the Bahamas. Eventually, after darkness had fallen and there was only a faint bluish glow towards the western horizon, Andrew spotted a large, sprawling lit-up area in the far distance.

'That's New Providence Island out there,' he said. 'It's pretty densely populated these days, so it is lit up like a Christmas tree at night.'

'What might this place have looked like at the time of Captain Flynn?' said Fiona. 'I think there were only a couple of other settlements here apart from Nassau. The whole island would have been completely dark.'

'Speaking of which,' said Andrew, pointing straight ahead. 'That's Nassau over there, and out to our left is the international airport. I am going to head over there and request a landing permission. I'll tell them our transponder has malfunctioned and that we're coming in from the island of Eleuthera just west of here. It's just a short helicopter trip, so hopefully they'll buy it.'

Nineteen

It was two minutes to midnight when the black, heavily armoured car that Blake had procured through a contact in the Haitian Ministry of the Interior rolled to a halt. It stopped on the westernmost quay inside the capital's port, which was managed by Haiti's national port authority. The port covered a vast area west of the centre of Port-au-Prince, and the once-busy freight terminal included dozens of large docks, quaysides, warehouses and container storage sites. Now, there were big open spaces where containers had once been stored, and just a single ship bringing in a consignment of fuel was lying by another dock several hundred metres away.

Towering over the quay were huge metal freight containers that had been stacked on top of each other like Lego bricks to look like tall, multicoloured apartment blocks without windows. The scene was dimly lit by a couple of floodlights that blinked occasionally, but it seemed to be completely deserted as Blake opened the rear passenger door and stepped out. He was followed by Ortega who had been at the wheel, and the Spaniard was wearing a black nylon jacket to conceal the various firearms he had strapped to his torso. His compatriot and former colleague Delgado from the Special Intervention Unit had been ordered to fulfil a different role, and he was now lying prone on top of a tall freight crane about a hundred metres further along the quayside. He had been there for over an hour, and in that time he had been able to observe no movement at all, indicating that the site was secure and that there were no signs of an ambush. Either the docks were just unusually quiet this night, or Marcellus had ordered it to be cleared for his upcoming meeting.

As Blake adjusted his expensive but casual-looking sandy brown suit, he felt no fear despite the location and the late hour. He had complete faith in Ortega and Delgado to protect him, but just to make sure, he himself carried a compact Ruger LC9 pistol under his suit jacket. This weapon, designed specifically as a small, concealed carry option for self-defence, had already accompanied him on many excursions throughout the Caribbean underworld, and he had fired it hundreds of times at the shooting range, but never once in anger. It fit perfectly in the palm of his hand, but due to its small size, its magazine contained only seven 9mm bullets. However, it afforded him a certain degree of confidence whenever he met up with various friends in low places. And tonight, since he was meeting an untrustworthy and ultra-violent gang boss in the chaotic hellhole that was Port-au-Prince, turning up unarmed would simply be foolish.

Blake smoothed down his jacket as he took a few measured steps away from the car and did a full turn to look around the area. Marcellus had suggested this as a meeting place since he controlled this part of the port, but Blake had decided that he needed to have his own plans for what was about to happen, given the slippery character of the Haitian kingpin. Seeing no movement anywhere, he glanced at his Patek Philippe wristwatch and then looked over at Ortega who was already scanning the area for threats.

'Anything?' said Blake in hushed tones as he turned his head to look in the direction of the crane where Delgado was ensconced.

Ortega put an index finger to his right ear to activate the comms system and lowered his head slightly to speak into the concealed mike. A few seconds later, he looked up at Blake.

'Nothing,' he said. 'Delgado is seeing no movement.'

Blake gave a small shake of the head. He should have known better than to expect Marcellus to be punctual, if he was even going to show up at all. For a moment, he contemplated the idea that the whole thing might have been a ruse to eliminate him, and an attempt by Marcellus to locate the Spanish treasure himself, but he quickly decided that there was no way the kingpin would be able to pull that off by himself. He might be violent and greedy and utterly deranged by his ridiculous voodoo nonsense, but he wasn't stupid, and he understood that Blake was his only option for getting his hands on a portion of the treasure. Blake, however, had no such incentives, and he had already decided on the most profitable course ahead for himself and his benefactor back in Castilla La Mancha in Spain.

Out of the corner of his eye, Blake spotted Ortega's hand move back up to his earpiece, and then the former UEI operative turned to face him.

'They're coming,' he said evenly.

'Good,' said Blake. 'Get ready. Both of you.'

Ortega spoke another few words to Delgado, and then he brought his hand back down, straightened his back and moved over to stand next to Blake.

'Ready,' he said.

In the next moment, a set of headlights appeared at the far southern entrance to the port, and a car began making its way slowly along the multiple quays towards the meeting point. From a distance, it was impossible to see what type of vehicle it was, but as it came closer, Blake could see that it was some sort of large SUV with room for more than a handful of people. The car came to a stop about twenty metres away from Blake and Ortega, and then it simply sat there with no sign of movement.

Unsure of what was about to happen, Blake felt a small tingle of fear and excitement all at the same time, and then all four doors of the SUV opened all at once, and a group of people spilt out. Among them was the tall and bulky Marcellus, who was wearing his usual attire consisting of dark trousers and a leather vest over a bare torso exposing his large pecs and his muscular arms. As he got out and walked slowly towards Blake, the four gun-toting men flanking him fanned out, with two on either side about a metre behind him. When he was five metres from Blake, he stopped and spread out his arms.

'Mister Blake,' he said without warmth. 'Good to see you again.'

'And you,' said Blake with a friendly nod, taking a couple of steps forward. 'You have the tracker?'

'Yes,' said Marcellus, raising a hand and snapping his fingers.

One of his men reached into a small leather satchel and extracted a black book-sized electronic device. He moved up next to Marcellus, handed it to the crime boss and took a couple of steps back.

'Here it is,' said Marcellus.

'Very good, said Blake, casting a quick glance over his shoulder towards the crane and then moving up to stand almost in front of Marcellus. 'May I see?'

Marcellus switched on the tracking unit, and a small screen with a moving map display lit up, casting a greenish glow up onto the kingpin's face from below. He then pressed a button to select the tracking device that had been attached to the Airbus H135, and then he handed the tracker to Blake, who was gratified to see the map showing a small red dot blinking somewhere in the Bahamas. On closer inspection, he realised that it was located exactly over Nassau, and a thin smile spread across his lips.

'Excellent,' he said. 'This will do the trick, I am sure.'

'I will let you have it,' said Marcellus, 'in exchange for a bigger cut.'

For a brief moment, the smile vanished from Blake's face, but then he nodded and resumed his affable demeanour.

'Alright,' he said. 'I suppose that's only fair. How much were you thinking?'

'Fifty percent,' said Marcellus completely deadpan, and Blake noticed that a couple of his men suddenly seemed to grip their weapons more tightly.

In your fucking dreams, thought Blake, struggling to maintain his cordial expression.

'How about thirty?' said Blake, deciding that a bit of haggling would make things appear genuine.

'Forty,' said Marcellus. 'Nothing less.'

'Alright,' smiled Blake, stretching out his hand. 'Fine. Let's settle on forty. Shake on it?'

Marcellus regarded Blake's hand and paused for a moment, but then he took it in his and gave it a vice-like squeeze, which Blake managed to ignore despite the pain. As the two men shook hands, Blake noticed that the tense demeanour of the goons seemed to melt away. Then Marcellus handed him the leather satchel.

'Perfect,' said Blake, sliding the tracking unit into the satchel. 'I will let you know when the task is complete, and then we can split the loot. Alright?'

Marcellus nodded.

'Good,' he said. 'But no tricks.'

Blake feigned being taken aback by the suggestion and broke into a wide smile.

'Tricks?' he repeated. 'Never. Trust me.'

He nodded at the kingpin, took a step back and slightly to one side, and then he brought up his right hand to his temple and performed a small salute. But instead of bringing the hand back down, it remained next to his head for a brief moment. In a quick movement, he spread out his fingers and then clenched his fist tightly.

An instant after the signal had been given, Marcellus' head exploded like a watermelon as the high-powered projectile from Delgado's sniper rifle ripped through his skull and burst out of the back of his head, taking a mist of brain matter and blood with it, part of which sprayed across one of his men with a wet slap. The loud report from the rifle's muzzle arrived a split second later, and the kingpin's body then seemed to remain upright for an unnaturally long time as his goons glared at their boss, momentarily stunned by the violent removal of his head. Then another shot rang out, and a fountain of blood exploded from the chest of one of Marcellus' men, and he was instantly knocked back by the force of the impact. At the same time, both Ortega and Blake reached for their weapons. Blake brought out his Ruger, and Ortega pulled two Glock 17s from their concealed holsters under his jacket. Ortega crouched low as he brought up the two pistols and began firing, and Blake threw himself to the ground while aiming in the general direction of the nearest opponent. Before the remaining goons could react, the quayside erupted in a cacophony of gunfire, Delgado sending shot after high-powered shot into the defenceless targets, and Blake and Ortega both firing rapidly at anything that moved until their magazines were empty. Within seconds, the members of Marcellus' small protection squad were all lying dead or bleeding out on the concrete, and Ortega swiftly moved forward to finish off anyone still alive with single well-placed shots to the head. When it was all over, a faint haze of smoke from their weapons drifted away on the breeze as Blake blinked and took in the scene with amazement. He lifted his head and looked around at the carnage and death on the quayside around him, and an intoxicated grin spread across his face as high-octane endorphins flooded his bloodstream.

'Holy fucking shit!' he breathed, his voice trembling with visceral excitement as he looked from under his tousled hair at the mayhem surrounding him. 'That was bloody spectacular!'

★   ★   ★

Having touched down on their designated helipad at Nassau's international airport, Andrew and Fiona logged the chopper's supposed transponder problem with the heliport's maintenance office and paid for a repair team to look into it the following day. The team was going to find nothing wrong with the unit, except that it had somehow been disabled manually in the onboard computer's communications menu. However, it helped mask their chaotic departure from Jamaica, and it would buy Andrew and Fiona some time to investigate Jack Flynn. Andrew was also hoping that it would smooth over the lack of aircraft identification as they had entered New Providence Island airspace, and as it turned out, the duty officer at the heliport did not appear to be too hot on regulations. He simply asked Andrew to fill out a form with basic details, which he then filed lazily as if this thing happened all the time, and then he bid them goodnight and wished them a pleasant stay in Nassau.

They exited the heliport terminal and walked to the airport's taxi stands, where they jumped into a cab to take them into the city. It was now late evening, and they decided to head for a hotel near Trinity Chapel in downtown Nassau. By the time they had checked in, they were both ravenously hungry and headed for a nearby upmarket restaurant. It turned out to have a roof terrace affording an unobstructed view of the Nassau Marina, which was full of dozens of expensive yachts and other pleasure craft. To their left, about a kilometre away, was the cruise port where a handful of enormous cruise ships were moored, and directly opposite the restaurant on the other side of the marina was a small island that was aptly named Paradise Island. The evening air was warm and pleasant, and there was a light breeze that occasionally rustled through the fronds of the palm trees that lined the promenade below. Over an expertly prepared meal of truffle mushroom tagliatelle served with white wine sauce and accompanied by a bottle of Sauvignon Blanc, the two of them sat back, and they both began to feel the tension of the dramatic events in Jamaica begin to drain away from them.

By the time desserts arrived, which for both of them consisted of carrot cake with frosting and maple syrup, they were both relaxed and well-fed, and Jamaica and Haiti now seemed a world away. As Fiona used her cake fork to scoop up the last crumbs of her cake, her left hand was already working the touchscreen on her phone. Andrew immediately recognised the slight frown and the way Fiona had set her mouth as being a surefire sign that something had occurred to her and that she was now busy exploring it.

'What are you looking at?' he said, picking up a dessert wine glass and sipping his Moscato.

'Remember how Jack Flynn's name showed up in the local diocese records?' she said, continuing her tapping.

'Sure,' he replied.

'Well,' she said. 'That's not the only place it shows up, as it turns out. There are legal records available from the local municipality going all the way back to those days. And interestingly, there appears to have been some sort of legal case launched against Flynn by a bishop here in 1723, two years after he took up the position as vicar at Trinity Chapel.'

'What sort of legal case?' said Andrew.

'It's all a bit opaque,' said Fiona. 'But from the looks of it, the new bishop at the time had found out about Flynn's former life as a pirate, and he wanted him kicked out of the clergy and fired as a vicar due to what he referred to as "moral deficiencies".'

'Well,' said Andrew, giving a thin smile and a shrug. 'You could say he had a point. Flynn was no saint, that's for sure.'

'Certainly not,' nodded Fiona. 'But apparently, the case never went forward?'

'Why not?' said Andrew. 'Did the bishop get cold feet?

'It seems like he never got the chance,' said Fiona, scrolling through a PDF document showing a scan of a page from the local news gazette published in early July 1723. 'The bishop was found murdered late one Sunday evening just a few weeks after the legal proceedings were initiated.'

'Really?' said Andrew slowly, raising an eyebrow. 'That seems like a highly suspicious coincidence.'

'No kidding,' said Fiona, reading on. 'He had been viciously stabbed dozens of times in an alley behind the Anglican Cathedral on George Street, just a couple of city blocks from where we are sitting.'

'Wow,' said Andrew. 'That must have been quite a shock to the town here.'

'Probably the whole of New Providence Island,' said Fiona. 'That's about as much of a high-profile murder case as you can get.'

'So, what happened to the legal case?' Andrew said.

'It was dropped,' said Fiona. 'And when a new bishop was appointed, no new case was ever opened.'

'Not to sound too much like a conspiracy theorist,' said Andrew, 'but there's no way in hell that was anything but cold-blooded murder. Just think about it. The former pirate Jack Flynn settles down here in Nassau to become a man of the cloth and embrace a life of peace and good deeds. But then suddenly, the moment someone threatens his new position, that person ends up murdered in spectacular fashion. That bishop was killed to stop the case from going forward and probably also to warn anyone else against trying any move against Flynn.'

'I think I agree,' said Fiona. 'It sort of fits a pattern. Remember how privateers and pirates became a kind of necessary evil for places like Port Royal in order for them to defend themselves against a Spanish invasion?'

'Sure,' said Andrew.

'Well,' said Fiona. 'It looks to me like Flynn dealt with the bishop the way the Port Royal pirates might have dealt with a new governor who didn't quite grasp the need for pirates in that port. Pretty much every single governor that the English king sent to Jamaica ended up realising that without pirates there was no Port Royal. And I would be surprised if those pirates didn't use threats of violence to make the point. It all makes perfect sense. And the sheer brutality of that murder was almost certainly meant as a statement. I guess Flynn was still the same man he had always been.'

'What if his whole vicar routine was just a front?' said Andrew. 'What if all it was ever designed to do was to allow him to quietly disappear from view after his pirating days had come to an end? Becoming part of the clergy would probably have been the best way to achieve that. It would allow him to slip behind the official veil of the church and do more or less as he pleased. And most people would probably stop asking questions about him for fear of offending the diocese. It's actually quite brilliant.'

'But what about the treasure?' said Fiona. 'There's no way he could have brought it here to Nassau.'

'I agree,' said Andrew. 'Which means that it is still out there somewhere.'

He gestured vaguely to the open sea in the distance beyond Paradise Island as Fiona leaned back in her chair and looked pensive for a moment.

'There's only one thing we can do now,' she said. 'We need to get inside Trinity Chapel and have a good look around. I know it's a long shot, but there just might be some clues in there. Or perhaps in the private residence of the vicar. It is in an adjacent building, and just like the chapel, it dates back to that time.'

'Well,' said Andrew, glancing down at his wristwatch, which was now showing close to midnight. 'There's no time like the present. Are you up for it?'

'Absolutely,' said Fiona with a nod and a wry smile. 'We're here now, right? Let's go and see what we can find.'

Twenty

Within ten minutes of leaving the restaurant, Andrew and Fiona arrived at the Trinity Chapel on Mount Royal Avenue, which was centrally located in Nassau's old town, close to where the first harbour had once been established in the middle of the 17th century. The old stone church had been built in an early gothic style with pointed arches, thin fluted columns on its façade, and a steeply pitched slate roof that rose almost as high as the tall rectangular bell tower that sported faux battlements on its flat roof. The well-maintained plot on which it sat was modest with a few low palm trees dotted around, and it was surrounded by a black wrought iron fence with gilded fleur-de-lis spear tops. Just inside the fence and next to the church was a tiny cemetery with only a few dozen tombstones, many of which looked very old. Beyond it was some sort of annexe that appeared to have been built at the same time as the church, and which had most likely served as a residence for the vicar in days gone by.

'This is it,' said Fiona, pointing past the fence. 'This is where Jack Flynn lived until his death in 1747. And his tombstone must be just in there.'

'Right,' said Andrew, looking along the street to make sure that no one was watching. 'Let's get in there.'

He moved over to stand next to the wrought iron fence, lowered himself slightly and clasped his hands together with the palms facing up to create a step for Fiona. As soon as she was over the fence, he gripped two of the gilded spear tops and jumped adeptly over to join her, landing on the soft grass edging that ran along the cemetery's perimeter. They quickly moved into the shadows of the palm trees and began examining the tombstones.

'It should be here somewhere,' said Fiona as they methodically began investigating each of the small monuments to prominent locals who had lived and died in Nassau going back to the days of the town's founding.

'Got it,' said Andrew after a couple of minutes. 'It's over here.'

Fiona turned her head to see him crouched next to an unassuming oval-topped tombstone with square shoulders carved from a single piece of limestone. The stone had once been light-coloured and smooth, but it was now a dark, pale grey, and its surface was heavily tarnished. It was also partly covered in moss and lichen, and it had minimal ornaments except for a simple cross carved into its front above a couple of lines of text.

'It's definitely this one,' he said. 'Come and look.'

Fiona joined him, crouched by his side, and let her fingertips run across the chiselled text as she read it aloud in hushed tones.

The Reverend Jack Flynn.
Born April 11, 1683.
Died October 26, 1747.

'You're right,' she said, musingly. 'Here lies the pirate who captured the Black Galleon. What secrets did he take with him into this grave?'

'What's that?' said Andrew, pointing to a small, barely visible carving just below the cross.

Fiona leaned closer to examine what appeared to be some sort of vertical, elongated symbol, and using her fingers to remove bits of lichen from it, she then realised what they were looking at.

'It's an hourglass,' she said. 'That's interesting.'

'What does that mean?' said Andrew.

'It's a century-old pirate symbol, she said. 'It's meant to symbolise that life is a fleeting thing and that we should make the most of it. I guess it was a type of mindset that summed up the life of a pirate pretty well.'

'Strange that it is on this tombstone, though,' said Andrew. 'Do you suppose Flynn had the tombstone made himself? It is almost as if he commissioned it to include that symbol as a two-fingers-up to anyone trying to fault him for his past. Even from beyond the grave.'

'I wouldn't put it past someone like him,' said Fiona. 'I feel like I've got to know him a bit, and this sort of irreverence is pretty much what I would have expected. A twisted sort of gallows humour, or whatever it is called after someone has actually died.'

'Let's find a way inside,' said Andrew, turning to look at the church.

'Right,' said Fiona, glancing towards the road, which was still quiet. 'I don't want to get spotted in here. We could really do without being charged with desecration of a religious site. I just hope we can get in without triggering an alarm.'

'I can't say I have made a habit of breaking into places of worship,' said Andrew. 'But I reckon they probably don't have the most sophisticated security measures available. Anyway, we're not actually desecrating anything. We're just having a little look around, out of hours.'

The two of them moved through the shadows to the back of the church where it met the annex. There was no access to the church itself, but there was a small door leading into the annexe. However, when Andrew gripped the cast iron door handle, it turned out to be locked.

'This lock is ancient,' he said. 'Give me a second.'

While Fiona waited, he moved along the exterior wall of the annexe while examining the ground, and after about ten metres he found what he was looking for. Bending down, he picked up a piece of stone that turned out to be roughly the top quarter of a tombstone that appeared to have broken many years ago. Returning to the door, he placed himself side-on to it and brought the tombstone piece up next to the door handle, then moved it sideways for a few practice runs.

'What was that you said about desecration?' said Fiona, eyeing the piece of the tombstone.

'Well,' said Andrew, grudgingly. 'Perhaps. Although, as far as I'm concerned, this is now just a piece of stone. Anyone coming?'

Fiona moved halfway back towards the street and stopped to listen. Then she turned to look at Andrew and gave a quick shake of the head.

'Here goes nothing,' he muttered to himself, and then he brought the stone piece out to his side, after which he rammed it hard onto the end of the door handle.

The stone, which weighed several kilos, smacked into the door handle with a crunch and a dull metallic clang, and its momentum punched the handle and the attached spindle inside the door right through the wood and out the other side. Andrew heard the handle clatter to the floor on the inside, and in the same instant, the door moved away from its frame and ended up slightly ajar. When he glanced back at Fiona, he saw her grimacing at the noise, but when she turned her head to look and listen for anyone approaching, she seemed to hear nothing, because she turned her head to look at him while giving him a quick thumbs up. He gestured silently for her to rejoin him, and a few seconds later, the two of them found themselves inside what had once been Reverend Jack Flynn's private residence.

They stood inside the foyer of the stone house for a moment, allowing their eyes to adapt to the relative darkness inside this ancient space that was lit very faintly by the streetlights out in the road past the cemetery. The air was dry and smelled of dust, and there was also a faint odour from the droppings of the mice who seemed to have made this their domain. After a few moments, the layout of the vicar's residence became apparent, and it turned out to be larger and more spacious than it had appeared from the outside. The ceiling was about two and a half metres above their heads, which would have been exceptionally high for a time when the average person was many inches shorter than today. The foyer continued into a corridor that led deeper into the house, and on either side were two doors leading into small rooms whose purpose could only be guessed at since the entire dwelling was now empty. It was clear that no one had lived here for a very long time. There was a thick layer of dust on the flagstone floor throughout the house, and none of the doorways were fitted with doors. It was as if the whole residence had been stripped bare many decades ago, most likely when the resident vicar of Trinity Chapel had moved to a more modern home somewhere else in Nassau. And ever since then, the old residence had likely been left empty and serving no use.

'This is all a bit creepy,' said Fiona. 'I'm not sure what I expected, but this isn't it.'

'Look through there,' said Andrew, having moved halfway along the corridor to where a shorter passage went off towards the church building. 'The old doorway into the church has been bricked up. So there's no way to get in from this side.'

'Damn it,' muttered Fiona, sounding disappointed. 'There's literally nothing here. It's all empty.'

'Let's have a look around,' said Andrew, risking using his phone light as a torch to light up the way as he pushed deeper into the house.

As they moved cautiously towards the end of the dusty corridor, dry bits of masonry and tiny flakes of plaster that had fallen from the ceiling crunched under their feet. They stopped to examine each room on either side, but there was no hint of what any of them had once been used for, and there was no indication that they would be able to find out anything more about Flynn in this long-abandoned place.

At the end of the corridor, they entered a room with two small windows facing out to a patch that might once have been a vegetable garden. Although also devoid of any furniture or other items that might have given away its former purpose, it was still the only recognisable room in the house on account of an alcove in the wall to their right. In years gone by, there would have been a stove there, and they could still see the now bricked-up circular outline of the chimney on the back wall of the alcove.

'This used to be the kitchen,' said Andrew, gesturing to another part of the wall between the two small windows. 'And there used to be a door to the outside here, but that's been bricked up too. I wonder how long this place has lain abandoned like this.'

Fiona moved to the alcove and placed her hands on her hips, looking around the room with a dejected expression.

'This is a dead end,' she said glumly. 'Maybe we were naïve thinking that we could just turn up here and find something after all this time.'

Andrew moved closer, placed an arm around her shoulder and was about to speak when the flagstone he stepped on produced a dull and barely audible clonk, and he also felt it shift almost imperceptibly under his foot. Fiona sensed it too, and without a word, the two of them looked down to the central flagstone that had been placed directly in front of the alcove. Only then did they realise that at roughly one metre on all sides, it was about twice as large as the other flagstones from which the kitchen floor had been made. They both crouched down to examine it, and Andrew used his torch to shine a light on it. As Fiona ran her fingers across its rough surface, her hand suddenly stopped. She wafted away some dust and bits of dry dirt, and then she gasped as a small, chiselled symbol was revealed.

'An hourglass,' she said, staring intrigued at the ancient and now barely visible pirate symbol. 'Do you think…?'

'There's got to be something underneath this,' said Andrew. 'I felt the flagstone move, and it sounded like there's some sort of cavity.'

'What if Flynn buried something under this stone?' said Fiona, her eyes lighting up at the prospect. 'Like a bag of coins.'

'I'll be right back,' said Andrew resolutely as he got to his feet. 'Don't go anywhere.'

He made his way through the corridor and back out of the house, crossed the modest cemetery and walked to the wrought iron fence where he looked first left and then right along the street to make sure he wasn't being watched. Then he gripped one of the black-painted fence's iron bars, placed his feet firmly on the ground, and wrenched the bar free, complete with a gilded fleur-de-lis at one end. This minor act of vandalism produced an uncomfortably loud metallic snap as the bar came away from the fence, but within a few seconds, he was back inside the house and rejoined Fiona in the former kitchen. When he re-entered the room and Fiona spotted what he was carrying, he held up a hand as if to ward off what she was about to say.

'Sue me,' he said dryly. 'But there's no way I am leaving this place without finding out what's underneath that flagstone.'

Using his fingers to remove most of the dust and dirt in one of the joins between the hourglass-adorned flagstone and the stone next to it, he then gripped the iron bar and jammed the tip of the gilded fleur-de-lis into the groove. It produced a loud clang, but Andrew was undeterred. Lifting the bar once again, he brought its tip straight down into the groove where it wedged itself between the two flagstones. He then used the bar as a lever to begin to lift the flagstone free from the smooth stone floor. On the first attempt, he managed to lift it up only slightly before it slipped back down into place with a muffled thump. But on his second attempt, he managed to wedge the fleur-de-lis tightly into the groove and was able to lift one side of the flagstone free by enough for him to then jam his fingers into the gap and turn the entire stone over and onto the floor. Amid a small cloud of dust that whirled up into the air, illuminated by the light from his torch, the flagstone thudded dully onto the floor to reveal something neither of them had expected. Rather than finding an item left behind by Captain Jack Flynn, such as a stash of gold coins from the Black Galleon, Andrew and Fiona found themselves staring down into a pitch-black hole. On one side of it was a set of narrow stone steps that seemed to extend down steeply into the void.

'Bingo,' said Fiona, her face suddenly lighting up with excitement as she glanced at Andrew.

'Let's have a look,' said Andrew, kneeling by the opening and shining his torch into it. 'I can't see much. We need to go down there.'

He swung his legs into the opening, and then his feet found purchase on one of the narrow steps. He began climbing down one foot at a time and noticed that the steps had very high treads, giving the impression of a ladder rather than a conventional set of stairs. As he descended, Fiona brought out her own phone and switched on its torch, helping to light the way for him as he disappeared into the gaping hole. The air was dry but noticeably cooler down there, and there was a faint, musty and slightly organic smell, as if something had decomposed a long time ago and was now barely detectable.

When he arrived at the bottom of the steps, his feet touching another stone floor, he turned around to see a small room that was roughly half the size of the kitchen above him. It had a vaulted ceiling like that of a church crypt, and its exposed, light-coloured and neatly mortared stone walls were rough and somewhat uneven, but they were draped in grey curtains of what looked like ancient cobwebs. A varnished but dust-covered desk and a chair sat by the far wall, and there was an inkwell with a quill sticking up placed on one side of it next to what appeared to be some sort of leatherbound journal or ledger. On the adjacent wall was a small bookcase with a couple of books, various trinkets and what looked like stacks of loose paper or maps. A couple of ceramic candleholders were placed on the desk and in the bookcase, each with a tray and a handle to allow them to be moved around the room. And on the walls were several small, polished brass candle sconces that would have been able to light up the entire space with just a couple of small candles. On the floor next to the desk was a wooden chest roughly the size of a picnic basket with rusty-looking metal brackets and a large, sturdy-looking lock. However, there was a key sitting in the keyhole.

'What do you see?' Fiona called down through the hole, sounding slightly anxious yet also excited.

'Come down and have a look,' said Andrew. 'I think we've found Captain Flynn's man cave.'

★   ★   ★

'Wow!' said Fiona as she took in the subterranean space, which appeared to have lain untouched for more than three centuries. 'This place is incredible.'

'It's like a time capsule in here,' said Andrew.

He then allowed his torch to sweep across the walls and the various items in the room to finally settle on what looked to be a long sword with an ebony grip and an elaborately decorated silver pommel, hanging on a hook on one of the walls. Unlike the falchion cutlass typically used by pirates, which was curved and often widening from the grip before tapering towards the tip of the blade, this weapon was slender and almost straight, tapering smoothly from its pointed tip to its handguard.

'That's an impressive weapon,' he said, stepping over and lifting it off its hook and then turning it over in his hands. 'Amazing craftsmanship.'

He gripped the hard leather scabbard and pulled out the sword, and as it came out and its still sharp edge glinted in the light from their torches, it sang for a brief moment with a faint, metallic ringing. Peering closely at the blade near the handguard, he realised that the steel had been engraved with a short line of text.

Peering closer, he read aloud.

J. Flynn.
HMNS - 1703

Andrew's brow creased for a moment before he realised what the text meant.

'This was Flynn's official navy sword,' he eventually said. 'Probably awarded to him after he graduated as an officer. 'HMNS' is the original full name of the Navy. It means 'His Majesty's Naval Service'. And 1703 was four years before the creation of the Royal Navy.'

'So, he would have graduated as an officer of the English Navy,' said Fiona.

'Strange, don't you think?' said Andrew pensively. 'That Jack Flynn would keep his navy service weapon even after turning his back on king and country and becoming a marauding pirate. Had he been caught before taking the king's pardon, he would have been strung up like so many of his fellow pirates.'

'Yes, I suppose you're right,' said Fiona, nodding pensively. 'Perhaps there was a part of him that was still proud to have been an officer. Who knows?'

'I want to see what's in there,' said Andrew, replacing the sword on the hook and pointing at the wooden chest.

He stepped over and crouched next to the small chest, gripped the lid and opened it. Inside were hundreds of rough, slightly translucent, walnut-sized stones in red, green and blue, and it was only when Fiona joined him and held one of them up in front of her torch that it became clear to her what they were looking at. As she positioned stones of each colour directly in front of the torchlight one by one, the room was lit up in hues of blood red, forest green and a deep, rich blue.

'These are uncut and unpolished gemstones,' she said, placing one of the largest red stones in front of the torchlight. 'Most likely from Peru. This is a ruby. The others are emerald and sapphire.'

'From the Black Galleon?' said Andrew.

'Without a doubt,' said Fiona. 'Uncut gemstones like these were part of the treasure fleet cargo that was transported back to Spain by the conquistadors once a year. Only then were they cut and polished into the types of gems that we see in jewellery today.'

'But they are still valuable, aren't they?' said Andrew. 'Even in this state.'

'Absolutely,' said Fiona. 'Both then and now. I reckon just one of these stones could fetch several thousand pounds. And once they've been cut and polished, it is probably at least ten times that amount.

So even the uncut stones in this chest represent a serious amount of money.'

'Alright,' said Andrew. 'But surely this is just a small portion of the treasure from the Black Galleon, right?'

'No question about it,' said Fiona. 'But these would have been much easier to transport than, say, gold or silver, which are hundreds of times heavier and bulkier. The value in this chest probably equated to dozens of large chests full of pieces of eight, so this would have been a much more efficient way of transporting and storing the loot.'

'Which begs the question,' said Andrew. 'Where's the rest of the treasure?'

'Exactly,' nodded Fiona, getting back up and looking around the room. 'Maybe the answer is in here somewhere.'

She stepped over to the desk and sat down on the small, creaking wooden chair. She placed the torch on one side of the desk so that its light shone onto a space in front of her. Then she gently slid over the dust-covered leatherbound book and was about to open it when she realised that there was something small and circular lying on top of it. It was a silver ring. She picked it up and blew the dust from it, seeing then that there was an ornate family crest engraved into it.

'What's this?' she said, turning it over and examining it. 'This looks like Flynn's signet ring. And there's something engraved on the inside.

She held it closer to the torch and leaned forward, peering at the inside of the ring with narrowed eyes to read the inscription out loud.

James Morley Flynn - 1699

'What the…?' she began before turning to face Andrew with her mouth open. 'This is James Flynn's signet ring. Jack's older brother.'

'And that sword,' said Andrew, turning to look at the navy officer's sword hanging on the wall. 'Maybe that belonged to James as well.'

The two of them stared at each other for a moment as they both appeared to come to the same conclusion.

'Was it Jack who became a vicar and lived here?' Fiona finally said. 'Or was it James the whole time?'

'It would certainly explain both the sword and the ring,' said Andrew, gesturing towards the book. 'Let's have a look inside that thing.'

Fiona put down the signet ring and carefully opened the old book. The leather binding creaked slightly as she let the front cover fold over and rest gently on the desk, and then she leaned forward to gaze at the neat handwritten text inside. She skimmed the first few pages, turning them over as carefully as she could, and after a couple of minutes, she looked up at Andrew who had been studying the signet ring.

'This is quite an astonishing tale,' said Fiona. 'It's essentially a confession. Listen to this.'

Nassau. August, 1747.
Time is the ultimate foe, and I sense that I am now losing the battle with this, my final adversary. As I look back on my life, I feel the urge to set the record straight and come to terms with my past in my own

mind, and I shall endeavour to do so here to the best of my ability. I have lived a life of apparent piety for many years, but in truth, I am not who people here in Nassau believe I am. Nor am I who I had hoped to become when I was a young man. Whether the blame lies with me or with my brother Jack, I do not know, but without him, I would never have ended up in this place, for better or for worse.

'Holy cow!' said Andrew as Fiona glanced up at him with a wistful smile. 'It was James who wrote this. It was him who lived here all along, pretending to be Jack.'

'It would appear so,' said Fiona. 'Let me read the next bit to you.'

I had all but severed any ties with my brother after his embrace of piracy, and I believed that I would never see him again. However, fate played a cruel trick on me when I came face to face with him again on that ill-fated night in 1714 aboard El Castillo Negro in the harbour of Port Royal. As watch officer for the night, I was entrusted with the safekeeping of the treasure galleon and her cargo overnight as she awaited repairs on the following day.

I could never have imagined that anyone would be so bold as to attempt to capture her from under the guns of Port Royal, much less that it would be my own brother who would do so. He and his men killed the entire detachment of soldiers, and I was only spared because of my kinship with the ringleader. At the time, I felt such shame and anger, but I was nonetheless happy to be alive. When the Port Royal gunpowder store went up in flames and the galleon set sail and slipped out of the harbour, I was chained in the captain's quarters and in the depths of despair. I realised then that even if I lived, I would be forever disgraced as the officer on whose watch one of the largest prizes ever captured from the Spanish had slipped from the grasp of the Royal Navy. And there was every chance that I would be court-martialed and hanged for my negligence in protecting the King's treasure. Hopelessness enveloped me, but it soon turned to fury at the predicament my brother had placed me in, and I became desperate for some semblance of retribution. And the opportunity would come soon enough.

On the following morning, after our rendezvous with my brother's ship, the Marauder, we set sail from Jamaica. Although I was confined to the captain's quarters, where I was chained up and barely able to move, from the position of the ship relative to the sun, I was able to gather that we were sailing almost due east. After two days on the open sea, by which time we had put Port Royal and any pursuing Royal Navy vessels far behind us, we arrived at our destination. It was a small, uninhabited and unnamed island known to sailors simply as Lizard Island on account of the many small and colourful creatures that lived there. Here, I was brought onto the deck and transferred to the Marauder. My brother's crew then set about dismantling the galleon's masts and rigging, leaving only the hull intact. It was a momentous task that took more than a day, and I could not for the life of me understand the purpose. Only when I realised that we had anchored next to an enormous sea cave that stretched into the side of the flat and rocky island did I understand Jack's intentions. The men called it the Cave of Skulls due to the appearance of its interior, although I never saw it for myself. By the end of the second day, the stripped galleon with its treasure had been floated inside the cave to be hidden there. The crew then began emptying the ship's gunpowder store to create enormous explosive charges, which were placed around the mouth of the sea cave. Several large chests were then brought aboard the Marauder from the cave, and my brother told his crew that they had been filled with gemstones later to be shared equally among them all. However, for reasons I could not yet discern, he confided to me that they in fact contained nothing but rocks from the cave. Only Jack and a trusted boatswain named Larkin were inside the galleon when the chests were filled with gems, but when they were finally ready to be taken aboard the Marauder, my brother claimed that Larkin had attempted to murder him just as the chests were sealed. He told the crew that he had been forced to kill Larkin with his dagger, which led to much consternation and shock among the men. However, the plan proceeded, and the chests containing the rocks were then carried aboard. Everyone was back aboard the Marauder when the burning fuses finally reached the explosive charges, and when they blew, the entire cavemouth collapsed, sealing the galleon inside and hiding it entirely from view.

'So they hid the galleon in a cave and collapsed the entrance,' said Andrew. 'But why fill those chests with rocks? Was he trying to trick his crew out of their share, just like you said?'

'Sounds like it,' said Fiona. 'It explains perfectly why you found those strange rocks inside the wreck of the Marauder.'

'What an absolute bastard this Captain Flynn was,' said Andrew. 'No loyalty whatsoever to his own men. Anyway, none of this tells us anything about where this Lizard Island might be.'

'Right,' said Fiona, 'except that it appears to have been a couple of days sailing from Port Royal. But that could be a lot of different places. There are lots of islands inside that range. Anyway, there's more. Listen.'

Whether it was the thunderous explosion designed to hide the treasure galleon that gave my brother the idea, or whether he had already planned the whole thing, I will never know. However, many days later, when we had dropped anchor at the pirate den of Tortuga, my brother revealed his dastardly scheme to me. He was planning to blow up his own ship and kill the entire crew so that he could take all the treasure for himself, and he offered me a share and even released me from my chains to show that he was sincere. However, I would hear nothing of such a ploy, and the entire scheme was so diabolical that I could hardly believe it. I have no love of pirates, not even my own brother, but to kill the men who had been loyal to him through countless perilous raids at sea was simply dishonourable beyond measure, and so I attempted to dissuade him from his chosen course. However, nothing I said could change his mind, and as the evening wore on, he became furiously angry as he consumed ever more rum. He suddenly threw himself at me, pummeling me with his fists. When I fought back, he pulled a dagger from his side. The memories of the events that followed are a tangled mess, but I clearly remember standing over him as he lay dead with his own dagger plunged deep into his chest. I was covered in his blood and unable to fathom what I had done. This was my own brother lying dead before me, and by my hand had he lost his life.

This moment, as terrible as it was, would become truly pivotal to me. I realised that I had no way back to my old life, and that I now had a singular opportunity to take fate into my own hands and chart a course for the future, free of my past. In that moment, I decided to leave James Flynn behind and become my brother Jack.

I left the captain's quarters and headed below to where I knew the gunpowder storage was, and just as Jack had explained, there were fuses there already prepared for the deed that mere hours earlier I had deemed abhorrent but which I was now about to carry out. To my shame, I did not hesitate as I lit the fuse, but on the way back up to the deck, I was confronted by some of the crew. I killed anyone standing in my way, and I only just managed to escape over the side of the ship and plunge into the water as the powder store blew and ripped the Marauder to pieces. As I swam to shore under some mangrove trees near the town, I was sure that the entire crew had been killed, and I could see people in the town converge on the jetties to watch the burning remains of my brother's frigate. And in that moment, James Flynn was no more. Only Jack would live on, and that is who I have been ever since.

'Wow,' said Andrew, amazed as he looked around the room. 'He stole his brother's identity. And this was his secret den.'

'Clearly,' said Fiona. 'I suppose this hidden space was the only place where he could allow himself to be James again, if only for a little while in between pretending to be Reverend Jack. What a strange life to lead. Anyway, let me read this next bit.'

Masquerading as Jack proved very much easier than I expected, partly due to the scars on my face caused by the fiery explosion. I lived as Jack Flynn for many years, assembling a new crew and capturing several prizes. But on a number of occasions, I returned alone to Lizard Island to retrieve some of the treasure whenever I was short on funds. Setting out from Petit Goave, I could reach the island in less than two days, and once there, a secret passage into the cave allowed me to reach the treasure galleon and its cargo of riches.

However, the lure of the gold, silver and gemstones waned with the years, and so when a royal proclamation was announced in the year 1717 offering a pardon to all pirates in the colonies, I decided to finally leave that part of my life behind and become a vicar here in Nassau. My transformation into a man of the cloth was simpler than I had dared to hope, and I soon became well-respected by the townsfolk of Nassau. Only once was I compelled to protect my new life, but in a contest between a pirate and a bishop, the pirate will always prevail.

'So he *did* kill the bishop,' said Andrew, intrigued. 'This is as much of a confession as anyone is going to be able to find. The Reverend Flynn was not a reformed pirate. He was a Royal Navy officer who succumbed to exactly the same temptations as his swashbuckling brother. And from what you just read, it doesn't sound like he was remotely bothered by killing the bishop either. Some man of the cloth he was. Seems like he had a lot more in common with Jack than he liked to admit.'

'No kidding,' said Fiona with a faint smile. 'I'm pretty sure Saint Peter would have been none too pleased when James finally arrived at the pearly gates in 1747.'

'Is that the end of it?' said Andrew, glancing at the leatherbound journal.

'There are only a couple of paragraphs left,' said Fiona. 'Let me read them to you.'

My life has been an extraordinary one, and now that I am nearing the end, I cannot say if I would have wanted it to happen differently. My only regret is that it took me so long to realise that as much as I loathed what Jack had become, it was I, James, who was shackled by a life of servitude to the King. And it was my brother Jack who had found true freedom to live as he pleased. When I now look in the mirror, I see both myself and Jack, and I often find myself wondering if my recollections are my own, or if they are in fact merely Jack's life playing out inside my mind. We appear to have now become one. We were as close as two brothers could be when we were young, so perhaps it was always meant to be this way. However, only I am left, and soon I will go to meet him again. Perhaps he and I can find reconciliation in the next life.

'That's pretty heavy,' said Andrew. 'He seemed like a very conflicted man. At least in his old age.'

'I think that happens to a lot of people,' said Fiona. 'When we're young, most things seem obvious and straightforward. But as we get older, things become more nuanced, and suddenly everything ends up being a bit more complicated. I think that's probably what happened here.'

'Right,' said Andrew. 'As interesting as James Flynn's psychology might be, what I want to know is this. What and where is Lizard Island?'

'Yes,' said Fiona, reaching for the stack of old maps lying on the shelf of the bookcase and placing it gently on the desk in front of her. 'That seems to be the question now. Maybe there is a clue here.'

Taking the utmost care not to stress and tear the ancient maps, she placed the maps side by side on the desk until its surface was almost completely covered, and then the two of them began examining each one in detail, looking for any marks or annotations that might indicate where Lizard Island and Skull Cave could be found. However, none of the maps appeared to have been scribbled on, and there were neither marks nor lines that might provide a clue as to where Jack Flynn had hidden the Spanish treasure more than three hundred years earlier.

'Drat,' sighed Fiona, sounding disappointed. 'I really thought this would give us a hint.'

'Well, I guess 'X' doesn't always mark the spot,' said Andrew.

'We might need to get hold of a really detailed map of the Caribbean and see which islands it might be,' said Fiona. 'Lizard Island was just what the sailors used to call it, but it is bound to have an official name by now, wherever it is.'

'Should we take Flynn's journal with us?' said Andrew.

'Yes,' said Fiona resolutely. 'I think we definitely should. Once we don't need it any more, I am sure I can arrange for it to be handed over to the appropriate archaeological or historical society. But we should bring it with us for reference.'

'What about the gemstones?' said Andrew.

'We should leave them here,' said Fiona. 'They belong to whatever part of South America the Spanish conquistadors took them from.'

'Makes sense,' said Andrew. 'They'll be safe here until that can be sorted out.'

'OK,' said Fiona, looking around the small room as if reluctant to leave. 'It seems we've found what there is to find down here. I also need some sleep soon. I'm suddenly feeling exhausted.'

'Alright,' said Andrew, moving towards the steep steps leading back up to the former kitchen. 'We'll seal up the access when we leave.'

'Definitely,' said Fiona. 'We don't want anyone else poking around down here. Everything in this room ought to end up in a local museum.'

'Good idea,' said Andrew. 'Now, come on. Let's get out of here and get back to the hotel.'

Twenty-One

The next morning, they were awoken by the muffled sound of a cruise ship's foghorn as one of the enormous floating cities pulled away from the cruise port and left Nassau to continue its circuit around the Bahamas. The sun shone from a clear blue sky, and below them in the streets of the old town, they could hear the start of a new day of bustling tourist commerce begin.

Wearing a thin, white dressing gown that moved gently in the faint breeze, Fiona was standing on the balcony and looking out over the marina and the old town. In the golden light of the morning sun, Nassau now appeared very different from the night before. There were dozens of narrow, winding, cobbled streets with souvenir and artisan shops, a plethora of bars and restaurants, and many of the buildings, most of which were only two or three storeys tall, were painted in cheerful pastel colours of yellow, blue and green. Along the promenade were palm trees whose fronds moved softly in the breeze, and the pavements were already beginning to fill up with pedestrians, most of whom appeared to be American tourists.

'I wouldn't mind spending a day or two poking around in the shops here,' Fiona said to Andrew as he joined her.

He was holding cups of coffee that he had just made for them in the small in-room kitchenette, and as the weather was pleasantly warm already, he was wearing only his jeans and an open shirt.

'It's all very characterful,' she said, taking a sip from her cup. 'So much to see.'

'Yes, although a bit busy for my liking,' said Andrew, glancing at the massive floating apartment blocks moored in the cruise port. 'I can't imagine the locals are too thrilled with this many tourists every day of the year. But I guess it keeps the local economy healthy.'

As he spoke, Fiona's phone chimed on one of the bedside tables, and she went inside to fetch it while Andrew slurped his coffee and watched a couple of the yachts pulling away from their moorings and then slowly making their way out of the marina and east along Paradise Island towards the ocean.

'Where do you think we might be able to get our hands on a really good map of the Caribbean?' he called over his shoulder towards the balcony's open French doors. 'We need a very detailed one that shows all the small islands.'

'We might not have to,' said Fiona, re-emerging onto the balcony with her phone in her hands.

'What do you mean?' he said, turning to face her.

'I just received a message from the mineral sample laboratory at the Natural History Museum,' said

Fiona. 'They have completed the analysis of the rock sample from the Marauder, and they will be running the results through their database shortly to look for a match. We should have an answer later today.'

'That's great,' said Andrew. 'Let's cross our fingers and hope they can help pin down Lizard Island. What do you want to do while we wait?'

'I think I have an idea,' said Fiona, peering out east along the promenade towards a small, dark grey structure built virtually on the beach in the distance.

Half an hour later, the two of them were walking across a small parking lot about five hundred metres due east of the marina. Surrounded by palm trees and with two beaches protected by rock breakwaters and meeting at a sharp point that overlooked Nassau Harbour and the open ocean further east, they found a small fort built from large, neatly cut limestone blocks. Square in shape and with five-metre tall walls that sloped inwards slightly, the defensive fortification was roughly twenty-five metres on all sides. The limestone was severely weathered and stained grey and black by centuries of rain and saltwater spray from the nearby beaches, but its form left visitors in no doubt about its original purpose.

'This is called Fort Montague,' said Fiona as they approached. 'It was built in 1741, long after the Golden Age of Piracy had ended.'

'It looks a bit small,' said Andrew, regarding the diminutive fortification, which had a handful of bronze cannons placed on top of its walls.

'Yes, it's really more of a gun battery than a fort,' said Fiona. 'I think it had about twenty-three cannons fitted inside it when it was operational. But it was only ever intended to provide suppressing fire on any would-be attackers coming from the east. The town's main defensive structure was obviously Fort Nassau, which was the main fort back in town. And that fort was under the control of the pirates for about twenty years until Woodes Rogers arrived with the King's Pardon in his pocket. But that fort isn't there anymore. I think it was demolished in the late 19th century.'

'Did this fort ever see battle?' said Andrew, glancing up at the cannons.

'It did,' said Fiona. 'Once, during what's known as the Battle of Nassau, although it had nothing to do with pirates. It happened in 1776 during the American War of Independence when Nassau was under British control and there was a severe gunpowder shortage. The American revolutionaries decided to raid Nassau to get their hands on the gunpowder storage here. And apparently, Fort Montague had a huge amount of the stuff stored inside, so a group of American marines turned up and launched an amphibious assault right here on this beach. They raided the fort and stole all the gunpowder, which they then took back to the continental colonies to fight against the British.'

'Very clever,' said Andrew as he shielded his eyes from the sun and peered out across the beach and the azure blue waters towards the east. 'I'm sure the British never saw that raid coming, which is why it worked. Speaking of which, you know that the acronym SAS is short for Special Air Service, but it also has a different meaning.'

'Really?' said Fiona.

'Well, unofficially, anyway,' said Andrew. 'It's short for the words speed, aggression and surprise, which is what the Regiment always strives for. And that's exactly what the American Marines did here. It's been a winning tactic for centuries, if not millennia.'

A gentle and warm breeze drifted across the beach and onto the small lawn next to the parking lot as the two of them sat down on a bench in the shade of a couple of palm trees. After a couple of minutes, Fiona's phone chimed again, and she extracted it to see that there was another message from her contact at the Natural History Museum.

'That was quick,' she said. 'The analysis results are here already.'

'Alright,' said Andrew, moving closer. 'Let's have a look.'

Fiona opened the attached PDF document and began skimming through it.

'Let's see here,' she began. 'Various mineralogical profiles. Pyrite, feldspar, dolomite, clay, chalk, marl, limestone etc, etc. It's all very detailed.'

'Let's just skip to the conclusion,' said Andrew.

'Right,' she said. 'There's a short write-up here at the bottom by one of the lab technicians. The gist of it is that the rocks almost certainly originated from a raised atoll somewhere in the central Caribbean Sea. In other words, after building for millions of years, an area packed with coral reefs was raised above sea level by tectonic activity to become an island. But the limestone on this particular island seems to have a very unique composition since it contains exceptionally high levels of phosphates.'

'Phosphates?' said Andrew. 'What does that mean?'

'According to the lab technician,' said Fiona, 'it essentially means bird poo.'

'Really?' said Andrew, raising an eyebrow. 'Alright. So where is the rock from?'

'Well,' said Fiona. 'There's apparently only one place in the Caribbean where the rock composition fits the profile of the sample from the wreck of the Marauder, and that is a place called Navassa Island.'

'What and where is that?' said Andrew.

'It's a small uninhabited island roughly two-thirds of the way from Jamaica to Haiti,' said Fiona.

'That would fit with it taking Flynn about two days to get there from Port Royal,' said Andrew.

Within seconds, Fiona had found a map and several photos of the island on her phone, and its appearance was that of a flat, raised and rocky, teardrop-shaped plateau that seemed to protrude almost unnaturally from the surrounding ocean. It looked barren and dry, and its surface had only very little vegetation. In addition, most of its sides were near-vertical cliffs some twenty or thirty metres high, and as Andrew studied them, he gave a pensive nod.

'This could be it,' he said. 'Look at those rock faces. There are bound to be sea caves around the perimeter of the island, so it is at least possible that this is where the galleon was hidden.'

'Seems like it's been inhabited by large populations of birds for tens of thousands of years,' said Fiona, 'so it was used as a guano mine for a long time. Hence the richness in phosphates. And phosphates are used as fertiliser. It was actually access to this guano that caused the US to claim the island in 1857, despite

Haiti already having claimed it. And now it is officially listed as a disputed territory.'

'Well, whatever it is today,' said Andrew, 'it appears to have been of no interest to anyone back in the early 18th century, which is why Flynn chose it. He seems to have had the whole thing worked out in great detail.'

'Oh,' said Fiona, glancing up at him with a smile after reading a brief paragraph about the island. 'Guess what lives there too, apart from birds.'

'What?' said Andrew.

'Lizards,' said Fiona. 'Lots and lots of lizards.'

'I think we found it,' Andrew said, a smile playing on his lips. 'Now all we need to do is find the collapsed cave.'

'Well, yes,' Fiona said, somewhat hesitantly. 'But there might be a small issue with that.'

'Which is what?' said Andrew.

'Because the island is claimed by the US and the subject of a territorial dispute,' she said, 'any access is strictly prohibited. We would need a permit issued by the US military.'

'Right,' said Andrew, mulling over their options. 'Well, you did say that it is uninhabited, right?'

'Yes,' Fiona said. 'So?'

'So, who's going to stop us?' he said as a faintly mischievous smile spread across his face.

★ ★ ★

When Andrew and Fiona strapped back into the seats of the Airbus H135 and lifted off from Nassau's heliport, the sun was nearing its apex, and with a full fuel tank, they were ready to cover the almost eight-hundred-kilometre journey to Navassa Island. The weather was fair, and the estimated flight time was a touch under three hours. As Nassau and New Providence Island became a faint shimmer on the blue horizon behind them, Fiona turned to Andrew.

'I did a bit of digging on the way to the airport,' she said, 'and I discovered something really fascinating about Navassa Island.'

'Let's hear it,' said Andrew.

'Beginning in the 1860s,' Fiona said, 'there was a guano mining colony there for several decades, but it only operated in the most easily accessible areas, and so they clearly didn't find any sea caves with treasure hidden inside. But in a strange mirror of what happened in Haiti about half a century earlier, the African American contract labourers working there rebelled against their white overseers because of poor working conditions, and it actually ended in an armed confrontation where several of the overseers were killed.'

'Wow,' said Andrew, glancing at her with his hands gripping the controls and guiding the chopper on a southeasterly heading. 'What happened to the workers?'

'The case went to the US Supreme Court,' said Fiona, 'and a handful of them were sentenced to death. But not too long after that, the guano mine became unprofitable, and the island was abandoned for many decades until 1917. And this is where it gets interesting because, in a curious twist, Navassa Island's fate became intertwined with what happened in Panama near the River Chagres, which is where one could argue that the Golden Age of Piracy originally began with Henry Morgan's famous raid there.'

'How so?' said Andrew.

'As I said,' Fiona continued, 'Navassa Island lay deserted until 1917 because that was when the US government decided to build a lighthouse there. The reason was the fact that the Panama Canal had opened three years earlier, and there was now so much sea traffic passing through the Caribbean and the strait between Jamaica and Haiti that a safe sea route was necessary. So the first permanent structures were built there in the form of a fifty-metre-tall lighthouse and a small house for a lighthouse keeper. Apparently, it is still there, and it sits on a spot on the island that is about 70 metres above sea level. So that's how high the island is in some places.'

'Sounds like a lonely spot for someone to live and work,' said Andrew, 'although I guess I could see the appeal. Far away from everything else, just you and your own thoughts for a few months. Nice warm weather most of the year. Maybe it wasn't so bad.'

'Well, those lighthouse keepers were there for a lot longer than that,' said Fiona. 'Years at a time. So, I reckon it required a certain type of person to be able to do that without coming down with a serious case of cabin fever. Anyway, this is where things get really fascinating. You see, one of the lighthouse keepers who worked there for a number of years in the 1950s, a man named Jacob Warner, one day reportedly found a badly decomposed skeleton in a deep crevice on the southwestern side of the island. Now, at first, he thought it might have been the remains of one of the labourers from the old guano mine, but it turned out that it couldn't have been the case, because all the deaths of labourers were fully accounted for by the mining company, and their bodies were all brought back for burial to their home towns in America. No one was ever buried or left behind on Navassa.'

'How do we know all this?' said Andrew.

'Because the lighthouse keeper was removed from the island by his employer, the U.S. Coast Guard, in 1957,' said Fiona. 'Apparently, he had more or less lost his marbles and was exhibiting signs of delusions. That's what his medical report said. He had become convinced that there was a treasure hidden somewhere on the island, and he was so obsessed with the idea that he was eventually deemed psychologically unstable and essentially unfit for the duty of ensuring the safety of passing ships.'

'Bizarre,' said Andrew. 'Who was it that Warner had found?'

'That's the thing,' said Fiona. 'According to Warner's testimony to the Coast Guard, after they brought him back to the U.S., the skeleton's clothes had all virtually decomposed, but he had found an old dagger, a brass belt buckle and a few other metal items that had survived since the man died. And Warner swore that they appeared several centuries old. But he also said that he had found a handful of Spanish silver coins and some gemstones.'

'Really?' said Andrew, raising an eyebrow. 'That's a strange coincidence.'

'Exactly,' said Fiona. 'But Warner refused to show these to anyone or reveal precisely where he had found the dead man. And he claimed to have given the skeleton of that unfortunate soul a proper burial in a secret location somewhere on the island. Anyway, he was eventually deemed so mentally unstable that he was fired in short order and a new lighthouse keeper was appointed. But there were never any reports of any other similar finds on the island after that.'

'Silver coins and gemstones,' said Andrew, glancing at her. 'That sounds awfully familiar.'

'Well, it does to us,' Fiona agreed, 'but to anyone else, you might forgive them for thinking that Warner really had lost his mind and was just imagining things. Either way, this is another hint that Navassa could very well turn out to have become the final destination of the Black Galleon.'

'Well, it's certainly beginning to look that way,' said Andrew. 'Were you able to find out anything else about Jacob Warner?'

'No,' said Fiona. 'He died in 1974, and as far as I can work out, he left no written records of his time on the island.'

'I guess we'll just have to see what we can find when we get there,' said Andrew, peering out at the seemingly endless blue ocean stretching ahead of them. 'We've done it before.'

Twenty-Two

It was midafternoon when Fiona spotted Navassa Island in the far distance. At first, it appeared like a hazy mirage on the edge of what her eyes were able to perceive. Just a thin, ethereal sliver of faintly moving pale yellow and green that eventually coalesced into a solid form far away where the curvature of the Earth only just allowed her to see it.

'I think we're finally here,' she said, pointing ahead.

Andrew leaned forward and looked at the moving map display on the instrument panel, and then he peered through the chopper's glass bubble canopy. At about three kilometres long and two kilometres wide, the island's size was about twice that of Hyde Park in London, but it looked tiny from the air as they drew nearer. It was also almost perfectly flat, with its terrain rising only slightly from west to east, and its general appearance was true to its nature as a raised atoll. A part of the coral-covered seabed that, millions of years ago, had been raised by immense tectonic forces deep beneath the ocean inside the Earth's crust.

'Look there,' said Fiona, pointing to the easternmost part of the island where something tall and thin protruded up into the air. 'That's the lighthouse.'

The tall structure was a faintly truncated cone that seemed to rise up like a thin, tapering needle from the otherwise completely flat surface. When they were a few kilometres out, they could see the waves breaking on the sheer cliffs that surrounded almost the entire island and made access to its flat interior more than a little challenging. However, with a helicopter, they would be able to touch down more or less anywhere they wanted, and Andrew adjusted the chopper's heading to line up with a large clear area about a hundred metres from the lighthouse. Drawing closer, they could see a deep, several-hundred-metre-long natural trench that had formed in the rock, most likely as a result of some sort of localised release of tectonic tension in the island's crust. The trench was only a few dozen metres from the lighthouse, but it was likely many aeons old now and had long ago settled into an unmoving state.

As Andrew flared out the chopper and they came in to land, they could see the details of the square former lighthouse keeper's residence, whose thick white walls had been constructed from brick and concrete. It now had neither doors nor windows or even a roof, and they were able to look down into the structure and see the room layout.

'I didn't think it would be this big,' said Fiona, looking at the now completely derelict building. 'It would have easily been able to accommodate a small family. I wonder if any children once lived here. It would have been a spectacular place to grow up.'

'If I had grown up here,' said Andrew, nudging the control stick as he guided the chopper towards its landing spot, 'I would have spent every single day outside. And I would probably have found the Spanish treasure myself if it's actually here.'

A large, pale cloud of dust whirled up around the chopper as the vortex created by its main rotor tore at the low vegetation near the lighthouse. Eventually, the skids made contact with the dry, rocky ground, and Andrew then killed the engines and checked the fuel gauge. They had spent more than half of their available fuel, so a return journey to Nassau was out of the question. However, they would easily be able to reach Kingston in Jamaica.

After touching down under the powerful afternoon sun, the high-pitched whine of the turbofan engines died down, and the rotors gradually slowed and then stopped spinning. Andrew and Fiona then opened the cockpit doors and climbed down onto the arid, rocky ground where only small tufts of pale grass and patches of moss grew. All around them, they could hear the dry drone of cicadas and the buzzing of a multitude of other insects. The air was hot and dry, and aside from the insects and the small amounts of low vegetation, it seemed that hardly anything lived or grew on the island. However, within a few seconds, Fiona heard faint rustling coming from under a low, parched-looking bush. Moments later, a pale brown lizard some ten centimetres long scurried out from under the bush and sprinted away towards a few tufts of yellow grass nearby. As it ran, its tail was partially curled up over its back, instantly giving away what type of reptile it was.

'That didn't take long,' smiled Fiona, glancing at Andrew as he closed the door to the cockpit. 'That was a curly-tailed lizard. And where there's one, there are many.'

'What do they eat around here?' said Andrew, watching the reptile scamper into safety and disappear from view. 'This place seems dry as a bone.'

'Yes,' said Fiona. 'There's no natural water source here, which is why this place was more or less ignored for centuries. But the soil is obviously extremely fertile, even if it looks totally desiccated. So, the plants here can survive just on rainwater, and the lizards live off the insects. Navassa is almost like a small closed ecosystem, but only a small number of different types of creatures can survive here.'

Andrew turned and placed his hands on his hips as he looked up towards the top of the tall, smoothly tapering lighthouse. At the top was the lantern room, which somehow appeared to have retained all its glass panes over the years, and it was domed by a metal cupola that was a deep orange-red colour as rust had completely taken over the roof. Similarly corroded was the metal guardrail on the walkway that circled the outside of the lantern room, and underneath it was a series of three tall, slim and equidistantly placed windows that allowed light to enter the narrow structure's interior. He lowered his gaze to what had once been the lighthouse keeper's residence, and the single-storey building looked significantly more derelict and dilapidated up close than it had from the air. The constant beating down of the powerful tropical sun and the ever-present wind, salty sea spray and occasional rain had weathered the structure over the decades since its abandonment, to the point where it now looked badly ruined. With nothing but gaping holes where there had once been wooden doors and windows, the structure appeared oddly sad and forlorn.

'The house is barely standing anymore,' said Andrew. 'Come on. Let's have a look inside.'

They left the chopper and headed towards the only doorway leading inside, and they soon found themselves in what had once been a hallway. There was not a trace of anyone ever having lived there, and with its bare, slowly crumbling walls and nothing but blue sky above where the roof should have been, the house looked more like an incomplete and abandoned building site than a place that had once been home to a long sequence of lighthouse keepers spanning most of an entire century. Small bushes and tufts of yellow grass now grew in all the different rooms, and as they walked around inside it, they began to get a sense of the layout.

'This might have been part of the living quarters,' said Andrew, gesturing to one of the larger rooms. 'And I reckon that through there could have been bedrooms and maybe a kitchen and dining room. And I think the other side of the building might have been for an office and some other functional rooms for the lighthouse keeper.'

'It's pretty big,' said Fiona. 'More than enough for one person or even a whole family. If Warner was here by himself, which I think he was, then I could see why he might have gone a bit loopy. All alone in a house this large.'

'Yes,' said Andrew. 'You have to wonder what a man like that did with all that time. Running and maintaining the lighthouse couldn't possibly have taken up more than a couple of hours per day. So what else did he get up to around here?'

'Maybe he spent a lot of time exploring the island,' said Fiona. 'That's how he found that skeleton.'

'Well, there's hardly anything else to do around here,' said Andrew. 'He probably knew the whole place like the back of his hand.'

'If only he would have written something down about his discovery of that skeleton,' said Fiona wistfully. 'Everyone else thought he was crazy and imagining things, but I think he was telling the truth. I think he found someone who died here centuries ago.'

Suddenly, she froze for a moment, her mind racing as she turned to face Andrew.

'Wait a minute,' she said as her eyes widened. 'What if that skeleton was the remains of the boatswain James mentioned in his journal?'

'Larkin?' said Andrew.

'Yes,' said Fiona. 'The man Jack claimed had tried to kill him when they were loading the rocks into the chests. If Captain Flynn was going to trick his own crew and bring only rocks onboard the Marauder before killing them all at Tortuga, then Larkin would have been the only man standing in his way. Only he knew that the chests were full of rocks from inside that cave.'

'You're suggesting Larkin somehow survived being stabbed by Jack Flynn?' said Andrew.

'Yes,' said Fiona. 'And then after the Marauder had left, he somehow found a way out of the collapsed cave but died later in the crevice where Warner then found his remains.'

'It's plausible, I guess,' Andrew said with a pensive nod. 'It would explain the silver coins and the gems that he found with the skeleton.'

'What a terrible fate,' said Fiona as she imagined the scenario of the boatswain being attempted murdered by his own captain, only to then be left mortally wounded to die on a desert island with no source of fresh water. 'It doesn't even bear thinking about.'

'I think we've established that Jack Flynn was a real bastard,' said Andrew.

'Well, his brother wasn't much better,' said Fiona. 'Seems like it ran in the family. Anyway, there's nothing here to find but crumbling walls. Let's go back out and investigate the lighthouse tower.'

They headed back outside and walked around the virtually derelict main building to stand at the foot of the almost fifty-metre-tall lighthouse. It had once been painted white, but its exterior was now just bare and mottled-looking concrete that had been bleached by the power of the sun. The single entrance at its base was facing the main building, and a rusty but solid-looking steel door barred any entry.

'Damn it,' said Fiona. 'Doesn't look like we'll be able to get in.'

Andrew stepped closer and gripped the heavily corroded door handle, but the door didn't budge at all. It was securely locked, and on top of that, it looked as if the heavy corrosion had partly grafted it to the metal doorframe.

'Right,' he said, rubbing his chin for a few moments. 'Since we're already technically trespassing on U.S. government property, we might as well go all the way and add vandalism to the charge sheet.'

'Wait, what are you planning?' said Fiona dubiously, realising that Andrew wasn't about to let an old door stop him from climbing to the top of the tower.

'Give me a moment,' he said, showing Fiona the palm of his hand as he backed away and began turning towards the helicopter. 'I'll be right back.'

Moments later, he returned with the black holdall containing his weapons stash, and he extracted another one of the small, spherical hand grenades that he had stolen from the brothel in Port-au-Prince.

'This just might do the trick,' he said, placing the holdall away from the door and a few metres further along the lighthouse's curving exterior wall.

'Are you sure this is a good idea?' said Fiona.

'We haven't come this far only to back down from investigating this place properly,' said Andrew. 'This lighthouse is the only way to get a clear overview of the whole island. Who knows what we might be able to see from up there.'

'Right,' Fiona nodded grudgingly.

'This is an M67 fragmentation grenade,' said Andrew. 'So, best stand back.'

'No kidding,' said Fiona dryly, moving towards the holdall.

'The lethal blast range is roughly five metres,' said Andrew, 'but it can cause serious injuries out to about fifteen metres.'

'In other words,' said Fiona, 'just stay well clear.'

'As long as you don't have a line of sight to the grenade,' said Andrew, 'it can't hurt you when it goes off. I'm going to hook it to the door handle just above the lock, and then I've got four seconds to get into cover.'

'I just hope you know what you're doing,' said Fiona, sounding decidedly unenthusiastic, but knowing full well that if anyone was capable of handling explosives safely, it was Andrew. 'Am I going to be OK here?'

He looked from her to the door and back again, and then he nodded.

'Yes,' he said. 'That's fine. Just don't move from there. And it's going to be loud.'

Crouching next to the door, he used a carry strap from one of the AR-15s to tie the grenade to the door handle so that it dangled just in front of the lock's keyhole. Then, holding down the spoon, he pulled out the safety pin.

'Ready?' he called to Fiona, who was now out of sight from where he was sitting.

'As ready as I'll ever be,' said Fiona half-heartedly.

'Fire in the hole,' Andrew then called as he released the spoon and allowed it to fly off as the fuse ignited and began burning down through the grenade fuse channel.

He jumped to his feet and hurried out of the doorway and around the side of the lighthouse base to join Fiona who already had both hands covering her ears. Four seconds after the spoon had been ejected, the fuse reached the centre of the grenade where it instantly ignited the 180-gram high-explosive charge. The blast was as loud as Andrew had warned, and the dry, ear-splitting blast raced out from the doorway as the fragmentation grenade disintegrated and sent hundreds of small, sharp metal fragments flying off in all directions at well above the speed of sound. Roughly half of the fragments tore into the steel door, many of which ripped through the lock less than an inch away. The other half tore through the air and flew out and away from the lighthouse tower, some of them smacking into the exterior wall of the former lighthouse keeper's residence. In addition, the powerful shockwave punched straight into the area around the lock and shattered many of its internal components. The noise from the blast eventually dissipated out across the island and the surrounding sea, and when the dust had settled and most of the smoke had cleared, Andrew and Fiona walked back to inspect the result. The door handle was missing, and the door was now somewhat bent out of shape and slightly ajar, and acrid smoke from the explosive charge still hung in the air, slowly drifting away on the breeze.

'There we go,' said Andrew, sounding content. 'That worked perfectly.'

'Guns, I can just about handle,' said Fiona, sounding unconvinced, 'but explosives, I will never get used to.'

'That's probably a good thing,' said Andrew, pushing the door open. 'Come on.'

As it moved on its hinges, the door produced a shrill metallic screech, and bits of rust and masonry debris from the explosion fell off the doorframe and onto the ground. Andrew pushed firmly to open it, and when it swung inwards and opened fully, they were greeted by the sight of a circular concrete floor where a set of wooden boxes had been stacked. There were also a couple of fuel cans and an old generator, which for some reason had been left behind when the lighthouse was closed, stripped bare and abandoned many decades ago. Around the circumference of the floor, a rusty spiral staircase made of metal began winding its way upwards towards the top of the tower, and Fiona regarded it warily as they stepped inside.

'Do you think this is safe?' she said, craning her neck to look up through the centre of the metal helix towards the lantern room. 'It seems pretty heavily corroded.'

'Let's find out,' said Andrew, unperturbed as he moved towards the lower section where the steps met the concrete floor.

He placed a firm kick on the railing, and the entire staircase sang and vibrated as the force of the impact travelled upwards. Tiny flakes of rust began raining down around them, but the staircase appeared otherwise unaffected. Then he stepped onto the bottom step and stamped hard. Once again, bits of rusty metal flaked off, but the metal step was neither broken nor bent out of shape.

'It seems fine,' he said. 'The rust is just on the surface of the metal, but the structure seems strong enough. I'll go first. If it can take my weight, then it can take yours.'

With Fiona stepping closer and watching him, Andrew began cautiously climbing the staircase, putting one foot carefully in front of the other, and soon he had climbed up one whole revolution and was looking down at her.

'It seems fine,' he said. 'Follow me at your own pace.'

He kept climbing, and as he did so, the helix of the metal structure tightened as the tower narrowed. Every two revolutions, he passed one of the three windows that had been visible from the outside, and they afforded him an increasingly clear view of the eastern part of the island and the lighthouse keeper's residence below. Moving ever higher, the metal joints occasionally groaned, and the entire structure seemed to wobble slightly as he and Fiona made their way upwards. When he reached the final window, the tower's interior was less than ten metres across, and he could have reached out and almost touched the other side of the staircase on the opposite side. However, he remained in the middle of the steps and made sure to check every one of them for corrosion. All it would take was for him to put his weight on a single weak step, and then he might suddenly find himself crashing to the floor below.

When he reached the concrete landing and the low-ceilinged space under the lantern room at the top, he found himself drawing a sigh of relief, and then he leaned out just enough to be able to watch Fiona as she covered the final distance. When she joined him, she was panting, and her eyes were wide with uneasiness.

'I really didn't like that,' she said, giving him a smile despite herself. 'I feel much safer on this landing.'

'Let's have a look outside,' he said, and then he reached for the door handle on the metal door leading out to the walkway that ran the circumference of the tower just below the lantern room at the very top.

The door was similar to the one at the bottom of the tower, but it looked somewhat less bulky but more corroded. However, it wasn't locked by anything other than a deadbolt, and once Andrew had yanked that aside amid a screech of rusty metal, the door easily opened outward. They were immediately met by a gust of warm air as the more or less ever-present wind across the island found its way inside the tower again after many decades. As they moved through the doorway and back out into the late afternoon sun, it quickly became apparent that Fiona's battle with vertigo and her general fear of things failing or breaking was far from over. The walkway was made of concrete and part of the main tower structure, but the only thing keeping anyone from going over the side and plunging fifty metres to the ground was a rusty and rickety-looking metal railing that appeared disturbingly slender and weak.

'It's alright,' said Andrew, taking her hand and giving it a squeeze when he sensed her unease. 'There's barely any wind today, so just stay near the wall, and you'll be fine.'

'Easy for you to say,' said Fiona fretfully. 'You don't suffer from vertigo the way I do.'

'Step where I step,' he said reassuringly, keeping her hand in his. 'We'll do a quick tour around the tower and see what we can see. Alright?'

'OK,' nodded Fiona, clenching her jaw as she mustered the necessary courage. 'Fine. Let's go.'

Slowly and cautiously, they followed the curving walkway around to the opposite side of the tower from where they had an unobstructed view of almost the entire island. When they stopped to look out,

Fiona gradually regained her composure and no longer felt in the grip of anxiety.

'It's really beautiful up here,' she said, a guarded smile spreading across her lips as she looked out across the parched and rocky island. 'Barren and rugged, but beautiful all the same.'

The island's teardrop shape was now clearly visible from their vantage point, and in the far distance were containerships moving north and south along the sea lanes, although only their superstructures could be seen above the horizon due to the curvature of the Earth. The island sloped gently away from the raised plateau where the lighthouse was located, and it appeared that the low and scraggy vegetation they had already seen around the lighthouse extended to the entire island. Not a single tree or bush taller than a metre appeared to be growing there, but there were plenty of rocky mounds and outcroppings everywhere, especially around the island's perimeter where the almost vertical cliffs fell away between twenty and forty metres towards the sea below.

'Yes, it's very pretty,' said Andrew. 'But I don't see anything that might give away where the sea cave could be, or where Warner might have found the skeleton. We would have to search the entire perimeter of the island to find it. And the whole thing is nothing but steep cliffs. This could become a mammoth task.'

'Maybe there are some walking trails down there,' said Fiona, peering at the ground below, 'although I don't see any. But you would think that Warner and the other lighthouse keepers followed the same paths whenever they went walking here, right? And when

Warner made the discovery of the skeleton, it must have been close to one of those.'

'Good point,' said Andrew, trying and failing to spot anything that looked even remotely like a trail. 'But even if that is the case, it looks like they might have been completely overgrown and erased by the passage of time. This is a rough environment.'

'I guess we'll need to head back down to find out,' said Fiona.

'I just want to have a quick look at the lantern room,' said Andrew, glancing behind them and up at the cupola at the very top of the tower. 'I wonder if the lamp is still there.'

Walking carefully around the tower to the door to the interior, they headed back inside, where there was a short metal ladder leading up to the lantern room. It was sturdy and bolted securely in place, and they soon found themselves standing inside the lantern room with its large glass panes affording views on all sides, almost all of which were still intact. Only a couple of them had cracked, allowing the breeze to enter the small room. At its centre, there was a complex-looking metal mount where the huge lighthouse lamp had once been fixed, but it appeared to have been removed long ago when the last lighthouse keeper left the island.

'Wow,' said Fiona, turning slowly around and gazing out across the blue sea that surrounded the island in all directions. 'The view is even better from up here. You can almost imagine those beautiful full-rigged sailing ships passing by this place back in the 17th and 18th centuries. Sails fluttering in the wind, sailors climbing the rigging, and the captain on the aftercastle with the ship's wheel in his hands. I would love to be able to go back and experience the whole thing for myself.'

'I agree,' said Andrew. 'I am sure it was a hard life with a fairly low life expectancy, but the idea of being on the edge of the known world and being free to explore and create your own life here away from Old Blighty sure has its appeal. It's a bit like the frontiers of the Wild West in the US before the whole country was settled.'

Fiona regarded him probingly for a moment and pressed her lips together.

'What?' he said.

'That's almost exactly what Tobin told me when I went to meet with him at King's College,' she said.

'Well,' said Andrew. 'It may be that Tobin is a lying, duplicitous bastard, but that doesn't mean he's wrong about everything.'

'You know,' she said pensively. 'I kind of get the feeling that his double life as a daring treasure hunter, consorting with the bottom feeders of places like Port-au-Prince, is his way of achieving exactly that sort of opportunity to reinvent himself. It's a bit juvenile, to be honest.'

'Maybe,' shrugged Andrew. 'I can honestly say that I don't give a toss about his psychological makeup. As far as I am concerned, he's in league with the people who almost killed Ronil, so I class him as a bad guy. That's all I need to know.'

'Right,' said Fiona. 'Well said. Let's head back down and try to find a trail to follow.'

'Alright,' said Andrew, gesturing to the ladder. 'After you.'

While Fiona began climbing down, Andrew cast a final look towards the southwest where, according to Warner's account, he had come across the crevice with the skeleton. He was on the verge of turning to follow Fiona down the ladder when his eye caught something on the raised concrete edge that ran the circumference of the lantern room. He peered at it for a moment and then went to crouch next to it.

'Fiona?' he called. 'Come and have a look at this.'

Already halfway down the ladder, Fiona climbed back up and joined him, lowering herself next to him as he pointed to a small marking that had been etched into the concrete. It was a straight arrow about five centimetres long that pointed out towards the island from the lantern room's centre. Underneath it was etched a single letter.

'X,' said Fiona, her mouth falling slightly open as she peered at the marking before then turning to face Andrew. 'What was that you said back in Nassau about 'X' not marking the spot? Could this have been made by Warner?'

'If it was,' said Andrew, 'the man had a sense of humour.'

'Where is it pointing to?' said Fiona, trying to gauge the precise direction of the arrow.

Taking a step back and then lowering his head right down to the concrete edge to line it up with the arrow, Andrew closed one eye and shifted his focus from the arrow to the island terrain beyond.

'It seems to be pointing right between those two outcroppings out there,' he said, indicating with an extended arm and a vertical palm at a distant point on the edge of the island almost due southwest. 'Do you see them?'

With the afternoon sun now lower in the sky, Fiona stood up and gazed out through the window at the two rocky outcroppings that rose about ten metres above the surrounding terrain some four hundred metres away. Framed by the glistening blue sea, they seemed a pale greyish yellow, and both of them appeared almost completely devoid of vegetation. She hadn't noticed them before, but now that the arrow was pointing straight at them, they were almost all she could see.

'We need to get down there right now,' she said, excitement creeping into her voice. 'Before the sun sets. It's our best lead so far.'

'Alright,' said Andrew, getting to his feet. 'Let's go.'

Twenty-Three

After the two of them had reached the bottom and emerged from the lighthouse tower, Andrew returned to the helicopter and extracted one of the AR-15 assault rifles as well as his SD9 pistol from the black holdall. He also handed Fiona her SIG Sauer P365.

'Just in case there are creatures living here that are larger than lizards,' he said as she tucked the pistol under the belt of her jeans behind her back.

'I guess it's better to be prepared,' she said, realising that she felt mildly reassured by having the weapon on her again.

They set off away from the lighthouse and headed straight into the sun as they began traversing the rocky and uneven terrain. At first, keen to move in a straight line towards the outcroppings, they found themselves cutting through yellow grass and clumps of dry, thorny bushes, both of which appeared virtually lifeless. However, after a couple of minutes, their course suddenly merged with what looked like the remnants of a narrow walking trail. It was barely discernible and partially overgrown, but it was clear that it had once been used by humans, and it made traversing the terrain significantly easier as they neared their intended destination.

'See?' said Fiona, flashing a smile at Andrew. 'I told you these would be here.'

'Right,' said Andrew, cradling his AR-15 as he walked. 'I will make it easier for us to spot snakes as well.'

'Snakes?' said Fiona, suddenly sounding much less eager. 'You think there are snakes here?'

'Let's assume that there are,' said Andrew. 'Just watch where you place your feet.'

They continued along the faint trail that appeared to lead directly towards the outcroppings, but when, after about ten minutes, they were less than fifty metres away from them, it suddenly curved almost due west and appeared to continue on towards the far end of the island.

'We'll need to leave the trail,' Andrew said, putting the nylon strap attached to the AR-15 across his chest so that he could carry the bulky weapon on his back. 'It's the only way to see what's here.'

They made their way into dry, knee-high bushes and shrubs that snapped and crunched as they pushed through them, and as they did so, they could hear shuffling and rustling from under the vegetation as lizards and other creatures scurried away from the approaching two-legged giants. Soon, they found themselves in the dip between the two rocky outcroppings, and only about five metres ahead of them was the vertiginous thirty-metre drop to the sea and the crashing waves below. They could hear them clearly as they broke against the rocks, and the breeze was now noticeably stronger.

Andrew took another couple of steps forward through the shrubs, and then he suddenly realised that the ground was falling away into a narrow gap right in front of him. It ran between the two outcroppings, and it had been completely hidden by the vegetation.

'There's something here,' he said. 'A large fissure in the rock.'

As she joined him by his side, he began gripping the vegetation and pulling it free of what turned out to be a crevice that was about a metre wide and appeared to reach four metres straight down into the rock. It narrowed further towards the bottom, and when Andrew knelt next to the edge, he spotted something down there. He couldn't make out exactly what it was, but it appeared to be metallic. Taking off his assault rifle, he disconnected the nylon strap and handed the weapon to Fiona.

'Take this for a second,' he said. 'There's something down here. I want to see what it is.'

'Will you be able to get back up?' she said.

'That's what the strap is for,' he said. 'If you hold on to one end, you can help me climb back up.'

'OK,' she said. 'Be careful.'

Using the sides of the crevice to slow himself, Andrew's boots slid down over the dry walls of the crevice as he descended, and amid a faint cloud of dust and small, falling pieces of dry rock, he quickly reached the bottom where he knelt to pick something up. The cramped space was barely wide enough for him to fit, but he managed to lower himself and retrieve what turned out to be a small brass button. It was somewhat corroded, partly caked in dirt, and bulky for its size, and it instantly felt like something belonging to a different time.

'Look,' he said, holding it up for Fiona to see. 'I think this is the crevice where Warner found the skeleton. Looks like he missed something.'

'Wow,' said Fiona, sounding intrigued. 'Is there anything else down there?'

Andrew took several moments to look around and make sure that he wasn't missing anything down in the somewhat dark fissure, but he found nothing more.

'It doesn't look like it,' he finally said. 'Throw me the end of the strap?'

She did as he asked, and within a few seconds, he climbed back up and was standing on the edge with the brass button resting in the palm of his hand. Fiona picked it up and examined it, wiping the dirt from its face with her thumb to reveal a simple, curving geometric pattern.

'See these swirling floral designs?' she said. 'That's a very typical baroque pattern. This could easily be from the early 1700s.'

'Larkin,' said Andrew. 'It could be him, right?'

'I think so,' said Fiona, her eyes lighting up with excitement as she looked up at Andrew and a smile spread across her face. 'We must be close now. Really close.'

'I am going to walk out there and see what I can see,' said Andrew, glancing out towards the edge as he reattached the nylon strap to his AR-15 and slung it onto his back.

Placing his feet carefully on the treacherous and occasionally loose rocks as he went, he then pushed all the way out to the edge from where he was able to lean out and look down along the sides of the almost vertical cliffs. Standing there, exposed to the faint, salty spray being carried up on the wind from the breakers below, the gusts pulled at his clothes, and the loud noise from the waves crashing against the cliff face drowned out all other sounds. He took a long moment to look first left and then right, trying to spot anything that might look like a cave mouth, but all he saw were sheer, rugged cliffs and near-vertical drops to the frothy water below.

'See anything?' Fiona called ahead as the whirling wind near the edge tugged at him.

'I need to get closer,' Andrew called over his shoulder.

'Be careful,' she shouted, anxious that he might lose his footing, slip over the edge, and plummet into the sea.

He gave her a quick thumbs up and then began climbing down and out along a ledge to a small promontory that reached out another five metres or so directly beneath one of the two rocky outcroppings. The wind did its best to pull him from the cliff face, but he gripped the rocks tightly and made sure to have a secure purchase under at least one foot whenever he took another step. After about a minute, he reached the outer edge of the promontory and craned his neck this way and that to try to identify anything that didn't look natural. However, there was nothing but craggy cliffs in both directions as far as he could see, and all of them looked as if they had remained unchanged for millennia.

Giving a bitter shake of the head amidst the whirling wind and the salty taste of the air, he turned back towards the cleft between the two outcroppings, and that was when he suddenly realised what he was looking at. Of all the things he could see around him, it was the cleft that was unnatural, and so were the two rocky outcroppings. Once he saw it, it was clear as day. The outcroppings had once been one huge promontory, and the cleft between them had been created by some sort of collapse inward of the entire cliff face in this precise location. Looking down towards the crashing waves below, he realised that there was a slight slope to the cliff just beneath where the cleft was located, and just under the surface of the relatively shallow water were a large number of massive rocks that might have fallen down into it when the cliff had collapsed.

He took a long moment to make sure that he wasn't imagining things, but the more he looked at it, the firmer his conclusion became. This piece of the cliff face had somehow crumbled, and if James Flynn's account was to be believed, it was almost certainly the place where his brother Jack had ordered the mouth of an entire sea cave to be sealed using explosives.

'It's here,' he panted as he returned to Fiona who was relieved to have him back safely.

'What is?' she said.

'The sea cave,' he said, his eyes now lit with the excitement of what he had just come to realise. 'The

Cave of Skulls is literally right beneath our feet as we stand here.'

'Are you sure?' said Fiona, looking astonished as she looked involuntarily down at the ground by her feet. 'How do you know?'

'The whole cliff face has collapsed,' he said, 'and I don't think it was a natural event. There's nothing else that looks anything like it along this part of the island. I think it was brought down with explosives. Just as Reverend Flynn wrote.'

'Holy crap,' said Fiona. 'What do we do now? Did you see a way in?'

'No,' said Andrew, shaking his head. 'I couldn't see anything like that. There's nothing to indicate that there's a cavity under there, but I am sure that's the case. We should head a bit further west and see if there's a way down somehow. We might have to get all the way down to the sea to find it.'

'OK,' said Fiona. 'Lead the way.'

They continued on through the low, parched vegetation, which seemed to get thicker as they went, and after another five minutes, they came to a flat clearing where a number of boulders were dotted around on the pale, rocky ground. They were both sweating now from the effort of pushing through the scrubs, and as Andrew began making his way out towards the edge to have another look back towards the two outcroppings, Fiona slumped down on a small boulder and hung her head while she caught her breath. A couple of minutes later, Andrew returned, but when she glanced up at him, he shook his head to indicate that there was no way down from this spot either.

She got to her feet and began walking towards him, but after just two steps, she heard a muffled cracking sound like thick ice slowly breaking. Suddenly, her right foot disappeared into a hole, and as she fell down, the hole widened, and both of her legs vanished. She only managed to break her fall and stop her entire body from falling through by stretching out her arms, and as she let out a scream and looked up, she saw Andrew already in full sprint towards her. He launched himself through the air and landed heavily in front of her, immediately gripping both of her wrists and holding on tightly.

'Pull me out!' she gasped in a panic, her body no longer visible from the chest down. 'My feet are just dangling under here. Pull!'

Getting to his feet again, Andrew swiftly managed to heave her back out, and the two of them backed away from the hole while Fiona's heart felt as if it was about to beat its way out of her chest.

'Bloody hell,' she gasped, partly hunched over with her hands on her knees as she panted. 'There's a huge cavity under there.'

It took a few seconds for her to realise the implications of what she had just said, but as her heart began to return to normal and her breathing slowed once more, she rose and regarded Andrew silently for a long moment.

'The cave,' he finally said. 'There's a way in from up here.'

Cautiously, the two of them returned to the irregular hole in the dusty, rocky ground. It was just under a metre in diameter, and its edges appeared to be less than half a metre thick before a dark void seemed to open up beyond it. While Fiona stayed back by a couple of metres, Andrew lay down and began crabbing his way the final stretch to the edge of the hole as he might have done on a frozen lake. When he reached the edge, he seemed to freeze for a moment. Then he rolled over onto his side and looked back towards Fiona.

'We found it,' he said, an incredulous grin taking over his face. 'It's down there. We found the Black Galleon.'

★   ★   ★

Wrapped up in his own thoughts and barely aware of what was going on around him, Lawrence Blake, formerly known to his academic colleagues back in London as Marcus Tobin, was pondering the treasure and what he could do with it. Once again, the thought of leaving the dreary world of academia behind to fully embrace treasure hunting and his alter ego pulled at his heartstrings. Perhaps it was time to finally embrace that calling and leave his old life behind. He meditated on this question for a while, and then he decided that if he ended up getting his hands on the treasure from the Black Galleon, then he would regard that as a sign from the gods of wealth and fortune for him to finally cast off the moorings that bound him to the ordinary life of a King's College professor.

Having resolved to let fate decide his future in this manner, he then found himself contemplating bumping off Count Carlos Roberto Velazquez de Toledo. The count had been a lucrative client for many years now, but all good things must come to an end, and wasn't it better to decide for oneself when that end came, rather than waiting for someone else to impose it? He would obviously need to get both Ortega and Delgado onside, and that would probably take some persuading. But they had been happy to oblige with regards to Marcellus, so why not also the count if it meant tens of millions of dollars in ready cash straight into their pockets? And then he and the two highly trained former special forces operators would be able to embark on a no doubt fruitful collaboration in the future where they would get a cut of the profits instead of a miserly pay cheque from a pompous minor Spanish noble. It was almost certainly worth a try. However, first things first. The treasure wasn't his yet, although he was getting close now. Quite literally.

The glowing dot on the tracking unit's moving map display had stopped and been stationary for more than an hour now. And given its location, there had been no point in waiting any longer when he saw where it had come to a halt. Once he had seen it stopping over that tiny dot in the Caribbean Sea, he had decided for them to move out immediately. It was now almost certain that young Fiona had discovered where the treasure from El Castillo Negro was hidden, and whether she and her soldier companion found it before or after he arrived at the site was now irrelevant. Either way, he was going to make it his, and if he and his two hired hands were going to swoop in and take it, now was surely their chance.

Sitting in the co-pilot's seat, he looked up from the moving map display on the tracking unit and watched the waves of the Caribbean Sea race past outside. The main rotor was a blur above him as the sleek, high-speed AgustaWestland AW101 corporate helicopter tore across the ocean at an altitude of less than fifty metres in order to stay below civilian and military radar systems. Given where they were headed and what their purpose was, Blake wanted no one to be able to track their movements. The last thing he needed now was for some opportunist to turn up, or even worse, for the U.S. military to suddenly make an appearance.

Sitting next to him in the pilot's seat was Delgado who was competently flying the corporate chopper towards their destination, and in one of the passenger seats behind him was Ortega. Both of the two large men were heavily tooled up for a firefight, and they looked focused, mean and ready to go. Blake felt confident. Whatever happened today, neither Fiona Keane nor Andrew Sterling would be leaving Navassa Island alive.

Twenty-Four

Andrew gazed down through the hole in the rocky ground and into the virtually dark sea cave below. It soon became apparent just how large the cave was, and he estimated that it was perhaps twenty-five metres tall, at least as wide and roughly fifty metres long. Lying at the bottom was a massive hulking silhouette that was unmistakably the shape of the hull of a large galleon, its aftercastle being noticeably taller than its forecastle and waist, although it appeared to have no masts.

The late afternoon sun glaring into his eyes made it difficult for him to discern much detail from his perch on the edge of the hole, but he had no doubt about what he was looking at. This was El Castillo Negro. Shielding them with one hand and peering around the cave as much as his vantage point would allow him, it turned out that the hole was off to one side of the cave's ceiling, and it was near one of its irregular, rocky walls. After a few moments, he realised that there was a narrow rock shelf a couple of metres below where the hole had been created.

'I think we can get down here,' he said, turning to Fiona who stood back several metres clasping her hands with worry that more of the cave's ceiling might suddenly collapse.

'Is it safe?' she said.

'Yes, I think so,' said Andrew. 'It looks like you just happened to step on a small area where the rock had cracked and then become weaker over time. But the rest of the limestone here looks solid. I think there's a way for us to get down.'

'Right,' said Fiona, not sounding entirely convinced. 'I guess I'll take your word for it.'

'I'll go down first and have a look around,' said Andrew, unslinging his AR-15. 'Just to make sure it's safe, and then you can join.'

'OK,' said Fiona, cautiously moving closer to the edge as Andrew sat up and swung his lower legs down through the hole. 'I'll wait here. Will you be able to get back out again?'

'I think so,' said Andrew, taking off the assault rifle and placing it on the ground in order to be able to squeeze through the hole. 'It looks like there are plenty of places to grab onto. Wish me luck.'

The gap was only just wide enough for him to fit through, and dust and flakes of rock rained down around him as he passed it to hang in midair under the cave's ceiling right next to the irregular, sloping wall. Looking down, he saw the rock shelf directly beneath his feet, so he let go and landed adeptly on his feet in a crouched position a couple of metres below. When he stood back up, he found that he could almost reach the ceiling and that the wall next to him was uneven and full of small cracks and crevices that would allow him to easily climb back up later. Below him, the wall sloped away steeply, but he could see plenty of footholds and small shelves allowing for an easy path down to the bottom.

Standing in the gloom for a long moment to allow his eyes to adjust to the darkness, he was soon able to make out more detail of the interior, but utterly dominating the scene was the massive wooden hulk of the Spanish galleon. With no masts or rigging, it looked strangely diminished, but at more than forty metres in length and as much as fifteen metres in width and height, it was still an impressive sight. It lay with its bow facing him at an angle, and it was tilted and partly on its side, almost as when sailing ships would be deliberately beached in order to remove barnacles from under the waterline in a process known as careening. However, he knew that this couldn't have been what had happened here, and then it dawned on him that there was something else missing from the scene. Water. In order to get the ship inside the sea cave, it would have had to have been floated inside after its masts had been removed. And according to James Flynn's account, that was exactly what had happened. But the cave appeared completely dry. So where had the water gone?

'Andrew, are you alright?' Fiona called down through the hole, and her voice echoed around the murky, cavernous space for several seconds.

'Yes,' he said, craning his neck to look up. 'You need to come down and see this for yourself.'

With some trepidation, Fiona placed her legs back in the hole she had found herself plunging into just a few minutes earlier, and then she began carefully lowering herself down through it. When only her head and shoulders were still above ground and she was about to shift down to hang by her hands the way she had seen Andrew do, she suddenly thought she heard something. It was almost like a faint and distant rolling thunder, except it somehow didn't sound quite like that. And the skies were clear and there was little wind or any indication that the weather might be worsening. She stayed immobile for a few seconds, listening intently for the sound, but then it was gone. She decided that she had been imagining things, and her arms were beginning to tremble from the strain of holding her own weight in an awkward position. She allowed herself to slip down through the hole and hang by her hands for a moment before dropping down to the shelf where Andrew was ready and helped slow her fall.

After a few moments, her eyes were also becoming accustomed to the darkness. At first, the cave appeared almost pitch black to her. However, a bright shard of light lanced down through the hole and sliced through the cavernous space, illuminating the dust that had been sent whirling into the air as the two of them had entered. Soon, she too was able to see what remained of the Black Galleon in all its glory.

'Wow,' she breathed, unable to hold back a widening smile. 'We found it. We actually found it.'

'Impressive, isn't it?' said Andrew. 'Come on. Let's head down and take a closer look.'

Without too much trouble, they climbed down the side of the cave wall and stood on the bottom, which was covered by a thick layer of sand, and as Fiona bent down to pick up a handful, her brow creased as it ran through her fingers.

'It's dry,' she said. 'So, how did Flynn get the ship in here?'

'That's exactly what I was thinking,' said Andrew. 'Maybe the collapsed cavemouth sealed off the cave and the water inside evaporated over the centuries.'

'Wait,' said Fiona. 'That might be part of the reason, but I think there's another explanation.'

'What?' said Andrew, placing his hands on his hips as he looked up at the massive hull lying in front of them.

'Well,' said Fiona. 'There have been some pretty significant global temperature fluctuations over the past three hundred years, including what's known as the Little Ice Age. And this can lead to significant changes in sea levels. In other words, it is possible that the sea level is somewhat lower now than it was during the Golden Age of Piracy. And that could mean that back in those days this sea cave was flooded, but that the water has receded since then.'

'Either way,' said Andrew. 'The ship is in amazing condition. This cave is like a time capsule with the ship almost perfectly preserved.'

'Imagine an enormous ship in a bottle,' said Fiona. 'That pretty much captures what happened here. And the collapsed entrance is the proverbial cork that sealed everything inside.'

As she spoke, she turned a full circle, marvelling at the huge cave that had lain dark and empty for centuries. Peering into the gloom at the far end of the cave, she then saw several stalactites hanging from the ceiling. Here, small amounts of moisture had either seeped through from above during rain or condensed inside the cave to form these elongated, tapering stone icicles over tens of thousands of years, long before the first humans had ever set foot on what was then an unknown and nameless island. Below them were stalagmites that had formed directly below as the water had once dripped onto the floor of the cave. However, now, both sets of rock formations appeared bone dry, and it was only after she had been looking at them for a few seconds that Fiona recognised the shape they seemed to form. Protruding from the back wall in strangely symmetrical shapes created by two similar sources of trickling water, there appeared to be a pair of large eyes staring at her, and beneath them, the stalagmites conspired to appear like a jagged set of teeth. Altogether, the impression was of a gaunt and almost skeletal face glaring out from the cave wall.

'The Cave of Skulls,' she said, pointing at the strange vista. 'No wonder that's what they called this place.'

'Amazing,' said Andrew as he also began to recognise the eerie shapes. 'So it wasn't just some random made-up name. It really does describe this place.'

'Hey, look up there,' said Fiona, pointing to a spot high on the collapsed wall behind the ship where the cavemouth had once been. 'There's a light.'

'Oh yes,' said Andrew, peering up at it. 'It looks like another way in.'

'I guess this place wasn't completely sealed,' said Fiona. 'It just appears that way from the outside. It looks small, though. Only just large enough for someone to squeeze through.'

'That must have been how Larkin got out,' said Andrew. 'And maybe that's also how James Flynn was able to come back here and bring out more of the treasure whenever he needed it.'

'Well,' said Fiona. 'I'm just glad there seems to be more than one way out of here. Even though this place is big, I am still finding it a bit claustrophobic.'

They walked the length of the ship towards the stern and marvelled at the many gunports along its side, and even without its masts, the huge vessel towered over them. When they arrived at the large rudder at the back of the ship, they switched on their torches and looked up. Raising their gaze up high along the ship's stern, they were greeted by elaborately carved galleries and window frames with small windows leading into the captain's quarters, as well as a large, ornate wooden name plaque with 'El Castillo Negro' written across it in gilded and vaguely gothic-looking letters.

'I guess that settles it,' said Fiona with a satisfied smile. 'This is it. This is the ship Jack Flynn stole from Port Royal in 1714 and sailed off with into the night.'

'It's an incredible discovery,' said Andrew. 'Well done. This is all thanks to you.'

'I guess,' said Fiona, her contentedness tempered by a hint of concern. 'But as soon as the world learns about this, more people, and even countries, are going to be fighting over who the treasure belongs to.'

'Well,' said Andrew, looking up towards the windows above. 'Before we jump to any conclusions, I want to see it for myself. Come on. This is probably the best place to get up and inside the ship.'

Using the metal brackets on the rudder and then the wooden railings on the galleries above, much like Jack Flynn and his band of raiders had done three hundred years ago, Andrew climbed up to the first set of windows. Finding none of them open, he proceeded up to the next level, which he knew had to be the captain's quarters, but they were also sealed shut from the inside. With Fiona following behind at a distance of a couple of metres, he continued to the top of the aftercastle and hauled himself over the edge to stand on top of it. Due to the ship being partly on its side, the floorboards were slanting heavily, but he was able to find purchase with his boots. When Fiona arrived, he helped her up and over, and then they made their way along the tilting top deck and down the stairs to the main deck.

'Let's check out the captain's quarters,' said Andrew.

Using their torches to light the way, they proceeded through an open door and then through a low-ceilinged corridor into a large space with small windows and a wide oak desk bolted to the floor immediately in front of it. Most other things in the room, except for some shelves and a large wooden chest that had also been secured to the wooden floorboards, had slid over into a jumbled heap on one side of the room, as the ship had gradually tilted during the many years in the cave to now lie at something approaching a thirty-degree angle. However, Fiona spotted one additional item that was still fixed to where it had originally been secured.

'The chain,' said Fiona, pointing to a heavy metal chain that was hooked around one of the wooden columns holding up the ceiling and the top of the aftercastle. 'This must have been where Jack chained up his own brother. He really was a true lunatic.'

'Gold has done that to people for thousands of years,' said Andrew dryly. 'I'm sure it will happen an endless number of times in the future too.'

They stepped across the slanting floor to the desk, and Andrew moved around it to open the two drawers underneath. However, they both proved to be empty. Fiona then approached the wooden chest. It was just over a metre long and about half a metre tall and deep, and it was in remarkably good condition, except for the somewhat corroded iron hinges, handles, and the lock, all of which bore the signs of age. She opened the lid but found it empty except for a length of old hemp rope.

Then they examined the random items piled together in a heap on the lower side of the room. There were two chairs, remnants of a large, bundled-up rug, empty bottles that no doubt used to contain rum, a sextant, brass candleholders, a couple of oil lanterns, a globe that had fallen out of its wooden stand, fragments of maps that had almost completely decomposed, several tin tankards, as well as three cutlasses and a long musket similar to those famously used by the buccaneers of Tortuga.

'This is so interesting,' said Fiona, crouching to pick up the now somewhat corroded brass sextant. 'These items alone would be enough to create a small exhibition in a museum.'

'No gold or silver, though,' said Andrew. 'Come on. We should head down to the cargo hold and see what is there.'

As they exited the captain's quarters, crossed the main deck, and found a set of steps leading down into the bowels of the galleon, Fiona began to experience a mild case of vertigo and dizziness as her inner ears struggled to reconcile what they were sensing with what her eyes were seeing. The slanted floors of the lower decks played tricks on their ability to walk straight. However, items like lanterns or the thick lengths of hemp rope that had survived the years and were hanging off wooden girders would occasionally signal which way was down. They passed the gun decks, where two rows of massive bronze cannons were still secured behind their gunports, almost certainly unaffected by the passage of time and perfectly capable of being fired again.

Finally, they found themselves at the very bottom of the ship, just above the ballast, where a wooden walkway ran the length of the cargo hold. Allowing their torches to sweep across its interior, they could see that the space was divided into several sections. Bulkheads made from thick wooden planks separated them, and the first couple of sections had various types of cargo still inside them, although many had degraded and others had almost decomposed over the years. There were barrels and crates stacked everywhere, and there were piles of what had possibly once been sacks of foodstuff that had rotted, dried and deflated not long after being left there. They were now just piles of decomposed cloth and some dry, unidentifiable organic matter that looked almost black.

Moving further forward, they finally came to a large open space with about two dozen large wooden chests. Without a word, the two of them glanced briefly at each other, unspoken eagerness passing between them, and then Andrew crouched by one of the chests and heaved open the heavy wooden lid. As soon as it gaped open and the light from their two torches flooded inside, their surroundings were lit up in a golden light that washed out over the cargo hold.

'Holy crap!' Fiona exclaimed as she gawped at the huge haul of gold coins lying inside the chest. 'This is incredible. These look like doubloons. I've never seen so many in my life.'

As she regarded the treasure, her head began to spin with the implications of it. The gold from which these doubloons had been made had most likely been extracted from the mines of Central and South America centuries before the first Europeans arrived in the Caribbean. They had then been made into jewels and other ornaments by the Incas and Aztecs and other cultures in the Americas, only to be melted down and minted as coins by the conquistadors and then put on a ship to be brought back to Spain, whose king regarded them as his personal property. However, they had never made it that far, and here they had lain, undisturbed for three centuries. And during that time, the world outside the cave had passed through the Enlightenment and the Renaissance, the Age of Empires, then industrialisation, the emergence of democratic nation-states, two world wars, the space age and the nuclear arms race, finally ending up in the modern world of the internet and portable computers where two people could travel thousands of miles in a flying machine across islands and oceans to find this treasure once again.

'Wow,' said Andrew quietly, his eyes fixed on the coins as he reflected on the enormity of their find. 'This is quite something. Let's have a look at the other chests.'

One by one, they opened the remaining chests, and most of them turned out to be filled either with silver pieces of eight, raw uncut gems, or bars of unrefined gold and silver that had yet to be smelted and purified. By the end of it, they stood in the centre of that section of the cargo hold and gazed at the luminous display of riches laid out in front of them.

'How much do you think all this might be worth?' said Fiona.

'I'm not sure I would hazard a guess,' said Andrew. 'But if it isn't several hundred million of any currency you can think of, then I'd be very surprised. This is an absolute fortune.'

'Which begs the question,' said Fiona, her hands on her hips as she surveyed the enormous amount of wealth surrounding them. 'What do we do now? How do we even go about informing the proper authorities, whoever they really are? Do we even reveal this to anyone?'

'Well, it isn't ours,' said Andrew. 'It belongs to someone. And if we don't try to make sure it ends up with its rightful owners, then eventually someone else is going to find it and probably take it for themselves.'

'That's a very good point,' said Fiona, switching her phone to camera mode. 'I am going to take a bunch of pictures so we can prove that we haven't been imagining the whole thing.'

As she walked around the cargo hold to document their discovery, Andrew moved further towards the bow of the ship to a large square compartment that was separated from the rest of the cargo hold by thick wooden bulkheads. Using his torch and moving around to its front, he discovered a narrow entrance and soon found himself in a copper-clad space inside which a slightly acrid, sulphuric smell still lingered in the air after all this time. A smell that he knew only too well. This had once been the galleon's gunpowder store, and it would have been packed with cloth sacks full of the potent mixture of sulphur, charcoal and potassium nitrate, which in those days was known as saltpetre.

Turning around inside the compartment, he saw that there were a couple of the grey cloth sacks still lying on the floor in a dark corner. When he walked over and crouched down next to them, it became clear that they were ripped open and half empty, and they had clearly just been left there. Perhaps they had accidentally been torn when the gunpowder had been brought out to prepare the explosive charges that Flynn had used to collapse the cave. He reached down and pinched his fingers around some of it, bringing it up to his nose. It was still dry and gave off a potent odour, and he wondered if it might have retained its explosive chemical properties.

'Find anything?' said Fiona, appearing in the narrow doorway behind him.

'Some old bags with gunpowder,' he said. 'This whole compartment used to be full of them.'

'Wow,' said Fiona, shining her torch around the space. 'I've read of gunpowder stores exploding in the middle of naval battles and turning their ships into woodchips. And with a whole room like this full of that stuff, I can see why.'

'Well, that's what happened to a big chunk of the Marauder,' said Andrew, getting back onto his feet. 'There was hardly anything left of the front of the ship. But this whole compartment was emptied to blow up the cavemouth. Did you get your pictures?'

'Yes,' said Fiona. 'All done.'

'OK,' said Andrew. 'I think we should probably make our way back to civilisation now. The longer we spend on this island, the higher the risk of being detected and having a visit from the U.S. military.'

'I could easily spend a couple of days examining this whole ship,' said Fiona, a hint of disappointment in her voice. 'It's like an enormous museum frozen in time. But you're probably right. And we didn't bring much in the way of provisions.'

'I think we have a couple of litres of water left,' said Andrew. 'Just enough to last us until tomorrow morning. But I would rather not spend the night here. Our chopper will be visible from ships nearby, so we should get out of here.'

'Alright,' said Fiona. 'Let's go.'

Twenty-Five

Andrew and Fiona exited the gunpowder store and walked back past the treasure chests that were virtually overflowing with the immense riches stolen from the vast territories that were once called New Spain.

'I'd like to head back up to the captain's cabin and grab that globe we saw,' said Fiona. 'I think it would be fitting if that was the first item to be brought out of here. It could be a sort of centrepiece for an exhibition.'

'OK,' said Andrew as they left the treasure chests. 'After you.'

With Fiona leading the way, they continued along the narrow central walkway to the stairs leading back up to the decks above, and they then ascended past the two gundecks to step back out onto the main deck. Fiona immediately began heading back towards the captain's quarters just as Andrew followed her up onto the deck, but they had barely emerged when a man suddenly cried out, his words reverberating around the massive cave.

'There!' shouted the voice, which to Fiona was at once familiar and chilling. 'Shoot them!'

Andrew's head spun around to see Marcus Tobin standing up on the shelf under the access hole where he and Fiona had entered the cave about an hour earlier. The professor was wearing his signature white, open-collared shirt, beige slacks and brown hiking boots, and in his hand, he was cradling Andrew's AR-15. He was flanked on either side by two large and heavily armed men who immediately raised their automatic weapons to aim down towards Andrew and Fiona. It appeared that the trio had just made their way into the cave, and Andrew immediately recognised Tobin's companions as the two goons that they had already tangled with at Marcellus' mansion in Port-au-Prince, and one of them was unmistakably Laura Hartley's killer.

In the next instant, the two men opened fire, and bullets began peppering the deck around them, chewing up the main deck's floorboards. As Andrew threw himself back into cover inside the stairwell, Fiona broke into a panicked sprint and raced for the door to the aftercastle's interior. Pulling out his holstered SD9, Andrew immediately moved back up and leaned out with his pistol trained in the direction of the two shooters. Just as he lined up the iron sights on one of the men, he heard Fiona cry out behind him. Turning to look as a cold chill instantly swept over his entire body, he saw her fall to the deck, grabbing her lower leg and producing a long, high-pitched moan that sounded like a mixture of both pain and fury. With bullets smacking into the deck around her, she reached for her P365 and fired it repeatedly towards their attackers as she scrabbled frantically towards cover inside the door to the aftercastle that was now just a couple of metres away.

With fury rising inside him and his teeth clenched, Andrew immediately turned, took aim and began firing single shots in quick succession at the three men up on the rocky shelf. Tobin threw himself to the ground, but the two goons merely lowered themselves onto one knee but continued firing down at Andrew undeterred. Squeezing the trigger again and again, rapidly depleting the ammo in his magazine, the SD9 kicked in his hand as bullets tore through the air in both directions, and he felt the wake of one of them as it passed dangerously close to the right side of his neck. However, he kept firing, and two of his shots then smacked into the chest of the shooter on the left. They hit him dead centre, and his head seemed to wobble on his neck as his chest was pushed back twice by the kinetic energy of the projectiles. With a stunned and vacant look, the assault rifle fell out of the man's hands, and he tipped forward to fall over the edge of the shelf, tumbling limply roughly ten metres down across the jagged rocks and boulders to the cave floor. His dead body thudded into the ground amid a puff of dust, and then he lay still as a rapidly expanding pool of dark red blood began to colour the dry sand around.

As Fiona disappeared inside the aftercastle, Andrew kept firing until his magazine clicked empty, but his final two shots missed, and in that instant, Tobin seemed to have somehow found his courage, because he emerged from cover next to Laura's killer and opened fire with Andrew's AR-15. As Andrew withdrew back down into the staircase and out of view, he cursed himself bitterly for having left his most potent weapon up top. However, he could not have imagined that Tobin and his thugs would have been able to track them here. The only explanation was that there had to be a tracking device on their chopper, and he had no idea how that had happened.

Inside the aftercastle, Fiona had kicked the door shut behind her and scrambled away from it and into the captain's quarters. Her lower leg was bleeding profusely, matting her soaked trouser leg and making it cling to her skin amid a disconcertingly warm sensation. The bullet appeared to have gone right through her calf muscle without severing arteries or breaking bones, but there was a lot of blood. She tore a long strip from her trouser leg and quickly made herself an improvised tourniquet, which immediately seemed to stem most of the bleeding.

To her surprise, there was very little pain now, but she knew that this was because her body had gone into full fight-or-flight mode and flooded her system with endorphins in an aeons-old response designed to allow her to escape predators. And it appeared to be working, because despite the gunshot wound, all of her senses now felt as if they were operating at peak performance, and she found herself with a feeling of firing on all cylinders both physically and mentally.

However, she was now trapped inside the aftercastle, and with a lurking sense of panic slowly building inside her, she looked frantically around the space for another way out, or perhaps some sort of weapon to defend herself with. Seeing none, and realising that she would be unable to climb through a window and down the stern of the galleon, her eyes finally settled on the wooden chest, and she decided that her best option now was to try to hide. She climbed inside and closed the lid above her, and she bit her lip in dismay as the events of the past few minutes replayed in her mind. If only she had told Andrew about the vaguely thunder-like sound she had heard just before entering the cave, they could have been prepared, and things might then have turned out differently, because she realised now that what she had heard was the sound of far-off rotor blades coming from a helicopter carrying Blake and his two gunmen. But regrets counted for nothing now. All she could do was hope that Andrew would be able to deal with their attackers and then come and find her.

Out in the stairwell by the main deck, Andrew's mind was racing as he tried to come up with some way of turning the tables. He had already removed roughly half of the threat, but the other shooter was still out there, and he knew better than to underestimate anyone holding a gun. Even a novice could get lucky, and all it took was one shot from the AR-15 to end him in an instant. And then Fiona's fate would be sealed. With no ammo left and two assault rifles firing in his direction, he reluctantly decided to move further back down into the ship and consider his options.

As he descended to the upper gundeck, he pondered whether he might be able to get to the body of the dead shooter and take his weapon, but he quickly decided that it would be suicide. With two shooters in an elevated position, he probably wouldn't make it halfway there, even if one of them was an amateur. With a bitter grimace, he reluctantly accepted that a frontal counterattack was out of the question.

He then considered making for the captain's quarters, where Fiona was now holed up. If he could get to one of the cutlasses, he might be able to fight his way to a better weapon. But on reflection, that was also almost certain to fail. From now on, stealth and surprise would be his best assets. However, with the words stealth, aggression and surprise lighting up inside his mind as if bent into a neon sign, he gradually slipped into the same familiar mindset that he had employed countless times before. Rather than being the hunted, he was now going to be the hunter. No longer prey, he was going to take on the role of predator. And few people in the world had more experience or better training for that task than he did. From escape and evasion exercises in his early days during SAS selection, to jungle training in the rainforests of Brunei, to the many deployments with the Regiment in places like Iraq, Afghanistan and a host of other countries throughout the world, Andrew had always had a knack for stealth, using the natural environment to his advantage and setting up ambushes to eliminate enemy combatants. And that was exactly what he was going to do.

As quietly as he could, he moved down the next set of stairs to the lower gundeck, and finding a spot in the darkness, he took off his boots in what he knew was a strange echo of something that had once seemed completely normal on this very ship. During what was often called the Age of Sail, most seafaring people, including pirates, went barefoot whenever possible since it gave them a better grip on the decks and up in the rigging. Like those pirates of old,

Andrew quickly removed his boots and then his socks. He was now able to move around the ship's interior without making any noise at all, and he knew exactly where he needed to go.

★   ★   ★

Out in the cave, Lawrence Blake felt the excitement pulse through his body as he clutched the AR-15 and kept it trained on the point on the deck where he had last seen Fiona's companion, Andrew. With any luck, Fiona was now bleeding out inside the captain's quarters, and that would at least remove one pesky headache. However, Andrew was by far the bigger threat, but now that he was trapped inside the ship, Blake had devised a plan to neutralise him and end this crazy circus once and for all so he could get his hands on the treasure. With no doubt that the galleon below him was full of riches, Blake was now fully committed to doing whatever it took to claim it for himself. The loss of Delgado was unfortunate, but with Ortega now on the hunt, it would be a question of time before the two pests were dead and he would finally be able to see the treasure for himself.

While Blake provided cover, Ortega was making his way down to the bottom of the cave, cradling his assault rifle. Advancing cautiously with his weapon up and his knees slightly bent in case he suddenly had to move quickly, the Spaniard crouched briefly next to his fallen comrade, glanced down at his face with a bitter look, and then he picked one of the full spare magazines from Delgado's tactical vest. Slotting the mag into a pocket, Ortega pushed up to the side of the ship and moved along it to the stern where he slung the assault rifle onto his back and began climbing up the rudder. As he did so, he disappeared from view, and Blake was gratified and somewhat relieved to see him reappear on top of the Galleon's aftercastle at the other end of the cave.

Moving smoothly and with practised speed and purpose, Ortega continued down the steps to the main deck and headed inside the captain's quarters. Moments later, from inside, Blake heard a yelp and a scream coming from a female voice that he knew only too well. Soon after, Ortega re-emerged, holding a limping and moaning Fiona roughly by the hair in front of him as his weapon was pushed into her back. Grimacing as she hobbled along with Ortega behind her, Fiona was in obvious pain, but there was still a furious and defiant fire in her eyes.

'Well done!' Blake shouted to his remaining thug. 'Now, bring her down to me.'

While Blake climbed down to the cave floor, Ortega used his belt to tie Fiona's hands, and then he lifted her over the gunwale on the side of the ship and let her go. She immediately began sliding down the slanted side of the tilting ship until the hull curved away from her to the ground, and she landed heavily in the sand below. With the wind knocked out of her and moaning from the pain of the impact, she spat sand out of her mouth and raised her head to glower at the approaching professor. Despite being winded and her pain receptors throughout her body screaming at her to stop whatever she was doing, she was able to find enough air to speak to the treasure hunter who now crouched next to her with a self-satisfied smile.

'You little shit,' she spat. 'I trusted you.'

'I know,' he said, feigning sadness and a touch of pity. 'And you shouldn't have. I've known about the story of the Black Galleon for decades, but I never in my wildest dreams imagined that anyone might be able to find her. And yet here we are. All thanks to you.'

'You're a real arsehole, Tobin,' she sneered, wincing from the pain in her lower leg as she spoke.

'Blake, if you don't mind,' said Blake. 'I've decided to retire the old chap. He had a good run of it, but I feel that Blake has really come into his own these past few weeks.'

'You can change your name a hundred times,' said Fiona. 'It doesn't change who you are, you pathetic snake.'

'Alright,' said Blake reasonably, as if speaking to an angry child. 'I think that's quite enough with the insults. Get up. On your feet.'

He rose and backed away a couple of steps while keeping the AR-15 trained directly on her. Fiona groaned as she got back up and stood there with her hands tied, looking angrily out from under tousled hair at her former mentor and now captor.

'Find Andrew,' Blake called up to Ortega who said nothing but simply gave Blake a dark nod and then disappeared from view.

'That way,' said Blake, returning his gaze to Fiona and jerking the muzzle of the gun towards the cave wall where the stalactites hung from the ceiling. 'Move.'

Limping along slowly with her bloodied trouser leg flapping against her wounded right calf muscle, Fiona looked surreptitiously around the gloomy cave for anything that might help her escape her bonds or somehow neutralise Blake, but she could see nothing.

'That's enough,' said Blake as they reached an uneven and nearly vertical section of the cave wall next to the huge stalactite skull. 'Stop there.'

Not taking his weapon off her and moving around to her side as she turned to face the galleon, Blake stood with his back against the rocky wall half a pace behind her. She glanced sideways at him, and he shot her a knowing smile before calling out in a loud voice that echoed around the cavernous space.

'Mr Sterling,' he shouted, his clipped voice sounding authoritative and brimming with self-confidence. 'This is Lawrence Blake. If you would like to see your dear Fiona alive again, I would suggest that you surrender yourself and come out without your weapon.'

Glancing at Fiona once more, he gave her a confident nod, as if he was fully expecting Andrew to appear and give himself up any second now.

'You're dead,' whispered Fiona icily as her eyes bored ominously into his. 'You just don't know it yet.'

Blake did not respond but produced a smile and a shrug that said that he felt completely in control of the situation and that everything would work out for him eventually.

Moments later, Fiona spotted something moving very slowly behind Blake. It was a roughly one-metre-long snake that was about the width of her lower arm, and it was unhurriedly making its way along the wall inside a more or less horizontal cranny in the rock. She had always had a severe fear of snakes, bordering on a phobia, but she suddenly found her mind racing and soon came up with an idea.

★   ★   ★

Inside the galleon, Andrew was returning from the gunpowder store with both sacks of the pungent powder he had spotted earlier. They barely held together, and some of the gunpowder was trickling out onto the walkway as he made his way towards the stairs leading back up. Moving on his bare feet and without making a sound, he made his way to the lower gundeck. This was where he knew that he would find what he reckoned was the best position for what he had in mind.

Emerging onto the gundeck, he proceeded roughly halfway along the two rows of bronze cannons, and then he selected one on the side of the tilted vessel that was facing away from the stalactite skull and that was closest to the cave floor. On this side, the cannons were pointing downward at roughly a thirty-degree angle behind their closed gunports, and they were all securely locked in place as they had been during sea journeys when they were not in active use.

Andrew moved to the muzzle-loading cannon's gunport, quietly undid the latch, and pushed the port open. Then he leaned out through the gunport and shoved the two half-full cloth bags with gunpowder into the muzzle. Lifting a long wooden ramrod from a rack inside the ship, he then pushed the bags all the way to the bottom of the gun barrel. Reaching inside one of his pockets, he poured the last remaining handful of gunpowder into the touchhole and made sure to leave a small amount on top of the barrel right next to the hole. The trap was set. He was ready. All he needed to do now was attract his prey.

At that moment, he heard the voice of the man calling himself Lawrence Blake coming from outside the ship. Something about Fiona and surrendering himself. For a moment, he considered complying with Blake's demand, but he knew in his heart that it would be foolish and lethal. As much as he needed Fiona to be safe, he also knew that the only way to ensure that happening was for him to eliminate the threat from both Blake and his remaining thug. With Fiona being able to expose Blake as Tobin and the fraud that he really was, it was obvious that the treasure hunter wanted both of them dead, as his commands to his two goons had already revealed beyond any doubt.

Crouching immobile in the darkness next to the cannon and holding in his hand a grappling hook that he had found, Andrew waited and listened. After a few moments, he heard the sound of footsteps coming from the staircase further up inside the ship. Their sound told him that the shooter was moving slowly and cautiously and was trying to make as little noise as possible, but the old wooden decks creaked ever so slightly, and what sounded like heavy boots produced a muffled thump whenever they made contact with the wood.

Gripping the grappling hook ever more tightly in his hand in case the goon suddenly made an appearance, he listened intently, and as he had hoped, the footsteps suddenly stopped moving. Before heading down to the gunpowder store, he had opened the gunport nearest the staircase on the lower starboard side of the ship, and he had then found a length of rope, which he had tied to the cannon and tossed out through the gunport in as obvious a fashion as he could come up with. The aim was for the man hunting him to think that he had escaped and climbed out and down the rope to the cave floor below. All he could do now was hope that the goon would fall for the ruse. Was he going to think that Andrew had slipped out and climbed down? Or would he perhaps not even spot the open gunport and the rope, in which case Andrew might soon find himself toe to toe with a well-armed shooter holding only an ancient grappling hook as a weapon?

The answers to those two questions came soon enough because he suddenly heard the sound of a pair of heavy boots landing on the cave floor outside. The thug had fallen for his ploy. Andrew picked up the last spent bullet casing that he had extracted from his pistol's chamber, tossed it out of the gunport and then moved silently to the back of the gun barrel.

The small 9mm brass casing hit the ground below with a faint clink, and Andrew could now hear the man's footsteps as he moved cautiously along the side of the ship towards where the noise had come from. Feeling the tension in his whole body as the moment drew near, Andrew found himself sweating as he waited for the goon to come. When he finally spotted the armed shooter through the gunport, he appeared below on the cave floor and directly in front of the tilted cannon's muzzle. As soon as the opportunity was there, Andrew took it and lit his zippo lighter.

'Hey arsehole!' he called out, and Ortega's head instantly swivelled to look up and to the side towards the light and the voice. 'This is for Laura.'

Through the now dimly lit gunport, Ortega instantly spotted Andrew looking straight at him with a vicious stare from behind the cannon, but even before he had turned his head fully, Andrew had lowered the zippo lighter to the touch hole. Ortega was bringing his assault rifle around to open fire when the gunpowder on top of the barrel caught alight. In a split second, it burned its way down through the touch hole, almost instantly igniting the gunpowder Andrew had pushed up into the gun barrel.

Although the gunpowder had lost a small fraction of its potency over the centuries since it had been made, it was still highly combustible, and as the flame reached the main charge, the entire load ignited explosively, and a hellish torrent punched straight out of the cannon's muzzle with enormous force. It was in effect firing a blank, but the sheer force of the fiery blast would have been enough to propel a cannonball many hundreds of metres. When the explosive stream of hellfire rammed downward and straight into Ortega a split second later, almost all of his clothes were burnt to a crisp in an instant, and much of his skin and large chunks of his tissue were ripped from their bones as the force of the blast flung his body against the side of the cave where it impacted with a sickening, wet thud. What was left of him then fell to the floor in a steaming, smouldering heap of burnt flesh and broken bones that was virtually unrecognisable as human.

Inside the galleon on the gundeck, Andrew's ears were ringing from the blast, and he found himself temporarily blinded by the bright muzzle flash. He staggered back across the slanting gundeck for a moment and had to reach out for a thick, wooden support column to steady himself. Soon, however, he regained his senses, and then his mind turned to Fiona. Dropping the grappling hook onto the floor, he scrambled out of the gunport past the hot and still smoking muzzle of the bronze cannon, and then he let himself drop down and made his way over towards the body of the gunman. His assault rifle was lying on the ground roughly halfway there, and it appeared to be intact. Andrew picked it up, checked the magazine, and then turned and gritted his teeth. The tables were now finally turned.

★   ★   ★

When the deafening blast and the bright flash of light suddenly enveloped the entire cave and made its interior reverberate like an enormous rocky bell, Fiona had been standing next to Blake only about a metre away. Feigning dizziness and pain, she had backed up towards the wall and used the opportunity to move ever so slightly closer to the professor-turned-treasure hunter. She had been steeling herself for an uncertain outcome of her intended attempt to surprise her captor, but just as she was about to make her move, the cannon filled the cave with noise and orange light.

Blake was so shocked by the blast that he almost dropped his weapon, and as he instinctively crouched lower gawping at the fiery display from behind the galleon, Fiona quickly stepped behind him, grabbed the snake and flung it at his head. The three-inch-thick serpent ended up partially coiled around his neck, and Blake cried out in shock and surprise as it clung on for dear life, wrapping itself tightly around his throat. As he clawed clumsily at the slithering animal, Fiona saw her opportunity to escape. Ignoring the pain in her leg and the rest of her body, she sprinted awkwardly away from the stalactite skull towards the galleon, turning the corner around its bow and making it out of Blake's line of sight before he could open fire on her. Moments later, Blake's weapon produced a sustained burst of fire. However, no bullets landed near her, and she realised that he must have thrown the snake onto the ground and was now emptying his magazine into it in a panic. As soon as she was safely in cover behind the huge hull of the ship, she spotted a man with an assault rifle standing in the gloom ahead of her.

'It's me!' Andrew called to her, and she immediately felt her heart begin to beat once more as she panted in relief.

'Thank the stars,' she breathed, catching her breath as Andrew rushed over to her.

'Are you alright?' he said anxiously but in hushed tones, keen not to allow Blake to hear. 'You've been shot.'

'I'll be OK,' she responded, wheezing slightly. 'Just go get that bastard for me. Enough of this crap.'

'I couldn't agree more,' said Andrew darkly, yanking the assault rifle's charging bolt back to slot a round into the firing chamber. 'Stay here.'

'Oh, I'm not going anywhere,' said Fiona, slumping down onto the ground near the ship's hull. 'Just finish this now.'

Andrew bent down and gave her a quick kiss on the top of her head. Then he turned around resolutely and moved purposefully towards the bow of the galleon with the assault rifle cradled in his hands. Pushing further forward in a combat stance and taking care not to make unnecessary noise, he then approached the bow with his weapon up and ready to fire. For every step he advanced, he pointed the weapon at the parts of the cave that were just coming into view. When he reached the point from which he would be able to see the rest of the cave, including the stalactite skull, he leaned out and to the side, ready to open fire in case Blake had taken cover somewhere and was attempting an ambush. However, the cave appeared empty, but that was when Andrew heard the faint noise of feet scrabbling against stone and then the sound of small pieces of rock clattering down the side of the cave.

Cautiously moving further out but picking up the pace, Andrew rounded the galleon's bow to look up towards the opposite end of the cave where the noises had come from. As he raised his gaze and peered up into the gloom of the cave's interior, he suddenly spotted Blake clambering up the jagged rocks of the uneven collapsed cavemouth with surprising adeptness for a man of his age. It was immediately clear what Blake was doing. He was attempting to make a run for it and get out of the cave through the small sea-facing gap high up on the collapsed wall.

'Stop!' Andrew shouted as he brought up his weapon, and his command echoed briefly around the cave. 'One more step and I'll open fire.'

Blake heard the call and turned his head slightly to one side, but he kept climbing upward towards the gap, showing no intention of stopping or even slowing down. He was now only a couple of metres from the gap, and he was going to get through it within a matter of seconds unless Andrew did something drastic. He flicked the safety off and selected single-shot mode, lined up the iron sights to a point mere inches above Blake's head, and then he pulled the trigger.

The loud, dry crack of the assault rifle reverberated through the cave as the bullet tore through the air and smacked audibly into a rock within reach of Blake's hands as he climbed. Virtually anyone else would have stopped immediately, realising that the shooter could easily hit them and that the next bullet would most likely be their end. However, instead, Blake seemed to speed up, and then he suddenly turned his head and his upper body around, and in his hands was a pistol. He immediately raised it and began emptying the magazine as fast as he could in Andrew's direction. The shots were rushed and badly aimed, but there were enough of them for there to be a decent chance of at least one of them hitting its mark.

Instead of returning fire, Andrew scrambled back into cover under the hull of the galleon. If he had opened fire, it would almost certainly have resulted in Blake's death, and this was something he didn't want. Blake deserved to spend the rest of his life sitting in some miserable prison cell somewhere in the Caribbean while being eaten alive by fleas and lice and driving himself mad with visions and fantasies about the enormous treasure he lost on Navassa Island.

'Bloody hell!' Andrew groaned to himself as the bullets smacked into the ground near his feet. 'This guy is really starting to piss me off.'

High up on the cave wall, Blake was firing over and over again until his pistol clicked empty, and then he threw the weapon aside, and it clattered down across the rocks towards the bottom of the cave. He then spun around and resumed his frantic climb, putting every ounce of strength he had left into reaching the gap to the outside.

As soon as Andrew heard the series of shots suddenly end in the characteristic click of an empty gun, he moved out from cover and raised his weapon up towards the gap some twenty metres high on the wall at the other end of the cave. Silhouetted in the late afternoon sunlight pouring in from the outside, he saw Blake scrambling through the small gap. He lined up his assault rifle and fired twice, but as the supersonic projectiles covered the distance in a fraction of a second and punched out through the gap in the cave wall, Blake had just managed to get out and throw himself clear.

'Shit!' Andrew swore, and then he set off in a sprint towards the other end of the cave.

Racing past the galleon across the uneven, sandy cave floor, he did a quick mental count of his remaining ammo. When he had taken the assault rifle from Laura Hartley's killer, the magazine had only five rounds left. That meant that he now had three rounds to stop Blake, so he had to make them count. First, however, he had to catch up with the remarkably fit treasure hunter, and so as he reached the collapsed cavemouth, he began climbing upward as fast as he could.

'Fiona!' he yelled over his shoulder. 'I am going after him. Stay here.'

'OK,' came Fiona's reply from the other side of the galleon, her voice now sounding weak and somewhat pained. 'Don't let him get away.'

'I won't,' Andrew muttered resolutely to himself as he clambered upwards to the gap near the cave's ceiling. 'Not this time.'

When he passed through the gap to emerge in the glaring, orange sunlight, he found himself standing on a narrow ledge with an almost vertical drop right in front of him. Some twenty metres below, waves were crashing into the rockface, and wisps of fine spray were carried up to him on the wind. With the gusts tugging at his clothes and ruffling his hair, he turned to look east along the cliff face, and it became clear that this was the only way to get up onto the top of the island and back to the lighthouse. Walking carefully but as swiftly as he could manage along the treacherous path back to the top, he eventually made it back up to the cleft between the two large rocky outcroppings where he and Fiona had discovered Larkin's final resting place a couple of hours earlier.

The sun was now noticeably lower in the sky, and it was approaching the horizon as he began running and pushing through the low vegetation, heading for the lighthouse. When he crested a small rise after a couple of hundred metres and finally had sight of the lighthouse residence and the helicopter that he and Fiona had arrived in, he also saw that there was another chopper parked some fifty metres further out from the lighthouse. This one was a large corporate helicopter that was entirely black, and less than fifty metres from it was Blake running almost straight for it. Andrew was about to stop to take a shot at him, but then the fleeing treasure hunter disappeared behind the corner of the lighthouse keeper's residence.

Andrew's legs were pumping as he sprinted across the uneven terrain holding the assault rifle in both hands, and only then did he realise that it appeared to be coated in a thin film of some sort of liquid that could only have been Ortega's blood. Gritting his teeth as he covered the final hundred metres or so, he heard the familiar sound of a turbofan engine starting up, and when he rounded the corner of the building behind which his quarry had disappeared, he saw Blake sitting inside the black chopper's cockpit flicking switches as the whine of the engines grew louder and the rotor blades rapidly began to spin up. Behind him on the left-hand side, the chopper's sliding passenger door had been left open from when he and his two goons had disembarked earlier, but there was no way Andrew was going to reach it in time. The distance to the chopper was a little less than a hundred metres, but the main rotor was now a blur above the chopper's fuselage, and Andrew caught Blake looking up at him as he gripped the controls with a spiteful smile. Blake was going to be airborne in a few seconds.

Lowering himself onto one knee, Andrew brought up the assault rifle, lined up on his target and pulled the trigger. The first bullet smacked into the windshield almost dead centre on Blake's head, but incredibly, the glass held, and the projectile left only a white, cracked ring. It had to be some sort of bulletproof glass that had been installed in this particular type of corporate helicopter. He then shifted his aim and attempted to shoot through the side of the cockpit door where Blake's shoulder was visible through the side window. The bullet glanced off the metal and ricocheted off somewhere behind the chopper. He now had only one shot left. Unless he could disable a vital component on the aircraft, Blake would get away, and he would probably never see or hear about him again. He lined up the iron sights on the centre of the tail rotor, without which the chopper would end up taking off and immediately go into an uncontrollable spin around the main rotor's driveshaft. Amid the loud whine of the turbofan engine and the dust being whirled up around the helicopter, he narrowed his eyes, held his breath and took careful aim, and then he squeezed the trigger.

For the final time, the assault rifle's recoil kicked back into his shoulder, and he saw a small but bright spark fly off the metal cover on the tail rotor axle. However, the rotor kept spinning, and there was no change to the pitch of the engines or the ever-faster thudding of the rotors. The bullet had done nothing, and Blake was now about to lift off. Lowering the weapon, Andrew saw the treasure hunter sitting inside the cockpit and performing a mock salute, and then he reached down for the handle on the collective, ready to start pulling it back and lifting the chopper from the ground.

At that moment, Andrew suddenly had an idea. He spun around and bolted for the other helicopter, which was parked some twenty metres away. Upon reaching it, he flung aside the sliding door to the back, ripped open the black holdall and grabbed the last of the three hand grenades he had taken from the brothel in Port-au-Prince. With no time to lose, he rounded the cockpit and ran for the black chopper just as its skids lifted from the rocky ground amid a huge gyrating cloud of dust and tiny dry pieces of debris from the surrounding vegetation.

The helicopter was about ten metres from the ground when Andrew pulled the pin on the hand grenade. He sprinted the final stretch to get within throwing distance, and then he held the grenade out behind himself as his fingers released their grip on the spoon, which flew off as he ran. He hurled it with all the power he could muster, and it sailed in an arc through the air towards the chopper's open passenger door just as the aircraft began to turn and pitch down to accelerate out over the edge of the island to the surrounding sea.

As it turned out, Andrew had judged the distance and the grenade's travel time perfectly, because it flew through the door and clonked onto the floor of the chopper just over three seconds after he had released the spoon. It then rolled towards the back of the cabin as the chopper began to accelerate, and when it detonated, it was directly above one of the fuel tanks.

In an instant, the fiery explosion burst out violently through every gap and opening in the helicopter's fuselage, and the cockpit and most of the front of the aircraft were enveloped in a searing fireball while hundreds of sharp metal grenade fragments travelling faster than the speed of sound sliced through metal, carbon fibre, soft human tissue and brittle bones. The helicopter's momentum kept it moving forward through the air as it burned, but then gravity took over, and the flying inferno quickly arced downward over the rocky edge of the island, and the helicopter finally crashed into the frothy sea below. As Andrew ran over to look down, he saw only burning fuel and small pieces of floating debris on the surface as the wreck of the chopper sank beneath the swells and disappeared. Andrew watched the scene with steely eyes and was left in no doubt that both Marcus Tobin and Lawrence Blake were now dead. The bizarre double act had finally come to an end, and the treasure hunter and his goons would never harm anyone ever again.

Panting as he looked at the burning waters below for a long moment. Then he turned around to hurry back to the cave where Fiona was waiting for him to return, and where she would need his help to get out. With any luck, she might be able to get treated for her gunshot wound in a hospital in as little as six hours, but that would end up feeling like an eternity to her. Andrew had seen plenty of similar injuries, and he had experienced his fair share of them himself. But he needed Fiona to be safe and suffer as little pain as possible, so he left the lighthouse and the chopper behind and began running as fast as he could back across the rugged terrain to find her and bring her to safety.

★ ★ ★

The next morning, Andrew was sitting by Fiona's bedside in Kingston Public Hospital on North Street in the south of the city, some two kilometres from the harbour. From the window, he was able to look out across the southern part of the city towards some of the wharves, and in the distance on the other side of Kingston Harbour, he was just able to make out Port Royal at the end of the long isthmus that enveloped the island's large natural harbour.

The first rays of the morning sun were now streaming in through the window and caressing Fiona's face as she slept, and Andrew had sat in a chair next to her since she had been admitted late the previous evening. He had found himself having to concoct a story about being caught in a gangland shooting somewhere in one of Kingston's most unsavoury neighbourhoods, but the staff appeared to have accepted his story and had got straight to treating her leg wound. He had managed to sleep only a couple of hours in the uncomfortable chair by her bedside, and he was now starving, but none of that mattered. Fiona was safe, and the doctors had told him that she should be able to recover fully within a few weeks.

As he looked out through the window, he spotted a corporate helicopter taking off from the international airport in the distance. Its dark profile looked almost exactly like the chopper Blake and his goons had been flying, and he suddenly found himself feeling a surge of adrenaline being released into his bloodstream. However, he quickly managed to suppress this instinctive and involuntary reaction. Blake was dead, most likely now being eaten by fish and crustaceans, and so was Laura Hartley's killer, of whom there was precious little left after his explosive final moments. The third goon was probably now in the process of being consumed by the insects and the various small rodents that no doubt lived on Navassa Island. Within weeks, there would be nothing left, and that seemed to Andrew to be a fitting end to those men.

'A penny for your thoughts,' Fiona whispered, smiling weakly as he turned to look at her.

'You're awake,' he said, returning her smile self-consciously as he took her hand in his and gave it a gentle squeeze. 'I didn't realise.'

'I only just woke up now,' she said, her face looking somewhat gaunt and the dark areas around her eyes hinting at the physical and emotional stress of the past few days. 'I'd like to go back to sleep soon, though. I still feel shattered.'

'Sleep as much as you like,' said Andrew. 'We're not leaving this place until you're ready to go.'

'I want to go home soon,' said Fiona. 'Back to my little office in Hampstead where nothing much ever happens. I've had enough excitement to last me a while.'

'No kidding,' said Andrew. 'It's been a bit hectic. Anyway, tell me. How did you get away from Blake? I heard him shooting.'

'Snake,' said Fiona enigmatically.

'Snake?' he said.

'There was one in the cave,' she said, 'and I threw it at him.'

'But you hate snakes,' said Andrew, with a perplexed look. 'They usually have you rigid with fear.'

'That's because I have seen what their venom can do to tissue,' said Fiona. 'Necrosis should terrify anyone. But this one wasn't venomous. It must have been some local species of boa.'

'How do you know?' said Andrew.

'Because I'm terrified of snakes,' said Fiona, 'so I know a lot about them. Different types of boas look very different, but they are all quite bulky, and they all have a narrow, dark line running down the centre of their heads. And this one had a line like that.'

'Wow,' said Andrew with a small nod as he gave her hand another squeeze. 'Well done. But listen. You should try to get some more sleep now. I'll be right here when you wake up.'

Epilogue

Hampstead, London – two weeks later

When Andrew returned home to the house in their leafy London suburb after a meeting at his SAS unit's HQ on Sheldrake Place, he was expecting to find Fiona in the living room upstairs ensconced in some form of research. However, when he went up the stairs and entered the large open-plan kitchen, she was standing by the large kitchen island holding in her hands a bulbous bottle with a dark brown liquid. She was wearing light blue jeans and a pink knitted top, her face looked healthy, and her green eyes were greeting him with a look of anticipation.

'Hi,' she beamed. 'I got you something, just as a way of saying thank you for taking such good care of me over these past couple of weeks.'

'You don't have to thank me,' he said with an uncharacteristically bashful smile, walking over and placing his hands on her shoulders and giving her a kiss. 'I am just happy you're back to normal.'

'Well,' she said, handing him the bottle. 'I found this and thought it would be an appropriate gift. It's a Caribbean rum made from sugarcane grown in Jamaica. It supposedly has gunpowder in it, the way Blackbeard used to like it. Although, I suspect that's just a marketing ploy.'

'Thanks,' he said, taking the bottle into his hands and examining the label. 'It looks good.'

'Did you know,' she then said. 'Rum came about accidentally when the slaves brought to the Caribbean realised that molasses from sugar production ferments to create alcohol.'

'No,' he said. 'I did not know that. That's interesting. Although, I am more interested in tasting this. Do you want to have a small glass with me?'

'Yes,' said Fiona. 'But not yet. I want to show you something first.'

She fished her phone out of the back pocket of her jeans and opened an image gallery. Swiping a few times, she then showed it to Andrew. On the screen was a picture taken on a sunny day, and it showed a piece of road, a small section of a promenade and some palm trees, and in the background was a building that looked to be in the process of being renovated. Peering closely at the photo, Andrew then recognised the two people standing in front of something that appeared to be on the way to becoming a restaurant. They were young and smiling, and he immediately recognised both of them.

'Ronil and Roseline,' he said, finding himself breaking into a smile as he looked at Fiona.

'And look there,' she said, pointing to the background where a temporary sign had been put up. 'Opening soon. R&R's Restaurant.'

'They're really doing it,' said Andrew, as a wave of gladness and empathy surged through him. 'They are opening a restaurant together. That's great.'

'It totally made my day as well,' Fiona smiled. 'I'm so happy for them. They really deserve a bit of wind in their sails.'

'I couldn't agree more,' said Andrew, turning to fetch some glasses for the rum. 'Let's toast to that.'

'Wait,' Fiona said cryptically. 'There's one more thing I want to show you. It's in the garden. Come on.'

She took his hand and led him back down the stairs and through the downstairs TV room to the patio double doors leading out to the modest but neatly kept back garden. As they reached them, she turned around and looked up at him whilst taking both of his hands in hers.

'Do you remember after Laura's murder,' she said slightly subdued but with a faint air of hopeful anticipation in her voice, 'I said that there was nothing we could do about it?'

'Yes,' said Andrew. 'I think so.'

'Well,' she said, placing her hands on the door handles. 'It turns out that I was wrong. There's something we can do. And it's a really good thing.'

'OK,' said Andrew, looking perplexed. 'What do you mean?'

Holding him by one hand, she pushed open the double doors and led him outside, glancing back at him with a smile.

'Meet our new dog,' she said. 'He was Laura's dog. But now he needs a new home. A new family.'

As if on cue, a small black labrador emerged from under one of the low bushes, and when it spotted Andrew and Fiona, it raced over to them with its tongue hanging out of its mouth. It arrived wagging its tail so enthusiastically that it could barely stand, and Andrew couldn't help but break into a wide smile. As he bent down to say hello, the excitable puppy sniffed and licked his hands in a show of genuine excitement and affection, its tail still going like a windscreen wiper on full power.

'His name is Wilbur,' Fiona smiled as Andrew ruffled his ears. 'And I have a feeling that you two are going to be best buddies.'

THE END

NOTE FROM THE AUTHOR.

Thank you very much for reading this book. I hope you enjoyed it. If you did, I would be very grateful if you would give it a star rating on Amazon and perhaps even write a review.

I am always trying to improve my writing, and the best way to do that is to receive feedback from my readers. Reviews really do help me a lot. They are an excellent way for me to understand the reader's experience, and they also help me to write better books in the future.

Thank you.

Lex Faulkner